STREET MAGICKS

STREET MAGICKS

Edited by Paula Guran

PRIME BOOKS

Prime Books
Germantown, MD
www.prime-books.com

For more information, contact Prime Books:
prime@prime-books.com

Print ISBN: 978-1-60701-469-0
Ebook ISBN: 978-1-60701-475-1

Contents

Introduction: Practices and Paved Paths
Paula Guran

"The magic of the street is the mingling of the errand and the epiphany."
—Rebecca Solnit, *Wanderlust: A History of Walking*

Magicks? Just a way to convey the stories collected herein all feature some variety of magic. Not just an overall atmosphere of the supernatural or the paranormal, but an act or example of the existence of "real" magic in the world of the author's making.

As for *street* . . .

A street is, generally, a public thoroughfare (usually paved) with buildings on one or both sides of it. It might be a road, but roads exist for transportation and aren't defined by the edifices lining them. A street does more than provide a path: it is a shared space that facilitates social interaction. Streets are urban. "The street" also means the people who live, work, and gather in streets: the common people who are a repository of public attitudes, knowledge, and opinion.

Streets are places of celebration. We still honor our heroes and celebrate holidays with street parades. Religious processions are not as common as they once were, but many still exist. (And though it is often forgotten, Mardi Gras and Carnival are religious celebrations taken to the streets.) We still have funeral processions as well as street fairs and festivals.

These and other communal outpourings have long served to relieve the tensions of the people dwelling closely together and city life.

Until the early nineteenth century, streets were the primary stages available for music, drama, puppet shows, jugglers, and all forms of common entertainment. And, since the sixteenth century, *streetwalker* has meant a prostitute who solicits on the pavement.

Street peddlers were once common. Since they conducted business without stationary shops, mobility meant one's wares might include the less than legally acceptable or material of interest only to the lower echelons of society. Popular media like the penny dreadfuls and *Bibliothèque bleue* could be easily distributed by street hawkers, as could seditious and inflammatory pamphlets.

Town criers and bellman (so-called because they rang a hand bell to gain attention) once walked the streets as the only means of conveying legal proclamations, bylaws, and notices of market and other special days to mostly illiterate urban dwellers.

Even after the masses learned to read, current events were carried to the streets by newsboys who hawked newspapers by shouting out the most sensational headlines of the day. From the mid-nineteenth to the early twentieth century, these "newsies" were the primary distributors of newspapers to the general public.

Streets have, historically, provided forums for political discourse and even confrontations involving varying degrees of violence—including the taking up arms. Since the French Revolution, the streets have played a role in the downfall of authority. Not that revolutionaries or dedicated demonstrators were the only ones to use the streets as a public arena, so did those in power: martial might on parade can draw the common folk together in shared patriotic pride or frighten a regime's foes.

In current usage, "street" can have dichotomous meanings.

The Street, in the U.S., is used to allude to the financial and securities industry of the America. (From Wall Street, the eight-block stretch of Lower Manhattan that has been a hub for commerce and trade since the late eighteenth century.) The Street belongs to the wealthy.

However, beginning in the mid-nineteenth century, *being on/in the street* has meant being homeless. Since 1967, and probably before, *street people* has meant those who are poor, often homeless, who live in urban environments. The street is a place of last resort for with no wealth.

On one hand, *the street* is a source of style, chic, hipness: the perspective and creations of the urban young who are seen as constituting a fashionable, trend-setting subculture.

On the other, *the streets* can be viewed as disadvantaged area of a city;

an environment of poverty, dereliction, violence, and crime so pervasive that an oppositional culture—with values often intentionally antithetical to those of mainstream society—has evolved.

I suppose I could have simply said: *street* has many meanings; it can be an attitude as well as a location. But, then again, I could have gone on and on . . .

This score of stories all involve magic and streets in one way or another. They vary from the lighthearted to the somber, from the near realistic to the exotically fantastic, from the poetic to the vernacular. The incredible imaginations of the authors included have been inspired by hard-boiled detectives, *genius loci,* visual art, Scots and other folklore, the vicissitudes of Hollywood, the Holocaust, high adventure, noir, epic fantasy, nightlife, mysteries, runaway kids, the mythic, technology, human and inhuman nature, dreams, nightmares, and more. Some stories are fairly lengthy, others quite short, most somewhere in between.

There also seems to be a disproportionate number of bars and taverns in these twenty tales. I suppose streets have to lead somewhere.

I truly hope you enjoy this anthology. It has been fun finding the magicks and mapping the streets.

Paula Guran
Tu Bishvat
15 Shevat 5776

To paraphrase the author, Newford could be any contemporary North American city . . . except that magic lurks in its music, in its art, in the shadows of its grittiest streets, and enchantment can be found in the spaces between its people. Those people are like you and me, each looking for a bit of magic to shape their lives and transform their fate. Except, in Newford, they often find it.

Freewheeling
Charles de Lint

"There is apparently nothing that cannot happen."
—Attributed to Mark Twain

"There are three kinds of people: those who make things happen, those who watch things happen, and those who wonder, 'What happened?'"
—Message found inside a Christmas cracker

1

He stood on the rain-slick street, a pale fire burning behind his eyes. Nerve ends tingling, he watched them go—a slow parade of riderless bicycles.

Ten-speeds and mountain bikes. Domesticated, urban. So inbred that all they were was spoked wheels and emaciated frames, mere skeletons of what their genetic ancestors had been. They had never known freedom, never known joy; only the weight of serious riders in slick, leather-seated shorts, pedaling determinedly with their cycling shoes strapped to the pedals, heads encased in crash helmets, fingerless gloves on the hands gripping the handles tightly.

He smiled and watched them go. Down the wet street, wheels throwing up arcs of fine spray, metal frames glistening in the streetlights, reflector lights winking red.

The rain had plastered his hair slick against his head, his clothes were sodden, but he paid no attention to personal discomfort. He thought instead of that fat-wheeled aboriginal one-speed that led them now. The maverick who'd come from who-knows-where to pilot his domesticated brothers and sisters away.

For a night's freedom. Perhaps for always.

The last of them were rounding the corner now. He lifted his right hand to wave goodbye. His left hand hung down by his leg, still holding the heavy-duty wire cutters by one handle, the black rubber grip making a ribbed pattern on the palm of his hand. By fences and on porches, up and down the street, locks had been cut, chains lay discarded, bicycles ran free.

He heard a siren approaching. Lifting his head, he licked the raindrops from his lips. Water got in his eyes, gathering in their corners. He squinted, enamored by the kaleidoscoping spray of lights this caused to appear behind his eyelids. There were omens in lights, he knew. And in the night sky, with its scattershot sweep of stars. So many lights . . . There were secrets waiting to unfold there, mysteries that required a voice to be freed.

Like the bicycles were freed by their maverick brother.

He could be that voice, if he only knew what to sing.

He was still watching the sky for signs when the police finally arrived.

"Let me go, boys, let me go . . . "

The Pogues album *If I Should Fall from Grace with God* was on the turntable. The title cut leaked from the sound system's speakers, one of which sat on a crate crowded with half-used paint tubes and tins of turpentine, the other perched on the windowsill, commanding a view of rainswept Yoors Street one floor below. The song was jauntier than one might expect from its subject matter, while Shane MacGowan's voice was as rough as ever, chewing the words and spitting them out, rather than singing them.

It was an angry voice, Jilly decided as she hummed softly along with the chorus. Even when it sang a tender song. But what could you expect from a group that had originally named itself Pogue Mahone—Irish Gaelic for "Kiss my ass"?

Angry and brash and vulgar. The band was all of that. But they were honest, too—painfully so, at times—and that was what brought Jilly back to their music, time and again. Because sometimes things just had to be said.

"I don't get this stuff," Sue remarked.

She'd been frowning over the lyrics that were printed on the album's inner sleeve. Leaning her head against the patched backrest of one of Jilly's two old sofas, she set the sleeve aside.

"I mean, music's supposed to make you feel good, isn't it?" she went on.

Jilly shook her head. "It's supposed to make you feel something—happy, sad, angry, whatever—just so long as it doesn't leave you brain-dead the way most Top Forty does. For me, music needs meaning to be worth my time—preferably something more than 'I want your body, babe,' if you know what I mean."

"You're beginning to develop a snooty attitude, Jilly."

"Me? To laugh, dahling."

Susan Ashworth was Jilly's uptown friend. As a pair, the two women made a perfect study in contrasts.

Sue's blond hair was straight, hanging to just below her shoulders, where Jilly's was a riot of brown curls, made manageable tonight only by a clip that drew it all up to the top of her head before letting it fall free in the shape of something that resembled nothing so much as a disenchanted Mohawk. They were both in their twenties, slender and blue-eyed—the latter expected in a blond; the electric blue of Jilly's eyes gave her, with her darker skin, a look of continual startlement. Where Sue wore just the right amount of makeup, Jilly could usually be counted on having a smudge of charcoal somewhere on her face and dried oil paint under her nails.

Sue worked for the city as an architect; she lived uptown and her parents were from the Beaches where it seemed you needed a permit just to be out on the sidewalks after eight in the evening—or at least that was the impression that the police patrols left when they stopped strangers to check their ID. She always had that upscale look of one who was just about to step out to a restaurant for cocktails and dinner.

Jilly's first love was art of a freer style than designing municipal necessities, but she usually paid her rent by waitressing and other odd jobs. She tended to wear baggy clothes—like the oversized white T-shirt and blue poplin laced-front pants she had on tonight—and always had a sketchbook close at hand.

Tonight it was on her lap as she sat propped up on her Murphy bed, toes in their ballet slippers tapping against one another in time to the music. The Pogues were playing an instrumental now—"Metropolis"—which sounded like a cross between a Celtic fiddle tune and the old *Dragnet* theme.

"They're really not for me," Sue went on. "I mean if the guy could sing, maybe, but—"

"It's the feeling that he puts into his voice that's important," Jilly said. "But this is an instrumental. He's not even—"

"Supposed to be singing. I know. Only—"

"If you'd just—"

The jangling of the phone sliced through their discussion. Because she was closer—and knew that Jilly would claim some old war wound or any excuse not to get up, now that she was lying down—Sue answered it. She listened for a long moment, an odd expression on her face, then slowly cradled the receiver.

"Wrong number?"

Sue shook her head. "No. It was someone named . . . uh, Zinc? He said that he's been captured by two Elvis Presleys disguised as police officers and would you please come and explain to them that he wasn't stealing bikes, he was just setting them free. Then he just hung up."

"Oh, shit!" Jilly stuffed her sketchbook into her shoulderbag and got up.

"This makes sense to you?"

"He's one of the street kids."

Sue rolled her eyes, but she got up as well. "Want me to bring my checkbook?"

"What for?

"Bail. It's what you have to put up to spring somebody from jail. Don't you ever watch TV?"

Jilly shook her head. "What? And let the aliens monitor my brainwaves?"

"What scares me," Sue muttered as they left the loft and started down the stairs, "is that sometimes I don't think you're kidding."

"Maybe I'm not," Jilly said.

Sue shook her head. "I'm going to pretend I didn't hear that."

Jilly knew people from all over the city, in all walks of life. Socialites and bag ladies. Street kids and university profs. Nobody was too poor, or, conversely, too rich for her to strike up a conversation with, no matter where they happened to meet, or under what circumstances. Detective Lou Fucceri, of the Crowsea Precinct's General Investigations squad, she met when he was still a patrolman, walking the Stanton Street Combat Zone beat. Jilly was there, taking reference photos for a painting she was planning. When she had asked Lou to pose for a couple of shots, he tried to run her in on a soliciting charge.

"Is it true?" Sue wanted to know as soon as the desk sergeant showed them into Lou's office. "The way you guys met?"

"You mean UFO-spotting in Butler U. Park?" he replied.

Sue sighed. "I should've known. I must be the only person who's maintained her sanity after meeting Jilly."

She sat down on one of the two wooden chairs that faced Lou's desk in the small cubicle that passed for his office. There was room for a bookcase behind him, crowded with law books and file folders, and a brass coat rack from which hung a lightweight sports jacket. Lou sat at the desk, white shirt sleeves rolled halfway up to his elbows, collar open, black tie hanging loose.

His Italian heritage was very much present in the Mediterranean cast to his complexion, his dark brooding eyes and darker hair. As Jilly sat down in the chair Sue had left for her, he shook a cigarette free from a crumpled pack that he dug out from under the litter of files on his desk. He offered them around, tossing the pack back down on the desk and lighting his own when there were no takers.

Jilly pulled her chair closer to the desk. "What did he do, Lou? Sue took the call, but I don't know if she got the message right."

"I *can* take a message," Sue began, but Jilly waved a hand in her direction.

She wasn't in the mood for banter just now.

Lou blew a stream of blue-gray smoke towards the ceiling. "We've been having a lot of trouble with a bicycle theft ring operating in the city," he said. "They've hit the Beaches, which was bad enough, though with all the Mercedes and BMWs out there, I doubt they're going to miss their bikes a lot. But rich people like to complain, and now the gang's moved their operations into Crowsea."

Jilly nodded. "Where for a lot of people, a bicycle's the only way they can get around."

"You got it."

"So what does that have to do with Zinc?"

"The patrol car that picked him up found him standing in the middle of the street with a pair of heavy-duty wire cutters in his hand. The street'd been cleaned right out, Jilly. There wasn't a bike left on the block—just the cut locks and chains left behind."

"So where are the bikes?"

Lou shrugged. "Who knows. Probably in a Foxville chopshop having their serial numbers changed. Jilly, you've got to get Zinc to tell us who he was working with. Christ, they took off, leaving him to hold the bag. He doesn't owe them a thing now."

Jilly shook her head slowly. "This doesn't make any sense. Zinc's not the criminal kind."

"I'll tell you what doesn't make any sense," Lou said. "The kid himself. He's heading straight for the looney bin with all his talk about Elvis clones and Venusian thought machines and feral-fuc—" He glanced at Sue and covered up the profanity with a cough. "Feral bicycles leading the domesticated ones away."

"He said that?"

Lou nodded. "That's why he was clipping the locks—to set the bikes free so that they could follow their, and I quote, 'spiritual leader, home to the place of mystery.'"

"That's a new one," Jilly said.

"You're having me on—right?" Lou said. "That's all you can say? It's a new one? The Elvis clones are old hat now? Christ on a comet. Would you give me a break? Just get the kid to roll over and I'll make sure things go easy for him."

"Christ on a comet?" Sue repeated softly.

"C'mon, Lou," Jilly said. "How can I make Zinc tell you something he doesn't know? Maybe he found those wire cutters on the street—just before the patrol car came. For all we know he could—"

"He *said* he cut the locks."

The air went out of Jilly. "Right," she said. She slouched in her chair. "I forgot you'd said that."

"Maybe the bikes really did just go off on their own," Sue said.

Lou gave her a weary look, but Jilly sat up straighter. "I wonder," she began.

"Oh, for God's sake," Sue said. "I was only joking."

"I know you were," Jilly said. "But I've seen enough odd things in this world that I won't say anything's impossible anymore."

"The police department doesn't see things quite the same way," Lou told Jilly. The dryness of his tone wasn't lost on her.

"I know."

"I want these bike thieves, Jilly."

"Are you arresting Zinc?"

Lou shook his head. "I've got nothing to hold him on except for circumstantial evidence."

"I thought you said he admitted to cutting the locks," Sue said.

Jilly shot her a quick fierce look that plainly said, don't make waves when he's giving us what we came for.

Lou nodded. "Yeah. He admitted to that. He also admitted to knowing a hobo who was really a spy from Pluto. Asked why the patrolmen had traded in their white Vegas suits for uniforms and wanted to hear them sing 'Heartbreak Hotel.' For next of kin he put down Bigfoot."

"*Gigantopithecus blacki*," Jilly said.

Lou looked at her. "What?"

"Some guy at Washington State University's given Bigfoot a Latin name now. *Giganto—*"

Lou cut her off. "That's what I thought you said." He turned back to Sue.

"So you see, his admitting to cutting the locks isn't really going to amount to much. Not when a lawyer with half a brain can get him off without even having to work up a sweat."

"Does that mean he's free to go then?" Jilly asked.

Lou nodded. "Yeah. He can go. But keep him out of trouble, Jilly. He's in here again, and I'm sending him straight to the Zeb for psychiatric testing. And try to convince him to come clean on this—okay? It's not just for me, it's for him too. We break this case and find out he's involved, nobody's going to go easy on him. We don't give out rainchecks."

"Not even for dinner?" Jilly asked brightly, happy now that she knew Zinc was getting out.

"What do you mean?"

Jilly grabbed a pencil and paper from his desk and scrawled "Jilly Coppercorn owes Hotshot Lou one dinner, restaurant of her choice," and passed it over to him.

"I think they call this a bribe," he said.

"I call it keeping in touch with your friends," Jilly replied and gave him a big grin.

Lou glanced at Sue and rolled his eyes.

"Don't look at me like that," she said. "I'm the sane one here."

"You wish," Jilly told her.

Lou heaved himself to his feet with exaggerated weariness. "C'mon, let's get your friend out of here before he decides to sue us because we don't have our coffee flown in from the Twilight Zone," he said as he led the way down to the holding cells.

Zinc had the look of a street kid about two days away from a good meal. His jeans, T-shirt, and cotton jacket were ragged, but clean; his hair had the look of a badly mowed lawn, with tufts standing up here and there like exclamation points. The pupils of his dark brown eyes seemed too large for someone who never did drugs. He was seventeen, but acted half his age.

The only home he had was a squat in Upper Foxville that he shared with a couple of performance artists, so that was where Jilly and Sue took him in Sue's Mazda. The living space he shared with the artists was on the upper story of a deserted tenement where someone had put together a makeshift loft by the simple method of removing all the walls, leaving a large empty area cluttered only by support pillars and the squatters' belongings.

Lucia and Ursula were there when they arrived, practicing one of their pieces to the accompaniment of speakers pumping out a mixture of electronic music and the sound of breaking glass at a barely audible volume. Lucia was wrapped in plastic and lying on the floor, her black hair spread out in an arc around her head. Every few moments one of her limbs would twitch, the plastic wrap stretching tight against her skin with the movement. Ursula crouched beside the blaster, chanting a poem that consisted only of the line, "There are no patterns." She'd shaved her head since the last time Jilly had seen her.

"What am I doing here?" Sue asked softly. She made no effort to keep the look of astonishment from her features.

"Seeing how the other half lives," Jilly said as she led the way across the loft to where Zinc's junkyard of belongings took up a good third of the available space.

"But just look at this stuff," Sue said. "And how did he get that in here?" She pointed to a Volkswagen bug that was sitting up on blocks, missing only its wheels and front hood. Scattered all around it was a hodgepodge of metal scraps, old furniture, boxes filled with wiring and God only knew what.

"Piece by piece," Jilly told her.

"And then he assembled it here?"

Jilly nodded.

"Okay. I'll bite. Why?"

"Why don't you ask him?"

Jilly grinned as Sue quickly shook her head. The entire trip from the precinct station, Zinc had carefully explained his theory of the world to her, how the planet earth was actually an asylum for insane aliens, and that was why nothing made sense.

Zinc followed the pair of them across the room, stopping only long enough to greet his squat-mates. "Hi, Luce. Hi, Urse."

Lucia never looked at him.

"There are no patterns," Ursula said.

Zinc nodded thoughtfully.

"Maybe there's a pattern in that," Sue offered.

"Don't start," Jilly said. She turned to Zinc. "Are you going to be all right?"

"You should've seen them go, Jill," Zinc said. "All shiny and wet, just whizzing down the street, heading for the hills."

"I'm sure it was really something, but you've got to promise me to stay off the streets for a while. Will you do that, Zinc? At least until they catch this gang of bike thieves?"

"But there weren't any thieves. It's like I told Elvis Two, they left on their own."

Sue gave him an odd look. "Elvis too?"

"Don't ask," Jilly said. She touched Zinc's arm. "Just stay in for a while—okay? Let the bikes take off on their own."

"But I like to watch them go."

"Do it as a favor to me, would you?"

"I'll try."

Jilly gave him a quick smile. "Thanks. Is there anything you need? Do you need money for some food?"

Zinc shook his head. Jilly gave him a quick kiss on the cheek and tousled the exclamation point hair tufts sticking up from his head.

"I'll drop by to see you tomorrow, then—okay?" At his nod, Jilly started back across the room. "C'mon, Sue," she said when her companion paused beside the speaker where Ursula was still chanting.

"So what about this stock market stuff?" she asked the poet.

"There are no patterns," Ursula said.

"That's what I thought," Sue said, but then Jilly was tugging her arm.

"Couldn't resist, could you?" Jilly said.

Sue just grinned.

"Why do you humor him?" Sue asked when she pulled up in front of Jilly's loft.

"What makes you think I am?"

"I'm being serious, Jilly."

"So am I. He believes in what he's talking about. That's good enough for me."

"But all this stuff he goes on about . . . Elvis clones and insane aliens—"

"Don't forget animated bicycles."

Sue gave Jilly a pained look. "I'm not. That's just what I mean—it's all so crazy.

"What if it's not?"

Sue shook her head. "I can't buy it."

"It's not hurting anybody." Jilly leaned over and gave Sue a quick kiss on the cheek. "Gotta run. Thanks for everything."

"Maybe it's hurting him," Sue said as Jilly opened the door to get out. "Maybe it's closing the door on any chance he has of living a normal life. You know—opportunity comes knocking, but there's nobody home? He's not just eccentric, Jilly. He's crazy."

Jilly sighed. "His mother was a hooker, Sue. The reason he's a little flaky is her pimp threw him down two flights of stairs when he was six years old—not because Zinc did anything, or because his mother didn't trick enough johns that night, but just because the creep felt like doing it. That's what normal was for Zinc. He's happy now—a lot happier than when Social Services tried to put him in a foster home where they only wanted him for the support check they got once a month for taking him in. And a lot happier than he'd be in the Zeb, all doped up or sitting around in a padded cell whenever he tried to tell people about the things he sees.

"He's got his own life now. It's not much—not by your standards, maybe not even by mine, but it's his and I don't want anybody to take it away from him."

"But—"

"I know you mean well," Jilly said, "but things don't always work out the way we'd like them to. Nobody's got time for a kid like Zinc in Social Services. There he's just a statistic that they shuffle around with all the rest of their files and red tape. Out here on the street, we've got a system that works. We take care of our own. It's that simple. Doesn't matter if it's the Cat Lady, sleeping in an alleyway with a half-dozen mangy toms, or Rude Ruthie, haranguing the commuters on the subway, we take care of each other."

"Utopia," Sue said.

A corner of Jilly's mouth twitched with the shadow of a humorless smile.

"Yeah. I know. We've got a high asshole quotient, but what can you do? You try to get by—that's all. You just try to get by."

"I wish I could understand it better," Sue said.

"Don't worry about it. You're good people, but this just isn't your world. You can visit, but you wouldn't want to live in it, Sue."

"I guess."

Jilly started to add something more, but then just smiled encouragingly and got out of the car.

"See you Friday?" she asked, leaning in the door.

Sue nodded.

Jilly stood on the pavement and watched the Mazda until it turned the corner and its rear lights were lost from view, then she went upstairs to her apartment. The big room seemed too quiet and she felt too wound up to sleep, so she put a cassette in the tape player—Lynn Harrell playing a Schumann concerto—and started to prepare a new canvas to work on in the morning when the light would be better.

2

It was raining again, a soft drizzle that put a glistening sheen on the streets and lampposts, on porch handrails and street signs. Zinc stood in the shadows that had gathered in the mouth of an alleyway, his new pair of wire cutters a comfortable weight in his hand. His eyes sparked with reflected lights. His hair was damp against his scalp. He licked his lips, tasting mountain heights and distant forests within the drizzle's slightly metallic tang.

Jilly knew a lot about things that were, he thought, and things that might be, and she always meant well, but there was one thing she just couldn't get right. You didn't make art by capturing an image on paper, or canvas, or in stone. You didn't make it by writing down stories and poems. Music and dance came closest to what real art was—but only so long as you didn't try to record or film it. Musical notation was only so much dead ink on paper. Choreography was planning, not art.

You could only make art by setting it free. Anything else was just a memory, no matter how you stored it. On film or paper, sculpted or recorded.

Everything that existed, existed in a captured state. Animate or inanimate, everything wanted to be free.

That's what the lights said; that was their secret. Wild lights in the night skies, and domesticated lights, right here on the street, they all told the same tale. It was so plain to see when you knew *how* to look. Didn't neon and streetlights yearn to be starlight?

To be free.

He bent down and picked up a stone, smiling at the satisfying crack it made when it broke the glass protection of the streetlight, his grin widening as the light inside flickered, then died.

It was part of the secret now, part of the voices that spoke in the night sky. Free.

Still smiling, he set out across the street to where a bicycle was chained to the railing of a porch.

"Let me tell you about art," he said to it as he mounted the stairs.

Psycho Puppies were playing at the YoMan on Gracie Street near the corner of Landis Avenue that Friday night. They weren't anywhere near as punkish as their name implied. If they had been, Jilly would never have been able to get Sue out to see them.

"I don't care if they damage themselves," she'd told Jilly the one and only time she'd gone out to one of the punk clubs further west on Gracie, "but I refuse to pay good money just to have someone spit at me and do their best to rupture my eardrums."

The Puppies were positively tame compared to how that punk band had been. Their music was loud, but melodic, and while there was an undercurrent of social conscience to their lyrics, you could dance to them as well. Jilly couldn't help but smile to see Sue stepping it up to a chorus of, "You can take my job, but you can't take me, ain't nobody gonna steal my dignity." The crowd was an even mix of slumming uptowners, Crowsea artists, and the neighborhood kids from surrounding Foxville. Jilly and Sue danced with each other, not from lack of offers, but because they didn't want to feel obligated to any guy that night. Too many men felt that one dance entitled them to ownership—for the night, at least, if not forever—and neither of them felt like going through the ritual repartee that the whole business required.

Sue was on the right side of a bad relationship at the moment, while Jilly was simply eschewing relationships on general principle these days. Relationships required changes, and she wasn't ready for changes in her life just now. And besides, all the men she'd ever cared for were already taken and she didn't think it likely that she'd run into her own particular Prince Charming in a Foxville nightclub.

"I like this band," Sue confided to her when they took a break to finish the beers they'd ordered at the beginning of the set.

Jilly nodded, but she didn't have anything to say. A glance across the room caught a glimpse of a head with hair enough like Zinc's badly mowed lawn scalp to remind her that he hadn't been home when she'd dropped by his place on the way to the club tonight.

Don't be out setting bicycles free, Zinc, she thought.

"Hey, Tomas. Check this out."

There were two of them, one Anglo, one Hispanic, neither of them much more than a year or so older than Zinc. They both wore leather jackets and jeans, dark hair greased back in ducktails. The drizzle put a sheen on their jackets and hair. The Hispanic moved closer to see what his companion was pointing out.

Zinc had melted into the shadows at their approach. The streetlights that he had yet to free whispered, *careful, careful*, as they wrapped him in darkness, their electric light illuminating the pair on the street.

"Well, shit," the Hispanic said. "Somebody's doing our work for us." As he picked up the lock that Zinc had just snipped, the chain holding the bike to the railing fell to the pavement with a clatter. Both teenagers froze, one checking out one end of the street, his companion the other.

"'Scool," the Anglo said. "Nobody here but you, me, and your cooties."

"Chew on a big one."

"I don't do myself, puto."

"That's 'cos it's too small to find."

The pair of them laughed—a quick nervous sound that belied their bravado-then the Anglo wheeled the bike away from the railing.

"Hey, Bobby-o," the Hispanic said. "Got another one over here."

"Well, what're you waiting for, man? Wheel her down to the van."

They were setting bicycles free, Zinc realized—just like he was. He'd gotten almost all the way down the block, painstakingly snipping the shackle of each lock, before the pair had arrived.

Careful, careful, the streetlights were still whispering, but Zinc was already moving out of the shadows.

"Hi, guys," he said.

The teenagers froze, then the Anglo's gaze took in the wire cutters in Zinc's hand.

"Well, well," he said. "What've we got here? What're you doing on the night side of the street, kid?"

Before Zinc could reply, the sound of a siren cut the air. A lone siren, approaching fast.

The Chinese waitress looked great in her leather miniskirt and fishnet stockings. She wore a blood-red camisole tucked into the waist of the skirt, which made her pale skin seem ever paler. Her hair was the black of polished jet, pulled up in a loose bun that spilled stray strands across her neck and shoulders.

Blue-black eye shadow made her dark eyes darker. Her lips were the same red as her camisole.

"How come she looks so good," Sue wanted to know, "when I'd just look like a tart if I dressed like that?"

"She's inscrutable," Jilly replied. "You're just obvious."

"How sweet of you to point that out," Sue said with a grin. She stood up from their table. "C'mon. Let's dance."

Jilly shook her head. "You go ahead. I'll sit this one out."

"Uh-uh. I'm not going out there alone."

"There's LaDonna," Jilly said, pointing out a girl they both knew. "Dance with her."

"Are you feeling all right, Jilly?"

"I'm fine—just a little pooped. Give me a chance to catch my breath." But she wasn't all right, she thought as Sue crossed over to where LaDonna da Costa and her brother Pipo were sitting. Not when she had Zinc to worry about. If he was out there, cutting off the locks of more bicycles . . .

You're not his mother, she told herself. Except—

Out here on the streets we take care of our own.

That's what she'd told Sue. And maybe it wasn't true for a lot of people who hit the skids—the winos and the losers and the bag people who were just too screwed up to take care of themselves, not to be mentioned look after anyone else—but it was true for her.

Someone like Zinc—he was an in-betweener. Most days he could take care of himself just fine, but there was a fey streak in him so that sometimes he carried a touch of the magic that ran wild in the streets, the magic that was loose late at night when the straights were in bed and the city belonged to the night people. That magic took up lodgings in people like Zinc. For a week. A day. An hour. Didn't matter if it was real or not, if it couldn't be measured or cataloged, it was real to them. It existed all the same.

Did that make it true?

Jilly shook her head. It wasn't her kind of question and it didn't matter anyway. Real or not, it could still be driving Zinc into breaking corporeal laws—the kind that'd have Lou breathing down his neck, real fast. The kind that'd put him in jail with a whole different kind of loser.

The kid wouldn't last out a week inside.

Jilly got up from the table and headed across the dance floor to where Sue and LaDonna were jitterbugging to a tune that sounded as though Buddy Holly could have penned the melody, if not the words.

"Fuck this, man!" the Anglo said.

He threw down the bike and took off at a run, his companion right on his heels, scattering puddles with the impact of their boots. Zinc watched them go.

There was a buzzing in the back of his head. The streetlights were telling him to run too, but he saw the bike lying there on the pavement like a wounded animal, one wheel spinning forlornly, and he couldn't just take off.

Bikes were like turtles. Turn 'em on their backs—or a bike on its side—and they couldn't get up on their own again.

He tossed down the wire cutters and ran to the bike. Just as he was leaning it up against the railing from which the Anglo had taken it, a police cruiser came around the corner, skidding on the wet pavement, cherry light gyrating-screaming, *Run, run!* in its urgent high-pitched voice—headlights pinning Zinc where he stood.

Almost before the cruiser came to a halt, the passenger door popped open and a uniformed officer had stepped out. He drew his gun. Using the cruiser as a shield, he aimed across its roof at where Zinc was standing.

"Hold it right there, kid!" he shouted. "Don't even blink."

Zinc was privy to secrets. He could hear voices in lights. He knew that there was more to be seen in the world if you watched it from the corner of your eye, than head on. It was a simple truth that every policeman he ever saw looked just like Elvis. But he hadn't survived all his years on the streets without protection.

He had a lucky charm. A little tin monkey pendant that had originally lived in a box of Crackerjacks—back when Crackerjacks had real prizes in them. Lucia had given it to him. He'd forgotten to bring it out with him the other night when the Elvises had taken him in. But he wasn't stupid. He'd remembered it tonight.

He reached into his pocket to get it out and wake its magic.

"You're just being silly," Sue said as they collected their jackets from their chairs.

"So humor me," Jilly asked.

"I'm coming, aren't I."

Jilly nodded. She could hear the voice of Zinc's roommate Ursula in the back of her head—

There are no patterns.

—but she could feel one right now, growing tight as a drawn bowstring, humming with its urgency to be loosed.

"C'mon," she said, almost running from the club.

Police officer Mario Hidalgo was still a rookie—tonight was only the beginning of his third month of active duty—and while he'd drawn his sidearm before, he had yet to fire it in the line of duty. He had the makings of a good cop.

He was steady; he was conscientious. The street hadn't had a chance to harden him yet, though it had already thrown him more than a couple of serious uglies in his first eight weeks of active duty.

But steady though he'd proved himself to be so far, when he saw the kid reaching into his the pocket of his baggy jacket, Hidalgo had a single moment of unreasoning panic.

The kid's got a gun, that panic told him. The kid's going for a weapon. One moment was all it took.

His finger was already tightening on the trigger of his regulation .38 as the kid's hand came out of his pocket. Hidalgo wanted to stop the pressure he was putting on the gun's trigger, but it was like there was a broken circuit between his brain and his hand.

The gun went off with a deafening roar.

Got it, Zinc thought as his fingers closed on the little tin monkey charm. Got my luck.

He started to take it out of his pocket, but then something hit him straight in the chest. It lifted him off his feet and threw him against the wall behind him with enough force to knock all the wind out of his lungs. There was a raw pain firing every one of his nerve ends. His hands opened and closed spastically, the charm falling out of his grip to hit the ground moments before his body slid down the wall to join it on the wet pavement.

Goodbye, goodbye, sweet friend, the streetlights cried.

He could sense the spin of the stars as they wheeled high above the city streets, their voices joining the electric voices of the streetlights.

My turn to go free, he thought as a white tunnel opened in his mind. He could feel it draw him in, and then he was falling, falling, falling . . .

"Goodbye . . . " he said, thought he said, but no words came forth from between his lips.

Just a trickle of blood that mingled with the rain that now began to fall in earnest, as though it too was saying its own farewell.

All Jilly had to see was the red spinning cherries of the police cruisers to know where the pattern she'd felt in the club was taking her. There were a lot of cars here—cruisers and unmarked vehicles, an ambulance—all on official business, their presence coinciding with her business. She didn't see Lou approach until he laid his hand on her shoulder.

"You don't want to see," he told her.

Jilly never even looked at him. One moment he was holding her shoulder, the next she'd shrugged herself free of his grip and just kept on walking.

"Is it . . . is it Zinc?" Sue asked the detective.

Jilly didn't have to ask. She knew. Without being told. Without having to see the body.

An officer stepped in front of her to stop her, but Lou waved him aside. In her peripheral vision she saw another officer sitting inside a cruiser, weeping, but it didn't really register.

"I thought he had a gun," the policeman was saying as she went by. "Oh, Jesus. I thought the kid was going for a gun . . . "

And then she was standing over Zinc's body, looking down at his slender frame, limbs flung awkwardly like those of a ragdoll that had been tossed into a corner and forgotten. She knelt down at Zinc's side. Something glinted on the wet pavement. A small tin monkey charm. She picked it up, closed it tightly in her fist.

"C'mon, Jilly," Lou said as he came up behind her. He helped her to her feet.

It didn't seem possible that anyone as vibrant—as alive—as Zinc had been could have any relation whatsoever with that empty shell of a body that lay there on the pavement.

As Lou led her away from the body, Jilly's tears finally came, welling up from her eyes to salt the rain on her cheek.

"He . . . he wasn't . . . stealing bikes, Lou . . . " she said.

"It doesn't look good," Lou said.

Often when she'd been with Zinc, Jilly had had a sense of that magic that touched him. A feeling that even if she couldn't see the marvels he told her about, they still existed just beyond the reach of her sight.

That feeling should be gone now, she thought.

"He was just . . . setting them free," she said.

The magic should have died, when he died. But she felt, if she just looked hard enough, that she'd see him, riding a maverick bike at the head of a pack of riderless bicycles—metal frames glistening, reflector lights glinting red, wheels throwing up arcs of fine spray, as they went off down the wet street.

Around the corner and out of sight.

"Nice friends the kid had," a plainclothes detective who was standing near them said to the uniformed officer beside him. "Took off with just about every bike on the street and left him holding the bag."

Jilly didn't think so. Not this time.

This time they'd gone free.

~

Charles de Lint is a full-time writer and musician who makes his home in Ottawa, Canada. This author of more than seventy adult, young adult, and children's books, he has won the World Fantasy, Aurora, Sunburst, and White Pine Awards, among other honors. De Lint is also a poet, artist, songwriter, performer, and folklorist, and he writes a book-review column for *The Magazine of Fantasy & Science Fiction*.

~

Theradane is nowhere near our world, which is good: the beleaguered city is constantly beset by warring wizards and under assault from deadly magic raining from the sky. Its magic-soaked streets are seldom safe to traverse.

A Year and a Day in Old Theradane
Scott Lynch

1. Wizard Weather

It was raining when Amarelle Parathis went out just after sunset to find a drink, and there was strange magic in the rain. It came down in pale lavenders and coppers and reds, soft lines like liquid dusk that turned to luminescent mist on the warm pavement. The air itself felt like champagne bubbles breaking against the skin. Over the dark shapes of distant rooftops, blue-white lightning blazed, and stuttering thunder chased it. Amarelle would have sworn she heard screams mixed in with the thunder.

The gods-damned wizards were at it again.

Well, she had a thirst, and an appointment, and odd rain wasn't even close to the worst thing that had ever fallen on her from the skies over Theradane. As she walked, Amarelle dripped flickering colors that had no names. She cut a ghostly trail through fog that drifted like the murk beneath a pink and orange sea. As usual when the wizards were particularly bad, she didn't have much company. The Street of Pale Savants was deserted. Shopkeepers stared forlornly from behind their windows on the Avenue of Seven Angles.

This had been her favorite sort of night, once. Heavy weather to drive witnesses from the streets. Thunder to cover the noise of feet creeping over rooftops. These days it was just lonely, unpredictable, and dangerous.

A double arc of silvery lights marked the Tanglewing Canal Bridge, the last between her and her destination. The lights burned within lamps held by rain-stained white marble statues of shackled, hooded figures. Amarelle kept her eyes fixed on her feet as she crossed the bridge. She knew the plaques beneath the statues by heart. The first two on the left, for example:

BOLAR KUSS

TRAITOR

NOW I SERVE THERADANE ALWAYS

CAMIRA THOLAR

MURDERESS

NOW I SERVE THERADANE ALWAYS

The statues themselves didn't trouble her, or even the lights. So what if the city lit some of its streets and bridges with the unshriven souls of convicts, bound forever into melodramatic sculptures with fatuous plaques? No, the trouble was how those unquiet spirits whispered to passers-by.

Look upon me, beating heart, and witness the price of my broken oaths.

"Fuck off, Bolar," muttered Amarelle. "I'm not plotting to overthrow the Parliament of Strife."

Take warning, while your blood is still warm, and behold the eternal price of my greed and slaughter!

"I don't have a family to poison, Camira."

Amarelle, whispered the last statue on the left. *It ought to be you up here, you faithless bitch.*

Amarelle stared at that last inscription, just as she promised herself she wouldn't every time she came this way.

SCAVIUS OF SHADOW STREET

THIEF

NOW I SERVE THERADANE ALWAYS

"I never turned my back on you," Amarelle whispered. "I paid for sanctuary. We all did. We begged you to get out of the game with us, but you didn't listen. You blew it."

You bent your knees to my killers before my flesh was even cold.

"We all bought ourselves a little piece of the city, Scav. That was the plan. You just did it the hard way."

Some day you will share this vigil with me.

"I'm done with all that now. Light your bridge and leave me alone."

There was no having a reasonable conversation with the dead. Amarelle kept moving. She only came this way when she wanted a drink, and by the time she got off the bridge she always needed at least two.

Thunder rolled through the canyons of the streets. A building was on fire somewhere to the east, smoldering unnatural purple. Flights of screeching bat-winged beasts filled the sky between the flames and the low, glowing clouds. Some of them tangled and fought, with naked claws and barbed spears and clay jars of explosive fog. The objectives the creatures contended for were known only to gods and sorcerers.

Gods-damned wizards and their stupid feuds. Too bad they ran the city. Too bad Amarelle needed their protection.

2. The Furnished Belly of the Beast

The Sign of the Fallen Fire lay on the west side of Tanglewing Street. Was, more accurately, the entire west side of Tanglewing Street. No room for anything else beside the cathedral of coiled bones knocked down fifteen centuries before, back when wild dragons occasionally took offense at the growing size of Theradane and paid it a visit. This one had settled so artistically in death, some long-forgotten entrepreneur had scraped out flesh and scales and roofed the steel-hard bones right where they lay.

Amarelle went in through the dragon's mouth, shook burnt orange rain from her hair and watched wisps of luminous steam curl up from the carpet where the droplets landed. The bouncers lounging against eight-foot serrated fangs all nodded to her.

The tavern had doors where the dragon had once had tonsils. Those doors smelled good credit and opened smoothly.

The Neck was for dining and the Tail was for gambling. The Arms offered rooms for sleeping or not sleeping, as the renters preferred.

Amarelle's business was in the Gullet, the drinking cavern under the dead beast's ribs and spine, where one hundred thousand bottles gleamed on racks and shelves behind the central bar.

Goldclaw Grask, the floor manager, was an ebony-scaled goblin in a dapper suit woven from actual Bank of Theradane notes. He had one in a different denomination for every night of the week; tonight he wore fifties.

"Amarelle Parathis, the Duchess Unseen," he cried. "I see you just fine!"

"That one certainly never gets old, Grask."

"I'm counting glasses and silverware after you leave tonight."

"I'm retired and loving it," said Amarelle. She'd pulled three jobs at the Sign of the Fallen Fire in her working days. Certainly none for silverware. "Is Sophara on bar tonight?"

"Of course," said Grask. "It's the seventeenth. Same night of the month your little crew always gets together and pretends it's just an accident. Those of you who aren't lighting the streets, that is."

Amarelle glared. The goblin rustled over, reached up, took her left hand, and flicked his tongue contritely against her knuckles.

"I'm sorry," he said. "I didn't mean to be an asshole. I know, you paid the tithe, you're an honest sheep living under the bombardment like the rest of us. Look, Sophara's waving. Have one on me."

Sophara Miris had mismatched eyes and skin the color of rosewood, fine aquamarine hair and the hands of a streetside card sharp. When she'd paid her sanctuary tithe to the Parliament of Strife, she'd been wanted on three hundred and twelve distinct felony charges in eighteen cities. These days she was senior mage-mixologist at the Sign of the Fallen Fire, and she already had Amarelle's first drink half-finished.

"Evening, stranger." Sophara scrawled orders on a slate and handed it to one of the libationarians, whose encyclopedic knowledge of the contents and locations of all the bottles kept the bar running. "Do you remember when we used to be interesting people?"

"I think being alive and at liberty is pretty damn interesting," said Amarelle. "Your wife planning on dropping in tonight?"

"Any minute now," said Sophara, stirring equal parts liquor and illusion into a multi-layered concoction. "The self-made man's holding a booth for us. I'm mixing you a Rise and Fall of Empires, but I heard Grask. You want two of these? Or something else?"

"You feel like making me a Peril on the Sea?" said Amarelle.

"Yours to command. Why don't you take a seat? I'll be over when the drinks are ready."

Ten dozen booths and suspended balconies filled the Gullet, each carefully spaced and curtained to allow a sense of intimate privacy in the midst of grand spectacle. Lightning, visible through skylights between the ribs, crackled overhead as Amarelle crossed the floor. Her people had a usual place for their usual night, and Shraplin was holding the table.

Shraplin Self-Made, softly whirring concatenation of wires and gears, wore a tattered vermilion cloak embroidered with silver threads. His sculpted brass face had black gemstone eyes and a permanent ghost of a smile. A former foundry drudge, he'd taken advantage of the old Theradane law that a sentient automaton owned its own head and the thoughts therein. Over the course of fifteen years, he'd carefully stolen cogs and screws and bolts and wires and gradually replaced every inch of himself from the neck down until not a speck of his original body remained, and he was able to walk away from the perpetual magical indenture attached to it. Not long after that he'd found klepto-kindred spirits in Amarelle Parathis' crew.

"Looking wet, boss," he said. "What's coming down out there?"

"Weird water," said Amarelle, taking a place beside him. "Pretty, actually. And don't call me boss."

"Certain patterns engrave themselves on my ruminatory discs, boss." Shraplin poured a touch of viscous black slime from a glass into a port on his neck. "Parliament's really going at it tonight. When I got here purple fire was falling on the High Barrens."

"That's one advantage of living in our prosperous thaumatocracy," sighed Amarelle. "Always something interesting exploding nearby. Hey, here's our girls."

Sophara Miris had one hand under a tray of drinks and the other around Brandwin Miris' waist. Brandwin had frosted lavender skin that was no magical affectation and thick amber spectacles over golden eyes. Brandwin, armorer, artificer, and physician to automatons, had the death sentence in three principalities for supplying the devices that had so frequently allowed the Duchess Unseen's crew to evade boring entanglements in local judicial systems. The only object she'd ever personally stolen in her life was the heart of the crew's magician.

"Shraplin, my toy," said Brandwin. She touched fingertips with the automaton before sitting down. "Valves valving and pipes piping?"

"Fighting fit and free of rust," said Shraplin. "And your own metabolic processes and needs?"

"Well attended to," said Sophara with a smirk. "Shall we get this meeting of the Retired Folks' Commiseration and Inebriation Society rolling? Here's something phlegmatic and sanguine for you, Shraplin."

She handed over another tumbler of black ooze. The artificial man had no use for alcohol, so he kept a private reserve of human temperaments magically distilled into asphaltum lacquer behind the bar.

"A Black Lamps of Her Eyes for me," said Sophara. "A Tower of the Elephant for the gorgeous artificer. And for you, Your Grace, a Peril on the Sea and a Rise and Fall of Empires."

Amarelle hefted the latter, a thick glass containing nine horizontal layers of rose-tinted liquors, each layer inhabited by a moving landscape. These varied from fallow hills and fields at the bottom to great cities in the middle layers to a ruin-dotted waste on high, topped by clouds of foam.

"Anyone heard from Jade?" she said.

"Same as always," said Shraplin. "Regards and don't wait up."

"Regards and don't wait up," muttered Amarelle. She looked around the table, saw mismatched eyes and shaded eyes and cold black stones fixed on her in expectation. As always. So be it. She raised her glass, and they did likewise.

"Here's a toast," she said. "We did it and lived. We put ourselves in prison to stay out of prison. To absent friends, gone where no words nor treasure of ours can restore amends. We did it and lived. To the chains we refused and the ones that snared us anyway. We did it and lived."

She slammed the drink back, poured layers of foaming history down her throat. She didn't usually do this sort of thing to herself without dinner to cushion the impact, but hell, it seemed that kind of night. Lightning flashed above the skylights.

"Did you have a few on your way over here, boss?" said Shraplin.

"The Duchess is dead." Amarelle set her empty glass down firmly. "Long live the Duchess. Now, do I have to go through the sham of pulling my cards out and dealing them, or would you all prefer to just pile your money neatly in the center of the table for me?"

"Oh, honey," said Brandwin. "We're not using your deck. It knows more tricks than a show dog."

"I'll handicap myself," said Amarelle. She lifted the Peril on the Sea, admired the aquamarine waves topped with vanilla whitecaps, and in two gulps added it to the ball of fast-spreading warmth in her stomach. "There's some magic I can appreciate. So, are we playing cards or having a staring contest? Next round's on me!"

3. Cheating Hands

"Next round's on me," said Amarelle an hour and a half later. The table was a mess of cards, bank notes, and empty glasses.

"Next round's IN you, boss," said Shraplin. "You're three ahead of the rest of us."

"Seems fair. What the hell did I just drink, anyway?"

"A little something I call the Amoral Instrument," said Sophara. Her eyes were shining. "I'm not allowed to make it for customers. Kind of curious to see what happens to you, in fact."

"Water off a duck's back," said Amarelle, though the room had more soft edges than she remembered and her cards were not entirely cooperating with her plan to hold them steady. "This is a mess. A mess! Shraplin, you're probably sober-esque. How many cards in a standard deck?"

"Sixty, boss."

"How many cards presently visible in our hands or on the table?"

"Seventy-eight."

"That's ridiculous," said Amarelle. "Who's not cheating? We should be pushing ninety. Who's not cheating?"

"I solemnly affirm that I haven't had an honest hand since we started," said Brandwin.

"Magician," said Sophara, tapping her cards against her breast. "Enough said."

"I'm wearing my cheating hands, boss," said Shraplin. He wiggled his fingers in blurry silver arcs.

"This is sad." Amarelle reached behind her left ear, conjured a seventy-ninth card out of her black ringlets, and added it to the pattern on the table. "We really are getting old and decrepit."

Fresh lightning tore the sky, painting the room in gray-white pulses. Thunder exploded just overhead; the skylights rattled in their frames and even the great bone-rafters seemed to shake. Some of the other drinkers stirred and muttered.

"Fucking wizards," said Amarelle. "Present company excepted, of course."

"Why would I except present company?" said Brandwin, tangling the fingers of one hand in Sophara's hair and gracefully palming an eightieth card onto the table with her other.

"It's been terrible all week," said Sophara. "I think it's Ivovandas, over in the High Barrens. Her and some rival I haven't identified, spitting fire and rain and flying things all over the damn place. The parasol sellers have been making a killing with those new leather and chainmail models."

"Someone ought to stroll up there and politely ask them to give it a rest." Shraplin's gleaming head rotated slowly until he was peering at Amarelle. "Someone famous, maybe. Someone colorful and respected. Someone with a dangerous reputation."

"Better to say nothing and be thought a fool," said Amarelle, "than to interfere in the business of wizards and remove all doubt. Who needs a fresh round? Next one's still on me. I plan on having all your money when we call it a night, anyway."

4. The Trouble with Glass Ceilings

The thunder and lightning were continuous for the next hour. Flapping, howling things bounced off the roof at regular intervals. Half the patrons in the Gullet cleared out, pursued by the cajoling of Goldclaw Grask.

"The Sign of the Fallen Fire has stood for fifteen centuries!" he cried. "This is the safest place in all of Theradane! You really want to be out in the streets on a night like this? Have you considered our fine rooms in the Arms?"

There was a high-pitched sound of shattering glass. Something large and wet and dead hit the floor next to the bar, followed by a shower of skylight fragments and glowing rain. Grask squawked for a house magician to unmake the mess while the exodus quickened around him.

"Ahhh, nice to be off duty." Sophara sipped unsteadily from a tumbler of something blue and uncomplicated. The bar had cut her off from casting her own spells into drinks.

"You know," said Amarelle, slowly, "maybe someone really should go up there to the High Barrens and tell that old witchy bitch to put a leash on her pets."

The room, through her eyes, had grown softer and softer as the noisy night wore on, and had now moved into a decidedly impressionist phase. Goldclaw Grask was a bright smear chasing other bright smears across the floor, and even the cards on the table were no longer holding still long enough for Amarelle to track their value.

"Hey," she said, "Sophara, you're a citizen in good standing. Why don't we get you made a member of Parliament so you can make these idiots stop?"

"Oh, brilliant! Well, first I'd need to steal or invent a really good youth-binding," said the magician, "something better than the three-in-five I'm working now, so I can ripen my practice for a century or two. You might find this timeline inconvenient for your purposes."

"Then you'd need to find an external power locus to kick up your juice," said Brandwin.

"Yes," said Sophara, "and harness it without any other hazard-class sorcerers noticing. Oh, and I'd also need to go *completely out of my everfucking head*! You have to be a dead-eyed dirty-souled maniac to want to spend your extended life trading punches with other maniacs. Once you've seized that power, there's no getting off the merry-go-round. You fight like hell just to hold on or you get shoved off."

"Splat!" said Brandwin.

"Not my idea of a playground," said Sophara, finishing her drink and slamming the empty glass down emphatically.

An instant later there was a horrendous shattering crash. A half-ton of dark winged something, its matted fur rain-wet and reeking, plunged through the skylight directly overhead and obliterated their table. A confused blur of motion and noise attended the crash, and Amarelle found herself on the floor with a dull ache between her breasts.

Some dutiful, stubborn fraction of her awareness kicked its way to the surface of the alcoholic ocean in her mind, and there clutched at straws until it had pieced together the true sequence of events. Shraplin, of course—the nimble automaton had shoved her aside before diving across the table to get Sophara and Brandwin clear.

"Hey," said Amarelle, sitting up, "you're not drunk at all!"

"That was part of my cheating, boss." The automaton had been very nearly fast enough, very nearly. Sophara and Brandwin were safe, but his left leg was pinned under the fallen creature and the table.

"Oh, you best of all possible automatons! Your poor foot!" Brandwin crawled over to him and kissed the top of his brass head.

"I've got three spares at home," said Shraplin.

"That tears it," muttered Amarelle, wobbling and weaving back to her feet. "Nobody drops a gods-damned gargoyle on my friends!"

"I think it's a byakhee," said Brandwin, poking at the beast. It had membranous wings and a spear protruding from what might have been its neck. It smelled like old cheese washed in gangrene and graveyard dew.

"I think it's a vorpilax, love," said Sophara. She drunkenly assisted her wife in pulling Shraplin out from under the thing. "Consider the bilateral symmetry."

"I don't care what it is," said Amarelle, fumbling into her long black coat. "Nobody drops one on my card game or my crew. I'm going to find out where this Ivovandas lives and give her a piece of my mind."

"Haste makes corpses, boss," said Shraplin, shaking coils and widgets from the wreckage of his foot. "I was just having fun with you earlier."

"Stupid damn commerce-murdering wizards!" Goldclaw Grask arrived at last, with a gaggle of bartenders and waiters in train. "Sophara!

Are you hurt? What about the rest of you? Shraplin! That looks expensive. Tell me it's not expensive!"

"I can soon be restored to prime functionality," said Shraplin. "But what if I suggested that tonight is an excellent night for you to tear up our bill?"

"I, uh, well, if that wouldn't get you in trouble," said the goblin, directing waiters with mops toward the growing puddle of pastel-colored rainwater and gray ichor under the beast.

"If you give it to us freely," said Sophara, "it's not theft, and none of us break our terms of sanctuary. And Shraplin is right, Amarelle. You can't just go berate a member of the Parliament of Strife! Even if you could safely cross the High Barrens in the middle of this mess—"

"Of course I can." Amarelle stood up nearly straight and, after a few false starts, approximately squared her shoulders. "I'm not some marshmallow-muscled tourist, I'm the Duchess Unseen! I stole the sound of the sunrise and the tears of a shark. I borrowed a book from the library of Hazar and didn't return it. I crossed the Labyrinth of the Death Spiders in Moraska TWICE—"

"I know," said Sophara. "I was there."

" . . . and then I went back and stole all the Death Spiders!"

"That was ten years and an awful lot of strong drinks ago," said Sophara. "Come on, darling, I mixed most of the drinks myself. Don't scare us like this, Amarelle. You're drunk and retired. Go home."

"This smelly thing could have killed all of us," said Amarelle.

"Well, thanks to a little luck and a lot of Shraplin, it didn't. Come on, Amarelle. Promise us you won't do anything stupid tonight. Will you *promise* us?"

5. Removing All Doubt

The High Barrens, east of Tanglewing Street, were empty of inhabitants and full of nasty surprises from the battle in progress. Amarelle kept out of the open, moving from shadowed arch to garden wall to darkened doorway, stumbling frequently. The world had a fragile liquid quality, running at the edges and spinning on previously unrevealed axes. She was not drunk enough to forget that she had to take extra care and still far too drunk to realize that she ought to be fleeing the way she'd come.

The High Barrens had once been a neighborhood of mansions and topiary wonders and public fountains, but the coming of the wizard Ivovandas has sent the former inhabitants packing. The arguments of the Parliament of Strife had blasted holes in the cobblestones, cracked and dried the fountains, and sundered the mansions like unloved toy houses. The purple fire from before was still smoldering in a tall ruined shell of wood and brick. Amarelle sidestepped the street-rivers of melted lead that had once been the building's roof.

It wasn't difficult to find the manse of Ivovandas, the only lit and tended structure in the neighborhood, guarded by smooth walls, glowing ideograms, and rustling red-green hedges with the skeletons of many birds and small animals scattered in their undergrowth. A path of interlocked alabaster stones, gleaming with internal light, led forty curving yards to a golden front door.

Convenient. That guaranteed a security gauntlet.

The screams of terrible flying things high above made concentration even more difficult, but Amarelle applied three decades of experience to the path and was not disappointed. Four trapped stones she avoided by intuition, two by dumb drunken luck. The gravity-orientation reversal was a trick she'd seen before; she cartwheeled (sloppily) over the dangerous patch and the magic pushed her headfirst back to the ground rather than helplessly into the sky. She never even felt the silvery call of the tasteful hypnotic toad sculptures on the lawn, as she was too inebriated to meet their eyes and trigger the effect.

When she reached the front door, the golden surface rippled like a molten pool and a sculpted arm emerged clutching a knocker ring. Amarelle flicked a collapsible baton out of her coat and used it to tap the ring against the door while she stood aside. There was a brief pause after the darts had hissed through empty air, and then a voice boomed:

"WHO COMES UNBIDDEN TO THE DOOR OF THE SUPREME SPELLWRIGHT IVOVANDAS OF THE HONORABLE PARLIAMENT OF THERADANE? SPEAK, WORM!"

"I don't take shit from doors," said Amarelle. "I'm flattering your mistress by knocking. Tell her a citizen of Theradane is here to give her a frank and unexpurgated opinion on how terrible her aim is."

"YOUR ATTITUDE IS UNDERSTANDABLE AND NONETHELESS THOROUGHLY OFFENSIVE. ARCS OF ELECTRODYNAMIC FORCE WILL NOW BE APPLIED TO THE LOBES OF YOUR BRAIN UNTIL THEY ARE SCALDED PULP. TO RECEIVE THIS PRONOUNCEMENT IN THE FORM OF UNIVERSAL PICTOGRAMS, SCREAM ONCE. TO REQUEST MORE RAPID SENSORY OBLIVION, SCREAM TWICE AND WAIT TO SEE WHAT HAPPENS."

"The name is Amarelle Parathis, also known as the Duchess Unseen. Your mistress' stupid feuds are turning a fine old town into a shitsack misery farm and ruining my card games. Are you going to open up, or do I find a window?"

"AMARELLE PARATHIS," said the door. A moment passed. "YOUR NAME IS NOT UNKNOWN. YOU PURCHASED SANCTUARY FROM THE PARLIAMENT OF THERADANE TWO YEARS AND FOUR MONTHS AGO."

"Attadoor," said Amarelle.

"THE MISTRESS WILL RECEIVE YOU."

The sculpted hand holding the knocker withdrew into the liquid surface of the door. A dozen others burst forth, grabbing Amarelle by the throat, arms, legs, and hair. They pulled her off her feet and into the rippling golden surface, which solidified an instant later and retained no trace of her passage.

6. The Cabinet of Golden Hands

Amarelle awoke, thoroughly comfortable but stripped of all her weapons and wearing someone else's silk nightgown.

She was in a doorless chamber, in a feather bed floating gently on a pool of liquid gold that covered the entire floor, or perhaps was the entire floor. Ruby shafts of illumination fell from etched glass skylights, and when Amarelle threw back her covers they dissolved into wisps of aromatic steam.

Something bubbled and churned beneath the golden pool. A small hemisphere rose from the surface, continued rising, became a tall, narrow, humanoid shape. The liquid drained away smoothly, revealing a dove-pale albino woman with flawless auric eyes and hair composed of a thousand golden butterflies, all fluttering elegantly at random.

"Good afternoon, Amarelle," said the wizard Ivovandas. Her feet didn't quite touch the surface of the pool as she drifted toward the bed. "I trust you slept well. You were magnificent last night!"

"Was I? I don't remember . . . uh, that is, I remember some of it . . . am I wearing your clothes?"

"Yes."

"Shouldn't I have a hangover?"

"I took it while you slept," said Ivovandas. "I have a collection of bottled maladies. Your hangover was due to be the stuff of legends. Here be dragons! And by 'here,' I mean directly behind your eyeballs, probably for the rest of the week. I'll find another head to slip it into, someday. Possibly I'll let you have it back if you fail me."

"Fail you? What?" Amarelle leapt to her feet, which sank awkwardly into the mattress. "You have me confused with someone who knows what's going on. Start with how I was magnificent."

"I've never been so extensively insulted! In my own foyer, no less, before we even adjourned to the study. You offered penetratingly savage elucidation of all my character flaws, most of them imaginary, and then you gave me the firmest possible directions on how I and my peers were to order our affairs henceforth, for the convenience of you and your friends."

"I, uh, recall some of that, I think."

"I am curious about a crucial point, citizen Parathis. When you purchased sanctuary from the Parliament of Theradane, you were instructed that personal threats against the members of said parliament could be grounds for summary revocation of sanctuary privileges, were you not?"

"I . . . recall something with that flavor . . . in the paperwork . . . possibly on the back somewhere . . . maybe in the margins?"

"You will agree that your statements last night certainly qualified as personal threats?"

"My statements?"

Smiling, Ivovandas produced a humming blue crystal and used it to project a crisp, solid image into the air beside the bed. It was Amarelle, black-coated and soaked with steaming magic rain, gesturing with clutching hands as she raved:

"And another thing, you venomous milk-faced thundercunt! NOBODY drops a dead vorpilax on my friends, NOBODY! What you fling at the other members of your pointy-hatted circle jerk is your business, but the next time you trifle with the lives of uninvolved citizens, you'd better lock your doors, put on your thickest steel corset, and hire a food taster, you catch my meaning?"

The image vanished.

"Damn," said Amarelle. "I've always thought of myself as basically a happy drunk."

"I'm three hundred and ten years old," said Ivovandas, "and I learned some new words last night! Oh, we were having such fun, until I found myself personally threatened."

"Yes. So it would seem. And how were you thinking we might, ah, proceed in this matter?"

"Ordinarily," said Ivovandas, "I'd magically redirect the outflow of your lower intestine into your lungs, which would be my little way of saying that your sanctuary privileges had been revoked. However, those skills of yours, and that reputation . . . I have a contract suited to such a contractor. Why don't you get dressed and meet me in the study?"

A powerful force struck Amarelle from behind, knocking her off the bed, headfirst into the golden pool. Rather than swimming down she found herself floating up, rising directly through the floor of Ivovandas' study, a large room full of bookshelves, scrollcases, and lacquered basilisk-skin paneling. Amarelle was suddenly wearing her own clothes again.

On the wall was an oil painting of the bedroom Amarelle had just left, complete with a masterful rendering of Ivovandas floating above the golden pool. As Amarelle watched, the painted figure grew larger and larger within the frame, then pushed her arms and head out of it, and with a twist and a jump at last floated free in the middle of the study.

"Now," said Ivovandas. "To put it simply, there is an object within Theradane I expect you to secure. Whether or not your friends help you is of no concern to me. As an added incentive, if you deliver this thing to me quietly and successfully, you will calm a great deal of the, ah, public disagreement between myself and a certain parliamentary peer."

"But the terms of my sanctuary!" said Amarelle. "You got part of my tithe! You know how it works. I can't steal within the boundaries of Theradane."

"Well, you can't threaten me either," said Ivovandas. "And that's a moot point now, so what have you got to lose?"

"An eternity not spent as a street lamp."

"Admirable long-term thinking," said Ivovandas. "But I do believe if you scrutinize your situation you'll see that you're up a certain proverbial creek, and I am the only provisioner of paddles willing to sell you one."

Amarelle paced, hands shoved sullenly into her coat pockets. She and her crew needed the security of Theradane; they had grown too famous, blown too much cover, taken too many interesting keepsakes from the rich and powerful in too many other places. Theradane's system was simplicity itself. Pay a vast sum to the Parliament of Strife, retire to Theradane, and don't practice any of the habits that got you in trouble outside the city. Ever.

"Have some heart, Amarelle. It's not precisely *illegal* for me to coax a master criminal back into operations within the city limits, but I can't imagine my peers would let the matter pass unremarked if they ever found out about it. Do as I ask and I'll gladly smash my little blue crystal. We'll both walk away smiling, in harmonious equipoise."

"What do you want me to secure for you?"

Ivovandas opened a tall cabinet set against the right-hand wall. Inside was a blank tapestry surrounded on all sides by disembodied golden hands not unlike the ones that had hauled Amarelle across the threshold. The hands leapt to life, flicking across the tapestry with golden needles and black thread. Lines appeared on the surface, lines that rapidly became clear to Amarelle as the districts of Theradane and their landmarks: the

High Barrens, the Sign of the Fallen Fire, the Deadlight Downs, and a hundred others, stitch by stitch.

When the map was complete, one hand stitched in a final thread of summer-fire crimson, glowing somewhere in the northeastern part of the city.

"Prosperity Street," said Ivovandas. "In Fortune's Gate, near the Old Parliament."

"I've been there," said Amarelle. "What do you want?"

"Prosperity Street. In Fortune's Gate. Near the Old Parliament."

"I heard you the first time," said Amarelle. "But what do you . . . oh, *no*. You did not. You did *not* just imply that implication!"

"I want you to steal Prosperity Street," said Ivovandas. "The whole street. The entire length of it. Every last brick and stone. It must cease to exist. It must be removed from Theradane."

"That street is three hundred yards long, at the heart of a district so important and money-soaked that even you lunatics don't blast it in your little wars, and it's trafficked at every hour of every day!"

"It would therefore be to your advantage to remove it without attracting notice," said Ivovandas. "But that's your business, one way or the other, and I won't presume to give you instruction in your own narrow specialty."

"It. Is. A. STREET."

"And you're Amarelle Parathis. Weren't you shouting something last night about how you'd stolen the sound of the sunrise?"

"On the right day of the year," said Amarelle, "on the peak of the proper mountain, and with a great deal of help from some dwarves and more copper pipe than I can—damn it, it was very complicated!"

"You stole tears from a shark."

"If you can figure out how to identify a melancholy shark, you're halfway home in that business."

"Incidentally, what *did* you do with the Death Spiders of Moraska once you'd taken them?"

"I mailed them back to the various temples of the spider-priests who'd been annoying me. Let's just say that confinement left the spiders agitated *and* hungry, and that the cult now has very firm rules concerning shipping crates with ventilation holes. Also, I mailed the crates postage *due*."

"Charming!" cried Ivovandas. "Well, you strike me as just the sort of woman to steal a street."

"I suppose my only other alternative is a pedestal engraved 'Now I Serve Theradane Always.'"

"That, or some more private and personal doom," said Ivovandas. "But you have, in the main, apprehended the salient features of your choices."

"Why a street?" said Amarelle. "Before I proceed, let's be candid, or something resembling it. Why do you want this street removed, and how will doing so calm down the fighting between you and your . . . oh. Oh, hell, it's a locus, isn't it?"

"Yes," said Ivovandas. Her predatory grin revealed teeth engraved with hair-fine lines of gold in arcane patterns. "Prosperity Street is the external power locus of the wizard Jarrow, my most unbeloved colleague. It's how he finds the wherewithal to prolong this tedious contest of summoned creatures and weather. Without it, I could flatten him in an afternoon and be home in time for tea."

"Forgive me if this is a touchy subject, but I thought the nature of these loci was about the most closely-guarded secret you and your . . . colleagues possess."

"Jarrow has been indiscreet," said Ivovandas. "But then, he understands the knowledge alone is useless if it can't be coupled to a course of action. A street is quite a thing to dispose of, and the question of how to do so absolutely *stymied* me until you came calling with your devious head so full of drunken outrage. Shall we go to contract?"

The cabinet of golden hands unstitched the map of Theradane, and in its place embroidered a number of paragraphs in neat, even script. Amarelle peered closely at them. They were surprisingly straightforward, describing a trade of one (1) street for one (1) blue crystal to be smashed, but then . . .

"What the hell's this?" she said. "A deadline? A year and a day?"

"It's the traditional span for this sort of arrangement," said Ivovandas. "And surely you can see the sense in it. I prefer Jarrow de-fanged fairly soon, not five or ten or some nebulous and ever-changing number of years from now. I require you working with determination and focus. And you require some incentive other than simple destruction for failure, so there it all is."

"A year and a day," said Amarelle, "and I deliver the street, or surrender my citizenship and worldly wealth to permanent indenture in your service."

"It would be a comfortable and exciting life," said Ivovandas. "But you can avoid it if you're as clever as I hope you are."

"And what if I were to quietly report this arrangement to the wizard Jarrow and see if he could do better for me?"

"A worthwhile contemplation of treacherous entanglement symmetrical to my own! I salute your spirit, but must remind you that Jarrow possesses no blue crystal, nor do you or he possess the faintest notion of where my external locus resides. You must decide for yourself which of us would make the easier target. If you wish to be ruled by wisdom, you'll reach into your pockets now."

Amarelle did, and found that a quill and an ink bottle had somehow appeared therein.

"One street," she said. "For one crystal. One year and one day."

"It's all there in plain black thread," said Ivovandas. "Will you sign?"

Amarelle stared at the contract and ground her teeth, a habit her mother had always sternly cautioned her against. At last, she uncapped the bottle of ink and wet the quill.

7. Another Unexpected Change of Clothing

The usual tumult of wizardly contention had abated. Even Ivovandas and Jarrow seemed to be taking a rest from their labors when Amarelle walked out of the High Barrens under a peach-colored afternoon haze. All the clocks in the city sounded three, refuting and echoing and interrupting one another, the actual ringing of the hour taking somewhere north of two and a half minutes due to the fact that clocks in Theradane were traditionally mis-synchronized to confuse malicious spirits.

Amarelle's thoughts were an electric whirl of anxiety and calculation. She hailed a mechanavipede and was soon speeding over the rooftops of the city in a swaying chair tethered beneath the straining wings of a flock of mechanical sparrows. There was simply nowhere else to go for help;

she would have to heave herself before her friends like jetsam washed up on a beach.

Sophara and Brandwin lived in a narrow, crooked house on Shankville Street, a house they'd secured at an excellent price due to the fact that it sometimes had five stories and sometimes six. Where the sixth occasionally wandered off to was unknown, but while it politely declined their questions about its business it also had the courtesy to ask none concerning theirs. Amarelle had the mechanavipede heave her off into a certain third-floor window which served as a friends-only portal for urgent business.

The ladies of the house were in, and by a welcome stroke of luck so was Shraplin. Brandwin was fussing with the pistons of his replacement left foot, while Sophara sprawled full-length on a velvet hammock wearing smoked glasses and an ice-white beret that exuded analgesic mist in a halo about her head.

"How is it that you're not covered in vomit and begging for death?" said Sophara. "How is it that you consumed three times your own weight in liquor and I've got sole custody of the hangover?"

"I had an unexpected benefactor, Soph. Can you secure this chamber for sensitive conversation?"

"The whole house is reasonably safe," groaned the magician, rolling off the hammock with minimal grace and dignity. "Now, if you want me to weave a deeper silence, give me a minute to gather my marbles. Wait . . . "

She pulled her smoked glasses off and peered coldly at Amarelle. Stepping carefully around the mess of specialized tools and mechanical gewgaws littering the carpet, she approached, sniffing the air.

"Something wrong, dearest?" said Brandwin.

"Shhhh," said Sophara. She rubbed her eyes in the manner of the freshly-awake, then reached out, moved Amarelle's left coat lapel aside, and pulled a gleaming gold thread out of the black wool.

"You," she said, arching her aquamarine eyebrows at Amarelle, "have been seeing another wizard."

Sophara clapped her hands and an eerie hush fell upon the room. The faint sounds of the city outside were utterly banished.

"Ivovandas," said Amarelle. "I ran off and did something stupid last night. In my defense, I would just like to say that I was angry, and you were the one mixing the drinks."

"You unfailingly omni-bothersome bitch," said Sophara. "Well, this little thread would allow Ivovandas to eavesdrop, if not for my counterspell and certain fundamental confusions worked into the stones of this house. And where there's obvious chicanery, there's something lurking behind it. Take the rest of your clothes off."

"What?"

"Do it now, Amarelle!" Sophara retrieved a silver-engraved casket from a far corner of the room, clicked it open, and made urgent motions while Amarelle shed her coat.

"You see how direct she is?" Brandwin squeezed a tiny bellows to pressurize a tube of glowing green oil within Shraplin's leg. "We'd never have gotten anywhere if she'd waited for me to make the first move."

"You keep your eyes on your work," said Sophara. "I'll do the looking for both of us and give you details later."

"I sometimes think that 'friend' is just a word I use for all the people I haven't murdered yet," said Amarelle, hopping and twirling out of her boots, leggings, belts, vest, blouse, sharp implements, silk ropes, smoke capsules, and smallclothes. When the last stitch was discarded, Sophara slammed the casket shut and muttered spells over the lock.

As a decided afterthought, smiling and taking her time, she eventually fetched Amarelle a black silk dressing robe embroidered with blue-white astronomical charts.

"It seems to be my day to try on everyone else's clothes," she muttered.

"I'm sorry about your things," said Sophara. "I should be able to sweep them for further tricks, but Ivovandas is so far outside my weight class, it might take days."

"Never let a wizard get their hands on your clothes," said Brandwin. "At least not until she promises to move in with you. It ought to be safe to talk now."

"I'm not entirely sure how to say this," said Amarelle, "but the concise version is that I'm temporarily unretired."

She told the whole story, pausing only to answer Sophara's excited questions about the defenses and décor of Ivovandas' manse.

"That's a hell of a thing, boss," said Shraplin when Amarelle finished. The clocks within the house started chiming five, and didn't finish for some time. The city clocks were still sealed beyond Sophara's silence. "I thought we were up against it when that shark tears job landed on us. But a street!"

"I wonder how Jarrow figured out it was a locus." Sophara adjusted the analgesic hat, which had done her much good over the long course of Amarelle's story. "I wonder how he harnessed it without anyone interfering!"

"Keep it relevant, dreamer." Brandwin massaged her wife's legs. "The pertinent question is, how are we going to pull it off?"

"I only came for advice," said Amarelle hastily. "This is all my fault, and nobody else needs to risk their sanctuary because I got drunk and sassed a wizard."

"Let me enlighten you, boss," said Shraplin. "If you don't want me to follow you around being helpful, you must be planning to smash my head right now."

"Amarelle, you *can't* keep us out in the cold now! This mischief is too delicious," said Sophara. "And it's clearly not prudent to let you wander off on your own."

"I'm grateful," said Amarelle, "but I feel responsible for your safety."

"The Parliament of Strife craps destruction on its own city at random, boss." Shraplin spread his hands. "How much more unsafe can we get? Frankly, two and a half quiet years is adequate to my taste."

"Yes," said Sophara. "Hang your delicate feelings, Amarelle, you know we won't let you . . . oh, wait. You foxy bag of tits and sugar! You didn't come here just for advice! You put your noble face on so we'd pledge ourselves without the pleasure of seeing you beg!"

"And you fell for it." Amarelle grinned. "So it's agreed, we're all out of retirement and we're stealing a street. If anyone cares to let me know how the hell that's supposed to work, the suggestion box is open."

8. The Cheap Shot

They spent the first two days in measurement and surveillance. Prosperity Street was three hundred and seventeen yards long running north-south, an average of ten yards wide. Nine major avenues and fifteen alleys bisected it. One hundred and six businesses and residences opened onto it, one of which was a wine bar serving distillations of such quality that a third day was lost to hangovers and remonstrations.

They struck on the evening of the fourth day, as warm mist curled lazily from the sewers and streetlamps gleamed like pearls in folds of gray gauze. The clocks began chiming eleven, a process that often lasted until it was nearly time for them to begin striking twelve.

A purple-skinned woman in the coveralls of a municipal functionary calmly tinkered with the sign post at the intersection of Prosperity and Magdamar. She placed the wooden shingle marked PROSPERITY S in a sack and tipped her hat to a drunk, semi-curious goblin. Brandwin emptied three intersections of PROSPERITY S signs before the clocks settled down.

At the intersection of Prosperity and Ninefingers, a polite brass-headed drudge painted over every visible PROSPERITY S with an opaque black varnish. Two blocks north, a mechanavipede flying unusually low with a cargo of one dark-haired woman crashed into a signpost, an accident that would be repeated six times. At the legendarily confusing seven-way intersection where the various Goblin Markets joined Prosperity, a sorceress disguised as a cat's shadow muttered quiet spells of alphabetic nullifcation, wiping every relevant signpost like a slate.

They had to remove forty-six shingles or signposts and deface the placards of sixteen businesses that happened to be named after the street. Lastly, they arranged to tip a carboy of strong vitriol over a ceremonial spot in the pavement where PROSPERITY STREET was set in iron letters. When those had become PRCLGILV SLGFLL, they gave the mess a quick splash of water and hurried away to dispose of their coveralls, paints, and stolen city property.

The next day, Ivovandas was less than impressed.

"Nothing happened." Her gold eyes gleamed dangerously and her butterflies were still. "Not one femto-scintilla of deviation or dampening in the potency of Jarrow's locus. Though there were quite a few confused travelers and tourists. You need to steal the street, Amarelle, not vandalize its ornaments."

"I didn't expect it to be that easy," said Amarelle. "I just thought we ought to eliminate the simplest approach first. Never lay an Archduke on the table when a two will do."

"The map is not the territory." Ivovandas gestured and transported Amarelle to the front lawn of her manse, where the hypnotic toad sculptures nearly cost her even more lost time.

9. Brute Force

Their next approach took eleven days to plan and arrange, including two days lost to a battle between parliament wizards in the western sectors that collapsed the Temple-Bridge of the God of Hidden Names.

The street signs had been restored at the intersection of Prosperity and Languinar, the southernmost limit of Prosperity Street. The sunrise sky was just creeping over the edge of the city in orange and scarlet striations, and the clocks were or were not chiming seven. A caravan of reinforced cargo coaches drawn by armored horses halted on Languinar, preparing to turn north. The signs hanging from the coaches read:

NUSBARQ DESISKO AND SONS
HAZARDOUS ANIMAL TRANSPORT

As the caravan moved into traffic, a woman in a flaming red dress riding a mecharabbit hopped rudely into the path of the lead carriage, triggering an unlikely but picturesque chain of disasters. Carriage after carriage toppled, wheel after wheel flew from its hub, horse team after horse team ran neighing into traffic as their emergency releases snapped. The side of the first toppled carriage exploded outward, and a furry, snarling beast came bounding out of the wreckage.

"RUN," cried someone, who happened to be the woman in the red dress. "IT'S A SPRING-HEELED WEREJACKAL!"

A heartbeat later her damaged mecharabbit exploded, enveloping her in a cloud of steam and sparks. The red dress was reversible and Amarelle had practiced swapping it around by touch. Three seconds later she ran from the cloud of steam dressed in a black hooded robe. Shraplin, not at all encumbered by seventy-five pounds of fur, leather, and wooden claws, merrily activated the reinforced shock-absorbing leg coils Brandwin had cobbled together for him. He went leaping and howling across the crowd, turning alarm into panic and flight.

Twenty-two unplanned carriage or mechanavipede collisions took place in the next half-minute, locking traffic up for two blocks north of the initial accident. Amarelle didn't have time to count them as she hurried north in Shraplin's wake.

Another curiously defective carriage in the Nusbarq Desisko caravan cracked open, exposing its cargo of man-sized hives to the open air and noise. Thousands of Polychromatic Reek-Bees, scintillating in every color of the rainbow and fearful for the safety of their queens, flew forth to spew defensive stink-nectar on everything within buzzing distance. The faintest edge of that scent followed Amarelle north, and she regretted having eaten breakfast. Hundreds of people would be burning their clothes before the day was through.

All along the length of Prosperity Street, aural spells prepared in advance by Sophara began to erupt. Bold, authoritative voices ordered traffic to halt, passers-by to run, shops to close, citizens to pray for deliverance. They screamed about werejackals, basilisks, reek-bees, cradlerobber wasps, rabid vorpilax, and the plague. They ordered constables and able-bodied citizens to use barrels and carriages as makeshift riot-barricades at the major intersections, which some of them did.

Amarelle reached the alley after Ninefingers Way and found the package she'd stashed behind a rotten crate the night before. Soon she emerged from the alley in the uniform of a Theradane constable, captain's bars shining on her collar, steel truncheon gleaming. She issued useless and contradictory orders, fomented panic, pushed shopkeepers into their stores and ordered them to bar their doors. When she met actual constables, she jabbed them with the narcotic prong concealed on the end of her truncheon. Their unconscious bodies, easily mistaken for dead, added a piquant verisimilitude to the raging disquiet.

At the northern end of Prosperity Street, a constabulary riot wagon commanded by a pair of uniformed women experienced another improbable accident when it came into contact with the open fire of a careless street fondue vendor. Brandwin and Sophara threw their helmets aside and ran screaming, infecting dozens of citizens with disoriented panic even before the rockets and canisters inside the wagon began to explode. For nearly half an hour pinkish-white arcs of sneezing powder, soporific smoke, and eye-scalding pepper dust rained on Prosperity Street.

Eventually, two parliament wizards had to grudgingly intervene to help the constables and bucket brigades restore order. The offices of Nusbarq Desisko and Sons were found to be empty and their records missing, presumably carried with them when they fled the city. The spring-heeled werejackal was never located and was assumed taken as a pet by some wizard or another.

"What do you mean, nothing happened?" Amarelle paced furiously in Ivovandas' study the following day, having explained herself to the wizard, who had half-listened while consulting a grimoire that occasionally moaned and laughed to itself. "We closed the full length of Prosperity Street down for more than three hours! We stole the street from everyone on it in a very meaningful sense! The traffic didn't flow, the riot barriers were up, not a scrap of commerce took place anywhere—"

"Amarelle," said the wizard, not taking her eyes from her book, "I applaud your adoption of a more dynamic approach to the problem, but I'm afraid it simply didn't do anything. Not the merest hint of any diminishment to Jarrow's arcane resources. I do wish it were otherwise. Mind the hypnotic toads, as I've strengthened their enchantments substantially." She snapped her fingers, and Amarelle was back on the lawn.

10. The Typographic Method

Sophara directed the next phase of their operations, resigning her place as mage-mixologist indefinitely.

"It was mostly for easy access to the bar anyway," she said. "And they'd kiss my heels to have me back anytime."

A studious, eye-straining month and a half followed. Sophara labored over spell-board, abacus, grimoire, and journal, working in four languages and several forms of thaumaturgical notation that made Amarelle's eyes burn.

"I keep telling you not to look at them!" said Sophara as she adjusted the analgesic beret on Amarelle's head. "You haven't got the proper optical geometry! You and Brandwin! You're worse than cats."

Brandwin prowled libraries and civic archives. Amarelle broke into seventeen major private collections. Shraplin applied his tireless mechanical perception to the task of rapidly sifting thousands of pages in thousands of books. A vast pile of notes grew in Brandwin and Sophara's house, along with an inelegant but thorough master list of scrolls, pamphlets, tomes, and records.

"Any guide to the city," chanted Amarelle, for the formula had become a sort of mantra. "Any notes of any traveler, any records of tax or residence, any mentions of repairs, any journals or recollections. Have we ever done anything *less* sane? How can we possibly expect to locate every single written reference to Prosperity Street in every single document in existence?"

"We can't," said Sophara. "But if my calculations are anywhere near correct, and if this can work at all, we only need to change a certain critical percentage of those records, especially in the official municipal archives."

Shraplin and Brandwin cut panels of wood down to precise replicas of the forty-six street signs and the sixteen business placards they had previously tried to steal. They scraped, sanded, varnished, and engraved, making only one small change to each facsimile.

"I have the key," said Brandwin, emerging from her incense-filled workroom one night, bleary-eyed and cooing at a small white moth perched atop her left index finger. "I call it the Adjustment Moth. It's a very complex and efficient little spell I can cast on anything about this size."

"And what will they do?" said Amarelle.

"They'll become iterating work-enhancers," said Sophara. "It'd take us years to manually adjust all the records we're after. Enchanted with my spell to guide and empower them, we can send these little darlings out to do almost all of the work for us in one night."

"How many do we need?" said Shraplin.

Nine nights later, from carefully-selected points around the city, they loosed 3,449 of Sophara's Adjustment Moths, each of which fluttered into the darkness and thence into libraries, archives, shop cupboards, private studies, and bedside cabinets. The 2,625 Adjustment Moths that were not eaten by bats or appropriated as cat toys located a total of 617,451 references to the name 'Prosperity Street' and made one crucial change to each physical text. By sunrise they were all dead of exhaustion.

Amarelle and her crew replaced the forty-six street signs and sixteen business placards under cover of darkness, then pried up one of the (restored) ceremonial iron letters sunk into the pavement. PROSPERIT STREET, the survivors said. PROSPERIT, read the signs and placards. PROSPERIT STREET read the name of the place in every guidebook, private journal, lease, assize, and tax record in the city, save for a few in magically guarded sanctums of the Parliament of Strife.

Overnight, Prosperity Street had been replaced by its very close cousin, Prosperit Street.

"Amarelle," said Ivovandas, sipping daintily at a cup of molten gold she'd heated in a desk-side crucible, "I sympathize with your agitation at the failure of so original and far-ranging a scheme, but I really must stress the necessity of abandoning these fruitlessly metaphysical approaches. Don't steal the street's name, or its business, or its final 'Y.' Steal the street, wholly and physically!"

Amarelle groaned. "Back to the lawn?"

"Back to the lawn, my dear!"

11. After Amarelle, the Deluge

Twenty-seven days later, one of the natural storms of summer blew in from the west, a churning shroud of dark clouds looking for a brawl. As usual, the wizards of parliament preserved their individual territories and let the rest of Theradane fend for itself. It was therefore theoretically plausible that the elevated aqueduct that crossed Prosperity Street just north of Limping Matron Lane would choose that night to break under the strain.

Prosperity Street was already contending with plugs of debris clogging its sewer grates (these plugs granted unusual thickness and persistence by the spells of Sophara Miris) and with its own valley-like position at the foot of several more elevated neighborhoods. The foaming rush from the broken aqueduct turned a boot-soaking stream into a rather more alarming waist-high river.

Amarelle and her crew lurked in artificial shadows on a high rooftop, dutifully watching to ensure that no one, particularly children and goblins, suffered more than a soaking from the flood. The city hydromancers would eventually show up to set things right, but they were no doubt having a busy night.

"This is still a touch metaphysical, if you ask me," said Sophara.

"It's something of a hybrid approach," said Amarelle. "After all, how can it be a street if it's been physically turned into a canal?"

12. No

"No," said Ivovandas. Amarelle was returned to the lawn.

13. Instructive Measures

Half a year gone. Despite vandalism, riot, werejackals, clerical errors, and flood, Prosperity Street was more worthy of its name than ever. Amarelle strolled the pavement, feeling the autumn sun on her face, admiring the pale bronze leaves of Prayer-trees as they tumbled about in little clouds, inscribed with calligraphic benedictions for anyone whose path they crossed.

There was a stir in the crowds around her, a new cacophony of shouting and muttering and horse-hooves and creaking wheels. Traffic parted to the north, making way for a rumbling coach, half again as high and wide as anything on the street. It was black as death's asshole, windowless, trimmed with engraved silver and inlaid nacre. It had no horses and no driver; each of its four wheels was a circular steel cage in which a slavering red-eyed ghoul ran on four limbs, creating a forward impetus.

The singular coach moaned on its suspension as it swerved and lurched to a halt beside Amarelle. The ghouls leered at her, unbreathing, their flesh crisply necrotic like rice paper pressed over old oozing wounds. The black door flew open and a footstep fell into place. A velvet curtain still fluttered in the entrance to the coach, concealing whatever lay inside. A voice called out, cold as chloroform and old shame.

"Don't you know an invitation when you see one, citizen Parathis?"

Running from wizards in broad daylight without preparation was not a skill Amarelle had ever cultivated, so she stepped boldly into the carriage, ducking her head.

She was startled to find herself in a warm gray space at least forty yards on a side, with a gently curving ceiling lit by floating silver lights. A vast mechanical apparatus was ticking and pulsing and shifting in the middle of the room, something along the lines of an orrery, but in place of moons and planets the thin arms held likenesses of men and women, likenesses carved with exaggerated features and comical flaws. Amarelle recognized one of them as Ivovandas by the gold eyes and butterfly hair.

There were thirteen figures, and they moved in complex interlocking patterns around a model of the city of Theradane.

The carriage door slammed shut behind her. There was no sensation of motion, other than the almost-hypnotic sway and swing of the wizard-orrery.

"My peers," said the cold voice, coming now from behind her. "Like celestial bodies, transiting in their orbits, exerting their influences. Like celestial bodies, not particularly difficult to track or predict in their motions."

Amarelle turned and gasped. The man was short and lithe, his skin like ebony, his hair scrapped down to a reddish stubble. There was a scar on his chin and another on his jawline, each of them familiar to her fingers and lips. Only the eyes were wrong; they were poisoner's eyes, dead as glass.

"You have no fucking right to that face," said Amarelle, fighting not to shout.

"Scavius of Shadow Street, isn't it? Or more like 'wasn't it?' Came with you to Theradane, but we never got his sanctuary money. Blew it in some dramatic gesture, I recall."

"He got drunk and lost it all on a dice throw," she said, wetting her lips and forcing herself to say: "Jarrow."

"Pleased to meet you, Amarelle Parathis." The man wore a simple black jacket and breeches. He extended a hand, which she didn't take. "Lost it all on one throw? That was stupid."

"I'm not unacquainted with drunken mistakes myself," said Amarelle.

"And then he went and did something even more stupid," said Jarrow. "Earned a criminal's apotheosis. Transfigured into a street lamp."

"Please . . . take some other form."

"No." Jarrow scratched his head, shook a finger at her. "That's a fine starting point for the discussion I really brought you here for, Amarelle. Let's talk about behavior that might get someone transfigured into a street decoration."

"I'm retired."

"Sure, kid. Look, there's a very old saying in my family: 'Once is happenstance. Twice is coincidence. Three times is another wizard fucking with you.' You never spent much time near Prosperity Street before, did you? Your apartments are on Hellendal. South of Tanglewing Street. Right?"

"About the location of my apartments, of course."

"You've got iron in your spine, Amarelle, and I'm not here to prolong this or embarrass you. I'm just suggesting, to the room, if you like, that it would be a shame if any more unusual phenomena befell a part of Theradane that is of particular sentimental value to me. This is what your sanctuary money gets you. This is me being kind. Are you pretending to listen, or are you listening?"

"I'm listening."

"Here's a little something to further sharpen your hearing." A burlap sack appeared in Jarrow's hands and he threw it to her. It weighed about ten pounds, and the contents rattled. "The usual verification that I'm serious. You know how it works. Anyhow, in the best of all possible worlds, we never have to have a conversation like this again. What world do you want to live in, Amarelle Parathis?"

The air grew cold. The lights dimmed and receded into the corners of the room, vanishing like stars behind clouds. Amarelle's stomach tumbled, and then her boots were on pavement, the sound of traffic was all around her, and Prayer-tree leaves brushed her face.

The sun was high and warm, and the black coach was nowhere in sight.

Amarelle shook the sack open and cursed as Shraplin's head tumbled out. The edges of the pipes running out of his neck were burnt and bent.

"I don't know what to say, boss." His voice was steady but weak. "I'm embarrassed. I got jumped last night."

"What the hell did they do?"

"Nothing technically illegal, boss. They left my head the contents intact. As for the rest, let's just say I don't expect to see it again."

"I'm sorry, Shraplin. I'll get you to Brandwin. I'm so sorry."

"Quit apologizing, boss." Something whirred and clunked behind the automaton's eyes, and he gave a garbled moan. "But I have to say, my reverence for these high-level wizard types is speeding in what you might call a southerly direction."

"We need more help," whispered Amarelle. "If we're going to put the boot to this mess, I think it's high time we got the whole band back together."

14. The Unretirement of Jadetongue Squirn

She was tall for a goblin, not that that meant anything to most other species. Her scales were like black glass, her eyes like the sudden plunge to blue depths beyond a continental shelf. Her pointed ears were pierced with silver rings, some of which held writing quills she could reach up and seize at leisure.

They all went together to see her in her shadowed cloister at the Theradane Ministry of Finance and Provision, a place that stank of steady habits, respectability, and workers who'd died at their desks with empty in-boxes. She was not best pleased to receive them.

"We're not what we were!" Jade hissed when Amarelle had finished telling most of the story, safely inside the goblin's office and Sophara's sound-proof bubble. "Look at you! Look at the messes you've made! And look at me. How can I possibly help you? I'm an ink-stained functionary these days. I scribe ordinances and design engravings for bank notes."

Amarelle stared at her, biting her lip. Jadetongue Squirn had been jailed six times and escaped six times. You could walk nearly around the world by setting foot only in nations that still sought her for trial. Smuggler, negotiator, procurer of bizarre supplies, she was also the finest forger Amarelle had ever met, capable of memorizing signatures at a glance and reproducing them with either hand.

"We've missed you at our drinking nights," said Brandwin. "You were always welcome. You were always *wanted*."

"I don't belong anymore." Amarelle's voice was flat and she clung to her desk as though it could be a wall between herself and her old comrades. "I'm like a hermit crab that's pulled an office over itself. Maybe the rest of you were only kidding yourselves about retiring, but I'm the real thing. I haven't been coming out to see you because you'd expect Jadetongue Squirn, not this timid little person who wears her clothes."

"We're like a hand with a missing finger," said Amarelle. "We've got half a year to make three hundred yards of street vanish and we need that slick green brain of yours. You said it yourself—look at what a mess we've made so far! Look what Jarrow did to Shraplin."

Amarelle reached into a leather satchel. The automaton's head bounced on Jadetongue's desk a moment later, and she made a rattling noise in her throat.

"Ha ha! The look on your face!" said Shraplin.

"How about the look on *yours*, duncebucket?" she growled. "I ought to stuff you in a drawer for scaring me like that!"

"You see now why we have to have you back," said Amarelle. "Shraplin's the warning. Our next shot has to be for keeps."

"Three funny bitches and a smart-ass automaton sans ass," said Jade. "You think you can just walk in here, tug on my heartstrings, and snatch me out of my sad retirement."

"Yes," said Amarelle.

"We're still not what we were." She put a scaly hand on Shraplin's face, then spun him like a top. "I'm definitely not what I was. But what the hell. Maybe you're right, about needing help, at least."

"So, are you going to take a leave of absence or something?" said Shraplin, when he'd stopped saying "Whaaaaargabaarrrrrgggh!"

"A leave of absence? Are you sure you didn't damage the contents of your head?" Jadetongue glanced around at all the members of the crew. "Sweethearts, softskins, thimblewits, if you're determined to see this thing through, the municipal bureaucracy of Theradane is the *last* asset you want to toss carelessly over your shoulder!"

15. Honest Business

"I haven't asked you for anything to assist us in this whole affair," said Amarelle. "Not once. Now that needs to change."

"I'm not averse in theory to small favors," said Ivovandas, "given that the potential reward for your ultimate success is so personally tantalizing. But do understand, most of my magical resources are currently committed. Nor will I do anything overt enough to harden Jarrow's suspicions. He has the same authority to kill you outright that I do, if he can prove your violation of your sanctuary terms to our peers."

"We're starting a business," said Amarelle. "The High Barrens Reclamation Consortium. We need you to sign on as the principal stakeholder."

"Why?"

"Because nobody can sue you." Amarelle pulled a packet of paper out of her coat and set them on Ivovandas' desk. "We need a couple of wagons and about a dozen workers. We'll provide those. We're going to excavate wrecked mansions in the High Barrens on days when you and Jarrow aren't blasting at each other."

"Again, why?"

"There's some things we need to take," said Amarelle with a smile, "and some things we need to hide. If we do it in our names, the heirs of all the families that ran like hell when you settled here and started shooting at other wizards will line up in court to stop us. If you're the one in charge, they can't do a damned thing."

"I will examine these papers," said Ivovandas. "I will have them returned to you if I deem the arrangement suitable."

Amarelle found herself on the lawn. But three days later, the papers appeared in her apartments, signed and notarized. The High Barrens Reclamation Consortium went to work.

The Parliament of Strife ruled Theradane absolutely but were profoundly disinterested in the mundane business of cleaning the streets and sorting the paperwork. That much they left to their city's strangely feudal and secretive bureaucracy, who were essentially free to do as they pleased so long as the hedges were trimmed and the damage from the continual wizard feuding was repaired. Jade worked efficiently from within this edifice. She pushed through all the requisite paperwork, forged or purchased the essential permits, swept all the mandated delays and hearings under the rug, and then stepped on the rug.

Brandwin hired their crew, a dozen stout men and women. They were paid the going wage for their work, that much again for the occasional danger of proximity to Ivovandas' battles, and a triple portion for keeping their mouths shut. For a week or two they excavated carefully in the wreckage of once-mighty houses, concealing whatever they took from the ruins beneath tarps on their wagons.

Next, Brandwin and Shraplin spent a week refurbishing a trio of wagons as mobile vending carts. They extended wooden skirts around them to the ground, installed folding awnings and sturdy roofs, carved signs and painted them attractively. One of the wagons was kitted out as a book stall, the other two as food carts.

The labyrinth of bribes and permits needed to launch this sort of venture was even more daunting than the one that had preceded the excavation company. Jade outdid herself, weaving blackmail and intimidation into a tapestry of efficient palm-greasing. Whether the permit placards that hung from the vending carts were genuine articles or perfect copies was ultimately irrelevant. No procedural complication survived first contact with Jade's attention.

With four months remaining, Amarelle and Sophara went into legitimate business for themselves. Amarelle peddled books on Prosperity Street until noon, while Sophara plied her precision sorcery for appreciative breakfast crowds on Galban Street. She cooked frosted walnut cakes into the shape of unicorns and cockatrices, caused fresh fruit to squeeze itself into juice glasses, and made her figs and dates give rude speeches while her customers tried to eat them and laugh at the same time. In the afternoon, she and Amarelle switched places.

Some days, Brandwin would operate the third vending cart, offering sweets and beer, but for some time she was absorbed in a number of demanding modifications to Shraplin's body and limbs. These modifications remained hidden in the darkness of her workshop; Shraplin never went out in public wearing anything but one of his ordinary bodies.

One bright day on Prosperity Street, a stray breeze blew one of Amarelle's books open and fluttered its pages. She moved to close it and was startled to find a detailed grayscale engraving of Scavius' face staring up at her from the top page.

"Amarelle," said the illustration. "You seem to have an unexpected literary sideline."

"Can't practice my former trade," she said through gritted teeth. "Money's getting tight."

"So you're exploring new avenues, eh? New avenues? Not even a smile? Well, fine, have it your way. I ought to snuff you, you realize. I don't know who or what prompted the weirdness of the previous few months—"

Amarelle fanned the pages of the book vindictively. The illustration flashed past on each one, and continued talking smoothly when Amarelle gave up.

" . . . but the wisest and cleverest thing would be to turn your bones to molten glass and take no chances. Alas, I need evidence of wrongdoing. Can't just blast sanctuary tithers. People might stop giving us large piles of treasure for the privilege."

"My business partners and I are engaged in boring, legitimate commerce," said Amarelle.

"I know. I've been peeking up your skirts, as it were. Very boring. I thought we ought to have a final word, though. A little reminder that you should stay boring, or I can think of one story that won't have a happy ending."

The book slammed itself shut. Amarelle exhaled slowly, rubbed her eyes, and went back to work.

On the days wore, on the legitimate business went. The women began to move their vending carts more frequently, investing some of their profits in small mechanical equines to make this work easier.

With three months left in the contract, the carts that moved up and down Prosperity Street began to cross paths with carts from elsewhere in the city in a complicated dance that always ended with an unmarked High Barrens Reclamation Consortium wagon paying a quiet evening visit to one of the mansions they were excavating.

Another two months passed, and there was no spot on Prosperity Street that Amarelle or Sophara or Brandwin had not staked out at least temporarily, no merchant they hadn't come to know by name, no constable they hadn't thoroughly pacified with free food, good beer, and occasional gifts of books.

Three days before the contract was due to expire, a loud explosion shook the north end of Prosperity Street, breaking windows and knocking pedestrians to the curb. A mansion in a private court was found burning, already collapsing into itself. A huge black coach lay wrecked in the drive, its ghoul-cage wheels torn open, its roof smashed, its insides revealing nothing but well-upholstered seats and a carpeted floor.

The next day, Amarelle Parathis was politely summoned to the manse of the wizard Ivovandas.

16. Bottled Malady

"Am I satisfied? Satisfaction is a palliative," said Ivovandas, gold-threaded teeth blazing with reflected light, butterflies fluttering furiously. "Satisfaction is mild wine. Satisfaction is a tiny fraction of what I feel. Delight and fulfillment pounding in my breast like triumphant chords! Seventy years of unprofitable disdain from this face-changing reprobate, and now his misery is mine to contemplate at leisure."

"I'm so pleased you were able to crush him," said Amarelle. "Did you manage to get home in time for your tea afterward?"

The golden wizard ignored her and kept staring at the glass cylinder on her desk. It was six inches tall and half as wide, capped with a ground-glass stopper and sealed with wax the color of dried blood. Inside it was wretched Jarrow, shrunken to a suitable proportion and clad in rags. He had reverted (or been forced into) the shape of a cadaverous pale man with a silver-black beard.

"Jarrow," she sighed. "Jarrow. Oh, the laws of proportion and symmetry are restored to operation between us; my sustained pleasure balanced accurately against your lingering discomfort and demise."

"So obviously," said Amarelle, "you consider me to have stolen Prosperity Street in accordance with the contract?"

Jarrow pounded furiously against the glass.

"Oh, obviously, dear Amarelle, you've acquitted yourself splendidly! Yet the street is still there, is it not? Still carrying traffic, still hosting commerce. Before I retrieve your blue crystal, are you of a mind to indulge my former colleague and I with an explanation?"

"Delighted," said Amarelle. "After all our other approaches failed, we decided to try the painstakingly literal. Prosperity Street is roughly three thousand, one hundred and seventy square yards of brick and stone surface. The question we asked ourselves was: who *really* looks at each brick and each stone?"

"Certainly not poor Jarrow," said Ivovandas, "else he'd not find his bottle about to join my collection."

"We resolved to physically steal every single square yard of Prosperity Street, every brick and stone," said Amarelle. "Which yielded three problems. First, how to do so without anyone noticing the noise and tumult of our work? Second, how to do so without anyone objecting to the stripped and uneven mess made of the street in our wake? Third, how to provide the physical labor to handle the sheer volume and tedium of the task?"

"To answer the second point first, we used the High Barrens Restoration Consortium. They carefully fished through the mansions you two have destroyed in your feud to provide us with all the bricks and stones we could ever need.

"A large hollow space was constructed beneath each of our vending carts, which we first plied up and down assorted city streets, not just Prosperity, for an *interminable* length of time to allay suspicion that they were directly aimed at Jarrow's locus."

Jarrow banged his head repeatedly against the inside of his prison.

"Eventually we felt it was safe to proceed with our real business. The rest you must surely have guessed by now. The labor was provided by Shraplin, an automaton, whose meeting with Jarrow left him very eager to bear any trouble or tedium in the cause of his revenge. Shraplin utilized tool-arms custom-forged for him by Brandwin Miris to dig up the bricks and stones of the actual street, and to lay in their place the bricks and stones taken from the High Barrens mansions. At night, the detritus he'd scraped up by day was dumped into the ruins of those same mansions. As for why nobody ever heard Shraplin scraping or pounding away beneath our carts, all I can say is that our magician is highly adept at the production of sound-proof barriers to fit any space or need.

"All that was left to do," said Amarelle, stretching and yawning, "was to spend the months necessary to carefully position our carts over every square foot of Prosperity Street. Nobody ever noticed that when we moved on, the patches of street beneath us had changed subtly from the hour or two before. Eventually, we pried up the last brick that was genuinely important, and Jarrow's locus became just another city lane."

"Help me!" Jarrow cried, his voice high and faint as a whisper in the wind. "Get me away from her! I can be him for you! I can be Scavius! I can be anyone you want!"

"Enough from you, I think." Ivovandas slid his prison lovingly into a desk drawer, still smiling. She curled her fingers, and a familiar blue crystal appeared within them.

"You have suffered quite tenaciously for this," said Ivovandas. "I give it to you now as my half of our bargain, fairly begun and fairly concluded."

Amarelle took the glowing crystal and crushed it beneath her heel.

"Is that the end of it?" she said. "All restored to harmonious equipoise? I go on my way and leave you to your next few years of conversation with Jarrow?"

"In a manner of speaking," said Ivovandas. "While I have dutifully disposed of the crystal recording from last year's intemperate drunken visitation, I have just now secured an even more entertaining one in which you confess at length to crimes carried out in Theradane and implicate several of your friends by name."

"Yes," said Amarelle. "I did rather expect something like this. I figured that since I was likely to eat more treachery, I might as well have an appreciative audience first."

"I am the *most* appreciative audience! Oh, we could be so good for one another! Consider, Amarelle, the very reasonable bounds of my desires and expectations. I fancy myself fairly adept at identifying the loci in use by my colleagues. With Jarrow removed, there will be a rebalancing of the alliances in our parliament. There will be new testing and new struggles. I shall be watching very, very carefully, and inevitably I expect to have another target for you and your friends to secure on my behalf."

"You want to use us to knock off the Parliament of Strife, locus by locus" said Amarelle. "Until it's something more like the Parliament of Ivovandas."

"It might not happen in your lifetime," said the wizard. "But substantial progress could be at hand! In the meantime, I'll be quite content to let you remain at liberty in the city, enjoying your sanctuary, doing as you please. So long as you and your friends come when I call. Doubt not that I shall call."

17. The Work Ahead

Amarelle met them afterward on the Tanglewing Bridge, in the pleasant purple light of fading sunset. The city was quiet, the High Barrens peaceful, no fires falling from the clouds or screeching things sinking claws into one another.

They gathered in an arc in front of Scavius' statue. Sophara muttered and gestured with her fingers.

"We're in the bubble," she said. "Nobody can hear us, or even see us unless I . . . shut *up*, Scavius, I know you can hear us. You're a special case. How did it go down, Amarelle?"

"It went down like we expected," said Amarelle. "*Exactly* like we expected."

"I told you those kinds of sorcerers are all reflexively treacherous bags of nuts," said Sophara. "What's her game?"

"She wants us on an unpaid retainer so she can dig up the loci of more of her colleagues and send us after them."

"Sounds like a good way to kill some time, boss." Shraplin wound a crank on his chest, re-synchronizing some mechanism that had picked up a slight rattle. "I could stand to knock over a few more of those assholes. She'd save us a lot of work if she identified the loci for us."

"Couldn't agree more," said Sophara. "Now hold still."

She ran her fingers through Amarelle's hair, and after a few moments of searching carefully plucked out a single curling black strand.

"There's my little spy," said Sophara. "I'm glad you brought me that one Ivovandas planted on you, Am. I never would have learned how to make these things so subtle if I hadn't been able to pry that one apart."

"Do you think it will tell you enough?" said Brandwin.

"I honestly doubt it." Sophara slipped the hair into a wallet and smiled. "But it'll give me a good look at everything Amarelle was allowed to see, and that's much better than nothing. If we can identify her patterns and her habits, the bitch will eventually start painting clues for us as to the location of her own locus."

"Splat!" said Brandwin.

"Yeah," said Sophara. "And that's definitely my idea of a playground."

"I should be able to get some messages out of the city," said Jadetongue. "Some of the people we've got howling for our blood hate the Parliament of Strife even more. If we could make arrangements with them before we knock those wizards down, I'd bet we could buy our way back into the world. Theradane sanctuary in reverse, at least in a few places."

"I like the way you people think," said Amarelle. "Ivovandas as a stalking horse, and once we've got the goods on her we dump her ass in the river. Her and all her friends. Who's got the wine?"

Jade held out the bottle, something carnelian and bioluminescent and expensive. They passed it around, and even Shraplin dashed a ceremonial swig against his chin. Amarelle turned with the half-empty bottle and faced Scavius' statue.

"Here it is, you asshole. I guess we're not as retired as we might have thought. Five thieves going to war against the Parliament of Strife. Insane. The kind of odds you always loved best. Will you try to think better of us?

And if you can't, will you at least keep a few pedestals warm? We might have a future as street lamps after all. Have one on us."

She smashed the bottle against his plaque, and they watched the glowing, fizzing wine run down the marble. After a few moments, Sophara and Brandwin walked away arm in arm, north toward Tanglewing Street. Shraplin followed, then Jade.

Amarelle alone remained in the white light of whatever was left of Scavius. What he whispered to her then, she kept to herself.

She ran to catch up with the others.

"Hey," said Jade. "Glad you're back! You coming to the Sign of the Fallen Fire with us? We're going to have a game."

"Yeah," said Amarelle, and the air of Theradane tasted better than it had in months. "Hell *yeah* we're going to have a game!"

≈

Scott Lynch was born in Minnesota in 1978. His first novel, *The Lies of Locke Lamora*, was released in 2006 and was a finalist for the World Fantasy Award. His latest novel, *The Republic of Thieves*, hit the *New York Times* and *USAToday* bestseller lists. He is also a volunteer firefighter. Lynch and author Elizabeth Bear recently announced their engagement.

≈

Maps of San Francisco are, we are told, misleading: streets may not be streets or they may change names. In this magical place a cartographer looks desperately for hope in the fog and the folding of a map.

Caligo Lane
Ellen Klages

Even with the Golden Gate newly bridged and the ugly hulks of battleships lining the bay, San Francisco is well-suited to magic. It is not a geometric city, but full of hidden alleys and twisted lanes. Formed by hills and surrounded by water, its weather transforms its geography, a fog that erases landmarks, cloaking and enclosing as the rest of the world disappears.

That may be an illusion; most magic is. Maps of the city are replete with misdirection. Streets drawn as straight lines may in fact be stairs or a crumbling brick path, or they may dead end for a block or two, then reappear under another name.

Caligo Lane is one such street, most often reached by an accident that cannot be repeated.

In Barbary Coast bars, sailors awaiting orders to the Pacific hear rumors. Late at night, drunk on cheap gin and bravado, they try walking up Jones Street, so steep that shallow steps are cut into the middle of the concrete sidewalk. Near the crest of the hill, the lane may be on their right. Others stumble over to Taylor until they reach the wooden staircase that zigzags up a sheer wall. Caligo Lane is sometimes at the top—unless the stairs have wound around to end at the foot of Jones Street again. A lovely view of the bay is a consolation.

When it does welcome visitors, Caligo Lane is a single block, near the crest of the Bohemian enclave known as Russian Hill. Houses crowd one edge of a mossy cobblestone path; they face a rock-walled tangle of ferns and eucalyptus, vines as thick as a man's arm, moist earth overlaid with a pale scent of flowers.

Number 67 is in the middle, a tall, narrow house, built when the rest of the town was still brawling in the mud. It has bay windows and a copper-domed cupola, although the overhanging branches of a gnarled banyan tree make that difficult to see. The knocker on the heavy oak door is a Romani symbol, a small wheel wrought in polished brass.

Franny has lived here since the Great Fire. She is a cartographer by trade, a geometer of irregular surfaces. Her house is full of maps.

A small woman who favors dark slacks and loose tunics, she is one of the last of her line, a magus of exceptional abilities. Her hair is jet-black, cut in a blunt bob, bangs straight as rulers, a style that has not been in vogue for decades. She smokes odiferous cigarettes in a long jade-green holder.

The ground floor of number 67 is unremarkable. A small entryway, a hall leading to bedrooms and a bath. But on the right, stairs lead up to a single, large room, not as narrow as below. A comfortable couch and armchairs with their attendant tables surround intricate ancient rugs. A vast library table is strewn with open books, pens and calipers, and scrap paper covered in a jumble of numbers and notations.

Facing north, a wall of atelier windows, reminiscent of Paris, angles in to the ceiling. Seven wide panes span the width of the room, thin dividers painted the green of young spinach. Beyond the glass, ziggurats of stone walls and white houses cascade vertically down to the bay and Alcatraz and the blue-distant hills.

Visitors from more conventional places may feel dizzy and need to sit; it is unsettling to stand *above* a neighbor's roof.

Bookshelves line two walls, floor-to-ceiling. Many titles are in unfamiliar alphabets. Tall art books, dense buckram treatises, mathematical apocrypha: swaths of cracked, crumbling leather spines with gilt letters too worn to decipher. Four flat cases hold maps, both ancient and modern, in a semblance of order.

Other maps are piled and folded, indexed or spread about willy-nilly. They are inked on scraps of parchment, cut from old textbooks, acquired at service stations with a fill-up of gas. They show Cape Abolesco and

Dychmygol Bay and the edges of the Salajene Desert, none of which have ever been explored. On a cork wall, round-headed pins stud a large map of Europe. Franny moves them daily as the radio brings news of the unrelenting malignance of the war.

At the far end of the room, a circular staircase helixes up. Piles of books block easy access, less a barricade than an unrealized intent to reshelve and reorganize.

There will be much to do before the fog rolls in.

The stairs lead to the center of the cupola, an octagonal room with a hinged window at each windrose point. Beneath them is a sill wide enough to hold an open newspaper or atlas, a torus of horizontal surface that circles the room, the polished wood stained with ink, scarred in places by pins and tacks and straight-edged steel, scattered with treasured paperweights: worn stones from the banks of the Vistula, prisms, millefiori hemispheres of heavy Czech glass.

Even in a city of hills, the room has unobstructed views that allow Franny to work in any direction. A canvas chair on casters sits, for the moment, facing southwest. On the sill in front of it, a large square of Portuguese cork lies waiting.

Downstairs, on this clear, sunny afternoon, Franny sits at the library table, a postcard from her homeland resting beside her teacup. She recognizes the handwriting; the postmark is obscured by the ink of stamps and redirections. Not even the mailman can reliably find her house.

She glances at the card one more time. The delayed delivery makes her work even more urgent. She opens a ledger, leafing past pages with notes on scale and symbol, diagrams and patterns, and arcane jottings, turning to a blank sheet. She looks again at the postcard, blue-inked numbers its only message:

50°-02'-09" N 19°-10'-42" E

Plotting this single journey will take weeks of her time, years from her life. But she must. She glances at the pin-studded map. When geography or politics makes travel or escape impossible, she is the last resort. Each life saved is a mitzvah.

Franny flexes her fingers, and begins. Each phase has its own timing and order; the calculations alone are byzantine. Using her largest atlas she locates the general vicinity of the coordinates, near the small village of Oświecim. It takes her all night to uncover a chart detailed enough to show the topography with precision. She walks her calipers from point to point like a two-legged spider as she computes the progressions that will lead to the final map.

For days she smokes and mutters as she measures, plotting points and rhumb lines that expand and shrink with the proportions of the landscape. The map must be drawn to the scale of the journey. She feels the weight of time passing, but cannot allow haste, sleeping only when her hands begin to shake, the numbers illegible. Again and again she manipulates her slide rule, scribbles numbers on a pad, and traces shapes onto translucent vellum, transferring the necessary information until at last she has a draft that accurately depicts both entrance and egress.

She grinds her inks and pigments—lampblack and rare earths mixed with a few drops of her own blood—and trims a sheet of white linen paper to a large square. For a week, the house is silent save for the whisper of tiny sable brushes and the scritch of pens with thin steel nibs.

When she has finished and the colors are dry, she carries the map upstairs and lays it on the cork. Using a round-headed steel pin, she breaches the paper's integrity twice: a single, precise hole at the village, another at Caligo Lane. She transfers the positions onto gridded tissue, and pulls the map free, weighting its corners so that it lies flat on the varnished sill.

She has done what she can. She allows herself a full night's rest.

In the morning she makes a pot of tea and toast with jam, then clears the library table, moving her map-making tools to one side, and opens a black leather case that contains a flat, pale knife made of bone, and a portfolio with dozens of squares of bright paper. She looks around the room. What form must this one take?

Scattered among the dark-spined tomes are small angular paper figurines. Some are geometric shapes; others resemble birds and animals, basilisks and chimeras. Decades before he was exiled to Manzanar, a Japanese calligrapher and amateur conjurer taught her the ancient art of *ori-kami*, yet unknown in this country.

The secret of *ori-kami* is that a single sheet of paper can be folded in a nearly infinite variety of patterns, each resulting in a different transformation of the available space. Given any two points, it is possible to fold a line that connects them. A map is a menu of possible paths. When Franny folds one of her own making, instead of plain paper, she creates a new alignment of the world, opening improbable passages from one place to another.

Once, when she was young and in a temper, she crumpled one into a ball and threw it across the room, muttering curses. A man in Norway found himself in an unnamed desert, confused and over-dressed. His journey did not end well.

The Japanese army might call this art *ori-chizu*, "map folding," but fortunately they are unaware of its power.

Franny knows a thousand *ori-kami* patterns. Finding the correct orientation for the task requires a skilled eye and geometric precision. She chalks the position of the map's two holes onto smaller squares, folding and creasing sharply with her bone knife, turning flat paper into a cup, a box, a many-winged figure. She notes the alignment, discards one pattern, begins again. A map is a visual narrative; it is not only the folds but their sequence that will define its purpose.

The form this one wishes to take is a fortuneteller. American children call it a snapdragon, or a cootie-catcher. It is a simple pattern: the square folded in half vertically, then horizontally, and again on the diagonals. The corners fold into the center, the piece is flipped, the corners folded in again. The paper's two surfaces become many, no longer a flat plane, nor a solid object. A dimension in between.

When she creases the last fold, Franny inserts the index finger and thumb of each hand into the pockets she has created, pushes inward, then moves her fingers apart, as if opening and closing the mouth of an angular bird. Her hands rock outward; the bird's mouth opens now to the right and left. She rocks again, revealing and concealing each tiny hole in turn.

Franny nods and sets it aside. The second phase is finished. Now the waiting begins. She reads and smokes and paces and tidies. The weather is one element she cannot control.

Four days. Five. She moves the pins on the map, crosses off squares on her calendar, bites her nails to the quick until finally one afternoon she feels the fog coming in. The air cools and grows moist as it is saturated with the sea. The light softens, the world stills and quiets. She calms herself for the ritual ahead, sitting on the couch with a cup of smoky tea, listening to the muffled clang of the Hyde Street cable car a few blocks away, watching as the distant hills dissolve into watercolors, fade into hazy outlines, disappear.

The horizon lowers, then approaches, blurring, then slowly obliterating the view outside her window. The edge of the world grows closer. When the nearest neighbors' house is no more than an indistinct fuzz of muted color, she climbs the spiral stairs.

She stands before each window, starting in the east. The world outside the cupola is gone; there are no distances. Where there had once been landmarks—hillsides and buildings and signs—there is only a soft wall, as if she stands inside a great gray pearl.

San Francisco is a different city when the clouds come to earth. Shapes swirl in the diffused cones of street lamps, creating shadows inside the fog itself. Not flat, but three-dimensional, both solid and insubstantial.

When all the space in the world is contained within the tangible white darkness of the fog, Franny cranks open the northeast window and gently hangs the newly painted map on the wall of the sky. She murmurs archaic syllables no longer understood outside that room, and the paper clings to the damp blankness.

The map is a tabula rasa, ready for instruction.

The fog enters through the disruption of the pinholes.

The paper's fibers swell as they draw in its moisture.

They draw in the distance it has replaced.

They draw in the dimensions of its shadows.

Franny dares not smoke. She paces. Transferring the world to a map is both magic and art, and like any science, the timing must be precise. She has pulled a paper away too soon, before its fibers are fully saturated, rendering it useless. She has let another hang so long that the fog began to retreat again; that one fell to earth as the neighbors reappeared.

She watches and listens, her face to the open window. At the first whisper of drier air, she peels this map off the sky, gently easing one damp corner away with a light, deft touch. There can be no rips or tears, only the two perfect holes.

Paper fibers swell when they are wet, making room for the fog and all it has enveloped. When the fibers dry, they shrink back, locking that in. Now the map itself contains space. She murmurs again, ancient sounds that bind with intent, and lays the map onto the sill to dry. The varnish is her own recipe; it neither absorbs nor contaminates.

Franny closes the window and sleeps until dawn. When she wakes, she is still weary, but busies herself with ordinary chores, reads a magazine, listens to Roosevelt on the radio. The map must dry completely. By late afternoon she is ravenous. She walks down the hill into North Beach, the Italian section, and dines at Lupo's, where she drinks raw red wine and devours one of their flat tomato pies. Late on the third night, when at last the foghorn lows out over the water, she climbs the spiral stairs.

She stands over the map, murmuring now in a language not used for conversation, and takes a deep breath. When she is as calm as a still pond, she lights a candle and sits in her canvas chair. She begins the final sequence, folding the map in half, aligning the edges, precise as a surgeon, burnishing the sharp creases with her pale bone knife. The first fold is the most important. If it is off, even by the tiniest of fractions, all is lost.

Franny breathes, using the knife to move that flow through her fingers into the paper. Kinesis. The action of a fold can never be unmade. It fractures the fibers of the paper, leaving a scar the paper cannot forget, a line traversing three dimensions. She folds the map again on the diagonal, aligning and creasing, turning and folding until she holds a larger version of the angular bird's beak.

When the fog has dissolved the world and the cupola is cocooned, Franny inserts her fingers into the folded map. She flexes her hands, revealing one of the tiny holes, and opens the portal.

Now she stands, hands and body rigid, watching from the open window high above Caligo Lane. She sees nothing; soon sounds echo beneath the banyan tree. Shuffling footsteps, a whispered voice.

Motionless, Franny holds her hands open. She looks down. Beneath the street lamp stands an emaciated woman, head shorn, clad in a shapeless mattress-ticking smock, frightened and bewildered.

"Elzbieta?" Franny calls down.

The woman looks up, shakes her head.

Three more women step into view.

Beyond them, through a shimmer that pierces the fog, Franny sees other faces. More than she anticipated. Half a dozen women appear, and Franny feels the paper begin to soften, grow limp. There are too many. She hears distant shots, a scream, and watches as a mass of panicked women surge against the portal. She struggles to maintain the shape; the linen fibers disintegrate around the holes. Three women tumble through, and Franny can hold it open no longer. She flexes her trembling hands and reveals the other hole, closing the gate.

After a minute, she calls down in their language. *"Jestes teraz bezpieczna."* You are safe now. She reverses the *ori-kami* pattern, unfolding and flattening. This work goes quickly. A fold has two possibilities, an unfolding only one.

The women stand and shiver. A few clutch hands.

Franny stares at the place where the shimmer had been. She sees her reflection in the darkened glass, sees tears streak down a face now lined with the topography of age.

"Znasz moją siostrę?" she asks, her voice breaking. *Have you seen my sister?* She touches the corner of the depleted map to the candle's flame. *"Elzbieta?"*

A woman shrugs. *"Tak wiele."* She holds out her hands. So many. The others shrug, shake their heads.

Franny sags against the window and blows the ash into the night air. *"Idź,"* she whispers. *Go.*

The women watch the ash fall through the cone of street light. Finally one nods and links her arm with another. They begin to walk now, their thin cardboard shoes shuffling across the cobbles.

Slowly, the others follow. One by one they turn the corner onto Jones Street, step down the shallow concrete steps, and vanish into the fog.

∼

Ellen Klages was born in Ohio, and now lives in San Francisco. Her short fiction has appeared in anthologies and magazines including *The Magazine of Fantasy & Science Fiction*, *Black Gate*, and *Firebirds Rising*. Her story, "Basement Magic," won the Best Novelette Nebula Award. Several of her other stories have been on the final ballot for the Nebula, World Fantasy, and Hugo Awards, and have been reprinted in various "year's best" volumes. Her young adult novels—*The Green Glass Sea* and sequel *White Sands, Red Menace*—were both award winners and her collection, *Portable Childhoods*, was nominated for a World Fantasy Award.

∼

Bordertown is a city on the border between our human world and Elfland. Nothing there is ever quite what it seems. Neither magic nor technology follow any rules. Runaway kids from both sides of the border come there to find adventure and to find themselves—and usually find both harsh reality and incandescent magic.

Socks

Delia Sherman

Socks got her name from her feet. There was something wrong with them, or at least with the skin on them, and had been for as long as she could clearly remember—since she'd been in Bordertown, anyway. When Bossman had asked her how old she was, she'd guessed twelve, and when he'd asked her name, she'd looked down at her bare feet that were all scaly and yellow-white and murmured, "Socks." Bossman had laughed and patted her on the shoulder.

"You can stay tonight," he said in a soft drawl, "maybe tomorrow—any longer's up to squat meeting. But you gotta do something about them feet. They stink." And he took Socks and her feet, as he took all problems, to Queen B.

The squat was the second floor of an abandoned apartment building. A year or so earlier, Bossman and Queen B. had chased out the rats and the resident ghost, and gradually furnished the place with scavenged mattresses, a table, a few broken chairs, and eight scrawny kids who had washed up on the doorstep from time to time.

Bossman was the drummer in a band called Goblin Market. He was a handsome boy, his bright brown hair skinned back into a tail, his eyes a clear pale blue, his long body loosely jointed and carelessly graceful. Socks liked that he didn't seem to know it, that he didn't dress up his looks like the musicians and gang members did, though she did wonder about his rings. His right hand was heavy with them: two wide silver bands on his forefinger, a silver braid on his middle finger, and on his ring finger, a real knuckleduster an inch wide, chased and knobbed. Sometimes, when things got really tight, Queen B. would eye Bossman's rings and he'd shrug and say, "I'd sell them in a minute, babe. But we'd be in deep shit without them. You know that."

Queen B. ran the place, handled the money, cooked, made deals, dispensed justice, kept the peace. Queen B. was a year or two younger and would look younger yet as they both grew older.

He was human, and she was a halfie, for all the good it did her: a lovely, tall, billowy girl with white-gold hair and a body like the rolling hills of Elfland. Before Queen B. opened her mouth, Socks thought she was the most comfortable woman she'd ever seen, all lap and breasts and soft, enfolding arms. Then she spoke, and Socks knew that Queen B. might be a lot of things, but comfortable wasn't one of them.

"Foot rot," said Queen B. in a voice like a wind instrument.

"She'll have to wrap them in rags and put plastic bags over them if she's going to stay. They're ugly and they stink."

"What if it makes them worse?" asked a small boy who was sitting on the floor beside her, folding little cranes out of paper.

"Well, Hand, then they'll fall off, and Eye will carve her pretty wooden ones."

Alarmed, Socks looked at Bossman, who gave a don't-mind-her shrug and led her away to the kitchen. There he gave her a bowl of watery soup from a big pot, some rags, two plastic bags, and two pieces of string.

"Never quite know when Queenie's bullshitting and when she ain't," he said apologetically. "Better put these on in case she wasn't."

Socks wound the rags around her feet and covered them with the plastic bags, which she tied around her bare ankles with the string. The plastic made her slip and slide as she walked, but since walking fast hurt a lot, that didn't bother her. It also made the skin weep and itch fiercely, so about once a day, usually just before bedtime, she'd go outside someplace and remove the bags and the dirty rags. With the ooze dried to a yellow crust, her feet really did look like a pair of socks, their ragged pink hems pulled up over her ankle-bones. She'd scratch at the hems lightly because she couldn't help it, then wrap her feet up again in clean rags. Her feet didn't improve under this treatment, but they didn't get much worse either.

Over the next few days, Socks met the rest of the children. They were all weird in some way, although Eye and Map were the only ones whose weirdness showed. Map had a dark red blotch like a map covering half his face, and Eye was so walleyed that Socks could never tell whether he was looking at her or at someone behind her and to her right, or maybe at both. Hand was blind, but you couldn't tell that by looking at him any more than you could tell that Baby wasn't as quick on the draw as she could have been or that Christie never spoke, or that her bosom shadow Pet walked in her sleep. The twins, Art and Science, were almost not real, except for looking like a pair of identical toy bears, tawny and round.

Socks was terrified of Art and Science, who also had identical deep voices and identical thin shadows on their cheeks, and also of Map, who dyed his hair blue and called her "Baggie girl." All the boys frightened her, except Hand, who was small and blond and pointy-eared and folded squares of paper into bright animals that he sold outside Taco Hell or The Dancing Ferret. Among the girls, she liked Christie best because she had hair the color of a deep red rose and rainbow hands from her dye vats. But she was much too shy to speak to her.

Everyone had to work to keep the place going. Goblin Market didn't bring in much money. Queen B. said it was because there were so many bands in Bordertown that the new ones had a hard time getting gigs. After hearing them rehearse, Socks thought it might be because they weren't very good.

She couldn't exactly remember hearing music before, certainly not the loud, tumbling discords Goblin Market favored, but from the bottom of her soul she knew what it ought to sound like. It should sound peaceful as the hush of her pulse in her ears at night, free as distant horns, wild as the Bloods on a rampage, secret as a bird's nest. She felt what Goblin Market wanted to play, and the space between that and the noises they actually produced made her throat ache with frustration. She could do better. She knew that, too.

But when Queen B. asked her at the Squat Meeting what she could do to bring in money, she only ducked her head and shrugged.

"Speak up, girl," said Queen B. "You have to be able to do something. Sew?"

Socks shook her head. The squat made most of its bread and butter from the old clothes Christie sold from a barrow on Ho Street. Since Christie didn't talk, Pet did the actual selling. But it was Christie who made the business work, Christie with her long, deft fingers and her magical sense of fashion. She knew just when slumming Highborns would want jackets embroidered with ribbons or skirts with unevenly ripped hems, crazy-quilt shirts, or mirrored tunics. And she supplied them. Art, Science, Map, and Eye scrounged, scavenged, and begged inventory; Queen B. and Baby washed their gleanings; Hand, Pet, and Christie mended and modified them. There was always a pile of work to be done.

Pet snorted. "I'll just bet," she said. "Baggie girl." Socks rested her chin on her chest and blinked against tears.

They'd never let her stay if she couldn't contribute. And then what would she do?

"Lay off her, Pet," said Bossman. "Poor kid's hardly got here yet. Let her help wash. Any idiot can wash. Oh. Sorry, Baby."

Baby smiled up from the bundle of rags she was nursing in her arms. "Wash," she said. "Rub-a-dub. Baggie girl."

"Okay," said Queen B. "It's not much, but it'll do for now." She took Socks by the chin, forced her head up to meet her eyes.

They were almost colorless—a crystalline blue-white with black pupils, impossible to read. "You'd better put your thinking cap on, though. Helping Baby wash is perilously close to getting a free ride, and I don't believe in free rides."

Socks shivered, and then she saw that Queen B. was smiling, her full mouth curved and warm. She's not as hard as she talks, Socks thought.

Queen B. gave her chin a shake. "Don't look so frightened," she said softly. "I'm not going to eat you or throw you out, either. It's just that all of us have a job, and mine's taking a hard line. You understand?"

"I understand," said Socks.

～

So Socks went to work washing second-hand clothes. The experience taught her something about Queen B.'s sense of humor, because washing clothes wasn't any way a free ride. The boys brought in their finds in huge bundles and dumped them in the pantry, where there was a big sink. Some of them stank worse than Sock's feet, and the wash water had to be lugged in from the kitchen. Socks was only grateful that one of the priority expenses was a heating spell.

Baby, who was a young woman to look at, anyway, was good at hauling water and wringing out heavy cloth, which was just as well, since Socks was neither very big nor very strong. But she was quick and responsible enough to be trusted with the strong-smelling solutions Science had invented to get out spots and lift the dye from things that Christie wanted to re-color. She had a good eye, too, and after a couple of days, Christie let her help with the dyeing.

That's what Socks was doing when the stranger girl arrived at the squat—hanging out a batch of freshly dyed silk shirts as Christie handed them to her. They were blue, "elf blue," Pet called it, a misty, elusive shade that was very in just now. Socks was leaning out the kitchen window, arms full of wet shirt and mouth full of clothespins, when she heard shouting.

If Baby hadn't come crowding up behind her to see what the noise was about, Socks wouldn't have seen the girl at all. She would have been behind the stove, hiding from the shouting, which had an angry music to it that sang to her of blood, of rending, and of death. But Baby was crushing her over the windowsill, squealing, "Elf-pack! Elf-pack!" in high hysteria, and so Socks had to watch the girl turn the corner of the alley, slide, recover, and glance wildly around her. The shouting swelled behind her, triumphant and shrill.

She must have been running a long time, long enough to outrun her street-smarts anyway, to turn so foolishly down an unfamiliar alley. She was very thin and elvin-tall. Her hair was dark and lank, her face brown and shadowed above a tight leather jacket and shredded jeans.

The girl stumbled forward a few steps as if hoping that the blank walls she saw all around her were an illusion. Then she shrugged, wrapped her arms tight around her ribs, faced the alley mouth, and waited.

An elf skidded around the corner, took in the girl and the blind alley, and grinned. His chains, the scarlet streak in his hair, the row of golden rings lining one pointed ear probably revealed to the initiated which pack he ran with. Socks knew only that he was not alone.

The elf said something at once liquid and harsh, and took a step forward. The girl backed up, which seemed to amuse him.

The rest of the gang had appeared by now, scarlet streaks like blood among their white hair, faces feral with anticipation of the kill. The girl dropped her arms to her sides and lifted her chin.

As if the gesture had released her, Socks screamed. The girl spun around, her eyes flying up to Socks and the kitchen window and the drainpipe running down the side of the old tenement. A second later, she was pelting towards it.

Everything seemed to happen at once. The gang came out of their blood-daze; the girl reached the drainpipe and began to scramble up it as the gang swarmed under her, furiously getting in each other's way. Socks leaned farther out the window to see the girl clinging just below the sill, wide-eyed and shaking, clearly unable to make the last effort that would bring her to safety. Socks wrapped her arms under the leather-clad shoulders, but she hadn't the strength to haul her in. They were cheek to cheek, the girl's rat-tailed hair blinding her eyes. The world shrank to a wild, sharp smell in Socks' nose, a panicked breathing in her ear, a bony body quivering in her grasp.

Just as Socks thought she'd have to let go, she heard a grunt and felt a heave, and she was sprawled on the kitchen floor with the girl, listening to Queen B. shouting out the window, her woodwind voice brassy with rage. Socks didn't recognize any of the words.

Bossman shut the kitchen window with a bang while Queen B. glared down at the girl, who pulled her feet under her and crouched as if ready to leap up and run.

"I suppose you want shelter," said Queen B.

The girl gave a tiny shrug. "Don't do me any favors," she said.

"We already done you one," Bossman pointed out reasonably.

"Yeah," said the girl. "Thanks." She unfolded herself from her crouch. "I'll be going now."

"Whoa," said Bossman. "You can't go out there. They'll be waiting for you."

"What do you care?"

"We rescued you. That makes us responsible for you."

"Will you stop feeling responsible if I pay you off?" Her lips parted and the tip of her tongue showed between them. Since her lips were cracked and one eye discolored and swollen, the effect was more goblinesque than seductive. "I know some tricks will make us more than even."

Bossman lowered his eyes to his rings. "Shit," he said.

"You look like chopped liver, girl," said Queen B. "And he's spoken for."

The girl looked Queen B. over. She took her time about it, her hands clasped behind her and her nose high, arrogant as an elflord. When the silence had begun to drag, she shook her head.

"He's yours? You sure must have something heavy on him. He's pretty enough to get a woman who won't squash him when she rolls over in bed."

Queen B.'s hand bunched itself into a fist and her eyes narrowed. "Easy, babe," said Bossman. "Little shitface is just scared, that's all. It takes some people that way, makes 'em nasty." He turned to the girl. "That right, ain't it? You didn't mean to badmouth Queen B. here. You just scared and mad about it, ain'tcha?"

The girl eyed him, opened her mouth; closed it again, shrugged. "Sorry," she said ungraciously. "I didn't mean anything by it."

"See that you didn't," said Bossman. "First rule around here's same as the last. We got plenty people riding us. We don't ride each other."

"Sure. I said I was sorry." And all at once, she looked sorry, and much younger than Socks had thought: dark and small and painfully thin, as if she'd never had a full meal in her life. Her wrists stuck way out from her rusty jacket, long and bony and covered with bright woven bracelets. She was incredibly grimy, her bare feet black and her skin gray with street dirt, her hair plastered to her skull, the leather of her jacket stiff and cracked. She was also, Socks realized, incredibly beautiful. When she turned against the window so that you couldn't see the dirt and the bruises, the delicate molding of her head came clear, the sharp curve from wide temples to pointed chin, the graceful line of her neck and back.

Socks stared until the stranger's eyes met hers.

By some trick of light, they glowed at her, bright as an animal's caught in a car's headlights, wild and curiously blank. Yet Socks knew that they saw her, knew her and what she was and all about her, all in an instant. She covered her own eyes with her hands and went away into a white place where nobody knew her and nobody could touch her. It wasn't very interesting, but it was safe. Her feet pricked and ached with the cold.

After a moment, the pressure of the stranger's gaze lightened. Socks returned to the crowded kitchen and Bossman's voice saying, "I don't know. We're pretty stretched. Soup's about as watered as it'll go. And we'll need another mattress, more blankets. Everybody pays their way here, much as they can. You willing to do that?"

"Yes, I'm willing," said the stranger. Her voice was no longer a sullen growl, but young and determined—a hero's voice. Bossman smiled.

Queen B., ever practical, said, "Doing what?"

"Turning tricks," she answered in the same practical tone.

"Not out of this squat, you don't," said Queen B. "That's our third rule. No ass-peddling."

"How many rules this place got? I don't like rules."

"Four," said Queen B. "One and three you know. Number two is that everyone has to work. Number four is, if you have a hassle with somebody in the squat, you bring it to Bossman or me and we decide what to do, no argument. You can't live with that, you're out."

"I don't know."

"Well, I don't know either," said Queen B. "If you decide you want to stay, we'll have a meeting about you. Bossman's got too kind a heart for his own good. In the meantime, you're as dirty as a mudslide, and a Wharf Rat would be ashamed of those clothes. Clean yourself up—Socks will show you where—and get some clothes out of inventory."

The stranger grinned, something between triumph and relief.

"And don't be getting any notions that you've got around me, girl," Queen B. added. "I'd do the same for my worst enemy's ugly dog, and that's the truth."

A little while later, Socks was shuffling down the hall to the bathroom, hardly daring to look at the girl padding beside her. "Socks, eh?" said the girl. "Funny name for a kid. But it suits you, you know? Like a cat's name. You look kinda like a cat."

"Do I?" asked Socks, startled out of her shyness.

"Yeah. An alley cat—not the mean kind, the shy kind. You know what I mean?"

Socks nodded. A cat, even a stray cat, was a much nicer thing to be than a Baggie girl, and somehow right. She stole a look at the girl, who was smiling at her, not mocking like she'd smiled at Queen B., but open and friendly. Given how dirty the rest of her was, her teeth were remarkably white.

Socks felt herself blush. "Towels are here," she murmured, indicating a crazy wooden cabinet. "The hot water spell's kind of weird, so you got to go easy."

"Thanks." Without waiting for Socks to leave, the girl stripped off her jacket and grabbed the grayish undershirt under it to pull it over her head like a child. The woven bracelets shifted on her wrists, showing skin rubbed raw and bloody. Her back was marked in a checkerboard of thin, precise cuts.

Socks gasped, half reached out to touch one of the welts. "Was that the elves?"

"Shut up!" The girl tucked her wrists into her armpits and glowered. Socks covered her mouth with both hands and cowered.

The girl's face softened. "Listen, kid," she said, not unkindly. "I'm grateful you rescued me and everything, but I hate it when people ask me questions. You get behind that, we can be friends. Now, get out so I can use up some of that hot water."

The squat had four rooms more or less, depending on whether you counted the big walk-in closet that was Queen B. and Bossman's private space. No one slept in the kitchen unless they had a heavy case of the Garbos, which left two rooms for eight kids to sleep in. During the day the mattresses were piled against a wall.

Whenever people were tired, they'd drag a mattress to wherever they fancied, get a blanket from the pile, and go to sleep.

There were six mattresses. Christie and Pet always shared, as did the twins. Until Socks came, Baby, Hand, Map, and Eye had sometimes slept alone, sometimes not, depending on whether they were feeling lonely.

After, Baby shared with Hand. No one wanted to share with Socks and her foot rot, nor, as it turned out, with the stranger girl.

"You can share with me," offered Socks when Map and Eye had made it clear, by sprawling themselves kitty-cornered across their mattresses, that they intended to sleep alone. "I don't snore. Honest."

"What's it to you, where I sleep?" asked the girl sharply. "You got the hots for me or something?" Then, awkwardly, at Socks' look of blank incomprehension, "I didn't say that. Thanks."

They rolled up in their blankets, Socks politely curled on the edge farthest from her bedmate. In the faint glow reflected from the alley lamp, she lay listening to the sounds of the squat settling in for the night. Hand and Baby were asleep. Under the window, Christie and Pet rustled and murmured. A rhythmic tenor buzzing drifted out of the common room: either one of the twins or Map—Socks could never decide which. Tonight, she was aware of the stranger breathing quietly beside her, a warm still presence in the half-light.

Socks was dreaming. The girl had slipped from her hands, and they were clinging to each other's wrists. Socks felt the woven bracelets rasping her fingers. The girl was too heavy for her, was pulling her out the window head-first into a pack of elves with chains around their necks and cars that came to sharp points above their long-muzzled faces. They whined eagerly beneath the stranger's dangling feet. The girl's lace was blank, almost serene with terror, her trembling so intense it was nearly imperceptible.

Her hands opened. Socks gripped as hard as she could, but the slender hands slipped through hers. The whining of the pack swelled. Socks' eyes flew open.

She'd taken a deep breath and another, glad the dream was over, glad she wasn't alone in the dark, before she realized that the whining hadn't faded with the feral elf faces. Beside her, the stranger girl was curled into a tight ball, her chin tucked into the crook of her arm, the hand resting palm-up on her neck. Her hair trailed dark coils across her face. For a moment Socks listened to the thready, hopeless sound and watched the fingers work, curling, scrabbling, flattening as if against some invisible surface, repulsing something Socks could not see. Socks shivered. This couldn't go on. Hesitantly, she touched the stranger's shoulder.

The girl jerked and curled up tighter. "Please, please, please, please," she begged. "No, no, please, no. I'll be good. I promise. Please."

Once she started, she said it over and over, breathless and low, punctuated by increasingly frantic whimpers and bleats of pain.

Socks grew cold, and her feet prickled and ached. She closed her eyes and wished, but the comforting white silence would not come.

From under the window, a sleepy voice complained. "What the . . . ?"

"Whozzat?" That was Hand.

A twin called out from the common room. "Whoever it is, get her to shut up."

"Yeah," said the other twin. "We're trying to sleep here."

Baby began to whimper in sympathy.

"She's still asleep," said Socks, high and panicked.

"Then wake her up," said Eye.

This wasn't easy, especially since the stranger struggled and moaned whenever Socks touched her. And when at last she stopped, she didn't really wake up, just uncurled, swore blearily, rolled over on her stomach, and was still. Socks was still, too, except for a tiny, constant shudder that lasted until at last she fell asleep.

Squat meetings were not called, they happened. Border magic, Science called it, how everyone knew when to turn up in the common room and why. Queen B. would laugh when he said so, and tell him he just didn't know much about how communities work, which was true enough. But it felt like magic to Socks. Especially today, when she was logy with dreams that left nothing behind them but a foul taste in her mind.

The stranger girl had slept late and had been sullenly silent after she got up, taking her bowl into the common room to eat alone. She was perched in the open window licking oatmeal off her fingers when people started drifting in. Queen B. and Bossman pulled a pair of crates into a bench by the front door; Pet, Christie, Baby, and Hand piled mattresses into a sofa; Art, Science, Map, and Eye plopped themselves down on the floor. Socks found a corner by the window where she could watch without being seen. Nobody said a word as a beat passed and another before the stranger put down her bowl and turned to face them with the same calm she'd shown the elf pack.

"Well?" asked Queen B.

"Well?" The girl echoed Queen B.'s tone exactly.

Bossman sighed. "You wanna stay or what?"

"Don't know. Depends."

Pet spoke up. "Sure does depend. Mostly on whether or not we want you around."

"Yeah," said Science. "So far, you haven't exactly blown us away."

Art nodded. "What he said. You haven't even told us what to call you."

The girl hesitated. "My name's Perdita," she said at last.

"Damn fancy name for a Wharf Rat," said Queen B.

"I'm not a Wharf Rat."

"Your name's not Perdita, either."

The stranger—Perdita—cocked up her pointed chin. "It is, too, and who are you anyway, to say it's not? You expect me to believe that your name's Queen B.? What kind of a name is Queen B.? Or Hand, or Eye, or Socks? The only one of you with something that sounds like a real name is Christie, and I'll bet all the tea in China that's not the name she was born with."

There was a silence. "Fair enough," said Queen B. "Perdita it is, if you say so. But you have to show us some good will here."

"Why?" asked Perdita. "I bet nobody else had to tell the story of their life for a lumpy mattress and a bowl of stone soup."

"No. Nobody else showed up here with Claws on their tail, either."

Bossman nodded. "You come carrying some pretty heavy baggage, girl. We gotta be sure it don't blow up in our face." Perdita shrugged. "Okay, but you won't believe me."

"You better tell us anyway," said Bossman.

Perdita locked her hands behind her back and began her talc.

She kept her eyes steadily on Queen B. as she told them of her highborn mother who had run away out of her palace in Elfland clear through the Borderlands and out into the World.

"Aren't there any lowborns in Elfland?" asked Pet wearily.

Perdita's lips pulled back from her teeth. "Not as lowborn as you, rag-picker. What is it with you guys, anyway?" she said, her eyes darting from face to face. "You make me talk, then you won't listen to me."

"That's cause you're talking bullshit," said Map, which started everybody arguing until Bossman clapped his hands.

"Hush up!" he said, his soft voice edged with impatience. The children looked at him sheepishly. He rubbed his face with both hands, and his rings caught the sun like mirrors. Socks saw Perdita blink and frown.

"She's right," he said. "Let her talk. Your mother was a runaway. Go on."

And Perdita went on like a child trying to get through her lesson as quickly as possible before she lost her nerve or forgot any of it, telling them how her mother had fallen in love with a black saxophone player and borne him a daughter, Perdita. "I guess she went kind of crazy after I came along because she dyed her hair black and ran away with me. We ran for the next ten years, passing as human, begging, stealing when we had to. It was a little easier after she stole the van. At least then we always had a place to sleep."

"What did she do about the license plates?" asked Science suspiciously. "Everybody knows you can't steal something like that without they trace you by the license plates."

"Magic," said Perdita.

"Not out in the World, man," objected Eye. "Magic don't work in the World any better'n machines work in Elfland."

Perdita grew sullen. "My mother could do anything, as long as she was straight. Anyway, I was just a baby. Seemed like magic to me. You want to hear this or not?"

"We want to hear it," said Bossman.

"As I was saying. We drove at night, mostly. Mama would keep us both awake with old songs and movie plots."

"What's a movie?" asked Hand.

"A story you can see," said Perdita, "over and over again."

"Why'd you drive at night?" asked Map.

"We drove at night to outrun the humans. Mama said that humans slept at night because they were afraid of the dark and we weren't because we were of the True Blood."

"I bet your Mama was afraid of the dark herself," said Pet. "I sure would be, sleeping in a stolen van with a kid that screams all night."

"Shut up, Pet," said Queen B. unexpectedly. "She's not the first screamer we've had. As I recall, you were one yourself, once upon a time. Go on, Perdita. I can't wait to hear what happens next."

Perdita clasped her hands in front of her. "You don't believe me," she said, sounding very young. "You think I'm making all this up." She started to play nervously with her gaudy wristlets; the welts showed red and purple between the woven bands. "I've made up my mind," she said. "I don't want to stay in your old squat. I don't need anyone laughing at my mother."

"Chill, girl," said Queen B. impatiently. "Nobody's laughing at your mother. Tell your story. We'll decide later whether we believe it or not."

Perdita hesitated, poised on the balls of her feet. Watching her, Socks remembered that she'd seen a fox once. Perdita reminded her of that fox, beautiful and vulnerable. She'd leave, go back out on the streets, get killed sure as anything, all because she didn't understand that Queen B. was just doing her job.

Socks could hear the concern behind the hard words, but someone like Perdita might think that she was just being mean. So Socks, who never, ever spoke up in meetings, said, "I believe you, Perdita."

At the sound of her voice, everybody looked at her. Ten pairs of eyes—brown, blue, gray, hazel, long, round, squinty—turned on her in surprise, as though a chair had spoken. Socks' heart started to beat so hard it nearly suffocated her, but she repeated, "I believe you, Perdita. Every word. And I want to hear the rest."

"Isn't much more to tell," said Perdita. "We drove around, I got older, she told me stories about Bordertown, she died, I found my way here."

Her shuttered face dared them to ask her what her mother had died of. Queen B. cleared her throat. "And the Claws?"

All at once, Perdita's face grew sharp and sly. "The Claws," she said. "Fuckers. They did me real rough, so I fixed their leader so he couldn't anymore." An unpleasant smile bared her white, white teeth. "Made him madder'n hell."

"I ain't sure I follow you," said Bossman. "Ain't sure I want to. They likely to swear blood feud?"

Perdita shrugged. "How the hell would I know? I tied a knot in their leader's dick. Want to see what made me do it?" She pushed the bracelets up her wrists with a flourish, displaying the raw sores. "There's more where a lady don't show in public. Want to see that, too?"

Queen B. gnawed her lip, then said, "Boychild, you think those pretty geegaws on your fingers can charm the Claws into calling it quits if our little sorceress here agrees to . . . ah . . . untie Beltane's dick?"

"Maybe," said Bossman. "You willing, Perdita?" He sounded like he wouldn't blame her if she wasn't.

"No way," said Perdita, grinning.

"Then you're out," said Queen B., flat and final.

They glared at each other, black eyes against crystal, Perdita a shadow against Queen B.'s shining bulk. Socks wasn't surprised that Perdita broke first, shrugged, and said, "Okay. If you can keep him off me."

Bossman stroked the bare fingers of his left hand over the array of silver on his right. "As long as you're under my roof," he said, "you're as safe as you can be in this town. Outside, Beltane can hassle you, but I'll see he don't hurt you. That good enough?"

"You're just full of surprises," said Perdita. "Okay. It's a deal. I'm tired of running." She glanced at Socks, smiled thinly. "I guess I have to stay anyway, work off my debt."

"It's not as simple as that, girl. You have to tell us what you intend to do to earn your keep around here. We have enough ragpickers, dyers, and menders. You have to come up with something new. Other than what you've been doing to date."

"You mean tricking?" asked Perdita innocently. "Okay. I'll tell stories."

"You already do that," said Science.

"I liked her story," said Hand unexpectedly. "I'd give her a penny or a clover for it, if I had one."

"Easy to spend money you don't have," said Eye. "I wouldn't give her the time of day for that bullshit."

Perdita seemed to shrink into herself, to grow denser. "Tales my mother taught me," she said, and there was a different note to her voice, a subtle, pleading music. "Pretty tales. Tales for humans and tales for the Blood. Tales of past and future joy. They'll pay to hear them, my oath on it. And if they don't, you'll only have lost some oatmeal and a night's sleep."

"That seems fair enough," said Bossman. "Whaddya think, Queenie?"

"That she's as mad as the River and twice as dangerous," said Queen B. "But I could never resist a challenge. I vote give her a chance. What do the rest of you vote?"

Hand, Christie, and Socks voted to let Perdita stay and try her storytelling. Art said he didn't much care either way, and Pet said she guessed she'd go along with Christie, but she didn't much like it. Science, Map, and Eye voted wholeheartedly against.

"I guess you're in, then," said Bossman.

"For tonight," said Queen B.

"Thanks." Perdita shaded the word just this side of rudeness, then shook herself and tried again. "Thank you. I always depend on the kindness of strangers."

"Hmph," said Queen B.

"Now. A teller needs a singer," said Perdita, making titles of the words: Teller. Singer. "One of you will have to sing for me." Gravely, she surveyed them, pointed at last to Socks, who was picking at the plastic frill at her ankles. "You. Sing for me."

Socks shook her head without looking up. "Can't sing."

"Can, too." Perdita's voice was intimate. "'Course you can. More sweetly than the crimson martlets of Elfland."

"Everybody will look at me."

Perdita stepped over Map's outstretched legs, knelt by Socks, and touched her cheek with one well-chewed finger. "The song will hide you, little bird. Everyone will hear your music, but when they look to see who's made it, all they'll see is me."

Socks almost believed her. Certainly all she saw was Perdita, her black eyes wanting a song so badly that Socks just had to give her one.

> "Hark, hark, the dogs do bark,
> The beggars are coming to town.
> Some in rags and some in tags,
> And some in velvet gowns."

The sound that came from her was pure and high and sexless as a reed pipe. It turned the simple tune into a charm, a warning and an invocation against harm. When she finished, everyone was gaping at her. She hid her face in her hands.

"That'll do," said Perdita with vast satisfaction. "Now catch some Zs. We'll be up late tonight."

Perdita woke Socks at sunset. She herself had obviously been up for some time gauding herself out in bits and bobs of Christie's second-hand finery. She'd hung herself with scarves like a maypole. When she moved, they fell into pattern after shifting pattern of rust and yellow and pale blue. Her thickly curling hair hung loose with ribbons plaited into it here and there, and beads, and silver bells that chimed thinly when she moved her head.

"Your outfit's on the bed," she said. "It's not perfect for a Singer, but it'll do. Put it on."

Socks stared at the pile of material with dismay. "You didn't say I'd have to get dressed up!" she wailed.

"Try it on, anyway," said Perdita gently. "Who knows? You may like it. And if you don't, we'll just put a big bag over you and pretend you're not there."

Socks giggled, and allowed herself to be coaxed into a pair of wide black trousers and a voluminous tunic sewn with fluttering patches of rust, green, brown, and gold that made her look something like a pile of autumn leaves. As a finishing touch, Perdita wound a gauzy black scarf around her head. "A Teller's Singer has no face," she said. "A Teller's Singer is all voice."

Behind the scarf, Socks grinned. No face sounded good to her.

Perdita gave her a sisterly shove, then stooped to pick up a fat roll of heavy cloth from the floor and handed it to Socks. "Your mat," she said.

It was rough in Socks' hands, many-colored like the wristlets Perdita wore, awkward and heavy to carry. Perdita helped her balance it on her shoulder. "There. You look like a real Singer now. Let's hit the road."

Standing at the street door with the mat weighing down one shoulder, her feet stinging and prickling and her mouth muffled in gauze, all Socks wanted to do was creep back upstairs to Baby, to silent, red-haired Christie and their piles of old clothes. But Perdita was smiling like a child sharing a rich treat, her scarves tossing around her.

A Teller needs a Singer, Socks thought. Perdita needs me.

"Okay," she said. "Hit the road."

Perdita opened the door and they emerged onto Low Street.

It was twilight in Bordertown, the sky a deep, electric blue just tinged at its elfward edge with royal purple. There was a green and living scent on the air that reminded Socks that it was spring, even in Bordertown, even in Soho where few trees grew. A warm breeze pressed her veil against her face. At the end of the street, someone was singing: *"O, dear o! O, dear o! me husband's got no porridge in him. O, dear o!"*

Socks began to feel better.

They walked towards Water Street, Perdita skipping every few steps as though she couldn't help herself. "Everyone needs a stage name," she said abruptly. "How about Nightingale?"

"Nightingale," breathed Socks.

"Nightingale it is, then. Do you think you can carry the mat to Ho Street?"

Socks felt that she could carry the mat, and Perdita too, all the way to Ho Street, over Dragon's Claw Bridge, and up the Hill if Perdita asked her to, but contented herself with hiking the rolled-up cloth higher on her shoulder and shuffling after Perdita as briskly as her prickling feet would take her.

By Bordertown standards, it was still fairly early in the evening, but Water Street was already crowded and Mock Avenue an obstacle course. All Bordertown was out tonight, it seemed to Socks, laughing and swaggering and telling her to watch where she was going when they ran into her or the awkward, heavy roll over her shoulder. As they passed O'Malley Hall, every step was like walking on ice, and the strange, loud faces that parted and washed over her as she struggled forward were like pounding waves. Where were they going again? Had Perdita even said? What if Socks lost her in the crowd? What if she just sat down and died?

Socks looked up just in time to see a scarlet scarf whisking down a sidestreet and panicked utterly. "Perdita," she squeaked. "Wait for me!"

Perdita spun around, wove through a mixed party of artists in paint-stained T-shirts back to where Socks stood drooping under her burden.

"Baggins," she said. "The footless wonder. Saving lives our specialty. Now, don't get yourself all upset—I'm only teasing you. Hasn't anyone ever teased you before?" She gave the mat a pat. It shifted and was lighter.

"That's the best I can do," she said. "You *have* to carry it—you're the Singer. Hang in, Nightingale. We're almost there."

"There" was The Dancing Ferret, just beginning to wake up and stretch itself for the evening's exertions. A few cobalt-haired Hill-folk were lounging outside: elves trying to look human or humans trying to look elvin—Socks didn't dare look close enough to figure out which.

"Here," said Perdita, indicating a space under a spell-lamp. "Unroll the mat." And, as Socks looked at her blankly, "What're you waiting for? Winter?"

Fluttering with rags and tags, Socks felt more like a fool than a nightingale. She began to shiver as if it were winter indeed.

Perdita's face softened. "Nightingale," she said. "Song in the branches of night. Do what you were born to do. Unroll the mat and sing."

Her voice was an incantation, drawing in the world around it until nothing else existed. Safe behind her veil and Perdita's voice, Socks arranged the mat in the circle of light and sat on the back corner. Perdita stood in front of her, hands folded demurely at her waist, ribbons and scarves at rest, bells silent. The Hill-folk poked each other and stared.

"Sing," she whispered.

"Hark, hark . . . " Socks cracked the first note, rasped the second, slid into silence. Perdita's shoulders twitched.

"Sing."

Socks swallowed, wet her lips, closed her eyes behind the veil, gathered breath into her lungs, and sang. The notes rose through her throat, echoed in her mouth, and flew out into the open air like birds uncaged, rolling with joy in their freedom.

> "Hark, hark, the dogs do bark,
> The beggars are coming to town.
> Some in rags and some in rags,
> And some in velvet gowns.

Tales they bring, tales old and new,
Tales for elf and man.
Give them bread, give them wine,
Give them half-a-crown."

Having sung more words than she knew, Socks fell abruptly silent.

Perdita began to chant: "Tales old, tales new, I've got 'em all. What's your pleasure, gentles? A fairy tale?" She pouted an airy kiss at a tall, lanky human with pale hair half-obscuring the azure thunderbolt painted along one cheekbone. He scowled, then laughed and shrugged as Perdita spun so that her scarves flared around her like licking flame.

"An old one," someone cried out.

"As you like," Perdita began. "Once upon a time."

Socks was too cold and self-conscious to pay much attention to what Perdita was saying. She heard just enough to know that it was about a bear and an aged lord and a foundling child and a cave in the woods, and that it made her feel scared and safe all at the same time. When Perdita had finished it, a crowd of elves and humans, dressed for dancing, stood around them three deep. For perhaps three beats, all Socks could hear was the faint pulse of music from the warm-up band at Farrell Din's, then a murmur of applause and a patter of coin and dried leaves falling on the mat at Perdita's feet.

"Gather 'em up, mungfoot," Perdita muttered as she bowed, the joy in her voice turning the insult into a caress. "And roll up the mat. The pigeons are ripe for plucking tonight."

Three times that night Socks sang about the beggars and Perdita told about the bear and the foundling child. At the Wheat Sheaf, her audience laughed at the tale. At the Widening Gyre, they wept.

"Money for nothing," said Perdita happily as they gathered up their take. "Boys for free," sliding a glance up at a young elf who was watching her with a ferocious intensity. She slid her shoulder back and tilted her head so that the scarves molded her breast and the braided strands of her hair half-veiled her face. The elf licked his lips.

"Perdita," whispered Socks. "Perdita, you *promised*."

Perdita opened her eyes very wide, "It was only going to be for fun."

She stretched suddenly, shook herself decent. "No, perhaps not," she said. "I should sleep fine tonight without it." She whiffled her fingers at the elf, said something in Elvish that bared his teeth and clenched his fists. "Better run," she muttered and, scooping up the mat, dragged it and Socks home through the thinning streets to the squat.

Queen B. was pleased enough with the night's take that she used some of it to buy Perdita her own mattress. She also let Socks off most of her washing duties. In an incredibly short time, Socks' days fell into a pattern of sleeping late, telling Christie about her adventures, eating, putting on her Nightingale clothes, and limping through the night streets of Bordertown.

They'd walk along Low Street, Perdita bright-eyed and sniffing the air, her scarves restless behind her. At the corner of Mock Avenue, she'd stop and quiver for a moment, then trot off towards whatever club she liked the smell of. Once there, she'd simply stop and let the scarves settle around her slender body while Socks unrolled the mat and sang a come-hither-and-lend-us-an-ear song.

As soon as the passers-by began to slow down, Perdita would gather them in with her flexible voice and her dancing hands, building the audience and working it for a sentence or two before slipping into her story like a fox into a henhouse.

There was never such a storyteller as Perdita. Socks never remembered much about the stories themselves, except that they were always just the stories Socks most wanted to hear. And the way Perdita told them was miraculous. Every character she spoke for had a different voice, a different way of standing and moving, you could almost swear a different face. Sometimes she would draw the audience into the tale, questioning, answering, challenging, teasing, diverting the story around their responses, no matter how weird. Like the Mad River, her tales flowed with dreams, with eddies of horror and currents of beauty, never twice exactly the same. No one ever walked out on one of Perdita's tales. Hill-dweller, street rat, gang tough, human, halfie, elf, all stayed to hear her, and when at last she'd bow and fall silent, they shivered and blinked as if waking from sleep.

Once, though, in the middle of a long and complicated tale about a leaf and a jewel and a boy with one green eye, Socks thought that Perdita had gone too far.

They were set up in front of the Wheat Sheaf, a bit of Bordertown that would be forever Elfland. There were maybe four humans in the audience. Usually Socks didn't pay much attention to the pigeons, wound up in Perdita's spell as thoroughly as they.

Tonight, however, she was bored. A human boy standing near her was shifting from foot to booted foot; a couple of other humans were trading what-is-this-shit glances. On the other hand, the elves were so silent they didn't even seem to be breathing, staring at Perdita as if nothing existed in the world except her.

Realizing that they weren't paying her the least bit of attention, Socks studied the faces through her veil. They were a dressy crowd. One elf had powder on his cheekbones, a diamond dust that echoed the crystal brilliance of his long eyes. Then something—the stillness of his face, perhaps—told Socks that the glitter was not make-up, but tears.

Perdita made enough from that one Telling to buy meat for the soup and a new spell-box for Goblin Market's amps. She also insisted on treating the whole squat to a meal at Hell's Kitchen, complete with a bottle of elvin wine.

"Pushing the boat out, aren't you, girl?" said Queen B. when she saw the tall, tapered bottle. "Order a beer, Bossman. This shit'll be wasted on you." She turned the impossibly narrow flutes the horned waiter had set in front of Baby and Hand mouth down on the table. "No way, kids."

"Come on, Queenie-babe. Let 'em live a little." Although she hadn't touched the green-white liquid in her glass, Perdita already sounded drunk. "They gotta drink to my good fortune. And everybody should taste elf's tears before they die. They're a real groovy high. Aren't they, Socks?"

Socks nodded. A real groovy high, all right. Miraculous, inhuman, they'd fallen on Perdita like a glamor, making her too bright to approach. She'd taken flight as soon as the crowd dispersed, leaving Socks to haul the heavy mat and the heavier take through the stony streets of Bordertown all by herself. After they went to bed, Socks had heard her whispering in the dark: "Did you see that, Mom? I made the fuckers cry. Just for you, Mom. I made the fuckers cry."

Next day, Perdita had been so full of herself that she overflowed, asking Map where to find Bordertown on his stained face, calling Queen B. "Queen Blimp," shuffling Hand's carefully sorted stacks of bright paper. And when Socks had presented herself at nightfall, she'd said, "I'm not in the mood."

So they'd missed one night—two, now. Socks didn't think Perdita'd be in the mood to tell stories tonight, either. Her thin cheeks were burnished rose-gold in the ruddy light of Hell's Kitchen's enchanted flambeaux. She was proposing a toast.

"To the half-bloods!" she cried in her rich, carrying Teller's voice. Everyone raised their glasses. "May they all prove as barren as the mules they are."

Socks had taken a sip of wine before she really heard what Perdita had said. The elf's tears was acrid on her tongue, like peat smoke and grass. She coughed and set the glass down hastily.

Queen B. slapped her on the back. "I don't blame you, girl. That toast would choke a horse."

Art and Eye glared at Perdita, who giggled and flipped them a finger. Pet got up, worked her mouth, got out "Oh, *you!*" and stamped out. Christie followed her. Baby began to cry.

Bossman rubbed his nose. "You the damnedest girl I ever did meet," he said wearily. "Don't you care what you say?"

"Yes," said Perdita, suddenly sober. "I care very much."

After the dinner at Hell's Kitchen, nobody much felt like speaking to Perdita for a while. Apparently, she didn't much feel like speaking either. She lounged around on her mattress under the window in the common room, reading books she'd filched from heaven-knows-where, sleeping a lot, not going out. About a week later, when the soup and Queen B.'s temper were about as thin as they'd ever been, Pet and Art cornered Socks in the kitchen.

"You gotta do something, Socks. One more day of watching her highness eating bonbons and I'll kill her dead," said Pet.

"Queen B. said she could stay as long as she contributed," said Art. "And she's not holding up her end of the bargain any more. Somebody's got to tell her to get her ass in gear or out of here, one or the other."

"Why are you telling me this? Aren't you breaking rule three or whatever it is?"

Pet raised a black brow. "We never pay much attention to rule three, tell you the truth. And we're telling you because you can handle her."

Socks examined Art's teddy-bear face and Pet's squirrelly one, looking for signs of ridicule. They both met her eyes full-on, a little plaintive, expecting her to take care of things. Afraid to tell them no, afraid to tell them yes, Socks felt her heart pounding in her throat.

"She's going to cop out," said Pet disgustedly. "Not one of your better ideas, Art, asking the Baggie girl for help." "No," said Socks. "I'll do it. At least I'll try."

"Can't do more than that," said Art fairmindedly.

Socks put on Nightingale's autumn tunic and pants, gathered up Perdita's fiery scarves, and went to stand at the foot of the mattress where Perdita lay covered by a disreputable knitted afghan, reading. Perdita glanced up from her book, groaned, and rolled up into the afghan like a cocoon.

Go away," she said. "I'm all out of stories, okay? I'm storied out."

Socks sighed and wondered what to say next. She knew Perdita was lying—telling stories never put out her flame, but fanned it hotter and brighter. She didn't look out of stories; she looked out of temper and bored.

"It's a pretty night," said Socks coaxingly. "Lots of people out. Pet said she overheard a Trueblood talking about you, about how you were a real Storyteller like her mother told her about in Elfland, and how she wanted to hear you again."

"You only hear perfection once," said Perdita, then abruptly unrolled herself and stretched languidly. "My public," she drawled. "My vampire public. I suppose I must feed them." She giggled, disentangled herself from her woolly cocoon, snatched a rainbow-colored scarf from Christie's drying rack, and twisted it around her neck. "Let's go, kid. Time's a-wasting."

She was good that night, but mean. Her stories skated the thin edge of insult, turning like snakes to bite her listeners. The audiences laughed, but uneasily, and the rain of coins and four-leaf clovers was not so heavy as it might have been.

"What's wrong with you?" Socks asked on the long walk home. They'd gone all the way to Dragon's Claw Bridge; the mat was a leaden weight on her shoulders and each step like broken ice.

"You," said Perdita. "You couldn't catch a cue if it had a sticking-spell laid on it. And you were yowling like a horny cat. What happened to your sweet voice, Singer? Your foot rot go to your throat or something?"

Socks bent her head silently, any response she could think to make locked tight in her throat. She spent what was left of the night curled up beside the stove in the kitchen, breathing very gently and trying not to think of what Perdita had said, or the hard, bright, clipped voice in which she'd said it, or the way her eyes had glittered, beady and animal in her pointed face.

In the morning, Socks got up early and joined Baby at the wash-tub.

She felt absurdly pleased when Baby laughed and butted her head against her shoulder, and absurdly grateful that Christie couldn't ask her why she was back washing and drying. In fact, by the end of the day it was clear to her that the whole squat knew that Perdita had ditched her lame Singer, and none too gently, either. She noticed their small kindnesses— the red paper crane Hand left under her pillow, the scrap of rusty silk Christie tied around her neck, the way Queen B. called her "honey." Their friendliness made her misery a little more bearable.

Perdita spent less and less time at the squat. She showed up once every day or so to give Queen B. the take from her storytelling and to sleep, rolled head to toe in her afghan, muttering and tossing in uneasy dreams. When she was awake, all her words were toothed and edged like knives. She told no one where she'd when she stayed out all night or what she'd be doing. Map, out late scavenging, saw her with a new Singer, dressed, as Socks had been, in earthy rags and a dark veil. The height had suggested an elf, Art said. The voice could easily have been a man's or a woman's. They'd been walking arm and arm, very cozy.

"I don't expect she'll be back for a while," he said smugly. "Whoever it is, I hope they've had their shots."

Two mornings later, Perdita was back. Socks met her coming into the kitchen, yawning and stretching her arms up over her head. Socks shrank back by the stove and stared at her. She looked pale, hollow-checked, and bruised around the eyes. Horrified, Socks watched a sluggish drop of blood paint crimson down her arm. Between the bracelets, her wrists were red and black and swollen. There was a cut over one eye, too, and a shadowy bruise along her jaw.

Perdita put down her arms and glared at "her. "What're you gaping at?"

Socks took a deep breath. "I know you don't like questions," she said miserably.

Perdita fingered her woven bracelets, winced as the cotton rubbed her abraded wrists, clasped her hands behind her back.

"I'm not selling my ass, if that's what you're thinking," she said. "I promised. A friend got a little rough—that's all."

"A friend," said Socks, horrified out of her shyness. "A friend cut you up and hit you? You don't need friends like that."

"What do you know about what I need or don't need? You're just a kid with stinky feet. You can't find your ass with both hands and a road map. Saving my life doesn't give you the right to tell me how to live it."

Socks stared into Perdita's angry face, watching it shift and distort into a fox's snarling mask. She felt cold, which wasn't surprising, since it was snowing heavily, muting the fox's crimson presence under soft, white veils. For a moment she rested, suspended like a leaf in a block of ice, then a spurt of flame melted the white world, and the common room burst upon her in an overwhelming kaleidoscope of shapes and colors, centering on Perdita's bruised face. Socks closed her eyes. She was sitting on the floor, slid down beside the stove with her Baggied feet tucked painfully under her.

Fingers like a cat's sandpapery pads touched her cheeks.

"Look," said Perdita, very close and low. "I didn't mean to yell at you. Honest. You're just a kid—you don't know any better. And you're my friend." The fingers moved to her forehead. "Socks? Nightingale? You can't go away. I owe you."

"You're mad at me," whispered Socks.

"I'm over it. I won't yell again. I didn't know you'd go away like that."

Socks opened her eyes. "You called me back," she said. It came out like an accusation. "How'd you do that?"

Perdita shrugged, sat back on her heels. "I can do a lot of shit like that."

"Elf magic?"

Perdita hesitated. "I don't know," she said finally. "I just do it. My mother did, too, mostly to keep people from noticing that she was from the Realm. She did other stuff, too, useful stuff, like healing my arm the time boiling stuff got . . . spilled on it. Like that."

"She healed you?" said Socks. "Can you heal?"

"Sure. I've done it lots of times." Perdita chewed her lower lip. "Well, I could if I wanted to."

Suddenly Socks felt hot. She'd never felt hot before, only cold.

Hot made her want to hit, to hurt, to see her own pain reflected on Perdita's face. "Never mind," said Socks loudly. "Just never mind. Forget I said anything, okay?" She turned and limped with dignity towards the bathroom.

"Wait," said Perdita. Her voice had lost its jagged edge, and sounded to Socks like the voice of the girl who had told her that she sang more sweetly than the crimson martlets of Elfland. Socks stopped, but she didn't turn around.

"You've always been straight with me," said Perdita. "You've believed me and stood up for me. I'm . . . grateful for that."

"I don't want you to be grateful. I don't want a payback for liking you." Socks' throat closed against the rising heat. "Fuck gratitude," she said.

"I'll heal you."

Hot tears boiled in her eyes. "Fuck you."

"Because I like you. Because I have to."

The heat fell away from her and Socks turned around, shivering with reaction. Perdita's eyes were blurred, her mouth pursed around tears.

"If you want to," said Socks. "I don't care."

"I'll need the others," said Perdita. "They like you, too."

"No, they don't. I'm the Baggie girl. They think I'm stupid because my feet stink."

"I'm right and you're wrong," said Perdita. "You'll see."

Setting up the healing was like the old recipe for a rabbit stew: the hardest part was catching the rabbits. Perdita didn't help matters by refusing to tell Queen B. and Bossman about it, nor to explain to the others exactly what she had in mind. "It's a kid thing," was all she'd say. "For Socks. You have to trust me."

"Trust you?" Eye brought one scornful eye to bear on her. "Not as far as I could see you."

"I'm with Eye," said Science. "You've been nothing but a nuisance since you got here. You've got some angle with this healing business. We just got to figure out what it is. If you were straight about this, you'd let us tell Bossman."

"I can't," said Perdita. "Because of the rings."

"Now I don't like it even more," said Art. "Who are you planning on hurting, you need to get away from Bossman's rings?"

"Nobody. I'm not planning on hurting nobody. They just cramp my style a little: it's too complicated to explain. You have to trust me on this."

Pet snorted. "I vote no. And so does Christie." As she spoke, she put an arm around Christie's shoulders.

Christie shrugged it off again and shook her head until the rose-red mop flew. "N-n-no harm," she stammered. Her voice was thick and painful to listen to. "For S-s-s-ocks. *T-t-try.*"

All the children looked at her, Pet wide-eyed with astonishment. "Shit," she said. "In public, too. You feel that strong about it?"

Christie nodded. "Okay. You know these things. I don't. We'll do it. Perdita's way. But I still don't like it."

The boys took longer to persuade, but eventually they followed Christie's lead, although Art expressed one final reservation.

"You're wrong, Christie. It could do harm, if it doesn't work."

Socks spoke for the first time. "They're my feet. And they hurt."

They couldn't have the healing in the squat—they all knew that without being told. But there were plenty of other apartments in the building, some of them occupied, some of them empty except for rats and spiders. Perdita led her reluctant healers to one of these, two flights up at the back of the building.

The children hesitated in the door. The windows were shrouded by long rags of curtains and dust lay like snow. Perdita, carrying a candle stuck upright on a plate, stepped softly through the dust, which eddied around her bare feet and clung to the legs of her jeans. She set the dish down in the middle of the floor and lit the candle with a kitchen match. One by one, she took the children by the hand and led them into their places in a circle: Art, Christie, Hand, Socks, Baby, Science, Pet, Eye, Map. The flame folded and flared, touching the young faces with gold at cheek and brow. Pet wrinkled her nose at Christie across the circle, encountered such a solemn look that she ducked her head, subdued. Socks felt Perdita pass behind her, a shadow pressure at her back.

"Sit."

Perdita's voice, at once light and resonant, seemed to come from inside the circle, as though the candle flame had spoken.

They all sat in the dust, careful not to stir it up, pulling their knees up in front of them. Socks blushed at the break her plastic-bagged feet made in the circle of boots and sneakers. Under the bags, her skin pricked and throbbed. She closed her eyes. The after-image of the candle flame danced black against her lids, shrinking and swelling. Socks had a sudden vision of Perdita smiling, toothy and feral, gasped, opened her eyes to catch the gleam of her glance across the circle.

"Untie your laces."

Again, her voice spoke in the flame. Again everyone obeyed, fumbling at knots and lopsided bows in the tricksy light. Science helped Baby, who usually wore sandals, but who today was sporting a pair of brown lace-up old-lady shoes from Christie's stock.

"Tie the laces together."

A shadow at Socks' back told her that Perdita was pacing the bounds of the circle. To her right and her left, Baby and Hand painstakingly tied a lace to one of Christie's and Science's, then sat uncertainly holding the other lace in their hands and nothing to tie it to.

"Around her ankles."

The low words came just as Hand's delicate fingers looped his leather bootlace around her right ankle, on the bare skin above the Baggie. She felt it lying there, soft and snug, and a moment later, Baby's round, waxed lace around the other.

Perdita's voice, the flame's voice, murmured intimately in her ear and bones. "This little piggy was beaten. This little piggy left home. This little piggy forgot herself. This little piggy got none. This little piggy sang roundelays all the way home."

Socks' feet began to itch as if a thousand fire ants were nibbling and stinging her between her toes, under her nails, across her arches, along the length of her soles. She whimpered and gritted her teeth.

"Wicked," said the flame. "Bad girl. Bad."

Socks cringed and covered her face with her hands. Bad. Wicked. That's what she was. She deserved to suffer, deserved to feel each step as ice and knives, for all those evil things, those evil things she must have done, or why was she being punished?

"Not you."

"Yes," whispered Socks. "Yes. Me."

"Not you. Never you. Never, ever. I'm nobody, who are you? Don't tell me you're nobody, too. Hush, don't tell. Don't tell. Don't. Tell."

"Never," said Socks. "I promise."

"Promise," echoed the voice. "Tell."

Behind her closed lids, Socks saw a man to her left, a woman to her right, much bigger than she was, giants. The man was all black hair and red lips, with hard, bright eyes and dark hair on the back of his wide hands. The woman was brown hair and pink skin except for the places where the man's blackness had rubbed off on her arms and cheeks. They were holding the leaves of a giant magazine full of pictures. Its spine was propped against her own outstretched legs.

"Fox," said the woman's voice. "See the fox, Precious?"

"I don't know why you bother, Louise. She's too little to understand. It's just noises to her."

"That's not true, Peter. She understands everything, don't you, Precious? See the pretty fox, all red and black? Mr. Fox in the woods."

The crackle of stiff paper, a quick glimpse of a pink tongue lolling over jagged white teeth, of a white paw crushed between jagged black teeth, of a red brighter than the fox's rusty coat staining the snow. Then the magazine was dragged from her knees and thrown on the floor.

"How could they!" said the woman. "And they call this a family magazine!"

"Oh, for Pete's sake, Louise," said the man. "It's just a damn fox in a trap. You're not going to get all pious about it, are you? Because if you are, you can just forget about your precious family time." Socks started to whimper, hardly knowing what had frightened her. "What's the matter with her?" he said.

"The picture," the woman said hesitantly. "It's upset her."

"You've upset her, if she's really upset." He gave Socks a shake. "You," he snapped. "You shut up. There's nothing wrong with you—you're just trying to get attention."

Socks looked up at his red, moist face and his red mouth spitting out loud words and wailed.

The man stood up. "You want attention? He shouted. "Then I'll give you attention. But you won't like it."

"Peter," said the woman, pleading. "She's only a baby, Peter; she doesn't understand."

"She'll understand this."

Socks felt a blow raking across her face, a blow that shocked her momentarily into silence.

"See?" he said. "Nothing to it." Then he plucked the magazine from the floor and left.

"Baby?" said the woman, thick-voiced. "Precious?" Socks shivered, waiting for the white world to come and take away the burning in her cheek, the itch of healing scratches on her back and arms, the helpless pain in the woman's voice. Recently, she'd discovered that all she had to do was sit very still and quiet, and everything would all go away.

But this time everything didn't go away. She could feel warm light against her eyelids, painting the world the color of fresh blood. A slow pulse throbbed in each ankle, one a little faster than the other. A shadow touched her back, passed on.

"Little Tina Tucker sang for her supper. What did she eat? A brass belt buckle."

"Shut up," whispered Socks.

"Two-for-one night," said the flame. "Your feet and your memory."

Socks opened her eyes. She was alone, surrounded by flickers of gold and scarlet and blue, like being at the center of a flame.

She blinked. The flame softened, resolved into a fox with orange-gold fur and amused dark eyes.

"All I asked for was my feet," Socks complained to the eyes.

"You asked to be healed. You have to be careful, making bargains with me."

"A bargain? What bargain? You said you wanted to do it. You said you liked me."

"I did. I do. But it's a bargain anyway. That's the way it works."

"You mean I have to pay you back?"

"Yes."

Socks hunched into herself. "What do you want?"

"Out of here," said the fox. "There are too many strings on me here, too many rules and too many eyes. Queen B.'s tongue galls me and Bossman's rings bind me. I'm leaving."

"And you want me to help?"

"Relax, kid. Releasing me's not your job—I can do it myself. Besides, you're not strong enough yet to do me any good."

"What are you going to ask of me? How do I know I can do it?"

The fox cocked her head. "That's the question, isn't it? You have a year and a day to find an answer to it."

"Huh?"

"A year and a day." The fox sounded impatient. "It's when I'll come back for you. It's traditional. My mother told me." The fox rose, her fur ruffling with the movement, her tail flowing as she turned to go.

"Wait," said Socks. "I need to know what you want me to do."

"Sing, for starters," said the fox, and was gone in a burst of red-gold flame like a dragon's sigh.

"You okay?" Hand's voice in her ear, high and panicky. "You were, like, burning up. We were scared."

"Scared," said Baby, sounding it. "Fire."

Realizing that her eyes were closed, Socks opened them. Everything pulsed, spun, and fell into place—a shabby room, twilit through rotting curtains, a dead candle on a cracked plate, eight terrified faces. Baby was curled into Science's arms, and across the circle, Pet, Eye, and Map were concentrating very hard on disentangling their shoelaces. The candle was out, dead out.

"What happened?" asked Socks.

"Whoosh," sobbed Baby. "Fire."

Over her head, Science nodded. "We thought the place had caught on fire, and here we were, tied down so we couldn't move."

"It was more than the shoelaces." Pet's voice was shrill with panic. "We really couldn't move. It seemed to last forever." "But it didn't hurt," said Hand thoughtfully. "It wasn't even hot. I couldn't tell what was going on at first."

Eye elbowed Map in the ribs. "Not until Mr. Mercator Projection here started yelling."

"And then it just went out," said Art. "Poof! Like that." Science looked at Socks. "Well?"

"Well, what?"

"Your feet. The object of this exercise. How are they?"

"My feet." Socks looked down. Her feet were bare, resting among blackened scraps of fabric. They were white and smooth.

They no longer felt like fire ants or ice or knives. They felt like feet.

Baby let go of Science, wiped her nose on her arm, and peered at Socks' toes. "No more Socks," she said with satisfaction.

"No. No more Socks." There were thin spots in her memory still, where things like names and places and where she'd gone to school had fallen through. She remembered her father, though, his eyes, his belt, and the hard, bright flame of his rage. And she remembered running from a blue house with black shutters, barefoot and in her pajamas, running because her father was killing her mother and she couldn't stop him. The rest would come back to her eventually. Or maybe it wouldn't. At the moment, she was too wiped out to care.

Baby was tugging at her arm. "No more Socks," she repeated.

"Who, then?"

"Huh?"

"She's asking you what we should call you now that your Baggies are things of the past," Pet translated.

"It's a fair question," said Art.

"Yeah," said Map. "We gotta call you something."

Eye punched him in the ribs. "Why? Why can't she be the Nameless One? We don't have one of those?"

Hand began to giggle. "Ex-Socks?"

"Sockless."

"Silk Stockings."

Below their hysterical joking, a sly voice sounded in her ear.

"Everyone needs a stage name, Singer."

"Shut up, you guys." Her voice was a little defensive, but they heard it, and obediently fell silent. "You can call me Nightingale. And I'll sing for my supper."

~

Delia Sherman's three novels for adults are *Through a Brazen Mirror*, *The Porcelain Dove* (a Mythopoeic Fantasy Award winner), and *The Fall of the Kings* (with Ellen Kushner). Her novel, *The Freedom Maze*, won the Prometheus and Andre Norton Awards. Sherman's short fiction has appeared most recently in the anthologies *Teeth*, *Naked City*, and *Queen Victoria's Book of Spells*. A collection, *Young Woman in a Garden*, was published in 2014. She lives in New York City.

~

In the streets and skies of New York City, we find a man with an ancient curse, raw and dire, of birdhood and madness. A newer form of transformative magic is also discovered there.

Painted Birds and Shivered Bones
Kat Howard

The white bird flew through the clarion of the cathedral bells, winging its way through the rich music of their tolling to perch in the shelter of the church's walls. The chiming continued, marking time into measured, holy hours.

Maeve had gone for a walk, to clear her head and give herself the perspective of something beyond the windows and walls of her apartment. She could feel the sensation at the back of her brain, that almost-itch that meant a new painting was ready to be worked on. Wandering the city, immersing herself in its chaos and beauty would help that back of the head feeling turn into a realized concept.

But New York had been more chaos than beauty that morning. Too much of everything and all excess without pause. Maeve felt like she was coming apart at the seams.

In an effort to hold herself together, Maeve had gone to the Cathedral of St. John the Divine. There, she could think, could sit quietly, could stop and breathe without people asking what was wrong.

Midwinter was cold enough to flush her cheeks as she walked to the cathedral, but Maeve couldn't bear being inside—large as the church was, she could feel the walls pressing on her skin. Instead, she perched on a bench across from the fallen tower, and pulled her scarf higher around her neck.

Maeve sipped her latte, and leaned back against the bench, then sat up. She closed her eyes, then opened them again.

There was a naked man crouched on the side of the cathedral.

She dug in her purse for her phone, wondering how it was possible that such a relatively small space always turned into a black hole when she needed to find anything. Phone finally in hand, she sat up.

The naked man was gone.

In his place was a bird. Beautiful, white feathers trailing like half-remembered thoughts. Impressive, to be sure, especially when compared to the expected pigeons of the city. But bearing no resemblance to a man, naked or otherwise.

Maeve let her phone slip through her fingers, back into her bag, and sat up, shaking her head at herself. "You need to cut down on your caffeine."

"You thought what?" Emilia laughed. "Oh, honey. The cure for thinking that you see a naked man at the cathedral isn't giving up caffeine, it's getting laid."

"Meeting men isn't really a priority for me." Maeve believed dating to be a circle of Hell that Dante forgot.

"Maeve, you don't need to meet them. Just pick one." Emilia gestured at the bar.

Maeve looked around. "I don't even know them."

"That's exactly my point." Emilia laughed again. "Take one home, send him on his way in the morning, and I can guarantee your naked hallucinations will be gone."

"Fine." Maeve sipped her bourbon. "I'll take it under advisement."

Surprising precisely no one, least of all the woman who had been her best friend for a decade, Maeve went home alone, having not even attempted to take one of the men in the bar with her. She hung up her coat, and got out her paints.

Dawn was pinking the sky when she set the brush down and rolled the tension from her neck and shoulders.

The canvas was covered in birds.

Madness is easier to bear with the wind in your feathers. Sweeney flung himself into the currents of the air, through bands of starlight that streaked the sky, and winged toward the cloud-coated moon.

Beneath Sweeney, the night fell on the acceptable madness of the city. Voices cried out to each other in greeting or curse. Tires squealed and horns blared. Canine throats raised the twilight bark, and it was made symphonic by feline yowls, skitterings of smaller creatures, and the songs of more usual birds.

Not Sweeney's.

Silent Sweeney was borne on buffeting currents over the wild lights of the city. Over the scents of concrete and of rot, of grilling meat and decaying corners, of the blood and love and dreams and terrors of millions.

And of their madness as well.

Even in his bird form, Sweeney recognized New York as a city of the mad. Not that one needed to be crazy to be there, or that extended residency was a contributing factor to lunacy of some sort, but living there—thriving there—took a particular form of madness.

Or caused it. Sweeney had not yet decided which.

He had not chosen his immigration, but had been pulled over wind and salt and sea by the whim of a wizard. Exiled from his kingdom in truth, though there were no kings in Ireland anymore.

On he flew, through a forest of buildings built to assault the sky. Over bridges, and trains that hurtled from the earth as if they were loosed dragons. Over love and anger and countless anonymous mysteries.

Sweeney tucked his wings, and coasted to the ground at the Cathedral of St. John the Divine. The ring of church bells set the madness on him, sprang the feathers from his skin, true. But madness obeyed rules of its own devising, and the quietness of the cathedral grounds soothed him. He roosted in the ruined tower, and fed on seed scattered on the steps after weddings.

He had done so for years, making the place a refuge. There had been a woman, Madeleine, he thought her name was, who smelled of paper and stories. She had been kind to him, kind enough that he had wondered sometimes if she could see the curse beneath the feathers. She scattered food, and cracked the window of the room she worked in so that he might perch just inside the frame, and watch her work among the books.

Yes. Madeleine. He had worn his man shape to her memorial, there at the cathedral, found and read her books, with people as out of time as he was. She had been kind to him, and kindness was stronger even than madness was.

Maeve stood in front of the canvas, and wiped the remnants of sleep from her eyes with paint-smeared fingers.

It was good work. She had gotten the wildness of the feathers, and the way a wing could obscure and reveal when stretched in flight. She could do a series, she thought.

"I mean, it's about time, right?" she asked Brian, her agent, on the phone. "Be ambitious, move out of my comfort zone, all those things you keep telling me I need to do."

"Yes, but birds, Maeve?"

"Not still lifes, or landscapes, if that's what you're worried about."

"Well, not worried exactly . . . Look, send me pictures of what you're working on. I'll start looking for a good venue to show them. If it doesn't work, we'll call this your birdbrained period."

It hadn't been the resounding endorsement of her creativity that Maeve had been hoping for, but that was fine. She would paint now, and enthusiasm could come later.

She could feel her paintings, the compulsion to create, just beneath the surface of her skin. She gathered her notebook and pencils, and went out into the city to sketch.

Sweeney perched on a bench in Central Park, plucking feathers from his arms. He had felt the madness creeping back for days this time before the feathers began appearing. Sure, he knew it was the madness. His blood itched, and unless that was the cursed feathers being born beneath his skin, itchy blood meant madness.

Itchy blood had meant madness and feathers for close to forever now, hundreds of years since the curse had first been cast. Life was long, and so were curses.

Though when he thought about it, Sweeney suspected curses were longer.

Pigeons cooed and hopped about near the bench's legs, occasionally casting their glinting eyes up at him. Sweeney thumbed a nail beneath a quill, worried at it until he could get a good grip. The feather emerged slowly, blood brightening its edges. He sighed as it slid from his skin. Sweeney flicked the feather to the ground, and the pigeons scattered.

"Can't blame you. I don't like the fucking things, either." Sweeney tugged at the next feather, one pushing through the skin at the bend of his elbow. Plucking his own feathers wouldn't stop the change, or even slow it, but it gave him something to do.

"The curse has come upon me," he said. Blood caked his nails, and dried in the whorls and creases of his fingers.

And it would. The curse would come upon him, as it had time and time again, an ongoing atonement. He might be occasionally mad, and sometimes a bird with it, but Sweeney was never stupid. He knew the metamorphosis would happen. A bell would ring, and his skin would grow too tight around his bones, and he would bend and crack into bird shape.

Sooner, rather sooner indeed than later, if the low buzz at the back of his skull was any indication.

"But just because something is inevitable, doesn't mean that we resign ourselves to it. No need to roll over and show our belly, now." Sweeney watched the pigeons as they skritched about in the dirt.

There were those who might say that Sweeney's stubbornness had gone a long way to getting him into the fix he was currently in. Most days, Sweeney would agree with them, and on the days he wouldn't, well, those days he didn't need to, as his agreement was implied by the shape he wore.

You didn't get cursed into birdhood and madness because you were an even-tempered sort of guy.

"You guys all really birds, there beneath the feathers?" Sweeney asked the flock discipled at his feet.

The pigeons kept their own counsel.

Then the bells marked the hour, and in between ring and echo, Sweeney became a bird.

Dusk was painting the Manhattan skyline in gaudy reds and purples when Maeve looked up from her sketchbook. She had gotten some good studies, enough to start painting the series. She scrubbed her smudged hands against the cold-stiffened fabric of her jeans. She would get take out—her favorite soup dumplings—and then go home and paint.

The bird winged its way across her sightlines as she stood up. Almost iridescent in the dying light, a feathered sweep of beauty at close of day. Watching felt transcendent—

"Oh, fuck, not again." In the tree not a bird, but a man, trying his best to inhabit a bird-shaped space.

Maeve closed her eyes, took a deep breath, opened them again. Still: Man. Tree. Naked.

"Okay. It's been a long day. You forgot to eat. You have birds on the brain. You're just going to go home now"—she tapped the camera button on her phone—"and when you get there, this picture of a naked man is going to be a picture of a bird."

It wasn't.

Sweeney watched the woman pick up her paintbrush, set it down. Pick up her phone, look at it, clutch her hair or shake her head, then set the phone down and walk back to her canvas. She had been repeating a variation of this pattern since he landed on the fire escape outside of her window.

He had seen her take the picture, and wanted to know why. The people who saw him were usually quite good at ignoring his transformations, in that carefully turned head, averted eyes, and faster walking way of ignoring. Most people didn't even let themselves see him. This woman did. Easy enough to fly after her, once he was a bird again.

Sweeney wondered if perhaps she was mad, too, this woman who held the mass of her hair back by sticking a paintbrush through it, and who talked to herself as she paced around her apartment.

She wasn't mad now though, not that he could tell. She was painting. Sweeney stretched his wings, and launched himself into the cold, soothing light of the stars.

In the center of the canvas was a man, and feathers were erupting from his skin.

"Oh, yes. Brian is going to love it when you tell him about this. 'That series of paintings you didn't want me to do? Well, I've decided that the thing it really needed was werebirds.'"

It was good, though, she thought. The shock of the transformation as a still point in the chaos of the city that surrounded him.

The transformation had been a shock. The kind of thing you had to see to believe, and even then, you doubted. Such a thing should have been impossible to see.

And maybe that was the thread for the series, Maeve thought. Fantasy birds, things that belonged in fairy tales and medieval bestiaries, feathered refugees from mythology and legend scattered throughout a modern city that refused to see them there.

She could paint that. It would be a series of paintings that would let her do something powerful if she got them right.

Maeve sat at her computer, and began compiling image files of harpy and cockatrice, phoenix and firebird. There were, she thought, so many stories of dead and vengeful women returning as ghost birds, but nothing about men who did so. Not that she thought what she had seen was a ghost, or that she was trying some form of research-based bibliomancy to discern the story behind the bird (the man) she kept seeing, but she wouldn't have turned away an answer.

"And would it have made you feel better if you had found one? Because hallucinating a ghost bird in Manhattan is so much better than if you're just seeing a naked werebird? Honestly." She shook her head.

Though it wasn't a hallucination. Not with the picture on her phone. Why it was easier to think she was losing her mind than to accept that she had seen something genuinely impossible was something Maeve didn't understand.

She printed out reference photos for all the impossible birds she hadn't yet seen, and taped them over the walls.

In the beginning, when the curse's claws still bled him, and Sweeney had nothing to recall him to himself or his humanity, he would fly after Eorann, who had been his wife, before he was a bird. She was the star to his wanderings.

Eorann had loved Sweeney, and so she had tried, at the beginning, to break the curse. Unspeaking, she wove garments from nettles and cast them over Sweeney like nets, in the hopes that pain and silence spun together might force a bird back into a man's shape. Even had one perfect wing lingered as a reminder of his past and his errors, it would have been change enough. More, it would have been stasis, a respite from the constant and unpredictable change that, Sweeney discovered, was the curse's true black heart.

When that did not work, she had shoes made from iron, and walked the length and breadth of Ireland in an attempt to wear them out. But she was already east of the sun and west of the moon, the true north of her compass set to once upon a time. Such places are not given to the wearing out of iron shoes.

Eorann spun straw into gold, then spun the gold into thread that flexed and could be woven into a dress more beautiful than the sun, the moon, and the stars. She uncurdled milk, and raised from the dead a cow that gave it constantly, without needing food nor drink of its own. If there were a miracle, a marvel, or a minor wonder that Eorann could perform in the hopes of breaking Sweeney's curse, she did so.

Until the day she didn't.

"A wife's role may be many things, Sweeney. But it is not a wife's job to break a husband's curse, not when he is the one who has armored himself in it."

Those were the last words that Eorann had spoken to him. From the distance of time, Sweeney could admit now that she was right. Still, from the height of the unfeeling sky, he wished that she had been the saving of him.

"Well, they're different. That's certain," Brian said, walking between the canvases.

"If different means crap, just say so. I'm too tired to parse euphemisms."

Maeve only had one completed canvas—the man transforming into a bird. But she had complete studies of two others—a phoenix rising out of the flame of a burning skyline, and a harpy hovering protectively over a woman.

"They're darker than your usual thing, but powerful." Brian stepped back, walked back and forth in front of the canvas.

"They're good. I've a couple galleries in mind—I'll start making calls.

"You'll come to the opening, of course."

"No," Maeve said. "Absolutely not. Nonnegotiable."

"Look, the reclusive artist thing was fine when you were starting out, because you didn't matter enough for people to care about you. But we can charge real money for these. People who pay real money for their art aren't just buying a decoration for their wall, they're buying the story that goes with it."

Maeve was pretty sure no one wanted to buy the story of the artist who had a panic attack at her own opening. No, scratch that. She was absolutely sure someone would want to buy that story. She just didn't want to sell her paintings badly enough to give it to them.

"Well, then how about the story is I am a recluse. A crazy bird lady instead of a crazy cat lady. I live with the chickens. Whatever you need to say. But I don't interact with the people buying my work, and I don't go to openings."

"You're lucky I'm good at my job, Maeve."

"I'm good at mine, too."

Brian sighed. "Of course you are. I didn't mean to suggest otherwise. But I don't understand why you don't just buy yourself a pretty dress, and have fun letting rich people buy you drinks and tell you how wonderful you are.

"Let yourself celebrate a little. It's the fun part of the job, Maeve."

It wasn't, not for her. Of course, Brian wouldn't understand that. Maeve worked too hard to keep her panic attacks hidden. She had an entire portfolio of tricks to keep them manageable, and out of view.

Out of the apartment was fine, as long as she didn't have to interact with too many people. Crowds were okay as long as she had someone she knew with her, and she didn't have to interact with the people she didn't know. When she had to meet new people, she did so in familiar surroundings, either one on one, or in a group of people she already knew and felt comfortable with. Even then, she usually needed a day at home, undisturbed, after, in order to rest and regain her equilibrium.

A party where everyone would be strangers who wanted to pay

attention to her, who wanted her to interact with them, with no safety net of friends that she could fall onto, was impossible.

Even after Eorann had told Sweeney that she could not save him, it took him some time to realize that he would need to be the saving of himself. More time still, an infinity of church bells, of molting feathers, to understand that saving himself did not necessarily include lifting the curse.

In search of himself, of answers, of peace, long and long ago, Sweeney had undertaken a quest.

A quest is a cruel migration. This is the essence of a quest, no matter who undertakes it. But Sweeney had not known what to look for, save for the longing to see something other than what he was.

The Sangréal had been found once already, and though lost again, it was the kind of thing where the first finding mattered. The dragons were all in hiding, and Sweeney had never particularly thought they needed to be slain.

Nor had he known the map with which to travel by, save for one that would take him to a place other than where he was. He took wing. Over sea and under stone and then over the sea to sky.

Maeve saw the bird at the Cathedral of St. John the Divine again.

Cathedrals, churches, museums, libraries, they were useful sorts of places for her. When the walls of her apartment pressed too tightly, these were places she could go, and sit, and think, and not have to worry about people insisting that she interact with them in order to justify her presence.

"I came here for peace and quiet, you know. Not because I'm hoping to catch a glimpse of you naked."

The bird did not seem to have an opinion on that.

When she sat, Maeve specifically chose a bench that did not have a line of sight to the bird's current perch. Not like it couldn't fly, but it was the principle of the thing. And she really didn't want to see it become a naked man again.

Stories about artistic inspiration that came to life and then interacted with the artist were only interesting if they were stories. When they were your life, they were weird.

The bird landed next to her on the bench.

Maeve looked at her bird, at her sketchbook, and back at the bird.

"Fine. Fine. But do not turn into a man. Not in front of me. Just don't. If you think you're going to, leave. Please." She tore off a chunk of her croissant and set it on the bird's side of the bench. "Okay?"

Maeve was relieved when the bird did not answer.

There was a package from Brian waiting for her when she got home. The card read, "For the crazy bird lady."

Inside was a beautiful paper bird. A crane, but not the expected origami. Paper-made sculpture, not folded. Feathers and wings and beak all shaped from individual pieces of brightly colored paper. It was a gorgeous fantasy of practicality and feathers.

Maeve tucked it on a shelf, where she could see it while she painted.

He hadn't answered her today, the red-haired painter.

Sweeney could speak in bird form—he was still a man, even when feather-clad—but he had learned, finally, the value of silence.

This had not always been so. It had been speaking that had first called his curse down upon him.

He had called out an insult to Ronan. Said something he should not have, kept speaking when he should have driven a nail through his tongue to hold his silence.

Ronan had spoken then, too. Spoken a word that burnt the sky, and shifted the bones of the earth. A curse, raw and dire. That was the first time the madness fell upon Sweeney. The madness, and the breaking of himself into the too-light bones that made up a bird's wing.

When it came down to it, it was pride that cursed Sweeney into his feathers as sure as pride had melted Icarus out of his. Pride, and a too-quick temper, faults that dwelt in any number of people without changing their lives and their shapes, without sending them on a path of constant migration centered on a reminder of error.

Curses didn't much care that there were other people they could have landed on, just as comfortably. They fell where they would, then watched the aftermath unfold.

Some days were good days, days when Maeve could walk through her life and not be aware of any of the adjustments she performed to make it livable.

Tuesday was not one of those days.

She had taken the subway, something she did only rarely, preferring to walk. But a sudden hailstorm had driven her underground, and sent what seemed like half of the city after her.

Maeve got off at the second stop, not even sure what street it was. Her pulse had been racing so fast that her vision had gone gray and narrow. If she hadn't gotten out, away from all those people she would have collapsed.

Her notebook, her most recent sketches for her paintings, was left behind on the Uptown 2 train. It had to have been the train where it went missing. She had been sure it was in her bag when she left her apartment, and it was clearly not among the bag's upended contents now.

Forty-five minutes on the phone with MTA lost and found had done no more than she expected, and reassured her the odds of its return were small.

And though it had smelled fine—she had checked—the milk with which she had made the hot chocolate that was supposed to make her feel better had instead made her feel decidedly worse.

The floor of the bathroom was cool against her cheek. Exhausted and sick, Maeve curled in on herself, and fell into tear-streaked sleep.

The bird was in her dream, and that was far from the weirdest thing about it.

The sky shaded to lavender, the clouds like ink splotches thrown across it.

Then a head sailed across the waxing moon.

Sweeney cocked his own head, and shifted on the branch.

Another head described an arc across the sky, a lazy rise and fall.

Sweeney looked around. He could not tell where the heads were launching from, nor could he hear any sounds of distress.

Three more heads, in rapid succession, and Sweeney was certain he was mad again. He wished he were in his human form, so that he might throw back his own head and howl.

Five heads popped up in front of Sweeney, corks popping to the surface of the sea.

Identical, each to each, the world's strangest set of brothers.

They looked, Sweeney thought, cheerful. Certainly more cheerful than he would be, were he suddenly disconnected from the neck down.

Each head had been neatly severed. Or no. Not severed. They looked as if they were heads that had never had bodies at all. Smiling, clean-shaven, bright-eyed. No dangling veins or spines, no ragged skin. No blood.

Sweeney supposed the fact that the heads were levitating was no more remarkable than the fact that they were not bleeding. Still, it was the latter that seemed truly strange.

"Hail."

"And."

"Well."

"Met."

"Sweeney," said the heads.

"Er, hello," said Sweeney.

"A."

"Fine."

"Night."

"Isn't."

"It?" Their faces were the picture of benevolence.

"Indeed it is," said Sweeney.

"We."

"Would."

"Speak."

"With."

"You."

As they seemed to be doing that already, Sweeney simply bobbed his head.

"Do."

"You."

"Not."

"Remember."

"Us?" The heads circled around Sweeney.

He tried to focus, to imagine them with bodies attached. Nothing about them seemed familiar. He could not see past their duplicated strangeness. "Please forgive me, gentlemen, but I don't."

"We."

"So."

"Often."

"Forget."

"Ourselves."

"Or."

"Perhaps."

"We."

"Haven't."

"Met." They slid into line in front of him again, the last one bumping its left-side neighbor, and setting him gently wobbling.

"Can you read the future, then?" It seemed the most likely explanation, though nothing about this encounter was at all likely.

"Yes."

"And."

"No."

"Only."

"Sometimes."

Sweeney appreciated the honesty of the answer almost as much as he appreciated the thoroughness.

"Listen."

"Now."

"Sweeney."

"Listen."

"Well."

"No.

"One."

"Chooses."

"His."

"Quest."

"It."

"Is."

"Chosen."

"For."

"Him."

"All.

"Quests."

"End."

"In."

"Death."

"So does life," said Sweeney.

"Then."

"Choose."

"Yours."

"Well."

"Sweeney."

The heads cracked their jaws so wide, Sweeney wondered if they would swallow themselves. Then they began to laugh, and while laughing, whirled themselves into a small cyclone. Faster and faster it spun, until the heads were nothing but a laughing blur, and then were gone.

Sweeney, contemplative, watched the empty sky until dawn.

Maeve sat up, her head and neck aching from sleeping on the tile, her mouth tasting as if she had licked the subway station she fled from earlier that day.

Legs still feeling more like overcooked noodles than functioning appendages, she staggered into the kitchen, and poured the milk down the sink. It was a largely symbolic sort of gesture, performed only to make her head feel better—it certainly wouldn't undo the food poisoning or the resulting fucked up dream, but seeing the milk spiral down the drain was still a relief.

Talking heads flying around Central Park and conversing with a bird who was sometimes a man. It was like something out of a Henson movie, except without the good soundtrack.

Becoming involved enough in her work to dream about it was, on balance, a good thing. But there were limits. She was not putting disembodied heads into her paintings.

Maeve painted a tower, set into the Manhattan skyline. A wizard's tower, dire and ancient, full of spirals and spires, held together with spells and impossibility.

She hung the surrounding sky with firebirds, contrails of flame streaking the clouds.

Dawn came, but it was neither rebirth nor respite. Sweeney was still befeathered. He turned to the glow of the rising sun, and the tower that appeared there, as if painted on the sky.

Every wizard had a tower, even in twenty-first century New York. It was the expected, required thing, and magic had rules and bindings more powerful than aught else. It had to, made as it was out of words and will and belief. Certain things had to be true or the magic crumbled to dust and nothingness.

Sweeney cracked open his beak, and tore at the promise-crammed air.

A wizard's tower is protected by many things, but the most puissant are the wizard's own words of power. Even after they have cast their spells and done their work, the words of a wizard retain tracings of magic. Their echoes continue to cast and recast the spells, for as long as sound travels.

The words do not hang idle in the air. Power recognizes power, and old spells linger together like former lovers. Though the connections are no longer as bright as the crackle and spark of that first magic, they can never be entirely erased. They gather, each to each, and in their greetings, new magics are made.

Ronan had been a wizard for centuries now, perhaps millennia. A few very important years longer than Sweeney had been a bird.

He had fled Ireland in the coffin ships, with the rest of the decimated, starving population. His magic, the curse's binding, had pulled Sweeney along in his wake.

In the years since his arrival, magic had wrapped itself around Ronan's tower like fairy tale thorns, a threat, a protection, and a guarantee of solitude. A locus of power that sang, siren-like, to Sweeney, though he knew it was never what he sought.

Sweeney flew around the tower three times, then three, then three again, in the direction of unraveling. The curse, as it always had, remained.

"How many paintings do you have finished?"

"Five."

"How long will it take you to do, say, five or maybe seven more?"

"Why?"

"Drowned Meadow will give you gallery space, but I think these new pieces are strong enough you'd be better served if you had enough finished work to fill the gallery, rather than being part of a group showing."

"When would I need them finished by?"

Brian's answer made her wince, and mourn, once again, the loss of the sketchbook, and the studies it contained. Still.

"It's a good space. I'll get the pieces done."

"Excellent. I'll email you the contracts."

"Wait, that's what the naked bird guy looks like?" Emilia stood in front of the first painting in the series, the man transforming into a bird. "No wonder you keep seeing him around the city. He's hot."

"He's usually a bird."

"Still, yum. And is that drawn to scale?"

Maeve snorted. "Fine. The next time I see him, if he's being a person, I'll give him your number."

Emilia laughed, but she looked sideways at Maeve while she did. "So, are you seeing all of the things from your paintings?"

Emilia had moved to the newest painting in the series, a cockatrice among the tents at Bryant Park's Fashion Week, models turned to statues under its gaze.

"Do you think I would be here with you, discussing the attractiveness of a werebird, after having consumed far too much Ethiopian food, if I had really encountered a bird that can turn people to stone just by looking at them?"

Maeve looked at Emilia again. "Or no. It's not actually that you think that. You're just doing the sanity check."

"I don't think you're crazy. But you know you don't always take care of yourself before a show. And this one did start with you thinking that you saw a bird turn into a naked guy."

"Which, I admit, sounds odd. But you don't need to worry that I've started the New York Chapter of the Phoenix Watching Club."

"That sounds very Harry Potter. You haven't seen any wizards wandering around the city, have you? I mean, other than the guys who like to get out their wands on the subway." Emilia twisted her face into an expression of repulsed boredom.

"And you wonder why I don't like to leave the house."

"No wizards?"

"No wizards."

There were wizards in New York City, nearly everywhere. War mages, who changed history over games of speed chess. Chronomancers who stole seconds from the subway trains. And the city built on dreams was rife with onieromancers channeling desires between sleep and waking.

Even the wizard who had set the curse on Sweeney looked out over the speed and traffic of the city as he spoke his spells, shiftings and transformations, covering one thing in some other's borrowed skin, whether they will or no.

But though Ronan was here, and had been, he was not the direction to which Sweeney looked to break his curse. Wizards did not, under any but the most extreme circumstances, undo their own magic. Magic, magic that is practiced and cast, is at odds with entropy. Not only does it reshape order out of chaos, but it wrenches the rules for order sideways. It rewrites the laws, so that a man might be shifted to a bird, and back again, no matter how physics wails.

To make such a thing happen, though it might seem the work of an incantation and an arcane gesture, is the marriage of effort and will. And will, once wielded in such fashion, is not lightly undone.

But just because the wizard would not lift his curse did not mean that the spell might never be broken.

It just meant it would require a magic stronger than wizardry to break it.

Maeve's apartment was full of birds. Photographs papered the walls, layered over each other in collage, Escheresque spirals of wings that had never flown together fell in cascading recursive loops of impossible birds.

The statue from Brian was a carnival fantasy among articulated skeletons in shadowboxes, shivered bones set at precise angles of flight.

Her own bones ached as if wings mantled beneath the surface of her skin and longed to burst forth from her back.

The canvas before her was enormous, six feet in height and half again as wide, the largest she had ever painted. On it, a murmuration of starlings arced and turned across a storm-tossed sky.

Among the starlings were other birds. Bird of vengeance, storm-called, and storm-conjuring. The Erinyes.

The Kindly Ones.

More terrible than lightning, they harried the New York skyline.

Cramps spasmed Maeve's hands around her brushes, and her eyes burned, but still she layered color onto the canvas.

It was a kind of madness, she thought, the way it felt to finish a painting. The muscle-memory knowledge of exactly where the brush strokes went, even though this was nothing she had painted before. The fizzing feeling at the top of her head that told her what she was painting was right, was true. The adrenaline that flooded her until she couldn't sit, or sleep, or eat until it was finished.

Madness, surely. But a madness of wings, and of glory.

The skies of New York had grown stranger. Sweeney was used to the occasional airborne mystery. It wasn't as if he had ever thought himself the only sometimes-bird on the wing.

But a flock of firebirds had taken up residence in Central Park, and an exaltation of larks had begun exalting in Mandarin in the bell tower of St. Patrick's Cathedral.

He thought he had seen the phoenix, but perhaps it had only been a particularly gaudy sunset.

Magic all unasked for, and stuck about with feathers.

Though perhaps not magic unconjured.

Sweeney paged through a notebook, not lost on a train but slid from a messenger bag. He had wanted, he supposed, to see how she saw him.

Of course, he was in none of the sketches.

But its pages crawled with magic. It was rife in the shadows and shadings and lines of the sketches. Sweeney didn't know if it was wizardry or not, what he was looking at, but there was power in her drawings.

Perhaps enough power to unmake a curse.

"You're sure I can't convince you to come to the opening?" Brian asked. "Because I think people are really going to want to talk to you about these paintings, and Maeve, do not say 'my art speaks for itself.'"

"You have to admit, you pretty much asked me to."

"Maeve."

"They'll sell better if I'm not there."

"What would make you think that?"

Because if I'm there, I'll spend the entire evening locked in the bathroom, occasionally vomiting from panic, she thought. "Because if I'm not there, you can spin me as mysterious. Or better yet, perfect. Tell them what they want to hear without the risk that I'll show up with paint still in my hair."

"I have never once seen you with paint in your hair. And even if I had, artists are supposed to be absent-minded and eccentric. It's part of your charm."

"You told me I wasn't allowed to be absent-minded and eccentric anymore, remember? Not in this gallery. Not at these prices."

"I suppose I did. Still, this is your night, Maeve. If you want to be here, even if there is paint in your hair, you should come."

"I can assure you, Brian, I won't want to."

Sweeney could, if he concentrated enough, prevent the shift in form from man to bird from happening. Usually, he didn't bother—the change came when it would, and after all of these years, he had made peace with his spontaneous wings.

But he wanted to see the paintings. To see, captured in pigment and brushstroke the birds that Maeve had made a space for in New York's skies.

He wanted to see her, just once, in the guise and costume of a normal man.

More, he wanted to see if the magic that crackled across the pages of her notebook was in the paintings as well, to see if she could paint him free. A request that might allow him to once again be a normal man, instead of what he was: a creature cursed into loneliness and the wrong skin, whose only consolation was the further loneliness of flight.

Sweeney's difficulty was that while he could, by force of will, hold himself in human form, it let the madness push further into his consciousness. The longer he fought the transformation, the more he struggled to be shaped like a man, they less he thought like one.

Sweeney slid on his jacket. He checked to make sure his buttons matched, his fly was up, and his shoes were from the same pair. He hailed a cab, and hoped for the best.

On the night of the opening, Maeve was not at the gallery. She had been there earlier in the day to double-check the way the paintings had been hung, to see to all the last minute details, and to tell Brian, one more time, that she was absolutely not coming to the opening.

"Fine. Then at least put on a nice dress at home and have some champagne with a friend so I don't get depressed thinking about you."

"If that's what will make you happy, of course I will," she lied, offering a big smile, and accepting Brian's hug.

As the show opened, Maeve was wearing a T-shirt with holes in it, and eating soup dumplings. Which she toasted with a glass of the very fine champagne that Brian had sent over. Emilia had texted from the gallery that the "paintings are your best thing ever. So proud of you!" Comfort and celebration and a friend, even if far from what Brian imagined.

Strange to think that this show, which Brian thought could be big enough to change her career, began with seeing a bird turn into a naked man. Which was certainly the one story she could never tell when asked what inspired her work.

She hadn't seen the bird for a while now. Or, thankfully, the naked man. Some parts of the strangeness of the city were better left unexplained.

Too many answers killed the magic, and Maeve wanted the magic. Its possibilities were what made up for the discomfort and worry of every day life.

The lights were too bright and there were too many people. Sweeney bit the insides of his cheeks and walked through the gallery as if its floor were shattering glass.

The paintings. He thought they were beautiful, probably, or that they would be if he could ever stand still long enough to really look at them, to see them as more than blurs as he circled the gallery. He felt too hot, his skin ill-fitting, his heart racing like a bird's.

Sweeney clenched his fists, digging his nails into his palms, and forced his breath in and out until it steadied.

There.

Almost comfortably human.

Sweeney walked the room slowly this time, giving himself space to step back and look at the canvases.

Feathers itched and crawled beneath his skin.

And there he was.

The still point at the center of the painting, and feathers were bursting from his skin there, too, but there, it didn't look like madness, it looked like transcendence.

Sweeney heaved in a breath.

"It does have that effect on people."

Sweeney glanced at the man standing next to him, the man who hadn't seemed to realize it was Sweeney in the painting hanging before them.

"Are you familiar with Maeve's work? Maeve Collins, the artist, I mean," Brian said.

"Ah. A bit. Only recently. Is she here tonight?"

"Not yet, though I hope she'll make an appearance later. But if you're interested in the piece, I'd be happy to assist you with it."

"If I buy it, can I meet her?"

"I can understand why you'd make the request, but that's not the usual way art sales work."

And now the man standing next to him did step back and look at Sweeney. "Wait. Wait. You're the model for the painting. Oh, this is fantastic."

Feathers. Feathers unfurling in his blood.

"But of course you'd know Maeve already then."

"I don't." Sweeney braceleted his wrist, his left wrist, downed with white feathers, with his right hand. "But I think I need to."

He unwrapped his fingers, and extended his feathered hand to the man in the gallery, beneath the painting that was and wasn't him.

Brian looked down at the feathers. "I'll call her."

"I don't care how good the party is, Brian, I'm not coming."

"Your model is here, and he would like to meet you."

"How many vodka tonics have you had? That doesn't even make sense. I didn't use any models in this series."

"Not even the guy with feathers coming out of his skin? Because he's standing right in front of the painting, and it certainly looks like him, not to mention this thing where I'm watching him grow feathers on his arms, and what the fuck is going on here, Maeve?"

"What did you say?" The flesh on her arms rose up in goose bumps.

"You heard me. You need to get here.

"Now."

Maeve took a cab, and went in through the service entrance, where she had loaded the paintings earlier that week.

"Brian, what is—you!"

"Yes," Sweeney said, and in an explosion of feathers and collapsing clothes, turned into a bird.

Maeve sat with the bird while the celebration trickled out of the gallery. She had gathered up the clothes he had been wearing, and folded them into precise piles, stuffing his socks into the toes of the shoes, spinning the belt into a coil.

At one point, Brian had brought back a mostly empty bottle of vodka, filched from the bar. Maeve took a swig, and thought of taking another before deciding that some degree of sobriety was in order to counterbalance the oddity of the night.

The bird didn't seem interested in drinking either.

Maeve dropped her head into her hands, and scraped her hair back into a knot. When she sat up again, Sweeney was pulling on his pants.

"I am sorry about before. Stress makes me less capable of interacting with people."

Maeve laughed under her breath. "I can relate."

Brian walked back. "Oh, good. You're, ah, dressed again. Have you two figured out what's going on?"

"I am under a curse," Sweeney said. "And I think Maeve can paint me free of it. There is some kind of power in her work, something that I would call magic. I'd like to commission a painting from her to see if this is possible."

"That's—" Maeve bit down hard on the next word.

"Mad? Impossible?" Sweeney met her eyes. "So am I."

"I'm not magic," Maeve said.

"That may be. After all this time and change, I am not a bird, though I sometimes have the shape of one. Magic reshapes truth."

Maeve could see the bird in the lines of the man, in the way he held his weight, in the shape of the almost-wings the air made space for.

She could see the impossibility, too, of what was asked.

"Please," said Sweeney. "Try."

"I'll need you," Maeve said, "to pose for me."

"This has got to be the weirdest contract I have ever negotiated."

"Brian. You negotiated with a guy who had been a bird for a significant part of the evening. Even if it had been straight up sign here boilerplate, it still would have been the weirdest contract you ever negotiated."

"True."

"I'm surprised he didn't ask for a deadline." Maeve picked up one of the white feathers from the floor, ran it through her fingers. "Some way of marking whether this will work or not, rather than just waiting to find out."

"You say *whether* like you genuinely believe it's a possibility, Maeve.

"And yes, this has been a night of strangeness, but magic is not what happens at the end. The way this ends is that you're going to wind up painting a very nice picture for a guy who is, I don't know how, sometimes a bird, and he is still going to be sometimes a bird after it is signed and framed, and once it is, we will never speak of this again because it is just too weird.

"You're good, Maeve. But you're not a magician. So stop worrying about whether there's magic in your painting, because there isn't."

"You said people don't buy paintings just because of what's on the canvas, they buy the story they think the painting tells," Maeve said.

Brian nodded.

"Sweeney bought a story where magic might be what happens at the end. He's bought that hope.

"And that much, I can paint."

Maeve took a sketchbook and went back to the Cathedral of St. John the Divine. It seemed like the right place to start, even if she didn't put the church itself into her painting. Full circle, somehow, to try and end the transformation in the same place she had first witnessed it.

Spring had come early, the buds on the trees beginning to limn the branches with a haze of green. The crocuses unfurled their purples in among the feet of the trees, and an occasional bold daffodil waved yellow.

And this was transformation, too, Maeve thought. More regular, less astonishing than a man suddenly enfeathered, but change all the same.

Maeve sat beneath a branch of birdsong, and cleared her mind of the magic she had been asked to make. If the bird—if Sweeney was correct, it would be there anyway.

She opened her sketchbook, and began to draw.

Sweeney walked the streets of his city. It wasn't often that he wandered on foot, preferring to save his peregrinations for when he wore wings. But tonight, he did not want to be above the grease and char scents of food cooking on sidewalk carts, of the crunch of shattered glass beneath his shoes.

He wanted the pulse and the press of people he had never quite felt home among. They would be his home, if Maeve succeeded. Perhaps then he would feel as if he belonged.

He should have, perhaps, spent his night on the wing, the flight a fragment to shore against the ruin of his days once he could no longer fly. He would miss, every day of his life he would miss the sensation of the air as his feathers cut through it. But he would have a life.

Sweeney bought truly execrable coffee in an "I Love NY" cup, because at that moment, with every fiber of his being, Sweeney did.

"Can I ask," Maeve hesitated.

"How this happened," Sweeney said.

She looked up from her sketchbook. "Well, yes. I don't want to be rude, or ask you to talk about something that's hurtful, but maybe I'll know better how to paint you out of being a bird if I know how you became one in the first place."

"It was a curse."

"I thought that was the kind of thing that only happened in fairy tales."

Sweeney shrugged, then apologized.

"That's fine. I don't need you to hold the pose . . . And I'll stop interrupting." Maeve bent back to her sketchbook.

"It is like something from a fairy tale. I was angry. I spoke and acted without thought, and, in the way of these things, it was a wizard I insulted. He cursed me for what I had done."

"For over a thousand years since, this has been my life."

"I'm sorry. Even if it was your fault, over a thousand years of vengeance seems cruel."

Tension rippled over Sweeney's skin. He shrank in on himself, fingers curling to claws.

"What is it?"

Sweeney extended his arm. Feathers downed its underside. "I had hoped this wouldn't happen."

"Does it hurt?"

"Only in my pride. Which was the point of the thing, after all." He schooled his breathing, and Maeve watched him relax, muscle by muscle. Except for a patch near his wrist, the feathers fell from Sweeney's skin.

"May I?" Maeve asked.

Sweeney nodded.

Maeve stroked her hand over the feathers, feeling the softness, and the heat of Sweeney's skin beneath. Heart racing like a bird's she stepped closer and kissed him.

A beat passed, and then another.

Sweeney's hand fisted in her hair, and he shuddered a breath into her mouth. She struggled out of her clothes, not wanting to break the kiss, or the contact.

Feathers alternated with skin under Maeve's hands, and Sweeney traced the outlines of her shoulder blades as if she, too, had wings.

As they moved together, Sweeney was neither feathered nor mad. Maeve did not feel the panic of a body too close, only the joy of a body exactly close enough.

White feathers blanketed the floor beneath them.

Maeve looked at Sweeney. "I don't think the painting is going to work."

"Why?" He tucked her hair behind her ear.

"I mean, I think it will be a good painting. But I don't think it will be magic."

"I'm no worse than I am now if it isn't. All I ask is for a good painting, Maeve. Anything beyond that would be," he smiled, "magic."

The parcel arrived in Wednesday's post. Inside, the sketchbook Maeve had lost. In the front cover, a scrawled note: *Forgive me my temporary theft. It's long past time that I returned this.—S.* There was also a white feather.

She flipped through the pages and wondered what Sweeney had seen that convinced him her art was magic, the kind of magic that could help him. Whatever that thing had been, she couldn't see it.

Maeve kept the feather, but she slid the notebook into a fresh envelope to return it to Sweeney. Even if she couldn't give him freedom, she could give him this.

That done, Maeve took down all of the reference photos of mystical, fantastic birds that she had printed out and hung on her walls while painting the show for the gallery. She closed the covers of the bestiaries, and slid feathers into glassine envelopes, making bright kaleidoscopes of fallen flight.

She packed away the shadow boxes, the skeletons, the figurines, reshelved the fairy tales.

The return of the sketchbook had reminded her of one thing. If there were any magic she could claim, it was hers, pencil on a page, pigment on canvas. It came from her, not from anywhere else.

The only things Maeve left in sight were a white feather, a photo she had downloaded from her phone of a naked man perched in a tree, and the sketches she had made of Sweeney. Finally, she hung the recent sketches from the cathedral. She would have to go back there, she thought, before this was finished, but not yet. Not until the end.

At first, Sweeney thought it was the madness come upon him again. His skin itched as if there were feathers beneath it, but they were feathers he could neither see nor coax out of his crawling skin.

His bones ground against each other, too light, the wrong shape, shivering, untrustworthy. Not quite a man, not wholly a bird and uncertain what he was supposed to be.

The soar of flight tipped over the edge into vertigo, and he landed with an abrading slap of his hands against sidewalk.

And then he knew.

Maeve was painting. Painting his own, and perhaps ultimate, transformation.

Dizzy, he ran to where he had first seen her, the Cathedral of St. John the Divine.

Maeve hated painting in public. Hated it. People stood too close, asked grating questions, offered opinions that were neither solicited nor useful, and offered them in voices that were altogether too loud.

The quiet space in her head that painting normally gave here became the pressure of voices, the pinprick texture of other people's eyes on her skin.

She hated it, but this was the place she had to paint, to finish Sweeney's commission here at the cathedral. The end was the beginning.

On the canvas: the shadow of Sweeney rising to meet him, a man-shape grayed and subtle behind a bird. Sweeney, feathers raining around him as he burst from bird to man. A white bird, spiraling in flight, haunting the broken tower of the cathedral, a quiet and stormy ruin.

The skies behind Maeve filled with all manner of impossible birds. On the cathedral lawn, women played chess, and when one put the other in check, a man in a far away place stood up from a nearly negotiated peace.

Behind Maeve, Sweeney gasped, stumbled, fell. And still, she painted.

This time, it felt like magic.

The pain was immense. Sweeney could not speak, could not think, could barely breathe as he was unmade. Maeve was not breaking his curse, she was painting a reality apart from it.

Feathers exploded from beneath his skin, roiling over his body in waves, and disappearing again.

He looked up at the canvas, watched Maeve paint, watched the trails of magic in her brush strokes. In the trees were three birds with the faces and torsos of women, sirens to sing a man to his fate.

The church bells rang out, a sacred clarion, a calling of time, and Sweeney knew how this would end.

It was not what he had anticipated, but magic so rarely was.

Maeve set her brush down, and shook the circulation back into her hands. A white bird streaked low across her vision, and perched in front of one of the clerestory windows.

"Maeve."

She turned, and Sweeney the man lay on the ground behind her. "Oh, no. This isn't what I wanted."

She sat next to him, took his hand. "What can I do?"

"Just sit with me, please."

"Did you know this would happen, when you commissioned the painting?"

"I considered the possibility. I had to. Without the magic binding me into one spell or the next, the truth is I have lived a very long time, and I knew that death might well be my next migration."

Sweeney's next words were quieter, as if he was remembering them. "No one chooses his quest. It is chosen for him."

Sweeney closed his eyes. "This is just another kind of flight."

Maeve hung the finished painting on her wall. Outside, just beyond the open window, perched a white bird.

≈

Kat Howard is a speculative fiction writer, a former lawyer, and a fencer. Her short fiction has appeared in many venues, been nominated for awards, and included in "year's best" and "best of" anthologies. One of her stories was performed on NPR's *Selected Shorts* program. *Roses and Rot*, Howard's first novel, was recently published by Simon & Schuster's Saga Press. She currently lives in New Hampshire.

≈

A writer learns, as most who go there do, that there is no "Hollywood magic"
is an illusion and wherever you want to go on the streets of L.A. takes thirty
minutes. But he also discovers great stage illusions make us question the
nature of reality and—if you can only pause and listen—the world is full
of quiet magic.

The Goldfish Pond and Other Stories
Neil Gaiman

It was raining when I arrived in L.A., and I felt myself surrounded by a
hundred old movies.

There was a limo driver in a black uniform waiting for me at the
airport, holding a white sheet of cardboard with my name misspelled
neatly upon it.

"I'm taking you straight to your hotel, sir," said the driver. He seemed
vaguely disappointed that I didn't have any real luggage for him to carry,
just a battered overnight bag stuffed with T-shirts, underwear, and socks.

"Is it far?"

He shook his head. "Maybe twenty-five, thirty minutes. You ever been
to L.A. before?"

"No."

"Well, what I always say, L.A. is a thirty-minute town. Wherever you
want to go, it's thirty minutes away. No more."

He hauled my bag into the boot of the car, which he called the trunk,
and opened the door for me to climb into the back.

"So where you from?" he asked, as we headed out of the airport into
the slick wet neon-spattered streets.

"England."

"England, eh?"

"Yes. Have you ever been there?"

"Nosir. I've seen movies. You an actor?"

"I'm a writer."

He lost interest. Occasionally he would swear at other drivers, under his breath.

He swerved suddenly, changing lanes. We passed a four-car pileup in the lane we had been in.

"You get a little rain in this city, all of a sudden everybody forgets how to drive," he told me. I burrowed further into the cushions in the back. "You get rain in England, I hear." It was a statement, not a question.

"A little."

"More than a little. Rains every day in England." He laughed. "And thick fog. Real thick, thick fog."

"Not really."

"Whaddaya mean, no?" he asked, puzzled, defensive. "I've seen movies."

We sat in silence then, driving through the Hollywood rain; but after a while he said: "Ask them for the room Belushi died in."

"Pardon?"

"Belushi. John Belushi. It was your hotel he died in. Drugs. You heard about that?"

"Oh. Yes."

"They made a movie about his death. Some fat guy, didn't look nothing like him. But nobody tells the real truth about his death. Y'see, he wasn't alone. There were two other guys with him. Studios didn't want any shit. But you're a limo driver, you hear things."

"Really?"

"Robin Williams and Robert De Niro. They were there with him. All of them going doo-doo on the happy dust."

The hotel building was a white mock-gothic chateau.

I said good-bye to the chauffeur and checked in; I did not ask about the room in which Belushi had died.

I walked out to my chalet through the rain, my overnight bag in my hand, clutching the set of keys that would, the desk clerk told me, get me through the various doors and gates. The air smelled of wet dust and, curiously enough, cough mixture. It was dusk, almost dark.

Water splashed everywhere. It ran in rills and rivulets across the courtyard. It ran into a small fishpond that jutted out from the side of a wall in the courtyard.

I walked up the stairs into a dank little room. It seemed a poor kind of a place for a star to die.

The bed seemed slightly damp, and the rain drummed a maddening beat on the air-conditioning system.

I watched a little television—the rerun wasteland: *Cheers* segued imperceptibly into *Taxi*, which flickered into black and white and became *I Love Lucy*—then stumbled into sleep.

I dreamed of drummers intermittently drumming, only thirty minutes away.

The phone woke me. "Hey-hey-hey-hey. You made it okay then?"

"Who is this?"

"It's Jacob at the studio. Are we still on for breakfast, hey-hey?"

"Breakfast . . . ?"

"No problem. I'll pick you up at your hotel in thirty minutes. Reservations are already made. No problems. You got my messages?"

"I . . . "

"Faxed 'em through last night. See you."

The rain had stopped. The sunshine was warm and bright: proper Hollywood light. I walked up to the main building, walking on a carpet of crushed eucalyptus leaves—the cough medicine smell from the night before.

They handed me an envelope with a fax in it—my schedule for the next few days, with messages of encouragement and faxed handwritten doodles in the margin, saying things like *This is Gonna be a Blockbuster!* and *Is this Going to be a Great Movie or What!* The fax was signed by Jacob Klein, obviously the voice on the phone. I had never before had any dealings with a Jacob Klein.

A small red sports car drew up outside the hotel. The driver got out and waved at me. I walked over. He had a trim, pepper-and-salt beard, a smile that was almost bankable, and a gold chain around his neck. He showed me a copy of *Sons of Man*.

He was Jacob. We shook hands.

"Is David around? David Gambol?"

David Gambol was the man I'd spoken to earlier on the phone when arranging the trip. He wasn't the producer. I wasn't certain quite what he was. He described himself as "attached to the project."

"David's not with the studio anymore. I'm kind of running the project now, and I want you to know I'm really psyched. Hey-hey."

"That's good?"

We got in the car. "Where's the meeting?" I asked.

He shook his head. "It's not a meeting," he said. "It's a breakfast." I looked puzzled. He took pity on me. "A kind of pre-meeting meeting," he explained.

We drove from the hotel to a mall somewhere half an hour away while Jacob told me how much he enjoyed my book and how delighted he was that he'd become attached to the project. He said it was his idea to have me put up in the hotel—"Give you the kind of Hollywood experience you'd never get at the Four Seasons or Ma Maison, right?"—and asked me if I was staying in the chalet in which John Belushi had died. I told him I didn't know, but that I rather doubted it.

"You know who he was with, when he died? They covered it up, the studios."

"No. Who?"

"Meryl and Dustin."

"This is Meryl Streep and Dustin Hoffman we're talking about?"

"Sure."

"How do you know this?"

"People talk. It's Hollywood. You know?"

I nodded as if I did know, but I didn't.

People talk about books that write themselves, and it's a lie. Books don't write themselves. It takes thought and research and backache and notes and more time and more work than you'd believe.

Except for *Sons of Man*, and that one pretty much wrote itself.

The irritating question they ask us—us being writers—is: "Where do you get your ideas?" And the answer is: Confluence. Things come together.

The right ingredients and suddenly: *Abracadabra!*

It began with a documentary on Charles Manson I was watching more or less by accident (it was on a videotape a friend lent me after a couple of things I *did* want to watch): there was footage of Manson, back when he was first arrested, when people thought he was innocent and that it was the government picking on the hippies. And up on the screen was Manson—a charismatic, good-looking, messianic orator. Someone you'd crawl barefoot into Hell for. Someone you could kill for.

The trial started; and, a few weeks into it, the orator was gone, replaced by a shambling, apelike gibberer, with a cross carved into its forehead. Whatever the genius was was no longer there. It was gone. But it had been there.

The documentary continued: a hard-eyed ex-con who had been in prison with Manson, explaining, "Charlie Manson? Listen, Charlie was a joke. He was a nothing. We laughed at him. You know? He was a nothing!"

And I nodded. There was a time before Manson was the charisma king, then. I thought of a benediction, something given, that was taken away.

I watched the rest of the documentary obsessively.

Then, over a black-and-white still, the narrator said something. I rewound, and he said it again.

I had an idea. I had a book that wrote itself.

The thing the narrator had said was this: that the infant children Manson had fathered on the women of The Family were sent to a variety of children's homes for adoption, with court-given surnames that were certainly not Manson.

And I thought of a dozen twenty-five-year-old Mansons. Thought of the charisma-thing descending on all of them at the same time. Twelve young Mansons, in their glory, gradually being pulled toward L.A. from all over the world. And a Manson daughter trying desperately to stop them from coming together and, as the back cover blurb told us, "realizing their terrifying destiny."

I wrote *Sons of Man* at white heat: it was finished in a month, and I sent it to my agent, who was surprised by it ("Well, it's not like your other stuff, dear," she said helpfully), and she sold it after an auction— my first—for more money than I had thought possible. (My other books, three collections of elegant, allusive and elusive ghost stories, had scarcely paid for the computer on which they were written.)

And then it was bought—prepublication—by Hollywood, again after an auction. There were three or four studios interested: I went with the studio who wanted me to write the script. I knew it would never happen, knew they'd never come through. But then the faxes began to spew out of my machine, late at night—most of them enthusiastically signed by one Dave Gambol; one morning I signed five copies of a contract thick as a brick; a few weeks later my agent reported the first check had cleared and tickets to Hollywood had arrived, for "preliminary talks." It seemed like a dream.

The tickets were business class. It was the moment I saw the tickets were business class that I knew the dream was real.

I went to Hollywood in the bubble bit at the top of the jumbo jet, nibbling smoked salmon and holding a hot-off-the-presses hardback of *Sons of Man*.

So. Breakfast.

They told me how much they loved the book. I didn't quite catch anybody's name. The men had beards or baseball caps or both; the women were astoundingly attractive, in a sanitary sort of way.

Jacob ordered our breakfast, and paid for it. He explained that the meeting coming up was a formality.

"It's your book we love," he said. "Why would we have bought your book if we didn't want to make it? Why would we have hired you to write it if we didn't want the specialness you'd bring to the project? The you-ness."

I nodded, very seriously, as if literary me-ness was something I had spent many hours pondering.

"An idea like this. A book like this. You're pretty unique."

"One of the uniquest," said a woman named Dina or Tina or possibly Deanna.

I raised an eyebrow. "So what am I meant to do at the meeting?"

"Be receptive," said Jacob. "Be positive."

The drive to the studio took about half an hour in Jacob's little red car. We drove up to the security gate, where Jacob had an argument with the guard. I gathered that he was new at the studio and had not yet been issued a permanent studio pass.

Nor, it appeared, once we got inside, did he have a permanent parking place. I still do not understand the ramifications of this: from what he said, parking places had as much to do with status at the studio as gifts from the emperor determined one's status in the court of ancient China.

We drove through the streets of an oddly flat New York and parked in front of a huge old bank.

Ten minutes' walk, and I was in a conference room, with Jacob and all the people from breakfast, waiting for someone to come in. In the flurry I'd rather missed who the someone was and what he or she did. I took out my copy of my book and put it in front of me, a talisman of sorts.

Someone came in. He was tall, with a pointy nose and a pointy chin, and his hair was too long—he looked like he'd kidnapped someone much younger and stolen their hair. He was an Australian, which surprised me.

He sat down.

He looked at me.

"Shoot," he said.

I looked at the people from the breakfast, but none of them were looking at me—I couldn't catch anyone's eye.

So I began to talk: about the book, about the plot, about the end, the showdown in the L.A. nightclub, where the good Manson girl blows the rest of them up.

Or thinks she does. About my idea for having one actor play all the Manson boys.

"Do you believe this stuff?" It was the first question from the Someone.

That one was easy. It was one I'd already answered for at least two dozen British journalists.

"Do I believe that a supernatural power possessed Charles Manson for a while and is even now possessing his many children? No. Do I believe that something strange was happening? I suppose I must do. Perhaps it was simply that, for a brief while, his madness was in step with the madness of the world outside. I don't know."

"Mm. This Manson kid. He could be Keanu Reaves?"

God, no, I thought. Jacob caught my eye and nodded desperately. "I don't see why not," I said. It was all imagination anyway. None of it was real.

"We're cutting a deal with his people," said the Someone, nodding thoughtfully.

They sent me off to do a treatment for them to approve. And by *them*, I understood they meant the Australian Someone, although I was not entirely sure.

Before I left, someone gave me $700 and made me sign for it: two weeks *per diem*.

I spent two days doing the treatment. I kept trying to forget the book, and structure the story as a film. The work went well. I sat in the little room and typed on a notebook computer the studio had sent down for me, and printed out pages on the bubble-jet printer the studio sent down with it. I ate in my room.

Each afternoon I would go for a short walk down Sunset Boulevard. I would walk as far as the "almost all-nite" bookstore, where I would buy a newspaper.

Then I would sit outside in the hotel courtyard for half an hour, reading a newspaper. And then, having had my ration of sun and air, I would go back into the dark, and turn my book back into something else.

There was a very old black man, a hotel employee, who would walk across the courtyard each day with almost painful slowness and water the plants and inspect the fish. He'd grin at me as he went past, and I'd nod at him.

On the third day I got up and walked over to him as he stood by the fish pool, picking out bits of rubbish by hand: a couple of coins and a cigarette packet.

"Hello," I said.

"Suh," said the old man.

I thought about asking him not to call me sir, but I couldn't think of a way to put it that might not cause offense. "Nice fish."

He nodded and grinned. "Ornamental carp. Brought here all the way from China."

We watched them swim around the little pool.

"I wonder if they get bored."

He shook his head. "My grandson, he's an ichthyologist, you know what that is?"

"Studies fishes."

"Uh-huh. He says they only got a memory that's like thirty seconds long. So they swim around the pool, it's always a surprise to them, going 'I never been here before.' They meet another fish they known for a hundred years, they say, 'Who are you, stranger?'"

"Will you ask your grandson something for me ?" The old man nodded. "I read once that carp don't have set life spans. They don't age like we do. They die if they're killed by people or predators or disease, but they don't just get old and die. Theoretically they could live forever."

He nodded. "I'll ask him. It sure sounds good. These three—now, this one, I call him Ghost, he's only four, five years old. But the other two, they came here from China back when I was first here."

"And when was that?"

"That would have been, in the Year of Our Lord Nineteen Hundred and Twenty-four. How old do I look to you?"

I couldn't tell. He might have been carved from old wood. Over fifty and younger than Methuselah. I told him so.

"I was born in 1906. God's truth."

"Were you born here, in L.A.?"

He shook his head. "When I was born, Los Angeles wasn't nothin' but an orange grove, a long way from New York." He sprinkled fish food on the surface of the water. The three fish bobbed up, pale-white silvered ghost carp, staring at us, or seeming to, the O's of their mouths continually opening and closing, as if they were talking to us in some silent, secret language of their own.

I pointed to the one he had indicated. "So he's Ghost, yes?"

"He's Ghost. That's right. That one under the lily—you can see his tail, there, see?—he's called Buster, after Buster Keaton. Keaton was staying here when we got the older two. And this one's our Princess." Princess was the most recognizable of the white carp.

She was a pale cream color, with a blotch of vivid crimson along her back, setting her apart from the other two.

"She's lovely."

"She surely is. She surely is all of that."

He took a deep breath then and began to cough, a wheezing cough that shook his thin frame. I was able then, for the first time, to see him as a man of ninety.

"Are you all right?"

He nodded. "Fine, fine, fine. Old bones," he said. "Old bones."

We shook hands, and I returned to my treatment and the gloom.

I printed out the completed treatment, faxed it off to Jacob at the studio.

The next day he came over to the chalet. He looked upset.

"Everything okay? Is there a problem with the treatment?"

"Just shit going down. We made this movie with . . ." and he named a well-known actress who had been in a few successful films a couple of years before. "Can't lose, huh? Only she is not as young as she was, and she insists on doing her own nude scenes, and that's not a body anybody wants to see, believe me.

"So the plot is, there's this photographer who is persuading women to take their clothes off for him. Then he *shtups* them. Only no one believes he's doing it. So the chief of police—played by Ms. Lemme Show the World My Naked Butt—realizes that the only way she can arrest him is if she pretends to be one of the women. So she sleeps with him. Now, there's a twist . . . "

"She falls in love with him?"

"Oh. Yeah. And then she realizes that women will always be imprisoned by male images of women, and to prove her love for him, when the police come to arrest the two of them she sets fire to all the photographs and dies in the fire. Her clothes burn off first. How does that sound to you?"

"Dumb."

"That was what we thought when we saw it. So we fired the director and recut it and did an extra day's shoot. Now she's wearing a wire when they make out. And when she starts to fall in love with him, she finds out that he killed her brother. She has a dream in which her clothes burn off, then she goes out with the SWAT team to try to bring him in. But he gets shot by her little sister, who he's also been *shtupping*."

"Is it any better?"

He shakes his head. "It's junk. If she'd let us use a stand-in for the nude sequences, maybe we'd be in better shape.

"What did you think of the treatment?"

"What?"

"My treatment? The one I sent you?"

"Sure. That treatment. We loved it. We all loved it. It was great. Really terrific. We're all really excited."

"So what's next?"

"Well, as soon as everyone's had a chance to look it over, we'll get together and talk about it."

He patted me on the back and went away, leaving me with nothing to do in Hollywood.

I decided to write a short story. There was an idea I'd had in England before I'd left. Something about a small theater at the end of a pier. Stage magic as the rain came down. An audience who couldn't tell the difference between magic and illusion, and to whom it would make no difference if every illusion was real.

That afternoon, on my walk, I bought a couple of books on stage magic and Victorian illusions in the "almost all-nite" bookshop. A story, or the seed of it anyway, was there in my head, and I wanted to explore it. I sat on the bench in the courtyard and browsed through the books. There was, I decided, a specific atmosphere that I was after.

I was reading about the Pockets Men, who had pockets filled with every small object you could imagine and would produce whatever you asked on request. No illusion—just remarkable feats of organization and memory. A shadow fell across the page. I looked up.

"Hullo again," I said to the old black man.

"Suh," he said.

"Please don't call me that. It makes me feel like I ought to be wearing a suit or something." I told him my name.

He told me his: "Pious Dundas."

"Pious?" I wasn't sure that I'd heard him correctly.

He nodded proudly.

"Sometimes I am, and sometimes I ain't. It's what my mama called me, and it's a good name."

"Yes."

"So what are you doing here, suh?"

"I'm not sure. I'm meant to be writing a film, I think. Or at least, I'm waiting for them to tell me to start writing a film."

He scratched his nose. "All the film people stayed here, if I started to tell you them all now, I could talk till a week next Wednesday and I wouldn't have told you the half of them."

"Who were your favorites?"

"Harry Langdon. He was a gentleman. George Sanders. He was English, like you. He'd say, 'Ah, Pious. You must pray for my soul.' And I'd say, 'Your soul's your own affair, Mister Sanders,' but I prayed for him just the same. And June Lincoln."

"June Lincoln?"

His eyes sparkled, and he smiled. "She was the queen of the silver screen. She was finer than any of them: Mary Pickford or Lillian Gish or Theda Bara or Louise Brooks . . . She was the finest. She had 'it.' You know what 'it' was?"

"Sex appeal."

"More than that. She was everything you ever dreamed of. You'd see a June Lincoln picture, you wanted to . . . " he broke off, waved one hand in small circles, as if he were trying to catch the missing words.

"I don't know. Go down on one knee, maybe, like a knight in shinin' armor to the queen. June Lincoln, she was the best of them. I told my grandson about her, he tried to find something for the VCR, but no go. Nothing out there anymore. She only lives in the heads of old men like me." He tapped his forehead.

"She must have been quite something."

He nodded.

"What happened to her?"

"She hung herself. Some folks said it was because she wouldn't have been able to cut the mustard in the talkies, but that ain't true: she had a voice you'd remember if you heard it just once. Smooth and dark, her voice was, like an Irish coffee. Some say she got her heart broken by a man, or by a woman, or that it was gambling, or gangsters, or booze. Who knows? They were wild days."

"I take it that you must have heard her talk."

He grinned. "She said, 'Boy, can you find what they did with my wrap?' and when I come back with it, then she said, 'You're a fine one, boy.' And the man who was with her, he said, 'June, don't tease the help' and she smiled at me and gave me five dollars and said, 'He don't mind, do you, boy?' and I just shook my head. Then she made the thing with her lips, you know?"

"A *moue*?"

"Something like that. I felt it here." He tapped his chest. "Those lips. They could take a man apart."

He bit his lower lip for a moment, and focused on forever. I wondered where he was, and when. Then he looked at me once more.

"You want to see her lips?"

"How do you mean?"

"You come over here. Follow me."

"What are we . . . ?" I had visions of a lip print in cement, like the handprints outside Grauman's Chinese Theatre.

He shook his head, and raised an old finger to his mouth. *Silence.*

I closed the books. We walked across the courtyard.

When he reached the little fish-pool, he stopped.

"Look at the Princess," he told me.

"The one with the red splotch, yes?"

He nodded. The fish reminded me of a Chinese dragon: wise and pale. A ghost fish, white as old bone, save for the blotch of scarlet on its back—an inch-long double-bow shape. It hung in the pool, drifting, thinking.

"That's it," he said. "On her back. See?"

"I don't quite follow you."

He paused and stared at the fish.

"Would you like to sit down?" I found myself very conscious of Mr. Dundas's age.

"They don't pay me to sit down," he said, very seriously. Then he said, as if he were explaining something to a small child, "It was like there were gods in those days. Today, it's all television: small heroes. Little people in the boxes. I see some of them here. Little people.

"The stars of the old times: they was giants, painted in silver light, big as houses . . . and when you met them, they were still huge. People believed in them. They'd have parties here. You worked here, you saw what went on. There was liquor, and weed, and goings on you'd hardly credit. There was this one party . . . the film was called *Hearts of the Desert*. You ever heard it?"

I shook my head.

"One of the biggest movies of 1926, up there with *What Price Glory* with Victor McLaglen and Dolores del Rio and *Ella Cinders* starring Colleen Moore. You heard of them?"

I shook my head again.

"You ever heard of Warner Baxter? Belle Bennett?"

"Who were they?"

"Big, big stars in 1926." He paused for a moment. "*Hearts of the Desert*. They had the party for it here, in the hotel, when it wrapped. There was wine and beer and whiskey and gin—this was Prohibition days, but the studios kind of owned the police force, so they looked the other way; and there was food, and a deal of foolishness; Ronald Colman was there and Douglas Fairbanks—the father, not the son—and all the cast and the crew; and a jazz band played over there where those chalets are now.

"And June Lincoln was the toast of Hollywood that night. She was the Arab princess in the film. Those days Arabs meant passion and lust. These days . . . well things change.

"I don't know what started it all. I heard it was a dare or a bet; maybe she was just drunk. I thought she was drunk. Anyhow, she got up, and the band was playing, soft and slow. And she walked over here, where I'm standing right now, and she plunged her hands right into this pool. She was laughing and laughing and laughing . . .

"Miss Lincoln picked up the fish—reached in and took it, both hands she took it in—and she picked it up from the water, and then she held it in front of her face.

"Now, I was worried, because they'd just brought these fish in from China and they cost two hundred dollars apiece. That was before I was looking after the fish, of course. Wasn't me that'd lose it from my wages. But still, two hundred dollars was a whole lot of money in those days.

"Then she smiled at all of us, and she leaned down and she kissed it, slow like, on its back. It didn't wriggle or nothin', it just lay in her hand, and she kissed it with her lips like red coral, and the people at the party laughed and cheered.

"She put the fish back in the pool, and for a moment it was as if it didn't want to leave her—it stayed by her, nuzzling her fingers. And then the first of the fireworks went off, and it swum away.

"Her lipstick was red as red as red, and she left the shape of her lips on the fish's back.—There. Do you see?"

Princess, the white carp with the coral-red mark on her back, flicked a fin and continued on her eternal series of thirty-second journeys around the pool. The red mark did look like a lip print.

He sprinkled a handful of fish food on the water, and the three fish bobbed and gulped to the surface.

I walked back in to my chalet, carrying my books on old illusions. The phone was ringing: it was someone from the studio. They wanted to talk about the treatment. A car would be there for me in thirty minutes.

"Will Jacob be there?"

But the line was already dead.

The meeting was with the Australian Someone and his assistant, a bespectacled man in a suit. His was the first suit I'd seen so far, and his spectacles were a vivid blue. He seemed nervous.

"Where are you staying?" asked the Someone.

I told him.

"Isn't that where Belushi . . . ?"

"So I've been told."

He nodded. "He wasn't alone, when he died."

"No?"

He rubbed one finger along the side of his pointy nose. "There were a couple of other people at the party. They were both directors, both as big as you could get at that point. You don't need names. I found out about it when I was making the last Indiana Jones film."

An uneasy silence. We were at a huge round table, just the three of us, and we each had a copy of the treatment I had written in front of us. Finally I said: "What did you think of it?"

They both nodded, more or less in unison.

And then they tried, as hard as they could, to tell me they hated it while never saying anything that might conceivably upset me. It was a very odd conversation.

"We have a problem with the third act," they'd say, implying vaguely that the fault lay neither with me nor with the treatment, nor even with the third act, but with them.

They wanted the people to be more sympathetic. They wanted sharp lights and shadows, not shades of gray. They wanted the heroine to be a hero. And I nodded and took notes.

At the end of the meeting I shook hands with the Someone, and the assistant in the blue-rimmed spectacles took me off through the corridor maze to find the outside world and my car and my driver.

As we walked, I asked if the studio had a picture anywhere of June Lincoln.

"Who?" His name, it turned out, was Greg. He pulled out a small notebook and wrote something down in it with a pencil.

"She was a silent screen star. Famous in 1926."

"Was she with the studio?"

"I have no idea," I admitted. "But she was famous. Even more famous than Marie Provost."

"Who?"

"'A winner who became a doggies' dinner.' One of the biggest stars of the silent screen. Died in poverty when the talkies came in and was eaten by her dachshund. Nick Lowe wrote a song about her."

"Who?"

"'I Knew the Bride When She Used to Rock and Roll.' Anyway, June Lincoln. Can someone find me a photo?" He wrote something more down on his pad. Stared at it for a moment. Then wrote down something else. Then he nodded.

We had reached the daylight, and my car was waiting.

"By the way," he said, "you should know that he's full of shit."

"I'm sorry?"

"Full of shit. It wasn't Spielberg and Lucas who were with Belushi. It was Bette Midler and Linda Ronstadt. It was a coke orgy. Everybody knows that. He's full of shit. And he was just a junior studio accountant for chrissakes on the Indiana Jones movie. Like it was his movie. Asshole."

We shook hands. I got in the car and went back to the hotel.

The time difference caught up with me that night, and I woke, utterly and irrevocably, at four A.M.

I got up, peed, then I pulled on a pair of jeans (I sleep in a T-shirt) and walked outside.

I wanted to see the stars, but the lights of the city were too bright, the air too dirty. The sky was a dirty, starless yellow, and I thought of all the constellations I could see from the English countryside, and I felt, for the first time, deeply, stupidly homesick.

I missed the stars.

I wanted to work on the short story or to get on with the film script. Instead, I worked on a second draft of the treatment.

I took the number of Junior Mansons down to five from twelve and made it clearer from the start that one of them, who was now male, wasn't a bad guy and the other four most definitely were.

They sent over a copy of a film magazine. It had the smell of old pulp paper about it, and was stamped in purple with the studio name and with the word ARCHIVES underneath. The cover showed John Barrymore, on a boat.

The article inside was about June Lincoln's death. I found it hard to read and harder still to understand: it hinted at the forbidden vices that led to her death, that much I could tell, but it was as if it were hinting in a cipher to which modern readers lacked any key. Or perhaps, on reflection, the writer of her obituary knew nothing and was hinting into the void.

More interesting—at any rate, more comprehensible—were the photos. A full-page, black-edged photo of a woman with huge eyes and a gentle smile, smoking a cigarette (the smoke was airbrushed in, to my way of thinking very clumsily: had people ever been taken in by such clumsy fakes?); another photo of her in a staged clinch with Douglas Fairbanks; a small photograph of her standing on the running board of a car, holding a couple of tiny dogs.

She was, from the photographs, not a contemporary beauty. She lacked the transcendence of a Louise Brooks, the sex appeal of a Marilyn Monroe, the sluttish elegance of a Rita Hayworth. She was a twenties starlet as dull as any other twenties starlet. I saw no mystery in her huge eyes, her bobbed hair. She had perfectly made-up cupid's bow lips. I had no idea what she would have looked like if she had been alive and around today.

Still, she was real; she had lived. She had been worshipped and adored by the people in the movie palaces.

She had kissed the fish, and walked in the grounds of my hotel seventy years before: no time in England, but an eternity in Hollywood.

I went in to talk about the treatment. None of the people I had spoken to before were there. Instead, I was shown in to see a very young man in a small office, who never smiled and who told me how much he loved the treatment and how pleased he was that the studio owned the property.

He said he thought the character of Charles Manson was particularly cool, and that maybe—"once he was fully dimensionalized"—Manson could be the next Hannibal Lecter.

"But. Um. Manson. He's real. He's in prison now. His people killed Sharon Tate."

"Sharon Tate?"

"She was an actress. A film star. She was pregnant and they killed her. She was married to Polanski."

"*Roman* Polanski?"

"The director. Yes."

He frowned. "But we're putting together a deal with Polanski."

"That's good. He's a good director."

"Does he know about this?"

"About what? The book? Our film? Sharon Tate's death?"

He shook his head: none of the above. "It's a three-picture deal. Julia Roberts is semi-attached to it. You say Polanski doesn't know about this treatment?"

"No, what I said was—"

He checked his watch.

"Where are you staying?" he asked. "Are we putting you up somewhere good?"

"Yes, thank you," I said. "I'm a couple of chalets away from the room in which Belushi died." I expected another confidential couple of stars: to be told that John Belushi had kicked the bucket in company with Julie Andrews and Miss Piggy the Muppet, I was wrong.

"Belushi's dead?" he said, his young brow furrowing. "Belushi's not dead. We're doing a picture with Belushi."

"This was the brother," I told him. "The brother died, years ago."

He shrugged. "Sounds like a shithole," he said. "Next time you come out, tell them you want to stay in the Bel Air. You want us to move you out there now?"

"No, thank you," I said. "I'm used to it where I am."

"What about the treatment?" I asked.

"Leave it with us."

I found myself becoming fascinated by two old theatrical illusions I found in my books: "The Artist's Dream" and "The Enchanted Casement." They were metaphors for something, of that I was certain, but the story that ought to have accompanied them was not yet there. I'd write first sentences that did not make it to first paragraphs, first paragraphs that never made it to first pages. I'd write them on the computer, then exit without saving anything.

I sat outside in the courtyard and stared at the two white carp and the one scarlet and white carp. They looked, I decided, like Escher drawings of fish, which surprised me, as it had never occurred to me there was anything even slightly realistic in Escher's drawings.

Pious Dundas was polishing the leaves of the plants. He had a bottle of polisher and a cloth.

"Hi, Pious."

"Suh."

"Lovely day."

He nodded, and coughed, and banged his chest with his fist, and nodded some more.

I left the fish, sat down on the bench.

"Why haven't they made you retire?" I asked. "Shouldn't you have retired fifteen years ago?"

He continued polishing. "Hell no, I'm a landmark. They can *say* that all the stars in the sky stayed here, but *I* tell folks what Cary Grant had for breakfast."

"Do you remember?"

"Heck no. But *they* don't know that." He coughed again. "What you writing?"

"Well, last week I wrote a treatment for this film. And then I wrote another treatment. And now I'm waiting for . . . something."

"So what *are* you writing?"

"A story that won't come right. It's about a Victorian magic trick called 'The Artist's Dream.' An artist comes onto the stage, carrying a big canvas, which he puts on an easel. It's got a painting of a woman on it. And he looks at the painting and despairs of ever being a real painter. Then he sits down and goes to sleep, and the painting comes to life, steps down from the frame, and tells him not to give up. To keep fighting. He'll be a great painter one day. She climbs back into the frame. The lights dim. Then he wakes up, and it's a painting again . . . "

" . . . and the other illusion," I told the woman from the studio, who had made the mistake of feigning interest at the beginning of the meeting, "was called 'The Enchanted Casement.' A window hangs in the air and faces appear in it, but there's no one around. I think I can get a strange sort of parallel between the enchanted casement and probably television: seems like a natural candidate, after all."

"I like *Seinfeld*," she said. "You watch that show? It's about nothing. I mean, they have whole episodes about nothing. And I liked Garry Shandling before he did the new show and got mean."

"The illusions," I continued, "like all great illusions, make us question the nature of reality. But they also frame—pun, I suppose, intentionalish—the issue of what entertainment would turn into. Films before the had films, telly before there was ever TV."

She frowned. "Is this a movie?"

"I hope not. It's a short story, if I can get it to work.

"So let's talk about the movie." She flicked through pile of notes. She was in her mid-twenties and looked both attractive and sterile. I wondered if she was one the women who had been at the breakfast on my first day, a Deanna or a Tina.

She looked puzzled at something and read: *"I Knew the Bride When She Used to Rock and Roll?"*

"He wrote that down? That's not this film."

She nodded. "Now, I have to say that some of you treatment is kind of . . . contentious. The Manson thing . . . well, we're not sure it's going to fly. Could we take him out?"

"But that's the whole point of the thing. I mean, the book is called *Sons of Man*; it's about Manson's children. If you take him out, you don't have very much, do you? I mean, this is the book you bought." I held it up for her to see: my talisman. "Throwing out Manson is like, I don't know, it's like ordering a pizza and then complaining when it arrives because it's flat, round, and covered in tomato sauce and cheese."

She gave no indication of having heard anything I had said. She asked, "What do you think about *When We Were Badd* as a title? Two *d*'s in Badd."

"I don't know. For this?"

"We don't want people to think that it's religious *Sons of Man*. It sounds like it might be kind of anti-Christian."

"Well, I do kind of imply that the power that possesses the Manson children is in some way a kind of demonic power."

"You do?"

"In the book."

She managed a pitying look, of the kind that only people who know that books are, at best, properties on which films can be loosely based, can bestow on the rest of us.

"Well, I don't think the studio would see that as appropriate," she said.

"Do you know who June Lincoln was?" I asked her.

She shook her head.

"David Gambol? Jacob Klein?"

She shook her head once more, a little impatiently.

Then she gave me a typed list of things she felt needed fixing, which amounted to pretty much everything. The list was TO: me and a number of other people, whose names I didn't recognize, and it was FROM: Donna Leary.

I said Thank you, Donna, and went back to the hotel.

I was gloomy for a day. And then I thought of a way to redo the treatment that would, I thought, deal with all of Donna's list of complaints.

Another day's thinking, a few days' writing, and I faxed the third treatment off to the studio.

Pious Dundas brought his scrapbook over for me to look at, once he felt certain that I was genuinely interested in June Lincoln—named, I discovered, after the month and the president, born Ruth Baumgarten in 1903. It was a leatherbound old scrapbook, the size and weight of a family Bible.

She was twenty-four when she died.

"I wish you could've seen her," said Pious Dundas. "I wish some of her films had survived. She was so big. She was the greatest star of all of them."

"Was she a good actress?"

He shook his head decisively. "Nope."

"Was she a great beauty? If she was, I just don't see it."

He shook his head again. "The camera liked her, that's for sure. But that wasn't it. Back row of the chorus had a dozen girls prettier'n her."

"Then what was it?"

"She was a star." He shrugged. "That's what it means to be a star."

I turned the pages: cuttings reviewing films I'd never heard of—films for which the only negatives and prints had long ago been lost, mislaid, or destroyed by the fire department, nitrate negatives being a notorious fire hazard; other cuttings from film magazines: June Lincoln at play, June Lincoln at rest, June Lincoln on the set of *The Pawnbroker's Shirt*, June Lincoln wearing a huge fur coat—which somehow dated the photograph more than the strange bobbed hair or the ubiquitous cigarettes.

"Did you love her?"

He shook his head. "Not like you would love a woman . . . " he said.

There was a pause. He reached down and turned the pages.

"And my wife would have killed me if she'd heard me say this . . . "

Another pause.

"But yeah. Skinny dead white woman. I suppose I loved her." He closed the book.

"But she's not dead to you, is she?"

He shook his head. Then he went away. But he left me the book to look at.

The secret of the illusion of "The Artist's Dream" was this: it was done by carrying the girl in, holding tight onto the back of the canvas. The canvas was supported by hidden wires, so, while the artist casually, easily, carried in the canvas and placed it on the easel, he was also carrying in the girl. The painting of the girl on the easel was arranged like a roller blind, and it rolled up or down.

"The Enchanted Casement," on the other hand, was, literally, done with mirrors: an angled mirror which reflected the faces of people standing out of sight in the wings.

Even today many magicians use mirrors in their acts to make you think you are seeing something you are not.

It was easy, when you knew how it was done.

"Before we start," he said, "I should tell you I don't read treatments. I tend to feel it inhibits my creativity. Don't worry, I had a secretary do a précis, so I'm up to speed."

He had a beard and long hair and looked a little like Jesus, although I doubted that Jesus had such perfect teeth. He was, it appeared, the most important person I'd spoken to so far. His name was John Ray, and even I had heard of him, although I was not entirely sure what he did. His name tended to appear at the beginning of films, next to words like EXECUTIVE PRODUCER. The voice from the studio that had set up the meeting told me that they, the studio, were most excited about the fact that he had "attached himself to the project."

"Doesn't the précis inhibit your creativity, too?"

He grinned. "Now, we all think you've done an amazing job. Quite stunning. There are just a few things that we have a problem with."

"Such as?"

"Well, the Manson thing. And the idea about these kids growing up. So we've been tossing around a few scenarios in the office. Try this for size: there's a guy called, say, Jack Badd—two *d*'s, that was Donna's idea—" Donna bowed her head modestly.

"They put him away for satanic abuse, fried him in the chair, and as he dies he swears he'll come back and destroy them all.

"Now, it's today, and we see these young boys getting hooked on a video arcade game called *Be Badd*. His face on it. And as they play the game he like, starts to possess them. Maybe there could be something strange about his face, a Jason or Freddy thing." He stopped, as if he were seeking approval.

So I said, "So who's making these video games?"

He pointed a finger at me and said, "You're the writer, sweetheart. You want us to do all your work for you?"

I didn't say anything. I didn't know what to say.

Think movies, I thought. *They understand movies*. I said, "But surely, what you're proposing is like doing *The Boys from Brazil* without Hitler."

He looked puzzled.

"It was a film by Ira Levin," I said. No flicker of recognition in his eyes. "*Rosemary's Baby*." He continued to look blank. "*Sliver*."

He nodded; somewhere a penny had dropped. "Point taken," he said. "You write the Sharon Stone part, we'll move heaven and earth to get her for you. I have an in to her people."

So I went out.

That night it was cold, and it shouldn't have been cold in L.A., and the air smelled more of cough drops than ever.

An old girlfriend lived in the L.A. area and I resolved to get hold of her. I phoned the number I had for her and began a quest that took most of the rest of the evening. People gave me numbers, and I rang them, and other people gave me numbers, and I rang them, too.

Eventually I phoned a number, and I recognized her voice.

"Do you know where I am?" she said.

"No," I said. "I was given this number."

"This is a hospital room," she said. "My mother's. She had a brain hemorrhage."

"I'm sorry. Is she all right?"

"No."

"I'm sorry."

There was an awkward silence.

"How are you?" she asked.

"Pretty bad," I said.

I told her everything that had happened to me so far.

I told her how I felt.

"Why is it like this?" I asked her.

"Because they're scared."

"Why are they scared? What are they scared of?"

"Because you're only as good as the last hit you can attach your name to."

"Huh?"

"If you say 'yes' to something, the studio may make a film, and it will cost twenty or thirty million dollars, and if it's a failure, you will have your name attached to it and will lose status. If you say no, you don't risk losing status."

"Really?"

"Kind of."

"How do you know so much about all this? You're a musician, you're not in films."

She laughed wearily: "I live out here. Everybody who lives out here knows this stuff. Have you tried asking people about their screenplays?"

"No."

"Try it sometime. Ask anyone. The guy in the gas station. Anyone. They've all got them." Then someone said something to her, and she said something back, and she said, "Look, I've got to go," and she put down the phone.

I couldn't find the heater, if the room had a heater, and I was freezing in my little chalet room, like the one Belushi died in, same uninspired framed print on the wall, I had no doubt, same chilly dampness in the air.

I ran a hot bath to warm myself up, but I was even chillier when I got out.

White goldfish sliding to and fro in the water, dodging and darting through the lily pads. One of the goldfish had a crimson mark on its back that might, conceivably, have been perfectly lip-shaped: the miraculous stigmata of an almost-forgotten goddess. The gray early-morning sky was reflected in the pool.

I stared at it gloomily.

"You okay?"

I turned. Pious Dundas was standing next to me.

"You're up early."

"I slept badly. Too cold."

"You should have called the front desk. They'd've sent you down a heater and extra blankets."

"It never occurred to me."

His breathing sounded awkward, labored.

"You okay?"

"Heck no. I'm old. You get to my age, boy, you won't be okay either. But I'll be here when you've gone. How's work going?"

"I don't know. I've stopped working on the treatment, and I'm stuck on 'The Artist's Dream'—this story I'm doing about Victorian stage magic. It's set in an English seaside resort in the rain. With the magician performing magic on the stage, which somehow changes the audience. It touches their hearts."

He nodded, slowly. "'The Artist's Dream' . . . " he said. "So. You see yourself as the artist or the magician?"

"I don't know," I said. "I don't think I'm either of them."

I turned to go and then something occurred to me.

"Mister Dundas," I said. "Have you got a screenplay? One you wrote?"

He shook his head.

"You *never* wrote a screenplay?"

"Not me," he said.

"Promise?"

He grinned. "I promise," he said.

I went back to my room. I thumbed through my U.K. hardback of *Sons of Man* and wondered that anything so clumsily written had even been published, wondered why Hollywood had bought it in the first place, why they didn't want it, now that they had bought it.

I tried to write "The Artist's Dream" some more, and failed miserably.

The characters were frozen. They seemed unable to breathe, or move, or talk.

I went into the toilet, pissed a vivid yellow stream against the porcelain. A cockroach ran across the silver of the mirror.

I went back into the sitting room, opened a new document, and wrote:

> I'm thinking about England in the rain,
> a strange theatre on the pier: a trail
> of fear and magic, memory and pain.
>
> The fear should be of going bleak insane,
> the magic should be like a fairytale.
> I'm thinking about England in the rain.
>
> The loneliness is harder to explain—
> an empty place inside me where I fail,
> of fear and magic, memory and pain.
>
> I think of a magician and a skein
> of truth disguised as lies. You wear a veil.
> I'm thinking about England in the rain . . .
>
> The shapes repeat like some bizarre refrain
> and here's a sword, a hand, and there's a grail
> of fear and magic, memory and pain.
>
> The wizard waves his wand and we turn pale,
> tells us sad truths, but all to no avail.
> I'm thinking about England, in the rain
> of fear and magic, memory and pain.

I didn't know if it was any good or not, but that didn't matter. I had written something new and fresh I hadn't written before, and it felt wonderful.

I ordered breakfast from room service and requested a heater and a couple of extra blankets.

The next day I wrote a six-page treatment for a film called *When We Were Badd*, in which Jack Badd, a serial killer with a huge cross carved into his forehead, was killed in the electric chair and came back in a video game and took over four young men. The fifth young man defeated Badd by burning the original electric chair, which was now on display, I decided, in the wax museum where the fifth young man's girlfriend worked during the day. By night she was an exotic dancer.

The hotel desk faxed it off to the studio, and I went to bed.

I went to sleep, hoping that the studio would formally reject it and that I could go home.

In the theater of my dreams, a man with a beard and a baseball cap carried on a movie screen, and then he walked off-stage. The silver screen hung in the air, unsupported.

A flickery silent film began to play upon it: a woman who came out and stared down at me. It was June Lincoln who flickered on the screen, and it was June Lincoln who walked down from the screen and sat on the edge of my bed.

"Are you going to tell me not to give up?" I asked her.

On some level I knew it was a dream. I remember, dimly, understanding why this woman was a star, remember regretting that none of her films had survived.

She was indeed beautiful in my dream, despite the livid mark which went all the way around her neck.

"Why on earth would I do that?" she asked. In my dream she smelled of gin and old celluloid, although I do not remember the last dream I had where anyone smelled of anything. She smiled, a perfect black-and-white smile. "I got out, didn't I?"

Then she stood up and walked around the room.

"I can't believe this hotel is still standing," she said "I used to fuck here." Her voice was filled with crackles and hisses. She came back to the bed and stared at me, as a cat stares at a hole.

"Do you worship me?" she asked.

I shook my head. She walked over to me and took my flesh hand in her silver one.

"Nobody remembers anything anymore," she said. "It's a thirty-minute town."

There was something I had to ask her. "Where are the stars?" I asked. "I keep looking up in the sky, but they aren't there."

She pointed at the floor of the chalet. "You've been looking in the wrong places," she said. I had never before noticed that the floor of the chalet was a sidewalk and each paving stone contained a star and a name-names I didn't know: Clara Kimball Young, Linda Arvidson, Vivian Martin, Norma Talmadge, Olive Thomas, Mary Miles Minter, Seena Owen . . .

June Lincoln pointed at the chalet window. "And out there." The window was open, and through it I could see the whole of Hollywood spread out below me—the view from the hills: an infinite spread of twinkling multicolored lights.

"Now, aren't those better than stars?" she asked.

And they were. I realized I could see constellations in the street lamps and the cars.

I nodded.

Her lips brushed mine.

"Don't forget me," she whispered, but she whispered it sadly, as if she knew that I would.

I woke up with the telephone shrilling. I answered it, growled a mumble into the handpiece.

"This is Gerry Quoint, from the studio. We need you for a lunch meeting."

Mumble something mumble.

"We'll send a car," he said. "The restaurant's about half an hour away."

The restaurant was airy and spacious and green, and they were waiting for me there.

By this point I would have been surprised if I *had* recognized anyone. John Ray, I was told over hors d'oeuvres, had "split over contract disagreements," and Donna had gone with him, "obviously."

Both of the men had beards; one had bad skin. The woman was thin and seemed pleasant.

They asked where I was staying, and, when I told them, one of the beards told us (first making us all agree that this would go no further) that a politician named Gary Hart and one of the Eagles were both doing drugs with Belushi when he died.

After that they told me that they were looking forward to the story.

I asked the question. "Is this for *Sons of Man* or *When We Were Badd*? Because," I told them, "I have a problem with the latter."

They looked puzzled.

It was, they told me, for *I Knew the Bride When She Used to Rock and Roll*. Which was, they told me, both High Concept and Feel Good. It was also, they added, Very Now, which was important in a town in which an hour ago was Ancient History.

They told me that they thought it would be a good thing if our hero could rescue the young lady from her loveless marriage, and if they could rock and roll together at the end.

I pointed out that they needed to buy the film rights from Nick Lowe, who wrote the song, and then that, no, I didn't know who his agent was.

They grinned and assured me that wouldn't be a problem.

They suggested I turn over the project in my mind before I started on the treatment, and each of them mentioned a couple of young stars to bear in mind when I was putting together the story.

And I shook hands with all of them and told them that I certainly would.

I mentioned that I thought that I could work on it best back in England.

And they said that would be fine.

Some days before, I'd asked Pious Dundas whether anyone was with Belushi in the chalet, on the night that he died.

If anyone would know, I figured, he would.

"He died alone," said Pious Dundas, old as Methuselah, unblinking. "It don't matter a rat's ass whether there was anyone with him or not. He died alone."

It felt strange to be leaving the hotel.

I went up to the front desk.

"I'll be checking out later this afternoon."

"Very good, sir."

"Would it be possible for you to . . . the, uh, the groundskeeper. Mister Dundas. An elderly gentleman. I don't know. I haven't seen him around for a couple of days. I wanted to say good-bye."

"To one of the groundsmen?"

"Yes."

She stared at me, puzzled. She was very beautiful, and her lipstick was the color of a blackberry bruise. I wondered whether she was waiting to be discovered.

She picked up the phone and spoke into it, quietly.

Then, "I'm sorry, sir. Mister Dundas hasn't been in for the last few days."

"Could you give me his phone number?"

"I'm sorry, sir. That's not our policy." She stared at me as she said it, letting me know that she really was so sorry . . .

"How's your screenplay?" I asked her.

"How did you know?" she asked.

"Well—"

"It's on Joel Silver's desk," she said. "My friend Arnie, he's my writing partner, and he's a courier. He dropped it off with Joel Silver's office, like it came from a regular agent or somewhere."

"Best of luck," I told her.

"Thanks," she said, and smiled with her blackberry lips.

Information had two Dundas, P's listed, which I thought was both unlikely and said something about America, or at least Los Angeles.

The first turned out to be a Ms. Persephone Dundas.

At the second number, when I asked for Pious Dundas, a man's voice said, "Who is this?"

I told him my name, that I was staying in the hotel, and that I had something belonging to Mr. Dundas.

"Mister. My grandfa's dead. He died last night."

Shock makes clichés happen for real. I felt the blood drain from my face; I caught my breath.

"I'm sorry. I liked him."

"Yeah."

"It must have been pretty sudden."

"He was old. He got a cough."

Someone asked him who he was talking to, and he said nobody, then he said, "Thanks for calling."

I felt stunned.

"Look, I have his scrapbook. He left it with me."

"That old film stuff?"

"Yes."

A pause.

"Keep it. That stuff's no good to anybody. Listen, mister, I gotta run."

A click, and the line went silent.

I went to pack the scrapbook in my bag and was startled, when a tear splashed on the faded leather cover, to discover that I was crying.

I stopped by the pool for the last time, to say good-bye to Pious Dundas, and to Hollywood.

Three ghost-white carp drifted, fins flicking minutely, through the eternal present of the pool.

I remembered their names: Buster, Ghost, and Princess; but there was no longer any way that anyone could have told them apart.

The car was waiting for me, by the hotel lobby. It was a thirty-minute drive to the airport, and already I was starting to forget.

$\sim$

Neil Gaiman is the #1 *New York Times* bestselling author of more than twenty books, and the recipient of numerous literary honors. Originally from England, he now lives in the U.S.

$\sim$

The best-known street in Las Vegas is The Strip, but the roadway across the top of Hoover Dam (although in our world it is now closed to traffic) plays a role here too. The protagonist, Jack, is himself magical, as is—to an extent—his friend Stewart. So are, unfortunately, Goddess and Angel.

One-Eyed Jack and the Suicide King
Elizabeth Bear

It's not a straight drop. Rather, the Dam is a long sweeping plunge of winter-white concrete: a dress for a three-time Las Vegas bride without *quite* the gall to show up in French lace and seed pearls. If you face Arizona, Lake Mead spreads out blue and alien on your left hand, inside a bathtub ring of Colorado River limestone and perchlorate drainage from wartime titanium plants. Unlikely as canals on Mars, all that azure water rimmed in massive red and black rock; the likeness to an alien landscape is redoubled by the Dam's louvered concrete intake towers. At your back is the Hoover Dam visitor's center, and on the lake side sit two art-deco angels, swordcut wings thirty feet tall piercing the desert sky, their big toes shiny with touches for luck.

That angled drop is on your right. *À main droite.* Downriver. To California. The same way all those phalanxes and legions of electrical towers march.

It's not a straight drop. Hoover's much wider at the base than at the apex, where a two-lane road runs, flanked by sidewalks. The cement in the Dam's tunnel-riddled bowels won't be cured for another hundred years, and they say it'll take a glacier or a nuke to shift the structure. Its face is ragged with protruding rebar and unsmoothed edges, for all it looks fondant-frosted and insubstantial in the asphyxiating light of a Mojave summer.

Stewart had gotten hung up on an upright pipe about forty feet down the rock face beside the dam proper, and it hadn't killed him. I could hear him screaming from where I stood, beside those New Deal angels. I winced, hoping he died before the rescue crews got to him.

Plexiglas along a portion of the walkway wall discourages jumpers and incautious children: a laughable barrier. But then, so is Hoover itself—a fragile slice of mortal engineering between the oppressive rocks, more a symbol interrupting the flow of the sacred Colorado than any real, solid object.

Still. It holds the river back, don't it?

Stewart screamed again—a high, twisting cry like a gutted dog. I leaned against the black diorite base of the left-hand angel, my feet inches from this inscription: 2700 BC IN THE REIGN OF THE PHARAOH MENKAURE THE LAST GREAT PYRAMID WAS BROUGHT TO COMPLETION. I bathed in the stare of a teenaged girl too cool to walk over and check out the carnage. She checked me out instead; I ignored her with all the cat-coolness I could muster, my right hand hooked on the tool loop of my leather cargo pants.

With my left one, I reached up to grasp the toe of the angel. Desert-cooked metal seared my fingers; I held on for as long as I could before sticking them in my mouth, and then reached up to grab on again, making my biceps ridge through the skin. *Eeny, Meeny, Miney, Moe.* Eyepatch and Doc Martens, diamond in my ear or not, the girl eventually got tired of me. I saw her turn away from the corner of my regular eye.

They were moving cars off the Dam to let emergency vehicles through, but the rescue chopper would have to come from Las Vegas. There wasn't one closer. I checked my watch. Nobody was looking at me anymore, despite dyed matte-black hair, trendy goatee, and sunburned skin showing through my torn sleeveless shirt.

Which was the plan, after all.

I released the angel and strolled across the mosaic commemorating the dedication of the Dam. Brass and steel inlaid in terrazzo express moons and planets: Alcyone, B Tauri, and Mizar. Marked out among them are lines of inclination and paths of arc. The star map was left for future archaeologists to find if they wondered at the Dam's provenance: a sort of "we were here, and this is what we made you" signature scrawled on the bottom of a glue-and-glitter card. A hundred and twenty miles north of here, we're leaving them another gift: a mountain full of spent nuclear fuel rods, and scribed on its surface a similar message, but that one's meant to say "Don't Touch."

Some card.

The steel lines describe the precession of equinoxes and define orbital periods. They mark out a series of curves and angles superimposed across the whole night sky and the entire history of civilized mankind, cutting and containing them as the Dam cuts and contains the river.

It creeps me out. What can I say?

They Died to Make the Desert Bloom, an inscription read, across the compass rose and signs of the zodiac on my left, and near my feet Capella. And On this 30th day of the month of September in the year (Anno Dominicæ Incarnationis mcmxxxv) 1935, Franklin Delano Roosevelt, 32nd president of these United States of America dedicated to the service of our people this dam, power plant, and reservoir. A little more than ten years before Bugsy Siegel gave us the Flamingo Hotel and the Las Vegas we know and love today, but an inextricable link in the same unholy chain nonetheless. I try to be suitably grateful.

But Bugsy was from California.

I passed over or beside the words, never stopping, my ears full of Stewart's screaming and the babble of conversation, the shouts of officers, the wail of sirens. And soon, very soon, the rattle of a helicopter's rotors.

The area of terrazzo closest to the angels' feet is called the Wheel of Time. It mentions the pyramids, and the birth of Christ, and the Dam. It ends in the year AD 14,000. The official Dam tour recommends you stay home that day.

Alongside these dates is another:

EARLY PART OF AD 2100

Slipped in among all the ancient significances, with a blank space before it and the obvious and precise intention that it someday be filled to match the rest.

Stewart screamed again. I glanced over my shoulder; security was still distracted. Pulling a chisel from my spacious pocket, I crouched on the stones and rested it against the top of the inscription. I produced a steel-headed mallet into my other hand. When I lifted the eyepatch off my *otherwise* eye, I saw the light saturating the stone shiver back from the point of my chisel like a prodded jellyfish. There was some power worked into it. A power I recognized, because I also saw its potential shimmer through my right eye where my left one saw only the skin of my own hand. The Dam, and me. Something meant to look like something else.

Card tricks.

The lovely whistle stop oasis called Las Vegas became a minor metropolis—by Nevada standards—in large part by serving gambling, whiskey, and whores to the New Deal workers who poured these concrete blocks. Workers housed in Boulder City weren't permitted such things within town limits. On Friday nights they went looking for a place to spend some of the money they risked their lives earning all week. Then after a weekend in Sin City, they were back in harness seven hundred feet above the bottom of Black Canyon come Monday morning, nine A.M.

Ninety-six of them died on the Dam site. Close to three hundred more succumbed to black lung and other diseases. There's a legend some of them were entombed within the Dam.

It would never have been permitted. A body in the concrete means a weakness in the structure, and Hoover was made to last well past the date I was about to obliterate with a few well-placed blows. "Viva Las Vegas," I muttered under my breath, and raised the hammer. And then Stewart stopped screaming, and a velvety female purr sounded in my ear. "Jack, Jack, Jackie."

"Goddess." I put the tools down and stood up, face inches from the face of the most beautiful woman in the world. "How did you know where to find me?"

She lowered tar-black lashes across a cheek like cream and thrust a narrow swell of hip out, pouting through her hair. The collar of her sleeveless blouse stood crisp-pressed, framing her face; I wondered how she managed it in a hundred-twenty. "I heard a rumor you meant to deface my Dam," she said with a smile that bent lacquered lips in a mockery of Cupid's little red bow. The too-cool teenager was staring at Goddess now, brow wrinkled as if she thought Goddess must be somebody famous and couldn't quite place who. Goddess gets that reaction a lot.

I sighed. Contrived as she was, she was still lovelier than anything real life could manage. "You're looking a little peaked these days, Goddess. Producers got you on a diet again? And it's my Dam, honey. I'm Las Vegas. Your turf is down the river."

Her eyes flashed. Literally. I cocked an ear over my shoulder, but still no screaming. Which—dammit—meant that Stewart was probably dead, and I was out of time. Otherwise I would have bent down in front of her and done it anyway.

"It's not polite to ask a lady what she does to maintain her looks, darling. And I say Hoover belongs to L.A. You claim, what—ten percent of the power and water?" She took a couple of steps to the brass Great Seal of California there at the bottom of the terrazzo, front and center among the plaques to the seven states that could not live without the Colorado, and twice as big as the others. Immediately under the sheltering wings of a four-foot bas-relief eagle. She tapped it with a toe. The message was clear.

I contented myself with admiring the way her throat tightened under a Tiffany collar as I shrugged and booted my hammer aside. Out of my left eye, I saw her *otherwise*—a swirl of images and expectations, a casting-couch stain and a shattered dream streetwalking on Sunset Boulevard. "You still working by yourself, Goddess? Imagine it's been lonely since your boyfriend died."

Usually there are two or three of us to a city. And we can be killed, although something new comes along eventually to replace us. Unless the city dies too: then it's all over. Her partner had gotten himself shot up in an alleyway. Appropriate.

"I get by," she answered with a Bette Davis sigh.

I was supposed to go over and comfort her. Instead, I flipped my eyepatch down. Goddess makes me happy I don't like girls. She's a hazard to navigation for those who do. "I was just leaving. We could stop at that little ice cream place in Boulder City for an avocado-baconburger."

A surprised ripple of rutabaga-rutabagas ran through the crowd on the other sidewalk, and I heard officers shouting to each other. Stewart's body must have vanished.

"Ugh," Goddess said expressively, the corners of her mouth turning down under her makeup.

"True. You shouldn't eat too much in a sitting; all that puking will ruin your teeth." I managed to beat my retreat while she was still hacking around a suitably acid response.

Traffic wasn't moving across the dam yet, but I'd had the foresight to park the dusty-but-new F150 in the lot in Arizona, so all I had to do was walk across the Dam—on the lake side: there was still a crowd on the drop side—and haul Stewart (by the elbow) away from the KLAS reporter to whom he was providing an incoherently homosexual man-on-the-spot reaction. He did that sort of thing a lot. Stewart was the Suicide King. I kissed him as I shoved him into the truck.

He pulled back and caught my eye. "Did it work?"

"Fuck, Stewart. I'm sorry."

"Sure," he said, leaning across to open the driver's-side door. "You spend fifteen minutes impaled on a rusty chunk of steel and then I'll tell you, 'Sorry.' What happened?"

"Goddess."

He didn't say anything after that: just blew silky blond hair out of eyes bluer than the desert sky and put his hand on my knee as we drove south through Arizona, down to Laughlin, and came over the river and back up through the desert wastes of Searchlight and CalNevAri. In silence. Going home.

We parked the truck in the Four Queens garage and went strolling past the courthouse. The childhood-summer drone of cicadas surrounded us as we walked past the drunks and the itinerant ministers. We strolled downtown arm in arm, toward the Fremont Street Experience, daring somebody to say something.

The Suicide King and me. Wildcards, but only sometimes. In a city with streets named for Darth Vader and for Seattle Slew, we were the unseen princes. I said as much to Stewart.

"Or unseen queens," he joked, tugging me under the arch of lights roofing Fremont Street. "What happened back there?"

Music and cool air drifted out the open doorways of casinos, along with the irresistible chime of the slot machines that are driving out the table games. I saw the lure of their siren song in the glassy eyes of the gamblers shuffling past us. "Something must have called her. I was just going to deface a national landmark. Nothing special."

Someone jostled my arm on my *otherwise* side, blind with the eyepatch down. I turned my head, expecting a sneering curse. But he smiled from under a floppy mustache and a floppier hat, and disappeared into Binion's Horseshoe. I could pick the poker players out of the herd: they didn't look anesthetized. *That* one wasn't a slot zombie. There might be life in my city yet.

Stewart grunted, cleaning his fingernails with a pocketknife that wasn't street-legal by anyone's standards. Sweat marked half-moons on his red-striped shirt, armholes and collar. "And Goddess showed up. All the way from the City of Angels."

"Hollywood and Vine."

"What did she want?"

"The bitch said it was her fucking Dam." I turned my head to watch another zombie pass. A local. Tourists mostly stay down on the Strip these days, with its Hollywood assortment of two-dimensional mockeries of exotic places. Go to Las Vegas and never see it.

I'm waiting for the Las-Vegas themed casino: somewhere between Paris, Egypt, Venice and the African coast. Right in the middle of the Strip. This isn't the city that gave Stewart and me birth. But this is the city I now am.

"Is it?"

"I don't know. Hoover should be ours by rights. But it called her: that's the only thing that makes sense. And I'm convinced that empty date forges a link between Vegas and L.A. It's as creepy as the damned Mayan calendar *ending* in 2012."

He let go of my arm and wandered over to one of the antique neon signs. Antique by Vegas standards, anyway. "You ever think of all those old towns under the lake, Jack? The ones they evacuated when the reservoir started to fill?"

I nodded, although he wasn't looking and I knew he couldn't hear my head rattle, and I followed him through the neon museum. I think a lot about those towns, actually. Them, and the Anasazi, who carved their names and legends on every wind-etched red rock within the glow of my lights and then vanished without a whisper, as if blown off the world by that selfsame wind. And Rhyolite, near Beatty, where they're building the nuke dump: it was the biggest city in Nevada in 1900 and in 1907 it was gone. I think about the Upshot Knothole Project: these downtown hotels are the older ones, built to withstand the tremors from the above-ground nuclear blasts that comprised it. And I think too of all the casinos that thrived in their day, and then accordioned into dust and tidy rubble when the men with the dynamite came.

Nevada has a way of eating things up. Swallowing them without a trace.

Except the Dam, with that cry etched on its surface. And a date that hasn't happened yet. Remember. Remember. Remember me.

Stewart gazed upward, his eyes trained on Vegas Vic: the famous neon cowboy who used to wave a greeting to visitors cruising into town in fin-tailed Cadillacs—relegated now to headliner status in the Neon Museum. He doesn't wave anymore: his hand stays upraised stiffly. I lifted mine in a like salute. "Howdy," I replied.

Stewart giggled. "At least they didn't blow him up."

"No," I said, looking down. "They blew the fuck out of Bugsy, though."

Bugsy was a California gangster who thought maybe halfway up the Los Angeles highway, where it crossed the Phoenix road, might be a good place for a joint designed to convert dirty money into clean. It so happened that there was already a little town with a light-skirt history huddled there, under the shade of tree-lined streets. A town with mild winters and abundant water. *Las Vegas* means *the meadows* in Spanish. In the middle of the harsh Mojave, the desert bloomed. And there's always been magic at a crossroads. It's where you go to sell your soul.

I shifted my eyepatch to get a look *otherwise*. Vic shimmered, a twist of expectation, disappointment, conditioned response. My right eye showed me the slot-machine zombies as a shuffling darkness, Stewart a blinding white light, a sword-wielding specter. A demon of chance. The Suicide King, avatar of take-your-own-life Las Vegas with its record-holding rates of depression, violence, failure, homelessness, DUI. The Suicide King, who cannot ever die by his own hand.

"I can see why she feels at home here," Stewart said to Vic's neon feet.

"Vic's a he, Stewart. Unless that was a faggot 'she,' in which case I will send the ghosts of campiness—past present and future—to haunt your bed."

"She. Goddess. She seems at home here."

"I don't want her at home in my city," I snapped as if it cramped my tongue. It felt petty. And good. "The bitch has her own city. And sucks enough fucking water out of my river."

He looked at me shyly through a fall of blond bangs. I thought about kissing him, and snorted instead. He grinned. "Vegas is nothing but a big fucking stage set wrapped around a series of strip malls, anymore. What could be more Hollywood?"

I lit a cigarette, because everybody still smokes in Vegas—as if to make up for California—and took a deep, acrid drag. When I blew smoke back out it tickled my nostrils. "I think that empty inscription is what locks us to L.A."

Stewart laced his arm through mine again. "Maybe we'll get lucky and it will turn out to be the schedule for The Big One."

I pictured L.A. tumbling into the ocean, Goddess and all, and grinned back. "I was hoping to get that a little sooner. So what say we go back to the Dam tonight and give it another try?"

"What the hell do we have to lose?"

The trooper shone his light around the cab and the bed of the truck, but didn't make us get out despite three A.M. and no excuse to be out but stargazing at Willow Beach. Right after the terrorist attacks, it was soldiers armed with automatic weapons. I'm not sure if the Nevada State Police are an improvement, but this is the world we have to live in, even if it is under siege. Stewart, driving, smiled and showed ID, and then we passed through winding gullies and out onto the Dam.

It was uncrowded in the breathless summer night. The massive lights painting its facade washed the stars out of the desert sky. Las Vegas glowed in the passenger-side mirror from behind the mountains as Stewart parked the truck on the Arizona side. On an overcast night, the glow is greenish—the reflected lights of the MGM Grand. That night, clear skies, and it was the familiar city-glow pink, only brighter and split neatly by the ascending Luxor light like a beacon calling someone home.

I'd been chewing my thumb all evening. Stewart rattled my shoulder to get me to look up. "We're here. Bring your chisel?"

"Better," I said, and reached behind the seat to bring out the tire iron and a little eight-pound sledge. The sledge dropped neatly into the tool loop of my cargo pants. I tugged a black denim jacket on over the torn shirt and slid the iron into the left-hand sleeve. "Now I'm ready."

He disarmed the doors and struggled out of the leather jacket I'd told him was too hot to wear. "Why you always gotta break things you don't understand?"

"Because they scare me." I didn't think he'd get it, but he was still sitting behind the wheel thinking when I walked around and opened his door. The alarm had rearmed; it wailed momentarily but he keyed it off in irritation and hopped down, tossing the jacket inside. "It's got to relate to how bad things have gotten. It's a shadow war, man. This Dam is *for* something."

"Of course it's for something." Walking beside me, he shot me that blue-eyed look that made me want to smack him and kiss him all at once. "You know what they used to say about the Colorado before they built it—too thick to drink, and too thin to plow. The Dam is there to screw up the breeding cycles of fish, make it possible for men to live where men shouldn't be living. Make a reservoir. Hydroelectric power. Let the mud settle out. It's there to hold the river back."

It's there to hold the river back. "I was thinking just that earlier," I said as we walked across the floodlit Dam. The same young girl from that afternoon leaned out over the railing, looking down into the yawning, floodlit chasm. I wondered if she was homeless and how she'd gotten all the way out here—and how she planned to get back.

She looked up as we walked past arm in arm, something reflected like city glow in her eyes.

The lure of innocence to decadence cuts both ways: cities and angels, vampires and victims. Sweet-eyed street kid with a heart like a knife. I didn't even need to flip up my eyepatch to know for sure. "What's your name?" I let the tire iron slip down in my sleeve where I could grab it. "Goddess leave you behind?"

"Goddess works for me," she said, and raised her right fist. A shiny little automatic glittered in it, all blued steel with a viper nose. It made a forties' movie tableau, even to the silhouetting spill of floodlights and the way the wind pinned the dress to her body. She smiled. Sweet, venomous. "And you can call me Angel. Drop the crowbar, kid."

"It's a tire iron," I answered, but I let it fall to the cement. It rang like the bell going off in my head, telling me everything made perfect sense. "What the hell do you want with Las Vegas, Angel?" I thought I knew all the West-coast animae. *She must be new.*

She giggled prettily. "Look at you, cutie. Just as proud of your little shadow city as if it really existed."

I wished I still had the tire iron in my hand. I would have broken it across her face.

"What the fuck is that supposed to mean?" Stewart. Bless him. He jerked his thumb up at the spill of light smirching the sky. "What do you call that?"

She shrugged. "A mirage shines too, but you can't touch it. All you need to know is quit trying to break my Dam. You must be Jack, right? And this charming fellow here"—she took a step back so the pistol still covered both of us, even as Stewart dropped my hand and edged away. *Stewart*—"This must be the Suicide King. I'd like you both to work for me too."

The gun oscillated from Stewart's midsection to mine. Angel's hand wasn't shaking. Behind her, I saw Goddess striding up the sidewalk, imperious in five-hundred dollar high-heeled shoes.

"I know what happens," I said. "All that darkness has to go somewhere, doesn't it? Everything trapped behind the Dam. All the little ways my city echoes yours, and the big ones too. And Nevada has a way of sucking things up without a trace.

"The Dam is a way to control it. It's a way to hold back that gummy river of blackness. And Las Vegas is the reservoir that lets you meter it out and use when you want it.

"Let me guess. You need somebody to watch over Hoover. And the magic built into it, which will be complete sometime after the concrete cures."

Stewart picked up the thread as Goddess pulled a little pearl-handled gun out of her pocketbook as well. He didn't step forward, but I felt him interpose himself. *Don't! Don't.* "Let me guess," he said. "*The early part of 2100?* What happens then?"

"Only movie villains tell all in the final reel." Goddess had arrived.

Angel cut her off. "Gloating is passé." She smiled. "L.A. is built on failure, baby. I'm a carnivore. All that pain has to go somewhere. Can't keep it inside: it would eat me up sure as I eat up dreams. Gotta have it for when I need it, to share with the world."

"The picture of Dorian Gray," Stewart said.

"Call it the picture of L.A." She studied my face for a long time before she smiled. All that innocence, and all that cool calculated savagery just under the surface of her eyes. "Smart boys. Imagine how much worse I would be without it. And it doesn't affect the local ecology all that much. As you noted, Jackie, Nevada's got a way of making things be gone."

"That doesn't give you the right."

Angel shrugged, as if to say, *What are rights*? "All chiseling that date off would do is remove the reason for Las Vegas to exist. It would vanish like the corpse of a twenty-dollar streetwalker dumped in the high desert, and no one would mark its passing. Boys, you're not *real*."

I felt Stewart swelling beside me, soul-deep offended. It was my city. His city. And not some vassal state of Los Angeles. "You still haven't said what happens in a hundred years."

Goddess started to say something, and Angel hushed her with the flat of her outstretched hand. "L.A.," she said, that gesture taking in everything behind her—Paris, New York, Venice, shadows of the world's great cities in a shadow city of its own—"Wins. The spell is set, and can't be broken. Work for me. You win too. What do you say to that, Jack?"

"Angel, honey. Nobody really talks like that." I started to turn away, laying a hand on Stewart's arm to bring him with me. The sledgehammer nudged my leg.

"Boys," Goddess said. Her tone was harsh with finality.

Stewart fumbled in his pocket. I knew he was reaching for his knife. "What are you going to do," he asked, tugging my hand, almost dragging me away. "Shoot me in the back?"

I took a step away from Goddess, and from Angel. And then Stewart caught my eye with a wink, and—*Stewart!*—kept turning, and he dropped my hand . . .

The flat clap of a gunshot killed the last word he said. He pitched forward as if kicked, blood like burst berries across his midsection, front and back. I spun around as another bullet rang between my Docs. Goddess skipped away as I lunged, shredding the seam of my pants as I yanked the sledgehammer out. It was up like a baseball bat before Stewart hit the ground. I hoped he had his knife in his hand. I hoped he had the strength to open a vein before the wound in his back killed him.

I didn't have time to hope anything else.

They shot like L.A. cops—police stance, wide-legged, braced, and aiming to kill. I don't know how I got between the slugs. I felt them tug my clothing; one burned my face. But I'm One-Eyed Jack, and my luck was running. Cement chips stung my face as a bullet ricocheted off the wall and out over Lake Mead. Behind Angel and Goddess, a light pulsed like Stewart's blood and a siren screamed.

Stewart wasn't making any sound now and I forced myself not turn and look back at him. Instead, I closed the distance, shouting something I don't recall. I think I split Goddess' lovely skull open on the very first swing. I know I smashed Angel's arm, because her gun went flying before she ran. Ran like all that practice in the sands of Southern California came in handy, fit—no doubt—from rollerblading along the board walk. My lungs burned after three steps. The lights were coming.

Almost nobody *runs* in Las Vegas, except on a treadmill. It's too fucking hot. I staggered to a stop, dropped the hammer clanging as I stepped over Goddess' shimmering body, and went back for Stewart.

His blood was a sticky puddle I had to walk through to get to him. He'd pushed himself over on his side, and I could hear the whimper in his breath, but the knife had fallen out of his hand. "Jack," he said. "Can't move my fingers."

I picked it up and opened it. "Love. Show me where."

"Sorry," he said. "Who the hell knew they could shoot so fucking well?" It came up on his lips in a bubble of blood, and it had to be *his* hand. So I folded his fingers around the handle and guided the blade to his throat.

The sirens and lights throbbed in my head like a Monday-morning migraine. "Does it count if I'm pushing?"

He giggled. It came out a kicked whimper. "I don't know," he said through the bubbles. "Try it and see."

I pushed. Distorted by a loudspeaker, the command to stop and drop might have made me jump another day, but Stewart's blood was sudden, hot and sticky-slick as tears across my hands. I let the knife fall and turned my back to the road. Down by my boots, Stewart started to shimmer. We were near where Angel had been leaning out to look down the face of the Dam. The Plexiglas barriers and the decorated tops of the elevator shafts started five feet to my right.

"One-Eyed Jacks and Suicide Kings are wild," I muttered, and in two running steps I threw myself over the wall. Hell, you never know until you try it. A bullet gouged the wall top alongside the black streaks from the sole of my Doc.

The lights on the Dam face silvered it like a wedding cake. It didn't seem like such a long way to fall, and the river was down there somewhere. A gust of wind just might blow me wide enough to miss the blockhouse at the bottom.

If I got lucky.

From the outside northbound lane on the 95, I spotted the road: more of a track, by any reasonable standard. I dragged the white Ford pickup across the rumble strip and halted amid scattering gravel. It had still had Stewart's jacket thrown across the front seat after I bribed impound. Sometimes corruption cuts in our favor. A flat hard shape patted my chest from inside the coat's checkbook pocket, and the alarm armed itself a moment after I got out.

Two tracks, wagon wheel wide, stretched through a forest of Joshua trees like prickly old men hunched over in porcupine hats, abutted by sage and agave. The desert sky almost never gets so blue. It's usually a washed out-color: Mojave landscapes are best represented in turquoise and picture jasper.

A lot of people came through here—enough people to wear a road— and they must have thought they were going someplace better. California, probably. I pitched a rock at a toxic, endangered Gila monster painted in the animal gang colors of don't-mess-with-me and then I sat down on a dusty rock and waited. And waited. And waited, while the sun skipped down the flat horizon and the sky grayed periwinkle and then indigo. Lights rippled on across the valley floor, chasing the shadow of the mountain. From my vantage in the pass between the mountains, I made out the radioactive green shimmer of the MGM Grand, the laser-white beacon off the top of the Luxor, the lofted red-green-lavender Stratosphere. The Aladdin, the Venetian, the Paris. The amethyst and ruby arch of the Rio. New York, New York. And the Mirage. Worth a dry laugh, that.

Symbols of every land, drawing the black energy to Vegas. A darkness sink. Like a postcard. Like the skyline of a city on the back of a one-eyed jack in a poker deck with the knaves pulled out.

It glittered a lot, for a city in thrall.

There was a fifth of tequila in Stewart's coat. I poured a little libation on an agave, lifted up my eyepatch and splashed some in my *otherwise* eye. I took a deep breath and stared down on the valley. "Stewart," I said to my city. "I don't know if you're coming back. If anybody squeaks through on a technicality, man, it should be you. And I haven't seen your replacement yet. So I keep hoping." I hadn't seen Angel either. But I hadn't been down to the Dam.

Another slug of liquor. "Bugsy, you son of a bitch. You brought me here, didn't you? Me and Stew. You fixed the chains tight, the ones the Dam forged. And it didn't turn out quite the way you anticipated. Because sometimes we're wild cards, and sometimes we're not, and what matters is how you call the game."

I drank a little tequila, poured a little on the ground. If you're going to talk to ghosts, it doesn't hurt to get them drunk. Ask a vodun if you don't believe me.

My glittering shadow city—all cheap whore in gaudy paint that makes her look older, much older, and much, much tireder than she is— she'll suck up all the darkness that bitch Angel can throw at her, and I swear someday the Dam will burst and the desert will suck the City of Angels up too. Nevada has a way of eating things whole. Swallowing them without a trace. Civilizations, loved ones, fusion products.

There's a place to carve one more Great Event on the memoried surface of the Dam. And I mean to own that sucker, before Angel carves her city's black conquest in it. I've still got a hundred years or so to figure out how to do it.

Meanwhile, my city glitters like a mirage in the valley. Sin City. Just a shadow of something bigger. But a shadow can grow strangely real if you squint at it right, and sometimes a mirage hides real water.

This is my city, and I'm her Jack. I'm not going anywhere.

≈

Elizabeth Bear is the Hugo, Sturgeon, Locus, and Campbell Award-winning author of over a hundred short stories and twenty-seven novels, including *One-Eyed Jack*, which is expanded from this story. Her most recent novels are *Karen Memory* and—co-authored with Sarah Monette—*An Apprentice of Elves*) Recently engaged to author Scott Lynch, she lives in Massachusetts.

≈

Brit sees things above the streets of Seattle that others don't. Another crazy teenager, right? Or maybe it is drugs. Either way, get her to a shrink. Then someone else sees magic where no one else has glimpsed it.

Street Worm
Nisi Shawl

Down, down, down: dust and mud and mortar and steel plunged story upon story into the earth. Brit Williams clung to the chain link fence surrounding the construction site as if only the desperate strength of her thin brown fingers kept her from falling in.

She could see the pit's bottom—barely. Late afternoon in Seattle during the first week of February meant darkness owned the corners, shadows filled in all the low places and rose like dirty water to hide everything, eventually, even . . .

Dragging her eyes up along the building's still-exposed girders and beams, Brit spotted the giant nest, shining gray and silver in the last of the twilight. She hunched smaller in her good leather coat. But as far as she knew, the worm-like things that lived between those web walls couldn't see her.

"You all right, kid?"

The cops sure could, though. "Yeah," she lied, meeting the policewoman's eyes. White people liked that. "Just wanted a look before I got on the bus home." Did that sound suspicious? Had she said too much?

No. The cop let her walk downhill and cross the intersection without interference. She strode briskly into the cold drizzle as if she really did have somewhere to go.

Well, she did. If she'd only admit to her parents she was crazy, she could go home. She could fit herself right back into their careful, bougie lives.

Except she was sane. Brit was pretty sure of that.

No one else seemed to see the nests, though. Whereas for her, they were everywhere. Heading north on First Avenue she walked by three, all stuck to the sides of skyscrapers in the throes of renovation. People going the other way faced her and passed on, oblivious office workers and ignorant drunks. The traffic light ahead changed and Brit hurried out into the street to get away from a close one hanging only a few floors above the sidewalk. Behind the nest's pale sides, paler shapes writhed disgustingly, knotting together and sliding apart—she stopped to watch in fascination till a rough jolt to her shoulder and a muttered curse got her moving again. On the street's other side she checked her pants' front pocket. Her cash was still there.

But the clerk at the Green Tortoise Hostel wouldn't take it.

Brit tried. She showed him she really had enough money, laying a wrinkled twenty on the greasy counter and smoothing it out flat. The man shook his shaggy head like a refugee from a Scooby-Doo cartoon. "Nope. Not without proper ID."

Brit glared at him. She'd shown him that, too. "What ain't proper about—" She slapped her hand down on her fake driver's license fast, grabbing it back before he could confiscate it. His large hand rested awkwardly between them.

"Look, do you need help? Somewhere to stay the night?"

Wasn't that what she'd wanted to pay him for? If she hadn't been so damn short, he might not have asked how old she was. Lots of people told Brit she acted four, even five years older than her age. She could have passed for eighteen, easily—if she stood a little taller. But no.

"Problems at home? Let me call somebody—" He turned for the phone behind him and Brit bolted back outside.

Getting dark. The rain had slacked off, but the cold felt worse. At least she couldn't smell Shaggy's stale cigarette butts anymore.

She took in a deep breath, convincing herself she was better off. So much for Plan A. Plan B was more flexible. Okay, less well-formed. The basics were the same: Stay away from her parents till they gave up labeling her "disturbed." Skip the appointment they'd made for her tomorrow afternoon with a psychiatrist.

She plodded stoically uphill. East. And south, away from the Green Tortoise. The library would probably still be open, but Brit wasn't in the mood to read. Too hungry. She pushed open the door of the Hotel Monaco's restaurant and went in.

Warm air caressed her, carrying in its soft swirls the aromas of fresh bread, baked herbs and onions, roasting meat—

"May I help you?" The way the woman walking towards her spoke made it clear she didn't think helping Brit was in her power or anyone else's. Brit had eaten here before. Only lunch, though. Everybody on that shift was used to her, but obviously she was just another black kid to this high-heeled blonde. And obviously she was too young to be eating dinner alone. "Meeting another party?"

Brit's gaze swept around the room. The only other customers were a couple of old ladies in red and purple suits and bizarrely flowered hats. "Yeah. Spozed to be. Look like I'm early."

Mostly Brit talked the way she did to make Mom and Dad angry. Ebonics didn't fit in with their image as "professionals." Of course it pissed off her friend Iyata's mother Sylvie, too, but that only meant they had to meet at school half the time. Not such a hardship. And maybe the use of Ebonics reminded the blonde it was National Brotherhood Week or something: she showed Brit to a nice table and gave her a menu without any more questions.

She ordered a cup of tea to drink while she was "waiting." She sipped it slowly, trying to figure out what story she'd tell to explain why the imaginary adults didn't show up for their ostensible rendezvous with her. She'd need to fake a phone call . . .

The outside door opened again and she glanced up exactly as if she really was expecting to meet someone here. In came a round-bellied white man in a navy blue coat, his long gray hair in a ponytail. Probably friends with the two old ladies. "There she is!" he said, brushing past the hostess and heading straight for Brit. Not the old ladies. Brit.

"How's my little half-pint of cider half drunk up?" The strange man smiled and plopped down in her table's other chair. "Play along!" he whispered. "Pretend you know me till I get a chance to—"

"Ready to order?" The waiter had appeared from nowhere to stand by the table at attention. He had a green notepad in his hands and a mildly worried expression on his face.

Brit could get up and scream for him to call the cops. That'd be great—they'd take her right back home. Besides, this table-crasher guy suddenly looked familiar. She narrowed her eyes. An actor? It was coming back to her: the race-flipped production that The Conciliation Project had brought to her school—"Uncle Tom?"

One of the man's bushy eyebrows lifted. "Don't look so surprised! Didn't you get our message? Aunt Eliza came down with the flu and sent me by myself." He turned to the waiter as if just noticing him. "I'd like a Jungle Bird, if the bar's open."

"Yes, sir!" The waiter left, looking reassured.

When they were alone again "Uncle Tom" hunched forward and laid his arms on the table. "Thanks," he said. "That was pretty brave of you."

"Yeah, well, get any nearer and I'm leavin."

"Fair enough." He leaned back. "I guess I ought to be grateful you recognized me—from that play version of *Uncle Tom's Cabin*, I take it?"

Brit nodded. "But that don't mean I trust you no further than I can throw the chair you sittin in."

"Fair enough," he said again. The waiter returned carrying a glass round as the man's belly, full of ice and an orangey liquid. A section of a pineapple ring gripped its rim. He left again after taking their orders: lasagna for Brit, which was what she usually had at lunch, and quail for her supposed uncle.

"All right, before we're interrupted anymore, let me try to tell you what I'm doing talking to you. Did you ever read—or see—*The Shining*?"

Brit was tired of white people assuming she was stupid simply because she was dark-skinned. Another reason she'd started talking hood; before, they always said how she was so "articulate." "I can read!"

"Never said you couldn't. Lots of kids don't bother with books, though; young people nowadays seem to prefer movies. Anyway, the book and the movie *are* different: the Scatman Crothers character doesn't die at the end of the novel. But what both versions of the story got right was how some of us, some of us who can do special things, have this glow to us, this 'shining' if you will . . . like you."

Like her. "You sayin I'm magic."

"For lack of a better word, yes. Yes I am."

"How bout 'insane'? How bout 'hallucinatin'?" She was standing—her legs shook. She hoped it didn't show. She kept her voice low. "How bout 'depressed an delusional'? All kinda things people be sayin I am, an ain't none of em good—" On the edge of her field of vision she saw the waiter approaching with a basket of bread.

"Ima go the bathroom. When I come out you be gone." She picked up her backpack from where she'd dropped it and fled.

"Wait, let me finish—"

She slammed the restroom door behind her and turned on the water so she wouldn't have to hear what he was saying. Peed, wiped, flushed, washed her hands. Eyes on the mirror, she pulled out her pick and went to work on her short little fro. Then a touch-up to her liner and mascara— Mom and Dad didn't allow her to wear make-up, but Brit kept a supply for use away from home.

She took a long time, but when she emerged the man—she didn't even know his real name!—was sitting where she'd left him. Between her and the exit. He stood up as she walked by—he didn't attempt to stop her, though. All he did was say, "Sorry. I don't blame you for being scared."

That made her turn around. "I ain't scared!"

"No? Then maybe you'll sit down and eat quietly with me?"

Brit suddenly noticed that the hostess, the waiter, the old ladies— everyone in the whole restaurant was staring at her. She didn't need that kind of attention. With an angry look at "Uncle Tom" she sat back in her abandoned chair.

"Maybe put on a slightly less murderous expression?"

Brit closed her eyes and took three deep breaths like her dad was always counseling his clients to do. When she opened them there was a white card on the table in front of her. *Elias Crofutt* read the first line, in a flowing, cursive-like script. Below it, in much plainer letters: *Theater, Language, Hierophance*—whatever *that* was. Below those words was a phone number. All printed in dark purple ink.

"Ken Rodriguez—at the hostel—called my pager after you left so— precipitously."

Shaggy. "He had one a these?" she asked. "Why come?"

"Often there's trouble at home when a talent such as yours emerges.

I keep an eye out for kids at risk, and I have my contacts in likely spots watching for—"

"You got spies? You a nasty fuckin creeper!" Brit scraped her seat away from the table.

"Wait! Don't you want to know how I found you?"

Yes she did. The Green Tortoise was eight blocks away, too far for mere coincidence. And she'd never heard of this sort of operation in Seattle. Both her parents worked with teens—Dad as a psychiatrist, Mom as a social worker. It was why they were so sure they knew what was wrong with her. They were always warning her about things she'd never be enough of an idiot to get mixed up in; surely they would have mentioned running across a scheme like this? What if she could tell them about something they'd missed? That would make her look on top of everything—completely sane. She nodded cautiously.

"I was trying to tell you: you *shine*. I followed your light—" He stopped midsentence. The waiter brought salads and set them on the table in the abrupt, awkward silence.

Brit smothered her lettuce and carrot chips in ranch and picked up her fork, determined to get some food in her stomach. She'd been too busy arguing with her mom to eat this afternoon at home. "You was sayin." She crammed a loaded fork in her mouth.

"I keep an office at the Y."

So cross off staying there. That put a big dent in Plan B.

"When I called Kenny back he described you—not only what you were wearing but—well, it's like invisible fireworks coming out of the top of your head—"

"Riiight." Let the man spew out his new-age sewage. She would concentrate on getting some nourishment under her belt. One forkful at a time.

"I know how this sounds. Believe me. Or maybe it's more like sparklers than fireworks, because you leave a trail in the air for a minute or two . . . Well. Anyway. I can see it, though most can't."

Grimly, Brit swallowed and began chewing a third mouthful of crunchy, oil-coated salad. Plan C was even hazier in her mind than B. And this dude was seriously woo-woo.

Or maybe not. If she was sane, he could be, too. Maybe? Would he back her up? Would her parents believe him? Or would they call him nuts—politely—to his face?

The waiter came back with their entrees before she could decide. Steam wafted off her lasagna when she cut apart the crusty cheesy top layer. Too hot to eat yet. "What my fireworks look like?" she asked.

"White and gold with flecks of ruby-red," Crofutt replied promptly. Not hesitating as if he was making stuff up. "I've never seen anything quite like it."

"That mean you don't know what kinda magic I do?"

"Correct. But I can help you figure it out. If you need me to." He sliced meat off the quail's breast and ate a couple of bites before he spoke again. "Anything else you need, just ask. Money, weapons, somewhere to stay the night . . . "

There was being scared and then there was being smart. She flagged the waiter down. "Put this in a go box," she said, gesturing at her food. She dug out the same bill she'd offered Shaggy. Kenny. It ought to cover her share. Plus tip.

"Through already?"

Brit stood up and the man didn't try to stop her. "So through." She kept her voice low so no one else would notice her anger. "Here some cash to pay for my food. You can see I don't need your stinkin money. Don't need you runnin crystals up an down my body, neither, or whatever freaky thing get you off before you stranglin me—"

"No! You're wrong!" Crofutt protested. "Sit down—*please!*"

"I ain't!" She tilted her head to one side and grinned ferociously for the benefit of the waiter coming back with her boxed up lasagna. "Tell Aunt Eliza I hope she be better for church Sunday," she said, too sweetly. "Thanks for the offer, but I gotta go." She swung her pack onto her left shoulder, took the box from the waiter, and headed for the door.

Behind her Brit heard the white man getting up and following her. She made it almost to the door before she felt his touch on her coat sleeve. She whirled fast and he dropped the offending hand. But he held the other out to give her the card from the table. "You almost forgot this."

Rather than attract more attention she took it and shoved it in her coat pocket. "Good *night*."

"Be careful!" he shouted as she stepped outside. "It's—"

The door banged shut and cut the last words off. Full night had fallen and a freezing wind blew off the bay.

There was one spot Brit knew would be probably a little warmer. And empty. Not somewhere safe, exactly, but she was out of other options. She walked downhill again and turned north on Third to avoid the Green Tortoise. She wasn't paranoid; she didn't really think Shaggy would even know she was going by the building. It was just better not to take any chances.

She wasn't paranoid. Something told her to look back up the street at Third, though, and here came Crofutt, striding after her as fast as his fat self could go. Which was surprisingly fast.

The second door past the corner had an *Open* sign hanging behind its glass. Brit yanked it out of the way and hurried inside. She put a couple of rows of shelves between her and the window before she came to a halt.

This was a cigar store. A pretty swanky one, too. Shelves and shelves of boxes full of brown cylinders: fat, thin, dark, light, short, long, banded in gold, wrapped in cellophane, as various as people.

"May I help you?" The man asking that question this time sounded as if he might really want to. He looked nice, too. He had curly, medium long hair, black mixed with silver; smooth skin the color of one of his cigars; a nose curved like a bird's beak; a mustache lifted up at its ends by his smile.

"My dad birthday comin up," she improvised. Actually, that wouldn't be till June. "I wanna get him somethin extra cool."

"Of course. He is already a smoker? A connoisseur? I may know him. What's his name?"

"He only started round Christmas." What a tangled web. Would she have to make up a reason why he'd started then?

With a few more lies Brit stretched the visit out to half an hour. She bought a gold-plated cigar trimmer, a bead-covered lighter shaped like a butterfly, and six of the hugest cigars she could find. That took two of her hundreds.

It was worth it, though. When she left the shop there was no sign of Crofutt the Creeper. She continued north toward the Denny Triangle neighborhood, then walked east again on Stewart to Westlake, keeping out of the Belltown bar scene.

The crowds dwindled and disappeared. Someday, Mom said, this part of town was going to get bought up and gentrified. Meanwhile it was home mostly to what the planning commissions her parents monitored called "light industry": newspaper offices, award plaque engravers, embroidery factories, etc. Low brick buildings, their walls dull with old paint, all dark and empty now. Including the one where Brit was going to have to spend the night.

Kind of ironic, she thought, keeping her eyes on the ground as she walked the final yards to the building's back entrance. Her fight with Mom and Dad had been all about not coming anywhere near this place they bought for a teen center. No way. But here she was.

She would probably be okay. As long as she didn't look up.

The realtor's lockbox still dangled from the dead fluorescent lamp beside the door. Her parents didn't know she knew the combination. The key was still inside it.

The key undid the lock easily. The door creaked. Only a little, though. Could the giant wriggly things on the rooftop even hear anything?

Brit peered inside. Grayblue squares glowed dimly on the floor where the city's faint light had funneled in via the high, dirty windows. The pale patches wavered like reflections. A real hallucination? No.

The floor was under water.

Brit stepped cautiously in. The linoleum beneath the rubber soles of her Converse shoes squelched as if it was wet, but at least she didn't hear her feet full-on splashing. Not deep enough, maybe? She shut the door and felt in her pack for her flashlight.

Crouching, she aimed the light low, hoping no one would see it. Nearby, the beige tiles she remembered from her first reluctant visit glittered only faintly, as if covered in sweat. But in the wide room's middle, the row of poles supporting its ceiling rose from a shallow pool.

As she walked around the room's edge, Brit's mood sank lower and lower. Tops, there was maybe half an inch of water anywhere, but it went almost from wall to wall. Not real comfortable to sleep in. Her bag would be soaked in no time, wherever she put it down.

Four doors led off the main room on its far side. The first opened on a closet. She felt its floor to be sure. Dripping wet. The second and third doors were locked. The outside key didn't work on them.

The fourth door was locked, too—but with the deadbolt's knob on *this* side. Behind it a stair climbed up to a dark landing.

Brit frowned. From what she remembered, this place had just one story. Arriving on the landing she looked up from there and saw that the stairs stopped at a metal fire door with a push bar for its handle.

A door onto the roof. Where an enormous tent full of worms waited.

She couldn't go there. Anyway, outside she'd be cold and, if the rain came back, just as wet as lying on the flooded floor below. With a sigh she scuffed back down to the landing. Tiny, but so was she. She unrolled her bag and fluffed it out, slipped inside. Her coat folded up into a big pillow. She tucked it under her head and waited.

The landing was concrete. Dry. Hard. Dad said it took the average person fourteen minutes to fall asleep. She waited some more. And some more. And some more.

She checked her watch and sure enough she'd stayed awake a lot longer than fourteen minutes. Maybe she needed more padding. She opened her coat up and put it under the bag. Now she didn't have a pillow—her pack was too lumpy, filled with pretend birthday presents. She shouldn't crush the cigars. That left—her lasagna! She must have dropped it somewhere— no use trying to figure out the exact spot now. But with nothing else to do she backtracked mentally anyway and decided she'd left the box balanced on the rim of a trashcan when she re-tied her shoelaces. Maybe she was too hungry to sleep.

Maybe it was too early: only eight, and she usually went to bed around nine on a school night.

She switched from cradling her head on her left arm to her right.

No use going back over the fight with Mom, either, thinking of what she should have said. Like, "Why don't you trust me? Why don't you believe me?" Like, "Just because all the other teenagers you deal with are on drugs doesn't mean I have the same problem." Like, "I am *not* insane!"

Instead, after a while, she'd given up saying anything. Talking wasn't going to do any good. Brit decided she was simply going to have to disappear. Actions spoke louder than words. She would take off; that way she'd miss school, miss the "counseling" appointment scheduled right afterwards, miss her parents picking her up from there to drag her along to the infested building they'd bought.

So how ridiculous was it that she'd wound up spending the night in the same building, practically right next to a worm nest after all, on her own? Alone? In the dark?

Well, coming here hadn't been her first idea. Or even her second.

The problem was, everyone in Seattle who was supposed to help kids knew her mom and dad. Now she had a chance to think, a bus or a train ride seemed like her best option. To Yakima or Spokane, or somewhere no one would look. Soon as it got light she'd walk to the station. Before school started, so she'd be less suspicious.

But if she was going to leave town early tomorrow morning she'd better get to sleep soon. She checked her watch again: 10:00. Past time. Her alarm would start beeping at 6:00. She put the watch back away in her pencil bag and zipped that in a pocket she never used so it would be harder to find and hit snooze. Shoved her pack a couple of stairs up so she'd have farther to reach for it. But she could still hear it ticking.

Except her watch was digital.

It didn't tick.

Had someone followed her in? How? She knew she'd locked the door. And there hadn't been any other way—she'd gone all around everywhere. Except for those two locked doors.

She pulled the pack back down to the landing and held it to her ear to be sure. Nothing. Let go of it and listened again. Louder, now, and faster. And coming from above—the opposite direction of whatever was behind the doors. And faster. And louder. Like a shower of rocks. Like a storm of hail—was that it? A storm? Maybe she should retreat to the ground floor for safety. A hurricane could rip an old building like this apart—there hadn't been any predictions of a storm that bad, though. Had there?

She needed to see. But the worms were up there. Did the noise come from them? What were they doing?

She could find out looking from the street. She put her shoes on and grabbed the key and her flashlight. She turned that off at the bottom of the stairs for a moment and immediately stepped in a stray puddle. Great.

Sticking near the wall she reached the front door without further mishap. And of course it was locked like she'd left it.

But the ticking noise was loud, even down here. She went out on the sidewalk and it was worse.

At first Brit couldn't see anything weird. The sky glowed a silvery gray with the city's ambient light; it was filled with low, slow-moving clouds—no! Those were the worms! She'd never seen them outside their tents before. What were they crawling on? Like ghosts in a movie they looked sort of see-through, rippling along what she could gradually make out as branch-like structures—and filmy-looking—leaves? Fainter than the worms themselves, the "leaves" shimmered in a way that made Brit's heart ache oddly, as if she was reading a sad love story.

What about that ticking noise, though, which she could hear all around now? It sounded tinier than the tiniest hail, and—she put her hands out to be certain—nothing was hitting her. Straining her eyes, Brit could finally see hundreds of minuscule white specks dropping from the worms. They bounced noiselessly off her skin and coat—and presumably her head—and clicked against the ground.

Experimentally she tried to crush some of them beneath her right Converse. Silence. Not even the soft scrape of a rubber sole on the cement. But when she lifted her foot she'd smashed the white specks beneath it to a powder, and an acrid smell wafted up to her from the pavement, like mildew. What—

On the street's other side a parked van lit up for a second as its door opened and shut. The brief light showed a navy coat; a long, pale ponytail; a round, pink face—Crofutt! He'd followed her somehow. Via those fireworks and sparklers he'd babbled about?

"Hey! This isn't a good place," he shouted across the road. "You really ought to come with me—"

Who cared how he'd found her? Brit ran back inside the building and slammed the door shut and locked it.

Crofutt kept shouting. "Dreams are dying back these days, and I think the reason for that's somewhere around here."

Her shoes were wetter than ever. And her socks. First chance she got—

"They're dying back. Something's killing them, something dangerous."

Dry socks and shoes. Clean underwear. She'd forgotten to—

"Are you listening? If you don't come out I'm going to call the cops."

"Go head!" Brit yelled back. What had he been raving about? Dreams dying back, like some kind of occult crop? "I've got a right to be here!" Well, she did, sort of—her parents had signed the mortgage papers yesterday. "What they gonna say bout you stalkin a underage girl?"

That shut him up. Only for a moment.

"I'll call anonymously," Crofutt amended. "You shouldn't stay here. Not here."

An anonymous tip? How quickly would the cops respond? She might get away before they came.

And go where?

"At least tell me what you saw?" the man asked.

"What I—" She ought to stop answering him. It only encouraged him to keep talking.

"You were looking up. What did you see?"

Well, this was one person who would probably believe what she said.

Brit described the tents, the worms, the leaves and branches. The rain of specks. When she was done it was quiet again. Except for the ticking.

"That explains a lot." Crofutt wasn't shouting anymore. His voice felt close, like he was leaning on the door.

"Explain what?"

Crofutt had it all figured out. He called Brit a "Visioner," and said her power was translating the ways of "non-physical entities" into "concrete, manipulable analogies." It boiled down to her boiling down demons, angels—and other things, things without names, all the things most people couldn't see or understand—to simpler forms. The worms ate dreams— that was what the leaves were. The specks were their—excrement.

And so on. It was the nearest anyone had come to making sense, assuming she truly wasn't crazy. Brit felt completely willing to listen to Crofutt—through the door.

"Say you right," she finally half-admitted. "These worms eatin up everybody's hopes an dreams till ain't none left?"

"Pretty much. Then *they'll* vanish—leave, starve, however you lay out the concept. I've seen the effects of the cycle over and over—the sixties, the eighties—a lot of innocent people got hurt."

"I can look after myself okay," Brit assured him. Maybe he wasn't a creeper after all.

She still wasn't about to let him in, though. He could prove that another time, in the daylight, around other people.

And part of what he said didn't quite compute—"I can make these what you callin 'entities' do like I want by how I see em?"

"Sort of; what they do also influences how they appear to you—"

"Awright. So what these worms turn into after they eat up everyone dreams? Some kinda gigantic moth?"

"Hmmmm. Could be."

Images of Japanese monster movies flitted in and out of Brit's head. She let them come and go. What she really needed to figure out was how to keep the worms from stripping all the silver dream leaves from people's thought vines—that was what she had decided to name the translucent branches curling through the night: thought vines. Which could belong to anybody. They were tangled up but there must be a way to trace them to their roots, to their sources, which could be anyone. Even her parents. Even her.

Wet and hungry and tired—that didn't matter. She had left home to find a way to convince Mom and Dad that she wasn't a whack job. That she knew what she was doing. Which meant she had to know it.

She stopped answering Mr. Crofutt's questions, and after a while he stopped asking them. She walked straight across the puddle to the stairway where her stuff was, not caring anymore how soaked she got. Because of the idea forming in her achy mind.

If the "entities" had to act like worms once she'd made them take that shape, they had to die like them. Die like worms.

She remembered from her sixth-grade science report how to kill tent caterpillars. You could cut down their nests and grind them to a pulp with heavy boots.

Brit didn't have boots that big. Nobody did.

You could burn them out.

Could the nests only she saw catch fire? And if they did would the flames spread and burn down her parents' building? Would the fire she set burn her to death?

She rolled up her sleeping bag and stuffed it in the pack. She pulled out her watch. Midnight. A long, long time till morning. Maybe she'd go home. Slog over to the Westin and find a cab. That'd be a laugh. She wouldn't have accomplished anything except to piss off Mom and Dad.

She wasn't scared. She climbed the rest of the way up and opened the door.

The roof was flat and covered in gravel. Brit scrunched over to the edge where the tent stuck up, betting it would be empty. Sure enough, the webbed walls were blank. No writhing. All the worms were out devouring dreams.

She took her box knife from her pants pocket and slashed at the nest's nearest side, but the knife sank in past its hilt and left no trace, while her hand wouldn't penetrate the webbing at all, not even a fraction of an inch. She remembered one of the rules for magic in the torn-up book of a runaway staying at their house: you should never use the same tools for mundane and spiritual tasks.

Brit cut things open with her box knife all the time. Mundane things. That left the cigar trimmer.

She hadn't really been going to give it to Dad. She got it out of the pack and the shop's bag: a pair of scissors with short, round blades. They made a nice, neat hole in the tent's side.

She pushed her head into the hole before she could think too much about what she was doing. It was awful anyway. She cut and cut and cut, past layers and layers of webs. Like squirming deeper and deeper inside a haunted house. Arms, shoulders, chest, stomach—she wanted to throw up. Here came that salty taste and the extra spit squirting into her mouth.

She wiggled back out again and breathed through her mouth, hard. And heard a siren in the street below. That was the goad she needed. She grabbed up her pack and went back in the tent. Completely.

The siren died away in the distance. So Crofutt hadn't turned her in after all. When she was sure they really weren't coming to get her she wiggled back out again. Drizzle had begun to fall while she shuddered and gagged inside; she actually thought about staying inside the nest all night.

But she had no guarantee the worms would stay out eating till sunrise.

Instead she sat cross-legged on the cold, damp gravel. She took out and unrolled the bag and half unzipped it so it lay like a puffy, down mantilla on her head and neck and shoulders, and formed a little shelter on either side of her. She laid out her tools underneath it: the butterfly lighter, the six fat cigars, ends ritually trimmed, ready to burn.

Then she waited for the worms' return. It wouldn't do any good to destroy an empty nest.

She tried not to sleep but dozed off despite the cold and discomfort. Obviously that meant she wasn't one bit scared of the morning. The red dawn. The horrible vibrations shaking the nest as its denizens poured back inside, ignoring—as she'd hoped they would—the slits and slices she'd made in their home.

Drawing on it as deeply as she could, Brit lit the first cigar. When it was going strong she reversed it and put the glowing end inside her mouth, bending to blow a stream of fragrant smoke into the nest's heart.

At first the worms stirred at the intrusion, blind heads seeking nonexistent fresh air, but by the fourth cigar they settled down where they were. To rest. The fifth. To sleep. The sixth. To loosen the grips of their hooked legs, fall to the tent's floor, and die.

She tossed the mantilla over the hole she'd used, changing it to a shroud.

Dizzy and nauseated, Brit struggled to her numb feet. Up, up, up: light and air and hope towered height upon height into heaven. The sun rose clear of a band of clouds. Too bright to the south and east to tell how many more nests awaited destruction.

She stumbled to the roof's other end. Her shadow stretched north across the city. Beyond it lay her parents and her home. Warmth. Blessed dryness. Anger, undoubtedly. But she would apologize. Even go to the psychiatrist a few times if that was what they wanted. She'd tell them that she'd been wrong, that they were right. That she wasn't scared anymore, because there had never been anything to be scared of.

She would tell them where she'd spent the night. And let them think they understood.

~

Nisi Shawl's collection *Filter House* was a 2009 James Tiptree, Jr., Award winner; her stories have been published in *Strange Horizons*, *Asimov's Science Fiction Magazine*, and in anthologies including *The Year's Best Fantasy and Horror* and both volumes of the *Dark Matter* series. Shawl's Belgian Congo historical fantasy/steampunk novel *Everfair* will be published in August 2016 by Tor Books.

~

*An immortal duke is dead—at least for now, perhaps for good—and the
magic power he stole centuries ago is released into the many labyrinthine
streets of exotic Copper Downs.*

A Water Matter

Jay Lake

The Duke of Copper Downs had stayed dead.

So far.

That thought prompted the Dancing Mistress to glance around her at
the deserted street. Something in the corner of her eye or the lantern of
her dreams was crying out a message. Just as with any of her kind, it was
difficult to take her by surprise. Her sense of the world around her was
very strong. Even in sleep, her folk did not become so inert and vulnerable
as humans or most animals did. And her people had lived among men for
generations, after all. Some instincts never passed out of worth.

*His Grace is not going to come clawing up through the stones at my
feet*, she told herself firmly. Her tail remained stiff and prickly, trailing
gracelessly behind her in a parody of alarm.

The city continued to be restive. A pall of smoke hung low in the
sky, and the reek of burning buildings dogged every breath. The harbor
had virtually emptied, its shipping steering away from the riots and the
uncontrolled militias were all that remained of the Ducal Guard after the
recent assassination. The streets were an odd alternation of deserted and
crowded. Folk seemed unwilling to come out except in packs. If chance
emptied a square or a cobbled city block, it stayed empty for hours. The
hot, heavy damp did nothing to ease tempers.

At the moment, she strode alone across the purple-and-black
flagstones of the Greenmarket area. The smell of rotting vegetables was

strong. The little warehouses were all shuttered. Even the ever-present cats had found business elsewhere.

She hurried onward. The message that had drawn her onto the open streets had been quite specific as to time and place. Her sense of purpose was so strong she could feel the blurring tug of the hunt in her mind. A trap, that; the hunt was always a trap for her people, especially when they walked among men.

Wings whirred overhead in a beat far too fast for any bird save the bright tiny hummers that haunted the flowering vines of the temple district. She did not even look up.

The Dancing Mistress found at a little gateway set in the middle of a long stucco wall that bordered close on Dropnail Lane in the Ivory Quarter. It was the boundary of some decaying manse, a perimeter wall marking out a compound that had long been cut up into a maze of tiny gardens and hovels. A village of sorts flourished under the silent oaks, amid which the great house rotted, resplendent and abandoned. She'd been here a few times to see a woman of her people whose soul path was the knowledge of herbs and simples. But always, she'd come through the servants' gate, a little humped arch next to the main entrance that faced onto Whitetop Street.

This gateway was different. It clearly did not fit the wall in which it was set. Black marble pilasters were embedded in the fading ochre plaster of the estate's wall. The darkness within tried to pull her onward.

She shook away the sense of compulsion. In firm control of her own intentions, the Dancing Mistress slowly reached to touch the metal grate. Though the air was warm, the black iron was cold enough to sting her fingers down to the claw sheaths.

The way was barred, but it was not locked. The Dancing Mistress pushed on through.

The dark gate opened into a tangle of heavy vines. Ivy and wisteria strangled a stand of trees which had been reduced to pale, denuded corpses. Fungus grew in mottled shelves along the lower reaches of the bare trunks, and glistened in the mat of leaves and rot that floored the little grove. There was a small altar of black stone amid the pallid trunks, where only shadows touched the ground. An irregular block of ice gleamed atop the altar. It shed questing coils of vapor into the spring-warm air.

Her folk had no name for themselves—they were just people, after all. And it was one of her people who had written the note she'd found strung by spider webs against the lintel of her rented room. She had been able to tell by the hand of the writing, the scent on the page, the faint trail of a soul flavored with meadow flowers.

No one she knew, though, not by hand nor scent nor soul. While the Dancing Mistress could not readily count the full number of her folk in Copper Downs, it was still a matter of dozens amid the teeming humans in their hundreds and thousands.

This altar freezing amid the bones of trees was nothing of her people's.

A man emerged from the shadows without moving, as if the light had found him between one moment and the next. He was human—squat, unhandsome, with greasy, pale hair that twisted in hanks down his shoulder. His face had been tattooed with fingerprints, as though some god or spirit had reached out and grasped him too hard with a grip of fire. His broad body was wrapped in leather and black silk as greasy as his hair. Dozens of small blades slipped into gaps in his leather, each crusted in old blood.

A shaman, then, who sought the secrets of the world in the frantic pounding hearts of prey small and large. Only the space around his eyes was clean, pale skin framing a watery gaze that pierced her like a diamond knife.

"You walk as water on rock." He spoke the tongue of her people with only the smallest hint of an accent. That was strange in its own right. Far stranger, that she, come of a people who had once hunted dreams on moonless nights, could have walked within two spans of him without noticing.

Both those things worried her deeply.

"I walk like a woman in the city," she said in the tongue of the Stone Coast people. The Dancing Mistress knew as a matter of quiet pride that she had no accent herself.

"In truth," he answered, matching her speech. His Petraean held the same faint hint of somewhere else. He was no more a native here than she.

"Your power is not meant to overmatch such as me," she told him quietly. At the same time, she wondered if that were true. Very, very few humans knew the tongue of the people.

He laughed at that, then broke his gaze. "I would offer you wine and bread, but I know your customs in that regard. Still, your coming to meet me is a thing well done."

She ignored the courtesy. "That note did not come from your hand."

"No." His voice was level. "Yet I sent it."

The Dancing Mistress shivered. He implied power over someone from the high meadows of her home. "Your note merely said to meet, concerning a water matter." That was one of the greatest obligations one of her people could lay upon another.

"The Duke remains dead," he said.

She shivered at the echo of her earlier thought. "The power of his passing has left a blazing trail for those who can see it."

"You aver that he will not return."

The man shrugged away the implicit challenge. She had not asked his name, for her people did not give theirs, but that did nothing to keep her from wondering who he was. "Soon it will not matter if he tries to return or not," he said. "His power leaches away, to be grasped or lost in the present moment. Much could be done now. Good, ill, or indifferent, this is the time for boldness."

She leaned close, allowing her claws to flex. He would know what that signified. "And where do *I* fit into your plans, *man*?"

"You have the glow of him upon you," he told her. "His passing marked you. I would know from you who claimed him, who broke him open. That one—mage, warrior or witch—holds the first and greatest claim on his power."

Green!

The girl-assassin was fled now across the water, insofar as the Dancing Mistress knew. She was suddenly grateful for that small mercy. "It does not matter who brought low the Duke of Copper Downs," she whispered. "He is gone. The world moves on. New power will rise in his place, new evil will follow."

Another laugh, a slow rumble from his black-clad belly. "Power will always rise. The right hand grasping it in the right moment can avoid much strife for so many. I thought to make some things easier and more swift with your aid—for the sake of everyone's trouble."

"You presume too much," she told him.

"*Me?*" His grin was frightening. "You look at my skin and think to judge my heart. Humans do not have soul paths as your people do. You will not scent the rot you so clearly suspect within me."

The Dancing Mistress steeled herself. There was no way she could stand alone against this one, even if she had trained in the arts of power. "Good or ill, I will say no more upon it."

"Hmm." He tugged at his chin. "I see you have a loyalty to defend." "It is not just loyalty." Her voice was stiff despite her self-control, betraying her fear of him. "Even if I held such power within my grasp, I would have no reason to pass it to you." "By your lack of action, you have already handed the power to whomever can pluck it forth. Be glad it was only me come calling." He added in her tongue, *I know the scent of a water matter. I will not argue from the tooth.*"

"*Nor will I bargain from the claw.*" She turned and stalked toward the cold gate, shivering in her anger.

"'Ware, woman," he called after her, then laughed again. "We are not friends, but we need not be enemies. I would still rather have your aid in this matter, and not your opposition. Together we can spare much suffering and trouble."

She slipped between the black stone gateposts and into the street beyond, refusing for the sake of the sick fear that coiled in the bottom of her gut to hurry on her way.

There was no one out in the late afternoon, normally a time when the squares and boulevards would have been thronged, even in the quieter, richer quarters.

She walked with purpose, thinking furiously even as she watched for trouble. That shaman must have come from some place both rare and distant. There were tribes and villages of humans in every corner of the world of which she'd heard. Men lived in the frigid shadows high up in the Blue Mountains where the very air might freeze on the coldest nights, and amid the fire-warm plains of Selistan beyond the sea, and in the boundless forests of the uttermost east. Not to mention everywhere in between.

He was from somewhere in between, to be sure—the Leabourne Hills, perhaps, or one of the other places her people lived when they had not yet done as she had, drifting away to dwell among the cities of men. There was no other way for him to speak their tongue, to know of water matters, to command whatever binding or influence or debt had brought her the note with which he'd summoned her.

The Dancing Mistress had no illusions of her own importance, but it had been her specifically that he'd wanted. It seemed likely the man had counted her as the Duke's assassin.

That was troublesome. If one person made that deduction, however flawed it was, others could do the same. *A fear for another time,* she told herself. Had he learned her people's magics the same way the late Duke of Copper Downs had? By theft?

A sickening idea occurred to her. *Perhaps this greasy man had been an agent of the Duke.*

As if summoned by the thought, a group of Ducal guards spilled out of an alley running between the walled gardens of wealth.

She happened to be walking close along the deserted curb just across from them. They stopped, staring at her. The Dancing Mistress didn't break stride. *Act like you are in charge. Do not fear them.* Still, she risked a glance.

The leader, or at least the one with the biggest sword, had a fine tapestry wrapped across his shoulders as a cloak. Looters. Though they wore Ducal uniforms, their badges were torn off.

"Hey, kitty," one of them called, smacking his lips.

Corner, she thought. *There's a corner up ahead. Many of these houses are guarded. They wouldn't risk open violence here.*

Her common sense answered: *Why not?* They had certainly risked open looting.

Colors were beginning to flow in the corner of her eye. The hunt tugged at her. That ritual was anchored deep in the shared soul of her people, a violent power long rejected in favor of a quiet, peaceful life. The Dancing Mistress shook off the tremor in her claws as she turned a walled corner onto Alicorn Straight, passing under the blank-eyed gaze of a funerary statue.

They followed, laughing and joking too loudly among themselves. Weapons and armor rattled behind her. Not quite chasing, not quite leaving her alone.

The towers of the Old Wall rose amid buildings a few blocks to her east. If she could get there before the deserters jumped her, she might have a chance. Once past those crumbling landmarks, she would be in a much more densely populated and notably less wealthy area. In the Dancing Mistress' experience, aid was far more likely from those who had nothing than from those who held everything in their hands. The rich did not see anyone but their own glittering kind, while the poor understood what it meant to lose everything.

"Oi, catkin," one of the guards shouted. "Give us a lick, then."

Their pace quickened.

Once more colors threatened to flow. Her claws twitched in their sheathes. She would not do this. The people did not hunt, especially not in the cities of men. Walking alone, the gestalt of the hunt had no use, and when fighting by herself against half a dozen men, the subtle power it gave meant nothing.

They would have her down, hamstrings cut, and be at their rape before she could tear out one throat.

Speed was all she had left. Every yard closer they came was a measure of that advantage lost. The Dancing Mistress broke into a dead run. The guards followed like dogs on a wounded beggar, shouting in earnest, hup-hup-hupping in their battle language.

Still the street was empty.

She cut across the pavers, heading for Shrike Alley, which would take her to the Old Wall and the Broken Gate. There was no one, *no one*. How could she have been so stupid?

Fast as she was, at least one of the men behind her was a real sprinter. She could hear him gaining, somehow even chuckling as he ran. The Dancing Mistress lengthened her stride, but his spear butt reached from behind to tangle her ankles and she went down to a head-numbing crack against the cobbles.

The guard stood above her, grinning through several days of dark beard and the sharp scent of man sweat. "Never had me one of you before," he said, dropping away his sword belt.

She kicked up, hard, but he just jumped away laughing. His friends were right behind him with blades drawn and spears ready. *Seven on one,* she thought despairing. She would fight, but they would only break her all the faster for it.

The first man collapsed, stunned, his trousers caught around his knees. A second yelled and spun around. The Dancing Mistress needed nothing more than that to spur her to her opportunity.

There was small, small distance between dance and violence. Controlled motion, prodigious strength, and endless hours of practice fueled both arts. She stepped through a graceful series of spins, letting the edges of the hunt back in as her clawed kicks took two more of the guards behind the knees.

The shaman was on the other side of them, grinning broadly as he fought with an already-blooded yatagan. His movements held a shimmer edge that was far too familiar.

He gambled on me joining the counter-attack, she thought. It did not matter why. They made common cause in the moment, and tore another man's hip from its socket. The last three deserters scrambled away before turning to run hell for leather down the street.

The Dancing Mistress had never thought to see a human who could take on even the smallest aspect of the hunt. "I should have expected more of you." Her rescuer's voice was scarcely shuddering from the effort of battle.

She kept her own voice hard, saying in the tongue of the people, "*This does not bind us with water.*"

"*We are already bound. Think on what I have asked.*" He nodded, then strode purposeful away among the silent houses of the rich.

Shaking, the Dancing Mistress trotted toward the Old Wall, away from the groaning, weeping men.

She made her way to the Dockmarket. That area was quiet as well, given that the harbor was as empty as it ever had been in the decades since the

Year of Ice. Still, there were some humans about. Though the booths were shuttered and the alleys quiet as the Temple Quarter, the taverns stayed open. The breweries of Copper Downs had operated through flood, fire, pestilence and famine for more years than anyone had bothered to count. Political turmoil and a shortage of the shipping trade were hardly going to stop people from drinking.

There was a place off the alley known as Middleknife (or the Second Finger, depending on who you asked) behind a narrow door. It was as nameless as the people it served—mostly her folk, truth be told, but also a scattering of others who did not pass without a sidewise cast of human eyes elsewhere in Copper Downs. Many races had come out of the countries that rose skyward to the north in order to live in the shadows of the human polities along the Stone Coast.

The Dancing Mistress had always scorned solaces such as this. Still, she needed to be among her people tonight. There few enough places for that, none of them part of her daily life.

She slipped inside with a clench riding hard in her gut.

No smoke of tabac or hennep roiled within. No dice clattered, no darts flew. Only a dozen or so of the people in quiet ones, twos, and threes. They sat at tables topped by deep stoneware bowls in which forlorn lilies spun slowly, sipping pale liquid the consistency of pine sap from tiny cups that matched the great bowls. The place smelled of water, rock and trees.

Much like where she had been born.

She also saw a very narrow-bodied blue man in pangolin-skin armor alone at a table, crouched in a chair with his knees folded nearly to his chin. Though he did not look to weigh eight stone, she thought he must be seven feet tall at the least. There were even a few people who might have been human.

The barkeep, one of her people, glanced briefly at her. He then took a longer look before nodding slightly, a gesture they had all picked up in the city. She read it well enough.

Between any two of her people there was a scent, of soul and body, that once exchanged could not easily be forgotten. Much could be read there, in a language which did not admit of lies. This one was not sib-close, nor enemy-distant, but she saw the path of trust.

"You work in the Factor's Quarter," he said in Petraean.

"I did," she admitted. She'd trained slave girls and the forgotten younger daughters of rising houses. Sometimes they were one and the same. "Before all things fell just lately." And therein lay her story, the scent the shaman had been tracking.

"In any case, welcome." He brought out a wooden plate, as tradition dictated turned by someone's hand on a foot-powered lathe. There he spilled dried flower petals from a watered silk sack, three colors of sugar, and a trickle from a tiny cut-crystal decanter. Their hands crossed, brushing together as each of them dragged a petal through sugar and lifewater.

The Dancing Mistress touched sweetness to her lips and smiled sadly. This was what the traditional feast of welcome had degenerated into, here in the labyrinthine streets of Copper Downs. Even so, they were now opened to each other for a moment.

The barkeep nodded again then brushed his fingers across hers, releasing them both. "You are of Copper Downs, but you are not one of my regulars. What brings you here? The need for a scent of home?"

"A water matter." She sighed. "A difficult one, I am afraid."

He stiffened, the fur of his neck bristling slightly as his scent strengthened. "Whom?"

"A man. A *human* man. Not of the Stone Coast." She shifted languages. *"He spoke our tongue."*

"He knew of water matters?"

"It was he who named this business. He was looking for the . . .agent . . . behind the Duke's fall." She paused, choosing her words carefully against revealing too much of her complicity in the Duke's death. *"This is not my soul path. I do not bind power, nor do I loose it. But the thread came to me all the same. And this one knows far too much of us."* Her voice dipped. *"I even glimpsed the hunt within him."*

"I do not accuse you of an untruth, but that has never been. I would not have thought to have seen it." The barkeep looked past her shoulder, as one of the people often did when seeking to avoid embarrassment. *"There is a rumor that one of us was the undoing of the late Duke. Is that what this water matter follows?"*

"*In a sense, yes,*" the Dancing Mistress admitted. "But I was never in the palace," she added in Petraean.

"Of course not." He thought a moment. "Do you seek aid in this? Or is this your fate to follow alone?"

"I do not yet see my fate. I do not think this is it." She sighed, another human gesture. "I doubt my ability to handle this well, and I fear the consequences of failure."

"Abide then at the empty table near the hearth. Someone will come." He dipped into a slow bow straight from the high meadows of their birth. "I will see to it."

The Dancing Mistress stared into the cold fireplace. There were no ashes, though there was sufficient soot blackening the bricks to testify to regular use in colder months. The darkness before her brought the man in the shadows very much to mind.

He'd offered to spare the city much suffering. She knew that the Duke's loosened power was like lightning looking for a path to the ground. Her hope, shared with Federo and the others who had conspired with her, had been to weather that storm until the ancient bonds relaxed. If the city was lucky, it would vanish like mist on a summer morning. Then her people's centuries-long part in the madness of the Duke's tyranny would be over.

The shaman had other ideas about that power, but even so he had not set himself up as her enemy. Except he knew too much. He knew their tongue, their ways, the hunt.

He was a threat to her kind. Anything he did in Copper Downs would seem to be the work of her people to the priests and the wizard-engineers who infested this city like lice. He might as well slit all their throats one by one.

I arranged to kill a Duke so that we might reclaim our power, she thought. *What is one more man?* She knew the answer to that: no more than another, then another, until her soul path was slick with blood.

Once more the hunt pulled at her, bending the light at the edges of her vision. Long ago in the high meadows when her people foraged or fought, they could slip their thoughts and deeds together. A hunt was a group working as neither one nor another but all together, as termites will hollow out a tree or ants ford a river. What one heard, all heard; what another touched, all felt. Deep into the hunt, leaderless and conjoined, there was none to call a halt to slaughter, none to direct their steps, and so with the power of their mesh-mind the people could become like a fire in the forest.

They had given it up long ago, save in most extreme need. There was too much violence at their command, too much power. She had never heard of the hunt being cried within the walls of a human city. If these pasty, pale folk even suspected what her kind could do when stirred to mortal effort, they would be lucky to be only driven from the gates.

Her claws slipped free again. Her blood thrummed in her veins. The Dancing Mistress was afraid of what this man had stirred her to. And how could he not know of the hunt and what might happen?

He must know, she realized. *He'd just counted on finding the power first.* That man took chances, just as he'd attacked her assailants from behind, counting on her to rise and join into the fight. He gambled with lives, hers and his.

Interrupting her thought, one of the people sat down next to her. A stoneware cup was quickly placed before him. Moments later a woman of the people sat across. She briefly met the Dancing Mistress' eyes, then studied the lilies wilting in the stoneware bowl. Another soon came to fill their table. More cups followed.

So they were four. She took a sip of wine fermented from the flowers and fir sap of the high meadows.

The woman spoke, finally. She had scent of cinnamon about her. *"You are said to bear a water matter which has a claim upon all the people."*

"Yes," said the Dancing Mistress quietly. *"This thing tears at my heart, but there is a catamount among us."*

"I would not question your judgment." It was the taller of the men, who smelled of sage and tree bark. *"But I would know this threat."*

She gave him a long slow look. To raise the pursuit she meant to bring to bear, she must tell them the truth. Yet any word of her involvement in the Duke's death could mean her own.

Still, there was far more at stake than her small life.

"*There is a man. A human man*," she amended. "*He knows our ways better than do many of our own. He pursues a great evil. If he succeeds, the return of the Duke will be upon us all. If he fails, the price may well be laid at our door.*"

She went on to explain in as much detail as she could, laying out the events of the day and her conclusions from it.

For a while, there was silence. The four of them sipped their wine and dipped into the same stream of thoughts. It was a gestalt, edging toward the mesh-mind of the hunt. It was the way her people prepared themselves for deep violence.

"*And once again, death brings death.*" That was the shorter of the men, the fourth in their hunt, whom she already thought of as "the glumper" for the small noises he made in his throat as he sipped at the wine. "*If we send this shaman to follow his duke, who's to say there will not be more to follow him.*"

Sage-man spoke up, in Petraean now. "This is so soon. The Duke is yet freshly dead. He did not expect to pass. There cannot already be a great conspiracy to return him to life and power."

"I do not know it for a conspiracy," said the Dancing Mistress. "He stalks me, seeing me for the bait to call this power back. That does not mean he has sung for my life, but I cannot think he will scruple to claim it in his pursuit." She flashed to the uneasy memory of the man laying into her attackers, grinning over the bloody blade of his yatagan. He played some game that ran neither along nor against her soul path, crosswise as it might otherwise be.

Still, they all knew, as everyone of the people did, that the Duke of Copper Downs had stolen their magic, generations past. There were stories and more stories, details that varied in every telling, but since that time the numbers and power of her people—never great to start with—had diminished, while the Duke had whiled away centuries on his throne.

That someone was hunting power through the Dancing Mistress now, so soon after the Duke's fall, meant old, old trouble returning. The man being a high country shaman with too much knowledge of their kind was only a seal on that trouble.

The cinnamon-woman broke the renewed silence. "You have the right of it. If we stop the Duke's man now, we may crush the seed before the strangler vine has a chance to grow."

The glumper stared up from the cup of wine clutched his hands. *"Crushing is not our way."*

"Not now." The cinnamon-woman looked around, catching their eyes. "Once . . . "

"Once we were warriors," said the Dancing Mistress. "We called storms from the high crags." They all knew those stories, too. "If we cry the hunt now, we will spare lives."

"And what do we give up in following your plan?" asked the glumper. *"The old ways are gone for good reason."*

The Dancing Mistress felt anger rising within her, a core of fire beneath the cool sense of purpose she'd hewn to all her life. *"They are gone because of what the Duke took from us."*

He gave her a long stare. *"Did you ever think we might have given our power away with a purpose?"*

Even in argument, the mesh-mind was knitting together, the edges of the room gleaming and sharpening. The Dancing Mistress set down her cup. *"It is time,"* she said in their language. *"We will find this shaman and stop his scheming, before he drags all of us down into darkness."*

The moon glowed faintly through the low clouds, but the shadows outflanked the light at every turn. Torches burned at compound gates while lamps hung at intersections and in the squares. The nighttime streets of Copper Downs were streaked with smears of heat and scent.

The hunt slid through the evening like a single animal with four bodies. Her vision was complex, edges gleaming sharp at all distances and ranges. Odors told stories she could never read on her own, about the passage of time and the sweat of fear, passion, even the flat, watery smell of ennui. The very feel of the air on her skin as she ran had been magnified fourfold. She saw every door, every hiding place, every mule or person they passed, in terms of force and danger and claws moving close to the speed of thought.

The sheer *power* of the hunt was frightening in its intoxication.

They slipped through the city like a killing wind, heading toward the

Ivory Quarter and the black gate through which she'd passed before. She'd never run so fast, so effortlessly, with such purpose.

Why had her people not stayed like this always? she wondered. All the logic of civilization aside, surely this was what they'd been made for.

It seemed only moments before they'd crossed the city to the old ochre walls of the compound, now glowing in the moonlight. The ancient stucco seemed to suck the life of the world into itself, though the trees beyond and above the wall practically shouted to her expanded sensorium.

Three times in as many minutes they circled around the shadowed walls, and found no sign of the shaman's black gate. Not even a significant crack where it might have stood.

There was power aplenty in the world, but it was not generally spent so freely as this man had done. Opening that gate was the magical equivalent of a parlor trick: flashy, showy, a splash of self such as a child with a paintpot might make. But costly, very costly. The greatest power lay in subtlety, misdirection, the recondite support and extension of natural processes.

It was here, she thought, and the hunt took her meaning from the flick of her eyes, the set of her shoulders, the stand of her fur. They believed her. She knew that just as they'd known her meaning.

Together they drifted back to the main gate. It had stood propped open years before the Dancing Mistress had come to Copper Downs, but no one ever passed through it. The squatters who lived within used the servants' gate beside the main gate, and so observed the blackletter law of the city even as they had built their illegal homes upon the grounds. The trail of their passing back and forth glowed in the eyes of the hunt. It was human, but there was something of the people mixed in with it.

The hunt slipped through the narrow door one by one, their steps like mist on the furze within. The path followed the old carriage drive through a stand of drooping willows now rotten and overgrown with wisteria. Trails led off between the curtains of leaves and vines toward the hidden homes beyond.

There was no scent to follow here. The shaman might as well have been made of fog.

A thought passed between the hunt like breeze bending the flowers of a meadow: *An herbalist lives here, a woman of their people.*

She felt her claws stiffen. The wisdom of the hunt stirred, the mesh-mind reading clues where ordinary eyes saw only shadow.

Is the Duke in fact still dead?

It was the same question she'd almost asked herself on her way to this place the first time.

Sage-man twitched aside a mat of ivy and stepped into the darker shadows. A brighter trail well marked with the traces of one of her people led within. *Of course, cloaked in the magic of her people the shaman could also have left his tracks so.*

The Dancing Mistress nodded the rest of her hunt through—cinnamon-woman and the glumper—and followed last.

The hut was a shambles. Jars shattered, sheaves scattered, what little furniture there had been now smashed to splinters. While there didn't seem to be any quantity of blood, the stink of fear hung heavy in the close air, overlaying even the intense jumble of odors from scattered herbs and salves.

The glumper trailed his fingers through the leaves and powders and shattered ceramic fragments on the floor. He sniffed, sending a tingle through the Dancing Mistress' nose. *"I might have thought one of us had done this thing."* He had yet to speak a word of Petraean within her hearing. *"But knowing to search, I find there has been a human here as well. Wearing leather and animal fat. He first took her unawares, then he took her away."*

The shaman, the Dancing Mistress thought. Inside the mesh-mind, they shared her next question. *What path did he follow now?*

The hunt had the shaman's scent, and the herbalist's besides. It was enough.

A warm, damp wind blew off the water to carry the reek of tide rot and the distant echo of bells. Even the rogue squads of the Ducal guard seemed to be lying low, doubtless surrounded by wine butts, and hired boys wearing slitted skirts and long wigs. The city was deserted, waiting under the smell of old fires and dark magic.

That was well enough, the Dancing Mistress thought with the independent fragment of herself that still held its own amid the flow of the mesh-mind. It would not do for her people to be seen gliding over the cobbles at preternatural speed, moving silent as winter snowfall.

The hunt's grip on shaman's scent and herbalist's soul path was sufficient, even when running through fire-reek and the alley-mouth stench of dead dogs. They moved together, heeding the Dancing Mistress' will, following the glumper's trace on the scent, using cinnamon-woman's eyes, sage-man's hearing. Most of all they pursued the dread that stalked the night, the banked fires of the hunt flaring only to seek a single hearth within Copper Downs.

They followed a dark river of fear and purpose into the Temple Quarter. That had long been the quietest section of the city. Once it must have brawled and boiled with worshippers, for the buildings there were as great as any save the Ducal Palace. In the centuries of the Duke's rule, the gods of the city had grown withered and sour as winter fruit. People left their coppers in prayer boxes near the edges of the district and walked quickly past.

Even with the gods fallen on hard times, locked in the embrace of neglect and refusal, no one had ever found the nerve to tear down those decaying walls and replace the old houses of worship with anything newer and more mundane.

The hunt pursued the scent down Divas Street, along the edge of the Temple Quarter, before leading into the leaf-strewn cobwebs of Mithrail Street. They bounded into those deeper shadows where the air curdled to black water and the dead eyes of the Duke seemed to glitter within every stygian crevice.

They came to a quivering halt with claws spread wide before a narrow door of burnt oak bound with iron and ebony laths. Darkness leaked from behind it, along with a fire scent and the tang of burning fat.

The man-smell was strong here. They were obviously close to the shaman's lair, where the cloak of the people's power grew thin over his layered traces of daily use—sweat and speech and the stink of human urine. The doorway reeked of magic, inimical purpose and the thin, screaming souls of animals slit from weasand to wodge for their particles of wisdom.

That was his weakness, the Dancing mistress realized, surfacing farther from the hunt for a moment even as those around her growled.

He used the people's power only as a cover, nothing more. The shaman could build a vision of the world from a thousand bright, tiny eyes, but animals never saw more than they understood. Her people knew that to be a fool's path to wisdom.

Now he worked his blood magic on the herbalist, summoning the Dancing Mistress. He had drawn her here to cut her secrets from her. The mesh-mind overtook her once more in the rush of angry passion at that thought, and together the hunt brushed someone's claw-tipped hand on the cool wooden planks of the door.

"Come," the shaman called. His voice held confident expectation of her.

The hunt burst in.

The four of them were a surprise to the shaman. They could see that in his face. But his power was great as well. The ancient stone walls of this abandoned temple kitchen were crusted with ice. The herbalist hung by ropes from a high ceiling beam, her body shorn and torn as he'd bled her wisdom cut by cut, the way he'd bled it from a thousand tiny beasts of the field.

He rose from his fire, kicked a brazier and coals toward them, and gathered the air into daggers of ice even as the claws of the hunt spread across the room.

Though they called the old powers of their people, none of them had ever trained to stand in open battle. Their purpose was strong, but only the Dancing Mistress could move below a slicing blade or land a strike upon a briefly unprotected neck.

If not for their number they would have been cut down without thought. If not for the shaman's need to capture an essence from the Dancing Mistress he might have blown them out like candles. She knew then that he had set the thugs upon her that day so he could render aid, only to draw her in to him now, when suasion had failed him.

The fight came to fast-moving claws against restrained purpose. His ice made glittering edges that bent the vision of the mesh-mind. The blood of his sacrifices confused their scent. He moved, as he had on the street that day, with the brutal grace of one raised to war, working his magic even as he wielded his yatagan. The glumper's chest was laid open.

Cinnamon-woman had her ear shorn off. Sage-man's thought were flayed by a dream of mountain fire that slipped through the mesh-mind.

But for every round of blows the hunt took, they landed at least one in return. Claws raked the shaman's cheek with the sound of roses blooming. A kick traced its arc in blurred colors on their sight to snap bones in his left hand. A brand was shoved still burning brightly sour into his hair, so the grease there smoldered and his spells began to crack with the distraction of the pain.

The hunt moved in for the kill.

The Dancing Mistress once more emerged from the blurred glow of the hunt to find herself with claws set against the shaman's face. The cinnamon-woman twisted his right arm from his shoulder. She looked up at the herbalist, who dangled bleeding like so much meat in the slaughterhouse, and thought, *What are we now?* "Wait," she shouted, and with the pain of forests dying tore herself free from the mesh-mind.

Cinnamon-woman stared, blood streaming from the stump of her ear. The look sage-man gave the Dancing Mistress from his place bending back the shaman's legs would have burned iron. Their mouths moved in unison, the mesh-mind croaking out the words, "He does not deserve to live!"

"He does not have a right to our power," she countered. "But we cannot judge who should live and who should die."

The shaman bit the palm of her hand, his tongue darting to lick the blood, to suck her down to some last, desperate magic.

Steeling herself, the Dancing Mistress leaned close. Her claws were still set in his face. "I will take your wisdom as you have taken the wisdom of so many others. But I shall let you live to know what comes of such a price."

"Wait," he screamed through her enclosing palm. "You do not underst—"

With a great, terrible heave, she tore his tongue out with her claws. "We will not have the Duke back," the Dancing Mistress whispered venomously. She slit into him, plucking and cutting slivers from his liver and lights. The hunt kept the shaman pinned tight until blood loss and fear erased his resolve. Then the remainder of mesh-mind collapse. The cinnamon-woman began to tend to the glumper and the herbalist. Sage-man rebuilt the fire before ungently sewing shut the slits that the Dancing Mistress had made in the shaman's chest and belly.

Ice from the walls turned to steam as the Dancing Mistress fried the organ meats, the tongue and two glistening eyes in a tiny black iron pan graven with runes. The blinded shaman wept and gagged, spitting blood while he shivered by the fire.

When the bits were done the Dancing Mistress dumped them to the blood-slicked mess that was the floor. She ground the burnt flesh to mash beneath her feet, then kicked it into the coals. The shaman's weeping turned to a scream as his wisdom burned away.

"Our water matter is discharged," she whispered in his ear. "If your Duke's ghost comes to you seeking restoration, send him to knock at my door."

Then the Dancing Mistress gathered the herbalist into her arms. Cinnamon-woman and sage-man brought the glumper between them. The shaman they left to his fate, blind, mute and friendless among the lonely gods.

The Duke of Copper Downs was still dead, the Dancing Mistress reflected as the night faded around her. Oddly, she remained alive.

She sat at the door of the herbalist's hut. The woman slept inside, mewing her pain even amidst the thickets of her dreams. There was a new water matter here, of course. The ties among her people ever and always were broad as the sea, swift as a river, deep as the lakes that lie beneath the mountains. She was bound for a time to the herbalist by the steam that the hunt had burned from the shaman's icy walls.

That man did not have much of life left to him, but at least she had not claimed it herself. Her people had the right of things in centuries past, when they gave up their power. She only hoped that rumor of the hunt was small and soon forgotten by the citizens of Copper Downs.

The shadows beneath the rotten willows lightened with the day. The spiced scent of cookery rose around her, tiny boiling pots and bumptious roasts alike. The Dancing Mistress rose, stretched, and went to tend her patient.

∾

The author of ten novels, seven collections, and over three hundred short stories, **Jay Lake** (1964–2014) won the 2004 John W. Campbell Award for Best New Writer and garnered multiple Hugo, Nebula, and World Fantasy Award nominations. He also edited fifteen anthologies. In 2008, Lake was diagnosed with cancer. He acquired new fame as an outspoken cancer survivor and blogger, discussing the details of his illness and efforts to navigate the health care industry with frankness and, often, humor. His *Last Plane to Heaven: The Final Collection*, published by Tor in September 2014, won the 2015 Endeavor Award.

∾

Harry Dresden, a private investigator of paranormal crime, walks the streets of a supernatural Chicago armed with numerous powers of wizardry. He's also has a healthy appreciation of fermented beverages, so it is not a good idea to mess with Harry's favorite "beeromancer."

LAST CALL
Jim Butcher

All I wanted was a quiet beer.

That isn't too much to ask, is it—one contemplative drink at the end of a hard day of professional wizarding? Maybe a steak sandwich to go with it? You wouldn't think so. But somebody (or maybe Somebody) disagreed with me.

McAnally's pub is a quiet little hole in the wall, like a hundred others in Chicago, in the basement of a large office building. You have to go down a few stairs to get to the door. When you come inside, you're at eye level with the creaky old ceiling fans in the rest of the place, and you have to take a couple of more steps down from the entryway to get to the pub's floor. It's lit mostly by candles. The finish work is all hand-carved, richly polished wood, stained a deeper brown than most would use, and combined with the candles, it feels cozily cavelike.

I opened the door to the place and got hit in the face with something I'd *never* smelled in Mac's pub before—the odor of food being burned.

It should say something about Mac's cooking that my first instinct was to make sure the shield bracelet on my left arm was ready to go as I drew the blasting rod from inside my coat. I took careful steps forward into the pub, blasting rod held up and ready. The usual lighting was dimmed, and only a handful of candles still glimmered.

The regular crowd at Mac's, members of the supernatural community of Chicago, were strewn about like broken dolls. Half a dozen people lay on the floor, limbs sprawled oddly, as if they'd dropped unconscious in the middle of calisthenics. A pair of older guys who were always playing chess at a table in the corner both lay slumped across the table. Pieces were spread everywhere around them, some of them broken, and the old chess clock they used had been smashed to bits. Three young women who had watched too many episodes of *Charmed*, and who always showed up at Mac's together, were unconscious in a pile in the corner, as if they'd been huddled there in terror before they collapsed—but they were splattered with droplets of what looked like blood.

I could see several of the fallen breathing, at least. I waited for a long moment, but nothing jumped at me from the darkness, and I felt no sudden desire to start breaking things and then take a nap.

"Mac?" I called quietly.

Someone grunted.

I hurried over to the bar and found Mac on the floor beside it. He'd been badly beaten. His lips were split and puffy. His nose had been broken. Both his hands were swollen and purple—defensive wounds, probably. The baseball bat he kept behind the bar was lying next to him, smeared with blood—probably his own.

"Stars and stones," I breathed. "Mac."

I knelt down next to him, examining him for injuries as best I could. I didn't have any formal medical training, but several years' service in the Wardens in a war with the vampires of the Red Court had shown me more than my fair share of injuries. I didn't like the look of one of the bruises on his head, and he'd broken several fingers, but I didn't think it was anything he wouldn't recover from.

"What happened?" I asked him.

"Went nuts," he slurred. One of his cut lips reopened, and fresh blood appeared. "Violent."

I winced. "No kidding." I grabbed a clean cloth from the stack on the shelf behind the bar and ran cold water over it. I tried to clean some of the mess off his face. "They're all down," I told him as I did. "Alive. It's your place. How do you want to play it?"

Even through as much pain as he was in, Mac took a moment to consider before answering. "Murphy," he said finally.

I'd figured. Calling in the authorities would mean a lot of questions and attention, but it also meant that everyone would get medical treatment sooner. Mac tended to put the customer first. But if he'd wanted to keep it under the radar, I would have understood that, too.

"I'll make the call," I told him.

The authorities swooped down on the place with vigor. It was early in the evening, and we were evidently the first customers for the night shift EMTs.

"Jesus," Sergeant Karrin Murphy said from the doorway, looking around the interior of Mac's place. "What a mess."

"Tell me about it," I said glumly. My stomach was rumbling, and I was thirsty besides, but it just didn't seem right to help myself to any of Mac's stuff while he was busy getting patched up by the ambulance guys.

Murphy blew out a breath. "Well, brawls in bars aren't exactly uncommon." She came down into the room, removed a flashlight from her jacket pocket, and shone it around. "But maybe you'll tell me what really happened."

"Mac said that his customers went nuts. They started acting erratic and then became violent."

"What, all of them? At the same time?"

"That was the impression he gave me. He wasn't overly coherent."

Murphy frowned and slowly paced the room, sweeping the light back and forth methodically. "You get a look at the customers?"

"There wasn't anything actively affecting them when I got here," I said. "I'm sure of that. They were all unconscious. Minor wounds, looked like they were mostly self-inflicted. I think those girls were the ones to beat Mac."

Murphy winced. "You think he wouldn't defend himself against them?"

"He could have pulled a gun. Instead, he had his bat out. He was probably trying to stop someone from doing something stupid, and it went bad."

"You know what I'm thinking?" Murphy asked. "When something odd happens to everyone in a pub?"

She had stopped at the back corner. Among the remnants of broken chessmen and scattered chairs, the circle of illumination cast by her flashlight had come to rest on a pair of dark brown beer bottles.

"Ugly thought," I said. "Mac's beer, in the service of darkness."

She gave me a level look. Well. As level a look as you *can* give when you're a five-foot blonde with a perky nose, glaring at a gangly wizard most of seven feet tall. "I'm serious, Harry. Could it have been something in the beer? Drugs? A poison? Something from your end of things?"

I leaned on the bar and chewed that thought over for a moment. Oh, sure, technically it could have been any of those. A number of drugs could cause psychotic behavior, though admittedly it might be hard to get that reaction in everyone in the bar at more or less the same time. Poisons were just drugs that happened to kill you, or the reverse. And if those people had been poisoned, they might still be in a lot of danger.

And once you got the magical side of things, any one of a dozen methods could have been used to get to the people through the beer they'd imbibed—but all of them would require someone with access to the beer to pull it off, and Mac made his own brew.

In fact, he bottled it himself.

"It wasn't necessarily the beer," I said.

"You think they all got the same steak sandwich? The same batch of curly fries?" She shook her head. "Come on, Dresden. The food here is good, but that isn't what gets them in the door."

"Mac wouldn't hurt anybody," I said quietly.

"Really?" Murphy asked, her voice quiet and steady. "You're sure about that? How well do you really know the man?"

I glanced around the bar, slowly.

"What's his first name, Harry?"

"Dammit, Murph," I sighed. "You can't go around being suspicious of everyone all the time."

"Sure I can." She gave me a faint smile. "It's my job, Harry. I have to look at things dispassionately. It's nothing personal. You know that."

"Yeah," I muttered. "I know that. But I also know what it's like to be dispassionately suspected of something you didn't do. It sucks."

She held up her hands. "Then let's figure out what did happen. I'll go talk to the principals, see if anyone remembers anything. You take a look at the beer."

"Yeah," I said. "Okay."

After bottling it, Mac transports his beer in wooden boxes like old apple crates, only more heavy-duty. They aren't magical or anything. They're just sturdy as hell, and they stack up neatly. I came through the door of my apartment with a box of samples and braced myself against the impact of Mister, my tomcat, who generally declares a suicide charge on my shins the minute I come through the door. Mister is huge, and most of his mass is muscle. I rocked at the impact, and the bottles rattled, but I took it in stride. Mouse, my big shaggy dogosaurus, was lying full on his side by the fireplace, napping. He looked up and thumped his tail on the ground once, then went back to sleep.

No work ethic around here at all. But then, he hadn't been cheated out of his well-earned beer. I took the box straight down the stepladder to my lab, calling, "Hi, Molly," as I went down.

Molly, my apprentice, sat at her little desk, working on a pair of potions. She had maybe five square feet of space to work with in my cluttered lab, but she managed to keep the potions clean and neat, and still had room left over for her Latin textbook, her notebook, and a can of Pepsi, the heathen. Molly's hair was kryptonite green today, with silver tips, and she was wearing cutoff jeans and a tight blue T-shirt with a Superman logo on the front. She was a knockout.

"Hiya, Harry," she said absently.

"Outfit's a little cold for March, isn't it?"

"If it were, you'd be staring at my chest a lot harder," she said, smirking a little. She glanced up, and it bloomed into a full smile. "Hey, beer!"

"You're young and innocent," I said firmly, setting the box down on a shelf. "No beer for you."

"You're living in denial," she replied, and rose to pick up a bottle.

Of course she did. I'd told her not to. I watched her carefully.

The kid's my apprentice, but she's got a knack for the finer aspects of magic. She'd be in real trouble if she had to blast her way out of a situation, but when it comes to the cobweb-fine enchantments, she's a couple of lengths ahead of me and pulling away fast—and I figured that this had to be subtle work.

She frowned almost the second she touched the bottle. "That's . . . odd." She gave me a questioning look, and I gestured at the box. She ran her fingertips over each bottle in turn. "There's energy there. What is it, Harry?"

I had a good idea of what the beer had done to its drinkers—but it just didn't make sense. I wasn't about to tell her that, though. It would be very anti-Obi-Wan of me. "You tell me," I said, smiling slightly.

She narrowed her eyes at me and turned back to her potions, muttering over them for a few moments, and then easing them down to a low simmer. She came back to the bottles and opened one, sniffing at it and frowning some more.

"No taste-testing," I told her. "It isn't pretty."

"I wouldn't think so," she replied in the same tone she'd used while working on her Latin. "It's laced with . . . some kind of contagion focus, I think."

I nodded. She was talking about magical contagion, not the medical kind. A contagion focus was something that formed a link between a smaller amount of its mass after it had been separated from the main body. A practitioner could use it to send magic into the main body, and by extension into all the smaller foci, even if they weren't in the same physical place. It's sort of like planting a transmitter on someone's car so that you can send a missile at it later.

"Can you tell what kind of working it's been set up to support?" I asked her.

She frowned. She had a pretty frown. "Give me a minute."

"Tick tock," I said.

She waved a hand at me without looking up. I folded my arms and waited. I gave her tests like this one all the time—and there was always a time limit. In my experience, the solutions you need the most badly are always time-critical. I'm trying to train the grasshopper for the real world.

Here was one of her first real-world problems, but she didn't have to know that. So long as she thought it was just one more test, she'd tear into it without hesitation. I saw no reason to rattle her confidence.

She muttered to herself. She poured some of the beer out into the beaker and held it up to the light from a specially prepared candle. She scrawled power calculations on a notebook. And twenty minutes later, she said, "Hah. Tricky, but not tricky enough."

"Oh?" I said.

"No need to be coy, boss," she said. "The contagion looks like a simple compulsion meant to make the victim drink more, but it's really a psychic conduit."

I leaned forward. "Seriously?"

Molly stared blankly at me for a moment. Then she blinked and said, "You didn't *know*?"

"I found the compulsion, but it was masking anything else that had been laid on the beer." I picked up the half-empty bottle and shook my head. "I brought it here because you've got a better touch for this kind of thing than I do. It would have taken me hours to puzzle it out. Good work."

"But . . . you didn't *tell* me this was for real." She shook her head dazedly. "Harry, what if I hadn't found it? What if I'd been wrong?"

"Don't get ahead of yourself, grasshopper," I said, turning for the stairs. "You *still* might be wrong."

They'd taken Mac to Stroger, and he looked like hell. I had to lie to the nurse to get in to talk to him, flashing my consultant's ID badge and making like I was working with the Chicago cops on the case.

"Mac," I said, coming to sit down on the chair next to his bed. "How are you feeling?"

He looked at me with the eye that wasn't swollen shut. "Yeah. They said you wouldn't accept any painkillers."

He moved his head in a slight nod.

I laid out what I'd found. "It was elegant work, Mac. More intricate than anything I've done."

His teeth made noise as they ground together. He understood what two complex interwoven enchantments meant as well as I did—a serious player was involved.

"Find him," Mac growled, the words slurred a little.

"Any idea where I could start?" I asked him.

He was quiet for a moment, then shook his head. "Caine?"

I lifted my eyebrows. "That thug from Night of the Living Brews? He's been around?"

He grunted. "Last night. Closing." He closed his eyes. "Loudmouth."

I stood up and put a hand on his shoulder. "Rest. I'll chat him up."

Mac exhaled slowly, maybe unconscious before I'd gotten done speaking.

I found Murphy down the hall.

"Three of them are awake," she said. "None of them remember anything for several hours before they presumably went to the bar."

I grimaced. "I was afraid of that." I told her what I'd learned.

"A psychic conduit?" Murphy asked. "What's that?"

"It's like any electrical power line," I said. "Except it plugs into your mind—and whoever is on the other end gets to decide what goes in."

Murphy went a little pale. She'd been on the receiving end of a couple of different kinds of psychic assault, and it had left some marks. "So do what you do. Put the whammy on them and let's track them down."

I grimaced and shook my head. "I don't dare," I told her. "All I've got to track with is the beer itself. If I try to use it in a spell, it'll open me up to the conduit. It'll be like I drank the stuff."

Murphy folded her arms. "And if that happens, you won't remember anything you learn anyway."

"Like I said," I told her, "it's high-quality work. But I've got a name."

"A perp?"

"I'm sure he's guilty of something. His name's Caine. He's a con. Big, dumb, violent, and thinks he's a brewer."

She arched an eyebrow. "You got a history with this guy?"

"Ran across him during a case maybe a year ago," I said. "It got ugly. More for him than me. He doesn't like Mac much."

"He's a wizard?"

"Hell's bells, no," I said.

"Then how does he figure in?"

"Let's ask him."

Murphy made short work of running down an address for Herbert Orson Caine, mugger, rapist, and extortionist—a cheap apartment building on the south end of Bucktown.

Murphy knocked at the door, but we didn't get an answer.

"It's a good thing he's a con," she said, reaching for her cell phone. "I can probably get a warrant without too much trouble."

"With what?" I asked her. "Suggestive evidence of the use of black magic?"

"Tampering with drinks at a bar doesn't require the use of magic," Murphy said. "He's a rapist, and he isn't part of the outfit, so he doesn't have an expensive lawyer to raise a stink."

"How's about we save the good people of Chicago time and money and just take a look around?"

"Breaking and entering."

"I won't break anything," I promised. "I'll do all the entering, too."

"No," she said.

"But—"

She looked up at me, her jaw set stubbornly. "No, Harry."

I sighed. "These guys aren't playing by the rules."

"We don't know he's involved yet. I'm not cutting corners for someone who might not even be connected."

I was partway into a snarky reply when Caine opened the door from the stairwell and entered the hallway. He spotted us and froze. Then he turned and started walking away.

"Caine!" Murphy called. "Chicago PD!"

He bolted.

Murph and I had both been expecting that, evidently. We both rushed him. He slammed the door open, but I'd been waiting for that, too. I sent out a burst of my will, drawing my right hand in toward my chest as I shouted, *"Forzare!"*

Invisible force slammed the door shut as Caine began to go through. It hit him hard enough to bounce him all the way back across the hall, into the wall opposite.

Murphy had better acceleration than I did. She caught up to Caine in time for him to swing one paw at her in a looping punch.

I almost felt sorry for the slob.

Murphy ducked the punch, then came up with all of her weight and the muscle of her legs and body behind her response. She struck the tip of his chin with the heel of her hand, snapping his face straight up.

Caine was brawny, big, and tough. He came back from the blow with a dazed snarl and swatted at Murphy again. Murph caught his arm, tugged him a little one way, a little the other, and using his own arm as a fulcrum, sent him flipping forward and down hard onto the floor. He landed hard enough to make the floorboards shake, and Murphy promptly shifted her grip, twisting one hand into a painful angle, holding his arm out straight, using her leg to pin it into position.

"That would be assault," Murphy said in a sweet voice. "And on a police officer in the course of an investigation, no less."

"Bitch," Caine said. "I'm gonna break your—"

We didn't get to find out what he was going to break, because Murphy shifted her body weight maybe a couple of inches, and he screamed instead.

"Whaddayou want?" Caine demanded. "Lemme go! I didn't do nothin'!"

"Sure you did," I said cheerfully. "You assaulted Sergeant Murphy, here. I saw it with my own eyes."

"You're a two-time loser, Caine," Murphy said. "This will make it number three. By the time you get out, the first thing you'll need to buy will be a new set of teeth."

Caine said a lot of impolite words.

"Wow," I said, coming to stand over him. "That sucks. If only there was some way he could be of help to the community. You know, prove how he isn't a waste of space some other person could be using."

"Screw you," Caine said. "I ain't helping you with nothing."

Murphy leaned into his arm a little again to shut him up. "What happened to the beer at McAnally's?" she asked in a polite tone.

Caine said even more impolite words.

"I'm pretty sure that wasn't it," Murphy said. "I'm pretty sure you can do better."

"Bite me, cop bitch," Caine muttered.

"*Sergeant* Bitch," Murphy said. "Have it your way, bonehead. Bet you've got all kinds of fans back at Stateville." But she was frowning when she said it. Thugs like Caine rolled over when they were facing hard time. They didn't risk losing the rest of their adult lives out of simple contrariness—unless they were terrified of the alternative.

Someone or, dare I say it, something had Caine scared.

Well, that table could seat more than one player.

The thug had a little blood coming from the corner of his mouth. He must have bitten his tongue when Murphy hit him.

I pulled a white handkerchief out of my pocket, and in a single swooping motion, stooped down and smeared some blood from Caine's mouth onto it.

"What the hell," he said, or something close to it. "What are you doing?"

"Don't worry about it, Caine," I told him. "It isn't going to be a long-term problem for you."

I took the cloth and walked a few feet away. Then I hunkered down and used a piece of chalk from another pocket to draw a circle around me on the floor.

Caine struggled feebly against Murphy, but she put him down again. "Sit still," she snapped. "I'll pull your shoulder right out of its socket."

"Feel free," I told Murphy. "He isn't going to be around long enough to worry about it." I squinted up at Caine and said, "Beefy, little bit of a gut. Bet you eat a lot of greasy food, huh, Caine?"

"Wh-what?" he said. "What are you doing?"

"Heart attack should look pretty natural," I said. "Murph, get ready to back off once he starts thrashing." I closed the circle and let it sparkle a little as I did. It was a waste of energy—special effects like that almost always are—but it made an impression on Caine.

"Jesus Christ!" Caine said. "Wait!"

"Can't wait," I told him. "Gotta make this go before the blood dries out. Quit being such a baby, Caine. She gave you a chance." I raised my hand over the fresh blood on the cloth. "Let's see now—"

"I can't talk!" Caine yelped. "If I talk, she'll know!"

Murphy gave his arm a little twist. "Who?" she demanded.

"I can't! Jesus, I swear! Dresden, don't, it isn't my fault, they needed bloodstone and I had the only stuff in town that was pure enough! I just wanted to wipe that smile off of that bastard's face!"

I looked up at Caine with a gimlet eye, my teeth bared. "You ain't saying anything that makes me want you to keep on breathing."

"I *can't*," Caine wailed. "She'll *know*!"

I fixed my stare on Caine and raised my hand in a slow, heavily overdramatized gesture. *"Intimidatus dorkus maximus!"* I intoned, making my voice intentionally hollow and harsh, and stressing the long vowels.

"Decker!" Caine screamed. "Decker, he set up the deal!"

I lowered my hand and let my head rock back. "Decker," I said. "That twit."

Murphy watched me, and didn't let go of Caine, though I could tell that she didn't want to keep holding him.

I shook my head at Murphy and said, "Let him scamper, Murph."

She let him go, and Caine fled for the stairs on his hand and knee, sobbing. He staggered out, falling down the first flight, from the sound of it.

I wrinkled up my nose as the smell of urine hit me. "Ah. The aroma of truth."

Murphy rubbed her hands on her jeans as if trying to wipe off something greasy. "Jesus, Harry."

"What?" I said. "You didn't want to break into his place."

"I didn't want you to put a gun to his head, either." She shook her head. "You couldn't really have . . . "

"Killed him?" I asked. I broke the circle and rose. "Yeah. With him right here in sight, yeah. I probably could have."

She shivered. "Jesus Christ."

"I wouldn't," I said. I went to her and put a hand on her arm. "I wouldn't, Karrin. You know that."

She looked up at me, her expression impossible to read. "You put on a really good act, Harry. It would have fooled a lot of people. It looked . . . "

"Natural on me," I said. "Yeah."

She touched my hand briefly with hers. "So, I guess we got something?"

I shook off dark thoughts and nodded. "We've got a name."

Burt Decker ran what was arguably the sleaziest of the half-dozen establishments that catered to the magical crowd in Chicago. Left Hand Goods prided itself on providing props and ingredients to the black magic crowd.

Oh, that wasn't so sinister as it sounded. Most of the trendy, self-appointed Death Eater wannabes in Chicago—or any other city, for that matter—didn't have enough talent to strike two rocks together and make sparks, much less hurt anybody. The really dangerous black wizards don't shop at places like Left Hand Goods. You could get everything you needed for most black magic at the freaking grocery store.

But, all the same, plenty of losers with bad intentions thought Left Hand Goods had everything you needed to create your own evil empire—and Burt Decker was happy to make them pay for their illusions.

Me and Murphy stepped in, between the display of socially maladjusted fungi on our right, a tank of newts (PLUCK YOUR OWN *#%$ING EYES, the sign said) on the left, and stepped around the big shelf of quasi-legal drug paraphernalia in front of us.

Decker was a shriveled little toad of a man. He wasn't overweight, but his skin looked too loose from a plump youth combined with a lifetime of too many naps in tanning beds. He was immaculately groomed, and his hair was a gorgeous black streaked with dignified silver that was like a Rolls hood ornament on a VW Rabbit. He had beady black eyes with nothing warm behind them, and when he saw me, he licked his lips nervously.

"Hiya, Burt," I said.

There were a few shoppers, none of whom looked terribly appealing. Murphy held up her badge so that everyone could see it and said, "We have some questions."

She might as well have shouted, "Fire!" The store emptied.

Murphy swaggered past a rack of discount porn DVDs, her coat open just enough to reveal the shoulder holster she wore. She picked one up, gave it a look, and tossed it on the floor. "Christ, I hate scum vendors like this."

"Hey!" Burt said. "You break it, you bought it."

"Yeah, right," Murphy said.

I showed him my teeth as I walked up and leaned both my arms on the counter he stood behind. It crowded into his personal space. His cologne was thick enough to stop bullets.

"Burt," I said, "make this simple, okay? Tell me everything you know about Caine."

Decker's eyes went flat, and his entire body became perfectly still. It was reptilian. "Caine?"

I smiled wider. "Big guy, shaggy hair, kind of a slob, with piss running down his leg. He made a deal with a woman for some bloodstone, and you helped."

Murphy had paused at a display of what appeared to be small smoky quartz geodes. The crystals were nearly black, with purple veins running through them, and they were priced a couple of hundred dollars too high.

"I don't talk about my customers," Decker said. "It isn't good for business."

I glanced at Murphy. "Burt. We know you're connected."

She stared at me for a second, and sighed. Then she knocked a geode off the shelf. It shattered on the floor.

Decker winced and started to protest, but it died on his lips.

"You know what isn't good for business, Decker?" I asked. "Having a big guy in a gray cloak hang out in your little Bad Juju Mart. Your customers start thinking that the Council is paying attention, how much business do you think you'll get?"

Decker stared at me with toad eyes, nothing on his face.

"Oops," Murphy said, and knocked another geode to the floor.

"People are in the hospital, Burt," I said. "Mac's one of them—and he was beaten on ground held neutral by the Unseelie Accords."

Burt bared his teeth. It was a gesture of surprise.

"Yeah," I said. I drew my blasting rod out of my coat and slipped enough of my will into it to make the runes and sigils carved along its length glitter with faint orange light. The smell of wood smoke curled up from it. "You don't want the heat this is gonna bring down, Burt."

Murphy knocked another geode down and said, "I'm the good cop."

"All right," Burt said. "Jesus, will you lay off? I'll talk, but you ain't gonna like it."

"I don't handle disappointment well, Burt." I tapped the glowing-ember tip of the blasting rod down on his countertop for emphasis. "I really don't."

Burt grimaced at the black spots it left on the countertop. "Skirt comes in asking for bloodstone. But all I got is this crap from South Asscrack.

Says she wants the real deal, and she's a bitch about it. I tell her I sold the end of my last shipment to Caine."

"Woman pisses you off," Murphy said, "and you send her to do business with a convicted rapist."

Burt looked at her with toad eyes.

"How'd you know where to find Caine?" I asked.

"He's got a discount card here. Filled out an application."

I glanced from the porn to the drug gear. "Uh-huh. What's he doing with bloodstone?"

"Why should I give a crap?" Burt said. "It's just business."

"How'd she pay?"

"What do I look like, a fucking video camera?"

"You look like an accomplice to black magic, Burt," I said.

"Crap," Burt said, smiling slightly. "I haven't had my hands on anything. I haven't done anything. You can't prove anything."

Murphy stared hard at Decker. Then, quite deliberately, she walked out of the store.

I gave him my sunniest smile. "That's the upside of working with the gray cloaks now, Burt," I said. "I don't need proof. I just need an excuse."

Burt stared hard at me. Then he swallowed, toadlike.

"She paid with a Visa," I told Murphy when I came out of the store. "Meditrina Bassarid."

Murphy frowned up at my troubled expression. "What's wrong?"

"You ever see me pay with a credit card?"

"No. I figured no credit company would have you."

"Come on, Murph," I said. "That's just un-American. I don't bother with the things, because that magnetic strip goes bad in a couple of hours around me."

She frowned. "Like everything electronic does. So?"

"So if Ms. Bassarid has Caine scared out of his mind on magic . . . " I said.

Murphy got it. "Why is she using a credit card?"

"Because she probably isn't human," I said. "Nonhumans can sling power all over the place and not screw up anything if they don't want to. It also explains why she got sent to Caine to get taught a lesson and wound up scaring him to death instead."

Murphy said an impolite word. "But if she's got a credit card, she's in the system."

"To some degree," I said. "How long for you to find something?"

She shrugged. "We'll see. You get a description?"

"Blue-black hair, green eyes, long legs, and great tits," I said.

She eyed me.

"Quoting," I said righteously.

I'm sure she was fighting off a smile. "What are you going to do?"

"Go back to Mac's," I said. "He loaned me his key."

Murphy looked sideways at me. "Did he know he was doing that?"

I put my hand to my chest as if wounded. "Murphy," I said. "He's a friend."

I lit a bunch of candles with a mutter and a wave of my hand, and stared around Mac's place. Out in the dining area, chaos reigned. Chairs were overturned. Salt from a broken shaker had spread over the floor. None of the chairs were broken, but the framed sign that read Accorded Neutral Territory was smashed and lay on the ground near the door.

An interesting detail, that.

Behind the bar, where Mac kept his iceboxes and his wood-burning stove, everything was as tidy as a surgical theater, with the exception of the uncleaned stove and some dishes in the sink. Nothing looked like a clue.

I shook my head and went to the sink. I stared at the dishes. I turned and stared at the empty storage cabinets under the bar, where a couple of boxes of beer still waited. I opened the icebox and stared at the food, and my stomach rumbled. There were some cold cuts. I made a sandwich and stood there munching it, looking around the place, thinking.

I didn't think of anything productive.

I washed the dishes in the sink, scowling and thinking up a veritable thunderstorm. I didn't get much further than a light sprinkle, though, before a thought struck me.

There really wasn't very much beer under the bar.

I finished the dishes, pondering that. Had there been a ton earlier? No. I'd picked up the half-used box and taken it home. The other two boxes were where I'd left them. But Mac usually kept a legion of beer bottles down there.

So why only two now?

I walked down to the far end of the counter, a nagging thought dancing around the back of my mind, where I couldn't see it. Mac kept a small office in the back corner, consisting of a table for his desk, a wooden chair, and a couple of filing cabinets. His food service and liquor permits were on display on the wall above it.

I sat down at the desk and opened filing cabinets. I started going through Mac's records and books. Intrusive as hell, I know, but I had to figure out what was going on before matters got worse.

And that was when it hit me. Matters getting worse. I could see a mortal wizard, motivated by petty spite, greed, or some other mundane motivation, wrecking Mac's bar. People can be amazingly petty. But nonhumans, now—that was a different story.

The fact that this Bassarid chick had a credit card meant she was methodical. I mean, you can't just conjure one out of thin air. She'd taken the time to create an identity for herself. That kind of forethought indicated a scheme, a plan, a goal. Untidying a Chicago bar, neutral ground or not, was not by any means the kind of goal that things from the Nevernever set for themselves when they went undercover into mortal society.

Something bigger was going on, then. Mac's place must have been a side item for Bassarid.

Or maybe a stepping-stone.

Mac was no wizard, but he was savvy. It would take more than cheap tricks to get to his beer with him here, and I was betting that he had worked out more than one way to realize it if someone had intruded on his place when he was gone. So, if someone wanted to get to the beer, they'd need a distraction.

Like maybe Caine.

Caine made a deal with Bassarid, evidently—I assumed he gave her the bloodstone in exchange for being a pain to Mac. So, she ruins Mac's day, gets the bloodstone in exchange, end of story. Nice and neat.

Except that it didn't make a lot of sense. Bloodstone isn't exactly impossible to come by. Why would someone with serious magical juice do a favor for Caine to get some?

Because maybe Caine was a stooge, a distraction for anyone trying to follow Bassarid's trail. What if Bassarid had picked someone who had a history with Mac, so that I could chase after him while she . . . did whatever she planned to do with the rest of Mac's beer?

Wherever the hell that was.

It took me an hour and half to find anything in Mac's files—the first thing was a book. A really old book, bound in undyed leather. It was a journal, apparently, and written in some kind of cipher.

Also interesting, but probably not germane.

The second thing I found was a receipt, for a whole hell of a lot of money, along with an itemized list of what had been sold—beer, representing all of Mac's various heavenly brews. Someone at Worldclass Limited had paid him an awful lot of money for his current stock.

I got on the phone and called Murphy.

"Who bought the evil beer?" Murphy asked.

"The beer isn't evil. It's a victim. And I don't recognize the name of the company. Worldclass Limited."

Keys clicked in the background as Murphy hit the Internet. "Caterers," Murphy said a moment later. "High end."

I thought of the havoc that might be about to ensue at some wedding or bar mitzvah and shuddered. "Hell's bells," I breathed. "We've got to find out where they went."

"Egad, Holmes," Murphy said in the same tone I would have said "duh."

"Yeah. Sorry. What did you get on Bassarid?"

"Next to nothing," Murphy said. "It'll take me a few more hours to get the information behind her credit card."

"No time," I said. "She isn't worried about the cops. Whoever she is, she planned this whole thing to keep her tracks covered from the likes of me."

"Aren't we full of ourselves?" Murphy grumped. "Call you right back."

She did.

"The caterers aren't available," she said. "They're working the private boxes at the Bulls game."

I rushed to the United Center.

Murphy could have blown the whistle and called in the artillery, but she hadn't. Uniformed cops already at the arena would have been the first to intervene, and if they did, they were likely to cross Bassarid. Whatever she was, she would be more than they could handle. She'd scamper or, worse, one of the cops could get killed. So Murphy and I both rushed to get there and find the bad guy before she could pull the trigger, so to speak, on the Chicago PD.

It was half an hour before the game, and the streets were packed. I parked in front of a hydrant and ran half a mile to the United Center, where thousands of people were packing themselves into the building for the game. I picked up a ticket from a scalper for a ridiculous amount of money on the way, emptying my pockets, and earned about a million glares from Bulls fans as I juked and ducked through the crowd to get through the entrances as quickly as I possibly could.

Once inside, I ran for the lowest level, the bottommost ring of concessions stands and restrooms circling entrances to the arena—the most crowded level, currently—where the entrances to the most expensive ring of private boxes were. I started at the first box I came to, knocking on the locked doors. No one answered at the first several. At the next, the door was opened by a blonde in an expensive business outfit showing a lot of décolletage who had clearly been expecting someone else.

"Who are you?" she stammered.

I flashed her my laminated consultant's ID, too quickly to be seen. "Department of Alcohol, Tobacco, and Firearms, ma'am," I said in my official's voice, which is like my voice only deeper and more pompous. I've heard it from all kinds of government types. "We've had a report of tainted beer. I need to check your bar, see if the bad batch is in there."

"Oh," she said, backing up, her body language immediately cooperative. I pegged her as somebody's receptionist, maybe. "Of course."

I padded into the room and went to the bar, rifling bottles and opening cabinets until I found eleven dark-brown bottles with a simple cap with an *M* stamped into the metal. Mac's mark.

I turned to find the blonde holding out the half-empty bottle number twelve in a shaking hand. Her eyes were a little wide. "Um. Am I in trouble?"

I might be. I took the beer bottle from her, moving gingerly, and set it down with the others. "Have you been feeling, uh, sick or anything?" I asked as I edged toward the door, just in case she came at me with a baseball bat.

She shook her head, breathing more heavily. Her manicured fingernails trailed along the V-neck of her blouse. "I . . . I mean, you know." Her face flushed. "Just looking forward to . . . the game."

"Uh-huh," I said warily.

Her eyes suddenly became warmer and very direct. I don't know what it was exactly, but she was suddenly filled with that energy women have that has nothing to do with magic and everything to do with creating it. The temperature in the room felt like it went up about ten degrees. "Maybe you should examine me, sir."

I suddenly had a very different idea of what Mac had been defending himself from with that baseball bat.

And it had turned ugly on him.

Hell's bells, I thought. I knew what we were dealing with.

"Fantastic idea," I told her. "You stay right here and get comfortable. I'm going to grab something sweet. I'll be back in two shakes."

"All right," she cooed. Her suit jacket slid off her shoulders to the floor. "Don't be long."

I smiled at her in what I hoped was a suitably sultry fashion and backed out. Then I shut the door, checked its frame, and focused my will into the palm of my right hand. I directed my attention to one edge of the door and whispered, *"Forzare."*

Metal squealed as the door bent in its frame. With any luck, it would take a couple of guys with crowbars an hour or two to get it open again—and hopefully Bubbles would pitch over into a stupor before she did herself any harm.

It took me three more doors to find one of the staff of Worldclass

Limited—a young man in dark slacks, a white shirt, and a black bow tie, who asked if he could help me.

I flashed the ID again. "We've received a report that a custom microbrew your company purchased for this event has been tainted. Chicago PD is on the way, but meanwhile I need your company to round up the bottles before anyone else gets poisoned drinking them."

The young man frowned. "Isn't it the Bureau?"

"Excuse me?"

"You said *Department of Alcohol, Tobacco, and Firearms*. It's a *Bureau*."

Hell's bells, why did I get someone who could think *now*?

"Can I see that ID again?" he asked.

"Look, buddy," I said. "You've gotten a bad batch of beer. If you don't round it up, people are going to get sick. Okay? The cops are on the way, but if people start guzzling it now, it isn't going to do anybody any good."

He frowned at me.

"Better safe than sorry, right?" I asked him.

Evidently, his ability to think did not extend to areas beyond asking stupid questions of well-meaning wizards. "Look, uh, really you should take this up with my boss."

"Then get me to him," I said. "Now."

The caterer might have been uncertain, but he wasn't slow. We hurried through the growing crowds to one of the workrooms that his company was using as a staging area. A lot of people in white shirts were hurrying all over the place with carts and armloads of everything from crackers to cheese to bottles of wine—and a dozen of Mac's empty wooden boxes were stacked up to one side of the room.

My guide led me to a harried-looking woman in catering wear, who listened to him impatiently and cut him off halfway through. "I know, I know," she snapped. "Look, I'll tell you what I told Sergeant Murphy. A city health inspector is already here, and they're already checking things out, and I am *not* losing my contract with the arena over some pointless scare."

"You already talked to Murphy?" I said.

"Maybe five minutes ago. Sent her to the woman from the city, over at midcourt."

"Tall woman?" I asked, feeling my stomach drop. "Blue-black hair? Uh, sort of busty?"

"Know her, do you?" The head caterer shook her head. "Look, I'm busy."

"Yeah," I said. "Thanks."

I ran back into the corridor and sprinted for the boxes at midcourt, drawing out my blasting rod as I went and hoping I would be in time to do Murphy any good.

A few years ago, I'd given Murphy a key to my apartment, in a sense. It was a small amulet that would let her past the magical wards that defend the place. I hadn't bothered to tell her that the thing had a second purpose— I'd wanted her to have one of my personal possessions, something I could, if necessary, use to find her if I needed to. She would have been insulted at the very idea.

A quick stop into the men's room, a chalk circle on the floor, a muttered spell, and I was on her trail. I actually ran past the suite she was in before the spell let me know I had passed her, and I had to backtrack to the door. I debated blowing it off the hinges. There was something to be said for a shock-and-awe entrance.

Of course, most of those things couldn't be said for doing it in the middle of a crowded arena that was growing more crowded by the second. I'd probably shatter the windows at the front of the suite, and that could be dangerous for the people sitting in the stands beneath them. I tried the door, just for the hell of it and—

—it opened.

Well, dammit. I much prefer making a dramatic entrance.

I came in and found a plush-looking room, complete with dark, thick carpeting, leather sofas, a buffet bar, a wet bar, and two women making out on a leather love seat.

They looked up as I shut the door behind me. Murphy's expression was, at best, vague, her eyes hazy, unfocused, the pupils dilated until you could hardly see any blue, and her lips were a little swollen with kissing. She saw me, and a slow and utterly sensuous smile spread over her mouth. "Harry. There you are."

The other woman gave me the same smile with a much more predatory edge. She had shoulder-length hair so black it was highlighted with dark, shining blue. Her green-gold eyes were bright and intense, her mouth full. She was dressed in a gray business skirt-suit, with the jacket off and her shirt mostly unbuttoned, if not quite indecent. She was, otherwise, as Burt Decker had described her—statuesque and beautiful.

"So," she said in a throaty, rich voice. "This is Harry Dresden."

"Yes," Murphy said, slurring the word drunkenly. "Harry. And his rod." She let out a giggle.

I mean, my God. She *giggled*.

"I like his looks," the brunette said. "Strong. Intelligent."

"Yeah," Murphy said. "I've wanted him for the longest time." She tittered. "Him and his rod."

I pointed said blasting rod at Meditrina Bassarid. "What have you done to her?"

"I?" the woman said. "Nothing."

Murphy's face flushed. "Yet."

The woman let out a smoky laugh, toying with Murphy's hair. "We're getting to that. I only shared the embrace of the god with her, wizard."

"I was going to kick your ass for that," Murphy said. She looked around, and I noticed that a broken lamp lay on the floor, and the end table it had sat on had been knocked over, evidence of a struggle. "But I feel so *good* now . . . " Smoldering blue eyes found me. "Harry. Come sit down with us."

"You should," the woman murmured. "We'll have a good time." She produced a bottle of Mac's ale from somewhere. "Come on. Have a drink with us."

All I'd wanted was a beer, for Pete's sake.

But this wasn't what I had in mind. It was just wrong. I told myself very firmly that it was wrong. Even if Karrin managed, somehow, to make her gun's shoulder rig look like lingerie.

Or maybe that was me.

"Meditrina was a Roman goddess of wine," I said instead. "And bassarids were another name for the handmaidens of Dionysus." I nodded at the beer in her hand and said, "I thought maenads were wine snobs."

Her mouth spread in a wide, genuine-looking smile, and her teeth were very white. "Any spirit is the spirit of the god, mortal."

"That's what the psychic conduit links them to," I said. "To Dionysus. To the god of revels and ecstatic violence."

"Of course," the maenad said. "Mortals have forgotten the true power of the god. The time has come to begin reminding them."

"If you're going to muck with the drinks, why not start with the big beer dispensary in the arena? You'd get it to a lot more people that way."

She sneered at me. "Beer, brewed in cauldrons the size of houses by machines and then served cold. It has no soul. It isn't worthy of the name."

"Got it," I said. "You're a beer snob."

She smiled, her gorgeous green eyes on mine. "I needed something real. Something a craftsman took loving pride in creating."

Which actually made sense, from a technical perspective. Magic is about a lot of things, and one of them is emotion. Once you begin to mass-manufacture anything, by the very nature of the process, you lose the sense of personal attachment you might have to something made by hand. For the maenad's purposes, it would have meant that the mass-produced beer had nothing she could sink her magical teeth into, no foundation to lay her complex compulsion upon.

Mac's beer certainly qualified as being produced with pride—real, personal pride, I mean, not official corporate spokesperson pride.

"Why?" I asked her. "Why do this at all?"

"I am hardly alone in my actions, wizard," she responded. "And it is who I am."

I frowned and tilted my head at her.

"Mortals have forgotten the gods," she said, hints of anger creeping into her tone. "They think the White God drove out the many gods. But they are here. We are here. I, too, was worshipped in my day, mortal man."

"Maybe you didn't know this," I said, "but most of us couldn't give a rat's ass. Raining down thunderbolts from on high isn't exclusive territory anymore."

She snarled, her eyes growing even brighter. "Indeed. We withdrew and gave the world into your keeping—and what has become of it? In two thousand years, you've poisoned and raped the Mother Earth who gave you life. You've cut down the forests, fouled the air, and darkened Apollo's chariot itself with the stench of your smithies."

"And touching off a riot at a Bulls' game is going to make some kind of point?" I demanded.

She smiled, showing sharp canines. "My sisters have been doing football matches for years. We're expanding the franchise." She drank from the bottle, wrapping her lips around it and making sure I noticed. "Moderation. It's disgusting. We should have strangled Aristotle in his crib. Alcoholism—calling the god a *disease*." She bared her teeth at me. "A lesson must be taught."

Murphy shivered, and then her expression turned ugly, her blue eyes focusing on me.

"Show your respect to the god, wizard," the maenad spat. "Drink. Or I will introduce you to Pentheus and Orpheus."

Greek guys. Both of whom were torn to pieces by maenads and their mortal female companions in orgies of ecstatic violence.

Murphy was breathing heavily now, sweating, her cheeks flushed, her eyes burning with lust and rage. And she was staring right at me.

Hooboy.

"Make you a counteroffer," I said quietly. "Break off the enchantment on the beer and get out of my town, now, and I won't FedEx you back to the Aegean in a dozen pieces."

"If you will not honor the god in life," Meditrina said, "then you will honor him in *death*." She flung out a hand, and Murphy flew at me with a howl of primal fury.

I ran away.

Don't get me wrong. I've faced a lot of screaming, charging monsters in my day. Granted, not one of them was small and blond and pretty from making out with what might have been a literal goddess. All the same, my options were limited. Murphy obviously wasn't in her right mind. I had my blasting rod ready to go, but I didn't want to kill her. I didn't want to go hand-to-hand with her, either. Murphy was a dedicated martial artist, especially good at grappling, and if it came to a clinch, I wouldn't fare any better than Caine had.

I flung myself back out of the room and into the corridor beyond before Murphy could catch me and twist my arm into some kind of Escher drawing. I heard glass breaking somewhere behind me.

Murphy came out hard on my heels, and I brought my shield bracelet up as I turned, trying to angle it so that it wouldn't hurt her. My shield flashed to blue-silver life as she closed on me, and she bounced off it as if it had been solid steel, stumbling to one side. Meditrina followed her, clutching a broken bottle, the whites of her eyes visible all the way around the bright green, an ecstatic and entirely creepy expression of joy lighting her face. She slashed at me—three quick, graceful motions—and I got out of the way of only one of them. Hot pain seared my chin and my right hand, and my blasting rod went flying off down the corridor, bouncing off people's legs.

I'm not an expert like Murphy, but I've taken some classes, too, and more important, I've been in a bunch of scrapes in my life. In the literal school of hard knocks, you learn the ropes fast, and the lessons go bone-deep. As I reeled from the blow, I turned my momentum into a spin and swept my leg through Meditrina's. Goddess or not, the maenad didn't weigh half what I did, and her legs went out from under her.

Murphy blindsided me with a kick that lit up my whole rib cage with pain, and had seized an arm before I could fight through it. If it had been my right arm, I'm not sure what might have happened—but she grabbed my left, and I activated my shield bracelet, sheathing it in sheer, kinetic power and forcing her hands away.

I don't care how many aikido lessons you've had, they don't train you for force fields.

I reached out with my will, screamed, *"Forzare!"* and seized a large plastic waste bin with my power. With a flick of my hand, I flung it at Murphy. It struck her hard and knocked her off me. I backpedaled. Meditrina had regained her feet and was coming for me, bottle flickering.

She drove me back into the beer-stand counter across the hall, and I brought up my shield again just as her makeshift weapon came forward. Glass shattered against it, cutting her own hand—always a risk with a bottle. But the force of the blow was sufficient to carry through the shield and slam my back against the counter. I bounced off some guy trying to carry beer in plastic cups and went down soaked in brew.

Murphy jumped on me then, pinning my left arm down as Meditrina started raking at my face with her nails—both of them screaming like banshees.

I had to shut one eye when a sharp fingernail grazed it, but I saw my chance as Meditrina's hands—hot, horribly strong hands—closed over my throat.

I choked out a gasped, *"Forzare!"* and reached out my right hand, snapping a slender chain that held up one end of a sign suspended above the beer stand behind me.

A heavy wooden sign that read, in large cheerful letters, PLEASE DRINK RESPONSIBLY swung down in a ponderous, scything arc and struck Meditrina on the side of the head, hitting her like a giant's fist. Her nails left scarlet lines on my throat as she was torn off me.

Murphy looked up, shocked, and I hauled with all my strength. I had to position her before she took up where Meditrina left off. I felt something wrench and give way as my thumb left its socket, and I howled in pain as the sign swung back, albeit with a lot less momentum, now, and clouted Murphy on the noggin, too.

Then a bunch of people jumped on us and the cops came running.

While they were arresting me, I managed to convince the cops that there was something bad in Mac's beer. They got with the caterers and rounded up the whole batch, apparently before more than a handful of people could drink any. There was some wild behavior, but no one else got hurt.

None of which did me any good. After all, I was soaked in Budweiser and had assaulted two attractive women. I went to the drunk tank, which angered me mainly because I'd never gotten my freaking beer. And to add insult to injury, after paying exorbitant rates for a ticket, I hadn't gotten to see the game, either.

There's no freaking justice in this world.

Murphy turned up in the morning to let me out. She had a black eye and a sign-shaped bruise across one cheekbone.

"So let me get this straight," Murphy said. "After we went to Left Hand Goods, we followed the trail to the Bulls game. Then we confronted this maenad character, there was a struggle, and I got knocked out."

"Yep," I said.

There was really no point in telling it any other way. The nefarious hooch would have destroyed her memory of the evening. The truth would just bother her.

Hell, it bothered me. On more levels than I wanted to think about.

"Well, Bassarid vanished from the hospital," Murphy said. "So she's not around to press charges. And, given that you were working with me on an investigation, and because several people have reported side effects that sound a lot like they were drugged with Rohypnol or something—and because it was you who got the cops to pull the rest of the bottles—I managed to get the felony charges dropped. You're still being cited for drunk and disorderly."

"Yay," I said without enthusiasm.

"Could have been worse," Murphy said. She paused and studied me for a moment. "You look like hell."

"Thanks," I said.

She looked at me seriously. Then she smiled, stood up on her tiptoes, and kissed my cheek. "You're a good man, Harry. Come on. I'll give you a ride home."

I smiled all the way to her car.

≈

Jim Butcher is the *New York Times* bestselling author of the Dresden Files and the Codex Alera. *The Aeronaut's Windlass*, the first book in a new nine-book steampunk series, Cinder Spires, was published in September 2015.

≈

The streets of Atlanta surround a neglected city park in which there lies an artificial pond. Neither would be particularly notable . . except for an ancient bewitchment and the strange aquatic being that lives there.

Bridle
Caitlín R. Kiernan

It's not a wild place—not some bottomless, peat-stained loch hidden away between high granite cliffs, and not a secret deep spring bubbling up crystal clear from the heart of a Welsh or Irish forest where the Unseelie host is said to hold the trees always at the dry and brittle end of autumn, always on the cusp of a killing winter that will never come. It's only a shallow, kidney-shaped pool in a small, neglected city park. No deeper than a tall man's knees, water the color of chocolate milk in a pool bordered by crumbling mortar and mica-flecked blocks of quarried stone. There are fountains that seem to run both night and day, two of them, and I suppose one might well imagine this to be some sort of enchantment, twin rainstorms falling always and only across the surface directly above submerged, disgorging mechanisms planted decently or deceitfully out of sight. In daylight, the water rises from the cloudy pool and is transformed, going suddenly clean and translucent, a fleeting purity before tyrant gravity reasserts itself and the spray falls inevitably back into the brown pool, becoming once again only some part of the murky, indivisible whole. There are gnarled old willows growing close together, here and there along the shore, trees planted when my grandmother was a young woman. They lean out across the pool like patient fishermen, casting limp green lines leaf-baited for fish that have never been and will never be.

No one much comes here anymore. Perhaps they never did. I suspect most people in the city don't even know the park exists, steep-sided and unobtrusive, hidden on three sides behind the stately Edwardian-era houses along Euclid Avenue, Elizabeth Street, and Waverly Way. The fourth side, the park's dingy north edge, is bordered by an ugly redbrick apartment complex built sometime in the seventies, rundown now and completely at odds with everything else around it. I wonder how many grand old houses were sacrificed to the sledgehammers and bulldozers to make room for that eyesore. Someone made a lot of money off it once, I suppose. But I'm already letting myself get distracted. Already, I'm indulging myself with digressions that have no place here. Already, I'm trying to look away.

Last spring, they found the boy's body near the small stone bridge spanning one end of the pool, the end farthest from the brick apartment complex. Back that way, there are thick bunches of cattails and a few sickly water lilies and other aquatic plants I don't know names for. I've seen the coroner's report, and I know that the body was found floating face up, that the lungs were filled with water, that insects had done a lot of damage before someone spotted the corpse and called the police. No one questioned that the boy had drowned, and there was no particular suspicion of foul play. He had an arrest record—shoplifting, drugs and solicitation. To my knowledge, no one ever bothered to ask how he might have drowned in such shallow water. There are ways it could happen, certainly. He slipped and struck his head. It might have been as simple as that.

No one mentioned the hoof prints, either, but I have photographs of them. The tracks of a large unshod horse pressed clearly into a patch of red mud near the bridge, sometime before the boy's body was pulled from the pool. You don't see a lot of horses in this part of town. In fact, you don't see any. I'm writing this like it might be a mystery, like I don't already know the answers, and that's a lie. I'm not exactly a writer. I'm a photographer, and I don't really know how one goes about this sort of thing. I'm afraid I'm not much better with confessions.

I could have started by explaining that I happen to own one of those old houses along Euclid, passed down to me from my paternal grandparents. I could have begun with the antique bridle, which I found wrapped in a moth-eaten blanket, hidden at the bottom of a steamer trunk in the attic, or . . . I could have started almost anywhere. With my bad dreams, for example, the things I only choose to call my bad dreams out of cowardice. The dreams—no, the *dream*, singular, which has recurred too many times to count, and which is possibly my shortest and most honest route to this confession.

(No, I didn't *kill* the boy, if that's what you're thinking. I'm no proper murderess. It'll never be so simple as that. This is a different sort of confession.)

In the dream, I'm standing alone on the little stone bridge, standing there stark naked, and the park is washed in the light of a moon that is either full or very near to full. I have no recollection of getting out of bed, or of having left the house, or of the short walk down to the bridge. I'm cold, and I wonder why I didn't at least think to wear my robe and slippers. I'm holding the bridle from the trunk, which is always much heavier than I remember it being. Something's moving in the water, and I want to turn away. Always, I want to turn away, and when I look down I see that the drowned boy floating in the water smiles up at me and laughs. Then he sinks below the surface, or something unseen pulls him down, and that's when I see the girl, standing far out near the center of the pool, bathing in one of the fountains.

A week ago, I laid the pen down after that last sentence, and I had no intention of ever picking it up again. At least, not to finish writing this. But there was a package in the mail this afternoon—a cardboard mailing tube addressed to me—and one thing leads to another, so to speak. The only return address on the tube was *Chicago, IL 60625*. No street address or post-office box, no sender's name. And I noticed almost immediately that the postmark didn't match the Chicago zip. The zip code on the postmark was 93650, which turns out to be Fresno, California. I opened the tube and found two things inside. The first was a print of a painting I'd never seen before, and the second was a note neatly typed out and paper-clipped to a corner of the print, which read as follows:

A blacksmith from Raasay lost his daughter to the Each Uisge.
In revenge, the blacksmith and his son made a set of large

hooks, in a forge they set up by the lochside. They then roasted a sheep and heated the hooks until they were red hot. At last, a great mist appeared from the water and the Each Uisge rose from the depths and seized the sheep. The blacksmith and his son rammed the red-hot hooks into its flesh and, after a short struggle, dispatched it. In the morning there was nothing left of the creature apart from a foul jelly-like substance.

(*More West Highland Tales*; J. F. Campbell, 1883)

The print was labeled on the back, with a sticker affixed directly to the paper, as *The Black Lake* by Jan Preisler, 1904. It shows a nude young man standing beside a tall white horse at the edge of a lake that is, indeed, entirely black. The horse's mane is black, as well, as is its tail and the lower portions of it legs. The young man is holding some black garment I can't identify. The sticker informed me that the original hangs in the Nárdoni Gallerie in Prague. I sat and stared at it for a long time, and then I came back upstairs and picked up this pen again.

These are only words. Only ink on paper.

I had the dream again tonight, and now it's almost dawn, and I'm sitting in my study at my desk, trying to finish what I started.

And I am standing on the stone bridge in the park, standing naked under the full moon, and I can hear the fountains, all that water forced up and then spattering down again across the pool, which, in my dream, is as black as the lake in Preisler's painting. The girl's wading towards me, parting the muddy, dark water with the prow of her thighs, and her skin is white and her long hair is black, black as ink, the ink in this pen, the lake in a picture painted one hundred and two years ago.

Her eyes are black, too, and I can read no expression in them. She stops a few yards from the bridge and gazes up at me. She points to the heavy bridle in my hands, and I hold it out for her to see. She smiles, showing me a mouthful of teeth that would be at home in the jaws of some devouring ocean thing, and she holds both her arms out to me. And I understand what she's asking me to do, that she wants me to drop the bridle into the pool. I step back from the edge of the bridge, moving so slowly now I might as well be mired to the ankles in molasses; she takes another quick step towards me, and her teeth glint in the moonlight. I clutch the bridle more tightly than before, and the bit and curb chains jingle softly.

I found this online an hour or so after I opened the mailing tube and copied it down on a Post-it note, something from a website, "Folklore of the British Isles"—*There was one way in which a kelpie could be defeated and tamed; the kelpie's power of shape shifting was said to reside in its bridle, and anybody who could claim possession of it could force the kelpie to submit to their will.*

One thing leads to another.

In my dream, I have laid the bridle in the fallen leaves gathered about the base of a drinking fountain that hasn't worked in decades, setting it a safe distance from the water, and she's standing at the edge of the pool, waiting for me. I go to her, because I can't imagine what else I would ever do. She takes my hand and leads me down into the cold black water. She kisses me, presses her thin, pale lips to mine, and I taste what any drowning woman might taste—silt and algae, fish shit and all the fine particulate filth that drifts in icy currents and settles, at last, to the bottoms of lakes that have no bottoms. Her mouth is filled with water, and it flows into me like ice. Her piranha's teeth scrape against my cheek, drawing blood. She laughs and whispers in a language I can't understand, a language that I can somehow only vaguely even *hear*, and then she's forcing me down into the muck and weeds beneath the bridge. She cups my left breast in one hand, and I can see the webbing between her fingers.

And then . . .

Then we are riding wild through the midnight streets of the city, her hooves pounding loud as thunder on the blacktop, and no one we pass turns to look. No one sees. No one would dare. I tangle my fingers in her black mane, and the wind is a hurricane whisper in my ears. We pass automobiles and their unseeing drivers. We pass shops and restaurants and service stations closed up for the night. We race along a railroad track past landscapes of kudzu and broken concrete, and the night air smells of creosote and rust. I think the ride will surely never end. I pray that it will never end, and I feel her body so strong between my legs.

Beneath the stone bridge, she slides her fingers down and across my belly, between my legs. The mud squelches beneath us, and she asks me for the bridle, stolen from her almost two hundred years ago, when she was tricked into leaving her lake. She promises no harm will ever come to me, at least no harm from her, if only I will return the bridle, a bewitched and fairie thing that is rightfully hers and which I have no conceivable use for.

Her hooves against the streets seem to rattle the stars above us, seem to loosen them from their places in the firmament. I beg her to let the ride never end. I promise her everything, except the old bridle.

In the fetid darkness beneath the bridge, away from the glare of the moon, her eyes blaze bright as burning forests, and she slips two fingers deep inside me. More words I can't understand, and then more that I do, and I imagine myself crawling back to the spot where I left the bridle lying next to the broken drinking fountain. I imagine myself giving it to her.

Her hooves are thunder and cyclones, cannon fire and the splintering of bedrock bones deep within the hearts of ancient mountains. I am deaf and blind and there is nothing remaining in the universe except her. In another instant, my soul will flicker out, and she will consume even the memory of me.

And then I see the dead boy watching me, standing near the bridge and watching as she fucks me, or he's watching from a street corner as we hurry past. Holes where his eyes once were, holes the hungry insects and birds have made, but I know that he can see us, nonetheless. One does not need eyes to see such things. Indeed, I think, eyes only blind a woman or a dead boy to the truth of things as terrible as the white woman leaning over me or the black horse bearing me along deserted avenues. And he is a warning, and I see him dragged down and down into depths only the kelpie can find in a knee-deep pool in a city park. The air rushes from his lungs, bleeds from his mouth and nostrils, and streams back towards the surface. I see him riding her all the way to the bottom, and I push her away from me.

The night is filled with the screams of horses.

And I come awake in my bed, gasping and sweat-drenched, sick to my stomach and fumbling for the light, almost knocking the lamp off the table beside my bed. My skin is smeared with stinking mud, and there's mud on the white sheets and green-gray bits of weed caught in my wet hair. When I can walk, I go to the shower and stand beneath the hot water beating down on me, trying to forget again, and afterwards, I take the soiled sheets down to the washing machine in the basement. Again. And, the last part of this ritual, I find a flashlight and go to the trunk in the attic to be sure that the bridle is still there, wrapped safe inside its wool blanket.

∼

Caitlín R. Kiernan's award-winning short fiction has been collected, to date, in fourteen volumes, one of which, *The Ape's Wife and Other Stories* received the World Fantasy Award. Novels include *The Red Tree* and *The Drowning Girl: A Memoir* (winner of the James Tiptree, Jr. Award and the Bram Stoker Award, nominated for the Nebula, Locus, Shirley Jackson, World Fantasy, British Fantasy, and Mythopoeic awards). Mid-World Productions has optioned both to develop into feature films. Kiernan is currently writing the screenplay for *The Red Tree.*

∼

Fishmere is a crumbling town that never really came to much. There are some decent neighborhoods, but shadowy streets, vacant lots, and dead brick buildings eclipse them. It's also the only place to find the magic Spell of the Last Triangle.

The Last Triangle
Jeffrey Ford

I was on the street with nowhere to go, broke, with a habit. It was around Halloween, cold as a motherfucker in Fishmere—part suburb, part crumbling city that never happened. I was getting by, roaming the neighborhoods after dark, looking for unlocked cars to see what I could snatch. Sometimes I stole shit out of people's yards and pawned it or sold it on the street. One night I didn't have enough to cop, and I was in a bad way. There was nobody on the street to even beg from. It was freezing. Eventually I found this house on a corner and noticed an open garage out back. I got in there where it was warmer, lay down on the concrete, and went into withdrawal.

You can't understand what that's like unless you've done it. Remember that *Twilight Zone* where you make your own hell? Like that. I eventually passed out or fell asleep, and woke, shivering, to daylight, unable to get off the floor. Standing in the entrance to the garage was this little old woman with her arms folded, staring down through her bifocals at me. The second she saw I was awake, she turned and walked away. I felt like I'd frozen straight through to my spine during the night and couldn't get up. A splitting headache, and the nausea was pretty intense too. My first thought was to take off, but too much of me just didn't give a shit. The old woman reappeared, but now she was carrying a pistol in her left hand.

"What's wrong with you?" she said.

I told her I was sick.

"I've seen you around town," she said. "You're an addict." She didn't seem freaked out by the situation, even though I was. I managed to get up on one elbow. I shrugged and said, "True."

And then she left again, and a few minutes later came back, toting an electric space heater. She set it down next to me, stepped away and said, "You missed it last night, but there's a cot in the back of the garage. Look," she said, "I'm going to give you some money. Go buy clothes. You can stay here and I'll feed you. If I know you're using, though, I'll call the police. I hope you realize that if you do anything I don't like I'll shoot you." She said it like it was a foregone conclusion, and, yeah, I could actually picture her pulling the trigger.

What could I say? I took the money, and she went back into her house. My first reaction to the whole thing was to laugh. I could score. I struggled up all dizzy and bleary, smelling like the devil's own shit, and stumbled away.

I didn't cop that day, only a small bag of weed. Why? I'm not sure, but there was something about the way the old woman talked to me, her unafraid, straight-up approach. That, maybe, and I was so tired of the cycle of falling hard out of a drug dream onto the street and scrabbling like a three-legged dog for the next fix. By noon, I was pot high, downtown, still feeling shitty, when I passed this old clothing store. It was one of those places like you can't fucking believe is still in operation. The mannequin in the window had on a tan leisure suit. Something about the way the sunlight hit that window display, though, made me remember the old woman's voice, and I had this feeling like I was on an errand for my mother.

I got the clothes. I went back and lived in her garage. The jitters, the chills, the scratching my scalp and forearms were bad, but when I could finally get to sleep, that cot was as comfortable as a bed in a fairy tale. She brought food a couple times a day. She never said much to me, and the gun was always around. The big problem was going to the bathroom. When you get off the junk, your insides really open up. I knew if I went near the house, she'd shoot me. Let's just say I marked the surrounding territory. About two weeks in, she wondered herself and asked me, "Where are you evacuating?"

At first I wasn't sure what she was saying. "Evacuating?" Eventually, I caught on and told her, "Around." She said that I could come in the house to use the downstairs bathroom. It was tough, 'cause every other second I wanted to just bop her on the head, take everything she had, and score like there was no tomorrow. I kept a tight lid on it till one day, when I was sure I was going to blow, a delivery truck pulled up to the side of the house and delivered, to the garage, a set of barbells and a bench. Later when she brought me out some food, she nodded to the weights and said, "Use them before you jump out of your skin. I insist."

Ms. Berkley was her name. She never told me her first name, but I saw it on her mail, "Ifanel." What kind of name is that? She had iron-gray hair, pulled back tight into a bun, and strong green eyes behind the big glasses. Baggy corduroy pants and a zip-up sweater was her wardrobe. There was a yellow one with flowers around the collar. She was a busy old woman. Quick and low to the ground.

Her house was beautiful inside. The floors were polished and covered with those Persian rugs. Wallpaper and stained-glass windows. But there was none of that goofy shit I remembered my grandmother going in for: suffering Christs, knitted hats on the toilet paper. Every room was in perfect order and there were books everywhere. Once she let me move in from the garage to the basement, I'd see her reading at night, sitting at her desk in what she called her "office." All the lights were out except for this one brass lamp shining right over the book that lay on her desk. She moved her lips when she read. "Good night, Ms. Berkley," I'd say to her and head for the basement door. From down the hall I'd hear her voice come like out of a dream, "Good night." She told me she'd been a history teacher at a college. You could tell she was really smart. It didn't exactly take a genius, but she saw straight through my bullshit.

One morning we were sitting at her kitchen table having coffee, and I asked her why she'd helped me out. I was feeling pretty good then. She said, "That's what you're supposed to do. Didn't anyone ever teach you that?"

"Weren't you afraid?"

"Of you?" she said. She took the pistol out of her bathrobe pocket and put it on the table between us. "There's no bullets in it," she told me.

"I went with a fellow who died and he left that behind. I wouldn't know how to load it."

Normally I would have laughed, but her expression made me think she was trying to tell me something. "I'll pay you back," I said. "I'm gonna get a job this week and start paying you back."

"No, I've got a way for you to pay me back," she said and smiled for the first time. I was ninety-nine percent sure she wasn't going to tell me to fuck her, but, you know, it crossed my mind.

Instead, she asked me to take a walk with her downtown. By then it was winter, cold as a witch's tit. Snow was coming. We must have been a sight on the street. Ms. Berkley, marching along in her puffy ski parka and wool hat, blue with gold stars and a tassel. I don't think she was even five foot. I walked a couple of steps behind her. I'm six foot four inches, I hadn't shaved or had a haircut in a long while, and I was wearing this brown suit jacket that she'd found in her closet. I couldn't button it if you had a gun to my head and my arms stuck out the sleeves almost to the elbow. She told me, "It belonged to the dead man."

Just past the library, we cut down an alley, crossed a vacant lot, snow still on the ground, and then hit a dirt road that led back to this abandoned factory. One story, white stucco, all the windows empty, glass on the ground, part of the roof caved in. She led me through a stand of trees around to the left side of the old building.

From where we stood, I could see a lake through the woods. She pointed at the wall and said, "Do you see that symbol in red there?" I looked but all I saw was a couple of *Fucks*.

"I don't see it," I told her.

"Pay attention," she said and took a step closer to the wall. Then I saw it. About the size of two fists. It was like a capital *E* tipped over on its three points, and sitting on its back, right in the middle, was an *o*. "Take a good look at it," she told me. "I want you to remember it."

I stared for a few seconds and told her, "Okay, I got it."

"I walk to the lake almost every day," she said. "This wasn't here a couple of days ago." She looked at me like that was supposed to mean something to me. I shrugged; she scowled. As we walked home, it started to snow.

Before I could even take off the dead man's jacket, she called me into her office. She was sitting at her desk, still in her coat and hat, with a book open in front of her. I came over to the desk, and she pointed at the book. "What do you see there?" she asked. And there it was, the red, knocked-over *E* with the *o* on top.

I said, "Yeah, the thing from before. What is it?"

"The Last Triangle," she said.

"Where's the triangle come in?" I asked.

"The three points of the capital *E* stand for the three points of a triangle."

"So what?"

"Don't worry about it," she said. "Here's what I want you to do. Tomorrow, after breakfast, I want you to take a pad and a pen, and I want you to walk all around the town, everywhere you can think of, and look to see if that symbol appears on any other walls. If you find one, write down the address for it—street and number. Look for places that are abandoned, rundown, burned out."

I didn't want to believe she was crazy, but . . .

I said to her, "Don't you have any real work for me to do—heavy lifting, digging, painting, you know?"

"Just do what I ask you to do."

Ms. Berkley gave me a few bucks and sent me on my way. First things first, I went downtown, scored a couple of joints, bought a forty of Colt. Then I did the grand tour. It was fucking freezing, of course. The sky was brown, and the dead man's jacket wasn't cutting it. I found the first of the symbols on the wall of a closed-down bar. The place had a pink plastic sign that said *Here It Is*, with a silhouette of a woman with an Afro sitting in a martini glass. The *E* was there in red on the plywood of a boarded front window. I had to walk a block each way to figure out the address, but I got it. After that I kept looking. I walked myself sober and then some and didn't get back to the house till nightfall.

When I told Ms. Berkley that I'd found one, she smiled and clapped her hands together. She asked for the address, and I delivered. She set me up with spaghetti and meatballs at the kitchen table. I was tired, but seriously, I felt like a prince. She went down the hall to her office. A few minutes later, she came back with a piece of paper in her hand. As I pushed the plate away, she set the paper down in front of me and then took a seat.

"That's a map of town," she said. I looked it over. There were two dots in red pen and a straight line connecting them. "You see the dots?" she asked.

"Yeah."

"Those are two points of the Last Triangle."

"Okay," I said and thought, "Here we go . . . "

"The Last Triangle is an equilateral triangle; all the sides are equal," she said.

I failed math every year in high school, so I just nodded.

"Since we know these two points, we know that the last point is in one of two places on the map, either east or west." She reached across the table and slid the map toward her. With the red pen, she made two dots and then made two triangles sharing a line down the center. She pushed the map toward me again. "Tomorrow you have to look either here or here," she said, pointing with the tip of the pen.

The next day I found the third one, to the east, just before it got dark. A tall old house, on the edge of an abandoned industrial park. It looked like there'd been a fire. There was an old rusted Chevy up on blocks in the driveway. The *E*-and-*o* thing was spray-painted on the trunk.

When I brought her that info, she gave me the lowdown on the triangle. "I read a lot of books about history," she said, "and I have this ability to remember things I've seen or read. If I saw a phone number once, I'd remember it correctly. It's not a photographic memory; it doesn't work automatically or with everything. Maybe five years ago I read this book on ancient magic, *The Spells of Abriel the Magus*, and I remembered the symbol from that book when I saw it on the wall of the old factory last week. I came home, found the book, and reread the part about the Last Triangle. It's also known as Abriel's Escape or Abriel's Prison.

"Abriel was a thirteenth-century magus . . . magician. He wandered around Europe and created six powerful spells. The triangle, once marked out, denotes a protective zone in which its creator cannot be harmed. There's a limitation to the size it can be, each leg no more than a mile. At the same time that zone is a sanctuary, it's a trap. The magus can't leave its boundary, ever. To cross it is certain death. For this reason, the spell was used only once, by Abriel, in Dresden, to escape a number of people he'd harmed with his dark arts who had sent their own wizards to kill him. He lived out the rest of his life there, within the Last Triangle, and died at one hundred years of age."

"That's a doozy."

"Pay attention," she said. "For the Last Triangle to be activated, the creator of the triangle must take a life at its geographical center between the time of the three symbols being marked in the world and the next full moon. Legend has it, Abriel killed the baker Ellot Haber to induce the spell."

It took me almost a minute and a half to grasp what she was saying. "You mean, someone's gonna get iced?" I said.

"Maybe."

"Come on, a kid just happened to make that symbol. Coincidence."

"No, remember, a perfect equilateral triangle, each one of the symbols exactly where it should be." She laughed, and, for a second, looked a lot younger.

"I don't believe in magic," I told her. "There's no magic out there."

"You don't have to believe it," she said. "But maybe someone out there does. Someone desperate for protection, willing to believe even in magic."

"That's pretty far fetched," I said, "but if you think there's a chance, call the cops. Just leave me out of it."

"The cops," she said and shook her head. "They'd lock me up with that story."

"Glad we agree on that."

"The center of the triangle on my map," she said, "is the train-station parking lot. And in five nights there'll be a full moon. No one's gotten killed at the station yet, not that I've heard of."

After breakfast she called a cab and went out, leaving me to fix the garbage disposal and wonder about the craziness. I tried to see it her way. She'd told me it was our civic duty to do something, but I wasn't buying any of it. Later that afternoon, I saw her sitting at the computer in her office. Her glasses near the end of her nose, she was reading off the Internet and loading bullets into the magazine clip of the pistol.

Eventually she looked up and saw me. "You can find just about anything on the Internet," she said.

"What are you doing with that gun?"

"We're going out tonight."

"Not with that."

She stopped loading. "Don't tell me what to do," she said.

After dinner, around dusk, we set out for the train station. Before we left, she handed me the gun. I made sure the safety was on and stuck it in the side pocket of the brown jacket. While she was out getting the bullets she'd bought two chairs that folded down and fit in small plastic tubes. I carried them. Ms. Berkley held a flashlight and in her ski parka had stashed a pint of blackberry brandy. The night was clear and cold, and a big waxing moon hung over town.

We turned off the main street into an alley next to the hardware store and followed it a long way before it came out on the south side of the train station. There was a rundown one-story building there in the corner of the parking lot. I ripped off the plywood planks that covered the door, and we went in. The place was empty but for some busted-up office furniture, and all the windows were shattered, letting the breeze in. We moved through the darkness, Ms. Berkley leading the way with the flashlight, to a back room with a view of the parking lot and station just beyond it. We set up the chairs and took our seats at the empty window. She killed the light.

"Tell me this is the strangest thing you've ever done," I whispered to her.

She brought out the pint of brandy, unscrewed the top, and took a tug on it. "Life's about doing what needs to get done," she said. "The sooner you figure that out, the better for everyone." She passed me the bottle.

After an hour and a half, my eyes had adjusted to the moonlight and I'd scanned every inch of that cracked, potholed parking lot. Two trains a half-hour apart rolled into the station's elevated platform, and from what I could see, no one got on or off. Ms. Berkley was doing what needed to be done—namely, snoring. I took out a joint and lit up. I'd already polished off the brandy. I kept an eye on the old lady, ready to flick the joint out the window if I saw her eyelids flutter. The shivering breeze did a good job of clearing out the smoke.

At around three A.M., I'd just about nodded off, when the sound of a train pulling into the station brought me back. I sat up and leaned toward the window. It took me a second to clear my eyes and focus. When I did, I saw the silhouette of a person descending the stairs of the raised platform. The figure passed beneath the light at the front of the station, and I could see it was a young woman, carrying a briefcase. I wasn't quite sure what the fuck I was supposed to be doing, so I tapped Ms. Berkley. She came awake with a splutter and looked a little sheepish for having corked off. I said, "There's a woman heading to her car. Should I shoot her?"

"Very funny," she said and got up to stand closer to the window.

I'd figured out which of the few cars in the parking lot belonged to the young woman. She looked like the white-Honda type. Sure enough, she made a beeline for it.

"There's someone else," said Ms. Berkley. "Coming out from under the trestle."

"Where?"

"Left," she said, and I saw him, a guy with a long coat and hat. He was moving fast, heading for the young woman. Ms. Berkley grabbed my arm and squeezed it. "Go," she said. I lunged up out of the chair, took two steps, and got dizzy from having sat for so long. I fumbled in my pocket for the pistol as I groped my way out of the building. Once I hit the air, I was fine, and I took off running for the parking lot. Even as jumped up as I was, I thought, "I'm not gonna shoot anyone," and left the gun's safety on.

The young woman saw me coming before she noticed the guy behind her. I scared her, and she ran the last few yards to her car. I watched her messing around with her keys and didn't notice the other guy was also on a flat-out run. As I passed the white Honda, the stranger met me and cracked me in the jaw like a pro. I went down hard but held onto the gun. As soon as I came to, I sat up. The guy—I couldn't get a good look at his face—drew a blade from his left sleeve. By then the woman was in the car, though, and it screeched off across the parking lot.

He turned, brandishing the long knife, and started for me.

You better believe the safety came off then. That instant, I heard Ms. Berkley's voice behind me. "What's the meaning of this?" she said in a stern voice. The stranger looked up, and then turned and ran off, back into the shadows beneath the trestle.

"We've got to get out of here," she said and helped me to my feet. "If that girl's got any brains, she'll call the cops." Ms. Berkley could run pretty fast. We made it back to the building, got the chairs, the empty bottle, and as many cigarette butts as I could find, and split for home. We stayed off the main street and wound our way back through the residential blocks. We didn't see a soul.

I couldn't feel how cold I was till I got back in the house. Ms. Berkley made tea. Her hands shook a little. We sat at the kitchen table in silence for a long time.

Finally, I said, "Well, you were right."

"The gun was a mistake, but if you didn't have it, you'd be dead now," she said.

"Not to muddy the waters here, but that's closer to dead than I want to get. We're gonna have to go to the police, but if we do, that'll be it for me."

"You tried to save her," said Ms. Berkley. "Very valiant, by the way."

I laughed. "Tell that to the judge when he's looking over my record."

She didn't say anything else, but left and went to her office. I fell asleep on the cot in the basement with my clothes on. It was warm down there by the furnace. I had terrible dreams of the young woman getting her throat cut but was too tired to wake from them. Eventually, I came to with a hand on my shoulder and Ms. Berkley saying, "Thomas." I sat up quickly, sure I'd forgotten to do something. She said, "Relax," and rested her hand for a second on my chest. She sat on the edge of the cot with her hat and coat on.

"Did you sleep?" I asked.

"I went back to the parking lot after the sun came up. There were no police around. Under the trestle, where the man with the knife had come from, I found these." She took a handful of cigarette butts out of her coat pocket and held them up.

"Anybody could have left them there at any time," I said. "You read too many books."

"Maybe, maybe not," she said.

"He must have stood there waiting for quite a while, judging from how many butts you've got there."

She nodded. "This is a serious man," she said. "Say he's not just a lunatic, but an actual magician?"

"Magician," I said and snorted. "More like a creep who believes his own bullshit."

"Watch the language," she said.

"Do we go back to the parking lot tonight?" I asked.

"No, there'll be police there tonight. I'm sure that girl reported the incident. I have something for you to do. These cigarettes are a Spanish brand, Ducados. I used to know someone who smoked them. The only store in town that sells them is over by the park. Do you know Maya's Newsstand?"

I nodded.

"I think he buys his cigarettes there."

"You want me to scope it? How am I supposed to know whether it's him or not? I never got a good look at him."

"Maybe by the imprint of your face on his knuckles?" she said.

I couldn't believe she was breaking my balls, but when she laughed, I had to.

"Take my little camera with you," she said.

"Why?"

"I want to see what you see," she said. She got up then and left the basement. I got dressed. While I ate, she showed me how to use the camera. It was a little electronic job, but amazing, with telephoto capability and a little window you could see your pictures in. I don't think I'd held a camera in ten years.

I sat on a bench in the park, next to a giant pine tree, and watched the newsstand across the street. I had my forty in a brown paper bag and a five-dollar joint in my jacket. The day was clear and cold, and people came and went on the street, some of them stopping to buy a paper or cigs from Maya. One thing I noticed was that nobody came to the park, the one nice place in crumbling Fishmere.

All afternoon and nothing criminal, except for one girl's miniskirt. She was my first photo—exhibit A. After that I took a break and went back into the park, where there was a gazebo looking out across a small lake. I fired up the joint and took another pic of some geese. Mostly I watched the sun on the water and wondered what I'd do once the Last Triangle hoodoo played itself out. Part of me wanted to stay with Ms. Berkley, and the other part knew it wouldn't be right. I'd been on the scag for fifteen years, and now somebody's making breakfast and dinner every day. Things like the camera, a revelation to me. She even had me reading a book, *The Professor's House* by Willa Cather—slow as shit, but somehow I needed to know what happened next to old Godfrey St. Peter. The food, the weights, and staying off the hard stuff made me strong.

Late in the afternoon, he came to the newsstand. I'd been in such a daze, the sight of him there, like he just materialized, made me jump. My hands shook a little as I telephotoed in on him. He paid for two packs of cigs, and I snapped the picture. I wasn't sure if I'd caught his mug. He was pretty well hidden by the long coat's collar and the hat. There was no time to check the shot. As he moved away down the sidewalk, I stowed the camera in my pocket and followed him, hanging back fifty yards or so.

He didn't seem suspicious. Never looked around or stopped, but just kept moving at the same brisk pace. Only when it came to me that he was walking us in a circle did I get that he was on to me. At that point, he made a quick left into an alley. I followed. The alley was a short one with a brick wall at the end. He'd vanished. I walked cautiously into the shadows and looked around behind the dumpsters. There was nothing there. A gust of wind lifted the old newspapers and litter into the air, and I'll admit I was scared. On the way back to the house, I looked over my shoulder about a hundred times.

I handed Ms. Berkley the camera in her office. She took a cord out of her desk drawer and plugged one end into the camera and one into the computer. She typed some shit, and then the first picture appeared. It was the legs.

"Finding the focus with that shot?" she asked.

"Everyone's a suspect," I said.

"Foolishness," she murmured. She liked the geese, said it was a nice composition. Then the one of the guy at the newsstand came up, and, yeah, I nailed it. A really clear profile of his face. Eyes like a hawk and a sharp nose. He had white hair and a thick white mustache.

"Not bad," I said, but Ms. Berkley didn't respond. She was staring hard at the picture and her mouth was slightly open. She reached out and touched the screen.

"You know him?" I asked.

"You're wearing his jacket," she said. Then she turned away, put her face in her hands.

I left her alone and went into the kitchen. I made spaghetti the way she'd showed me. While stirring the sauce, I said to my reflection in the stove hood, "Now the dead man's back, and he's the evil magician?" Man, I really wanted to laugh the whole thing off, but I couldn't forget the guy's disappearing act.

I put two plates of spaghetti down on the kitchen table and then went to fetch Ms. Berkley. She told me to go away. Instead I put my hands on her shoulders and said, "Come on, you should eat something." Then, applying as little pressure as possible, I sort of lifted her as she stood. In the kitchen, I held her chair for her and gave her a cup of tea. My spaghetti was undercooked and the sauce was cold, but still, not bad. She used her napkin to dry her eyes.

"The dead man looks pretty good for a dead man," I said.

"It was easier to explain by telling you he was dead. Who wants the embarrassment of saying someone left them?"

"I get it," I said.

"I think most people would, but still . . . "

"This clears something up for me," I told her. "I always thought it was pretty strange that two people in the same town would know about Abriel and the Last Triangle. I mean, what's the chances?"

"The book is his," she said. "Years after he left, it just became part of my library, and eventually I read it. Now that I think of it, he read a lot of books about the occult."

"Who is he?"

"His name is Lionel Brund. I met him years ago, when I was in my thirties. I was already teaching at the college, and I owned this house. We both were at a party hosted by a colleague. He was just passing through and knew someone who knew someone at the party. We hit it off. He had great stories about his travels. He liked to laugh. It was fun just going to the grocery store with him. My first real romance. A very gentle man."

The look on her face made me say, "But?"

She nodded. "But he owned a gun, and I had no idea what kind of work he did, although he always had plenty of money. Parts of his life were a secret. He'd go away for a week or two at a time on some 'business' trip. I didn't mind that, because there were parts of my life I wanted to keep to myself as well. We were together, living in this house, for over two years, and then, one day, he was gone. I waited for him to come back for a long time and then moved on, made my own life."

"Now you do what needs to get done," I said.

She laughed. "Exactly."

"Lionel knows we're onto him. He played me this afternoon, took me in a circle and then was gone with the wind. It creeped me."

"I want to see him," she said. "I want to talk to him."

"He's out to kill somebody to protect himself," I said.

"I don't care," she said.

"Forget it," I told her and then asked for the gun. She pushed it across the table to me.

"He could come after us," I said. "You've got to be careful." She got up to go into her office, and I drew the butcher knife out of its wooden holder on the counter and handed it to her. I wanted her to get how serious things were. She took it but said nothing. I could tell she was lost in the past.

I put the gun, safety off, on the stand next to my cot and lay back with a head full of questions. I stayed awake for a long while before I eventually gave in. A little bit after I dozed off, I was half wakened by the sound of the phone ringing upstairs. I heard Ms. Berkley walk down the hall and pick up. Her voice was a distant mumble. Then I fell asleep for a few minutes, and the first thing I heard when I came to again was the sound of the back door closing. It took me a minute to put together that he'd called and she'd gone to meet him.

I got dressed in a flash, but put on three T-shirts instead of wearing Lionel's jacket. I thought he might have the power to spook it since it belonged to him. It took me a couple of seconds to decide whether to leave the gun behind as well. But I was shit scared so I shoved it in the waist of my jeans and took off. I ran dead out to the train-station parking lot. Luckily there were no cops there, but there wasn't anybody else either.

I went in the station, searched beneath the trestles, and went back to the rundown building we'd sat in. Nothing.

As I walked back to the house, I tried to think of where he would have asked to meet her. I pictured all the places I'd been to in the past few weeks. An image of Ms. Berkley's map came to mind, the one of town with the red dots and the triangles, east and west. I'd not found a triangle point to the west, and as I considered that, I recalled the point I had found in the east, the symbol spray-painted on the trunk of an old car up on blocks. It came to me—say that one didn't count because it wasn't on a building, connected to the ground. That was a fake. Maybe he knew somehow Ms. Berkley would notice the symbols and he wanted to throw her off.

Then it struck me: what if there was a third symbol in the west I just didn't see? I tried to picture the map as the actual streets it represented and figure where the center of a western triangle would be. At first it seemed way too complicated, just a jumble of frustration, but I took a few deep breaths, and, recalling the streets I'd walked before, realized the spot must be somewhere in the park across the street from Maya's Newsstand. It was a hike, and I knew I had to pace myself, but the fact that I'd figured out Lionel's twists and turns gave me a burst of energy. What I really wanted was to tell Ms. Berkley how I'd thought it through. Then I realized she might already be dead.

Something instinctively drew me toward the gazebo. It was a perfect center for a magician's prison. The moonlight was on the lake. I thought I heard them talking, saw their shadows sitting on the bench, smelled the smoke of Ducados, but when I took the steps and leaned over to catch my breath, I realized it was all in my mind. The place was empty and still. The geese called from out on the lake. I sat down on the bench and lit a cigarette. Only when I resigned myself to just returning to the house, it came to me I had one more option: to find the last point of the western triangle.

I knew it was a long shot at night, looking without a flashlight for something I couldn't find during the day. My only consolation was that since Lionel hadn't taken Ms. Berkley to the center of his triangle, he might not intend to use her as his victim.

I was exhausted, and although I set out from the gazebo jogging toward my best guess as to where the last point was, I was soon walking.

The street map of town with the red triangles would flash momentarily in my memory and then disappear. I went up a street that was utterly dark, and the wind followed me. From there, I turned and passed a row of closed factory buildings.

The symbol could have been anywhere, hiding in the dark. Finally, there was a cross street, and I walked down a block of row homes, some boarded, some with bars on the windows. That path led to an industrial park. Beneath a dim streetlight, I stopped and tried to picture the map, but it was no use. I was totally lost. I gave up and turned back in the direction I thought Ms. Berkley's house would be.

One block outside the industrial park, I hit a street of old four-story apartment buildings. The doors were off the hinges, and the moonlight showed no reflection in the shattered windows. A neighborhood of vacant lots and dead brick giants. Halfway down the block, hoping to find a left turn, I just happened to look up and see an unbroken window, yellow lamplight streaming out. From where I stood, I could only see the ceiling of the room, but faint silhouettes moved across it. I took out the gun. There was no decent reason why I thought it was them, but I felt drawn to the place as if under a spell.

I took the stone steps of the building, and when I tried the door, it pushed open. I thought this was strange, but I figured he might have left it ajar for Ms. Berkley. Inside, the foyer was so dark and there was no light on the first landing. I found the first step by inching forward and feeling around with my foot. The last thing I needed was three flights of stairs. I tried to climb without a sound, but the planks creaked unmercifully. "If they don't hear me coming," I thought, "they're both dead."

As I reached the fourth floor, I could hear noises coming from the room. It sounded like two people were arguing and wrestling around. Then I distinctly heard Ms. Berkley cry out. I lunged at the door, cracked it on the first pounce and busted it in with the second. Splinters flew, and the chain lock ripped out with a pop. I stumbled into the room, the gun pointing forward, completely out of breath. It took me a second to see what was going on.

There they were, in a bed beneath the window in the opposite corner of the room, naked, frozen by my intrusion, her legs around his back.

Ms. Berkley scooted up and quickly wrapped the blanket around herself, leaving old Lionel out in the cold. He jumped up quick, dick flopping, and got into his boxers.

"What the hell," I whispered.

"Go home, Thomas," she said.

"You're coming with me," I said.

"I can handle this," she said.

"Who's after you?" I said to Lionel. "For what?"

He took a deep breath. "Phantoms more cruel than you can imagine, my boy. I lived my young life recklessly, like you, and its mistakes have multiplied and hounded me ever since."

"You're a loser," I said and it sounded so stupid. Especially when it struck me that Lionel might have been old, but he looked pretty strong.

"Sorry, son," he said and drew that long knife from a scabbard on the nightstand next to the bed. "It's time to sever ties."

"Run," said Ms. Berkley.

I thought, "Fuck this guy," and pulled out the gun.

Ms. Berkley jumped on Lionel, but he shrugged her off with a sharp push that landed her back on the bed. "This one's not running," he said. "I can tell."

I was stunned for a moment by Ms. Berkley's nakedness. But as he advanced a step, I raised the gun and told him, "Drop the knife."

He said, "Be careful; you're hurting it."

At first his words didn't register, but then, in my hand, instead of a gun, I felt a frail wriggling thing with a heartbeat. I released my grasp, and a bat flew up to circle around the ceiling. In the same moment, I heard the gun hit the wooden floor and knew he'd tricked me with magic.

He came toward me slowly, and I whipped off two of my T-shirts and wrapped them around my right forearm. He sliced the air with the blade a few times as I crouched down and circled away from him. He lunged fast as a snake, and I got caught against a dresser. He cut me on the stomach and the right shoulder. The next time he came at me, I kicked a footstool in front of him and managed a punch to the side of his head. Lionel came back with a half dozen more slices, each marking me. The T-shirts on my arm were in shreds, as was the one I wore.

I kept watching that knife, and that's how he got me, another punch to the jaw worse than the one in the station parking lot. I stumbled backward and he followed with the blade aimed at my throat. What saved me was that Ms. Berkley grabbed him from behind. He stopped to push her off again, and I caught my balance and took my best shot to the right side of his face. The punch scored, he fell backward into the wall, and the knife flew in the air. I tried to catch it as it fell but only managed to slice my fingers. I picked it up by the handle and when I looked, Lionel was steam-rolling toward me again.

"Thomas," yelled Ms. Berkley from where she'd landed. I was stunned, and automatically pushed the weapon forward into the bulk of the charging magician. He stopped in his tracks, teetered for a second, and fell back onto his ass. He sat there on the rug, legs splayed, with that big knife sticking out of his stomach. Blood seeped around the blade and puddled in front of him.

Ms. Berkley was next to me, leaning on my shoulder. "Pay attention," she said.

I snapped out of it and looked down at Lionel. He was sighing more than breathing and staring at the floor.

"If he dies," said Ms. Berkley, "you inherit the spell of the Last Triangle."

"That's right," Lionel said. Blood came from his mouth with the words. "Wherever you are at dawn, that will be the center of your world." He laughed. "For the rest of your life you will live in a triangle within the rancid town of Fishmere."

Ms. Berkley found the gun and picked it up. She went to the bed and grabbed one of the pillows.

"Is that true?" I said and started to panic.

Lionel nodded, laughing. Ms. Berkley took up the gun again and then wrapped the pillow around it. She walked over next to Lionel, crouched down, and touched the pillow to the side of his head.

"What are you doing?" I asked.

Ms. Berkley squinted one eye and steadied her left arm with her right hand while keeping the pillow in place.

"What else?" said Lionel, spluttering blood bubbles. "What needs to be done."

The pillow muffled the sound of the shot somewhat as feathers flew everywhere. Lionel dropped onto his side without magic, the hole in his head smoking. I wasn't afraid anyone would hear. There wasn't another soul for three blocks. Ms. Berkley checked his pulse. "The Last Triangle is mine now," she said. "I have to get home by dawn." She got dressed while I stood in the hallway.

I don't remember leaving Lionel's building, or passing the park or Maya's Newsstand. We were running through the night, across town, as the sky lightened in the distance. Four blocks from home, Ms. Berkley gave out and started limping. I picked her up and, still running, carried her the rest of the way. We were in the kitchen, the tea whistle blowing, when the birds started to sing and the sun came up.

She poured the tea for us and said, "I thought I could talk Lionel out of his plan, but he wasn't the same person anymore. I could see the magic's like a drug; the more you use it, the more it pushes you out of yourself and takes over."

"Was he out to kill me or you?" I asked.

"He was out to get himself killed. I'd promised to do the job for him before you showed up. He knew we were onto him and he tried to fool us with the train-station scam, but once he heard my voice that night, he said he knew he couldn't go through with it. He just wanted to see me once more, and then I was supposed to cut his throat."

"You would have killed him?" I said.

"I did."

"You know, before I knifed him?"

"He told me the phantoms and fetches that were after him knew where he was, and it was only a matter of days before they caught up with him."

"What was it exactly he did?"

"He wouldn't say, but he implied that it had to do with loving me. And I really think he thought he did."

"What do you think?" I asked.

Ms. Berkley interrupted me. "You've got to get out of town," she said. "When they find Lionel's body, you'll be one of the usual suspects, what with your wandering around drinking beer and smoking pot in public."

"Who told you that?" I said.

"Did I just fall off the turnip truck yesterday?"

Ms. Berkley went to her office and returned with a roll of cash for me. I didn't even have time to think about leaving, to miss my cot and the weights, and the meals. The cab showed up and we left. She had her map of town with the triangles on it and had already drawn a new one—its center, her kitchen. We drove for a little ways and then she told the cab driver to pull over and wait. We were in front of a closed-down gas station on the edge of town. She got out and I followed her.

"I paid the driver to take you two towns over to Willmuth. There's a bus station there. Get a ticket and disappear," she said.

"What about you? You're stuck in the triangle."

"I'm bounded in a nutshell," she said.

"Why'd you take the spell?"

"You don't need it. You just woke up. I have every confidence that I'll be able to figure a way out of it. It's amazing what you can find on the Internet."

"A magic spell?" I said.

"Understand this," she said. "Spells are made to be broken." She stepped closer and reached her hands to my shoulders. I leaned down. She kissed me on the forehead. "Not promises, though," she said and turned away, heading home.

"Ms. Berkley," I called after her.

"Stay clean," she yelled without looking.

Back in the cab, I said, "Willmuth," and leaned against the window. The driver started the car, and we sailed through an invisible boundary, into the world.

∾

Jeffrey Ford's fifth story collection, *A Natural History of Hell*, will be published by Small Beer Press this summer. The author of eight novels—including the Edgar Award-winning *The Girl in the Glass* and the Shirley Jackson Award-winning *The Shadow Year*—Ford is a native New Yorker who now lives in Ohio.

∾

Young Tom's job is to wander the city's street collecting coins for a very old, very cruel god. The coins enable the god to walk those same streets and use his terrible magic.

Working for the God of the Love of Money
Kaaron Warren

"A cut or a bruise appears on your body," he says. "You don't remember where it came from. You go over your movements to identify the moment of injury and you worry about memory loss when the answer doesn't come, then you forget it. The matter fades as the bruise fades, as the cut heals.

"If you were to mark into your diary the times this occurred, you would not be kept busy over the course of a year. Around Christmas, most people would have a mark, other times would depend on the individual's areas of vulnerability. The anniversary of a death, perhaps, or an affair. A birthday or a good day at work, or a bad day leading to recklessness. Anything which may cause you to give a coin to a child with black hair, enormous purple eyes, teeth so white they reflect the sun as he grimaces. He is short (or tall, if you are short) and thin. He looks hungry, and you think his face will never leave you. But you forget him in an instant, you forget him as soon as you hand him the coin he has requested.

"You keep your fingers around your wallet or purse so he can't see the notes there, can't see your driver's license to come round to your address and ask for more. Can't see the picture of your lover or child so he can't think of them as his own. This is why you so rarely give coins. You don't trust the collectors. This is why the purple-eyed boy wants your coin so much.

"You hand over the coin and you forget the boy," he says, "and within a week or two you have an unexplained cut or bruise."

∽

The purple-eyed boy's name was Tom. He had been with the god for many years. He liked the work. It involved travel, and was an outdoor job. He rose as soon as the sun did, because he slept well. He slept in a broad bed, slept like a starfish, in a dark room. The god did not allow him to have a light in his bedroom.

"Night is for sleeping," said the god, "and sleep is important."

But the god's room was filled with light—it slid under his door like a living fungus, and Tom heard him snuffling and grunting in there all night.

He was an incurious child, turned that way by fear. The god liked to talk about the others who held the position before him.

"Better off not keeping any money for yourself," said the god. "I had a boy called Richard once, a boy like you. He worried about the money so much he choked on a coin, it swelled up and filled his throat so he couldn't breathe for all the money in the world."

Tom did not remember any other life than this. He did not think about the lives of other people. He always returned to the god after his day's work.

"Freedom is over-rated," the god told him. "I had a boy who looked like you once. Gerald wanted to talk about freedom but no one tells you anything when you're locked up in jail. Just the other inmates and all they tell you is how pretty you are, pretty pretty, how they love you and how lonely they are. Do you know about loneliness, Tom?" Tom nodded.

Tom knew the god did terrible things. He went out and did terrible things then came home to rest.

Each time, Tom would have to work hard, on the streets to collect the coins, then in the kitchen to melt them into a liquid the god could work with. He wasn't to rest during the melting time. Each coin had to be plopped into the cauldron and stirred, plop and stir, plop and stir, and there were thousands of coins at a time. If he paused in his stirring for a moment, the god would roar from wherever he was, and Tom's ears would burn.

Then Tom could rest for a day or two. Eat and sit in the garden, breathe and sit. The god stayed down in the basement, building his armor.

The god looked very handsome when he left home in his suit made of coins. He had gloves and socks, pants and a full jacket. He had a hat with a flap to cover his face. The whole thing glistened and shivered.

He would come back from a trip with rips and scratches, and give the suit to Tom to throw away. Tom would begin his job on the street again, collecting coins from the people.

It took a lot of coins to make a suit but the god could wait. He had patience.

"Where did that cut come from? You might remember the boy if I describe him to you. The eyes are purple, like the moment before dawn when you haven't slept, when you lay there all night and begged for sleep. The hair is black as the devil's soul. The teeth are white, they smile at you with love so you can't help but hand over a coin."

The god was very old, and very cruel. He only killed people who were loved. He wanted those left behind to suffer. He killed people whose greed brought them across his path, even if the greedy moment had occurred a long time ago, and the meeting was only a distant consequence. He took risks to complete his tasks—the god was very old, and very cruel— though truly the risks were not great, because he was in no danger, not with his suit on, not with people suffering cuts and bruises for him.

The closest he came to danger was when one of Tom's predecessors had become lazy and stolen coins from a church charity box. These coins had passed through fewer hands and provided a weak link. He had dived into the water with a little girl and stayed under, his golden fingers digging into her flesh, his eyes seeing well through the mesh of his mask. He watched her face, her eyes, felt her pathetic struggle.

Then he began to choke. The weakened suit only just gave him time to anchor the body into the mud in the bed of the river and rise carefully to the surface.

After he made his new suit, he disposed of his lazy assistant. He told Tom the stories of his predecessors because he wanted Tom to learn from their mistakes. Tom would stay young as long as he stayed loyal.

"He smells like lavender in an ancient closet or of your mother or of whatever makes you feel guilty."

Tom was a fearful boy and he did as the god told him. He listened when the god spoke and did not ask for food when he was hungry or sleep when he was tired.

The god began to trust him, to want to impress him. So Tom heard how the god spent his hours, then he began to accompany him on his outings.

Tom did not have the stomach for his employer's job. He did not like other people but he did not hate them either, and the sound of tears made him sad.

The god began to give him presents and more food, and sometimes Tom didn't have to work, he just wandered around the house, looking at his presents. He began to feel the god loved him, and one day, after an enormous meal of quail, seafood, chocolate, cake, cheese, over and over, the god smiled at him. They were slightly hysterical with food. The god described a moment of great pleasure and Tom laughed at the description of a man trying to resuscitate his wife, when she had a cut throat, she wasn't choking at all, and his air just blew straight out her neck!

They laughed, blowing and puffing for a while. Then Tom said, "Poor husband, though," and laughed again. The god did not laugh. He stared at Tom then left the table.

Tom thought of ways to leave the god, to kill him, or leave him dying, or tie him up and run away. He was made of flesh like everyone else, just strangely put together. He would die if you stabbed him, or smothered him. You could poison him and he would collapse and Tom would be the savior of many.

The god invited Tom in to watch the making of the suit, and Tom thought he had been forgiven.

The stuff was poured into a large vat, where it shimmered and steamed. Tom felt his skin burning as he watched, and later, when he looked in the mirror, he saw that his nose and cheeks were softly blistered.

"Now, you see, Tom? Can you smell it? Smell the greedy sweat from those people's palms?"

He handed Tom a coin.

"The special ingredient," he said. It was an ancient coin, dented by the centuries—a Roman coin.

"Don't find many of those on the street, hey, boy?" said the god. Tom preferred him to be silent. This joking, this camaraderie, was terrifying.

The god told Tom to drop the coin into the vat and short flames burst out, reaching for Tom. He jumped back.

"It's very hot," he whispered. "Very hot."

The god threw off his robe.

He was naked beneath. His skin was vast and white, his stomach distended as if from some huge feast (though he had not eaten, Tom was certain of that). His penis was engorged. Tom laughed at its hugeness. It couldn't be real. It was stuck on.

The god turned to face him.

"Can't have that," he said. The erection shrank into his body.

He climbed two steps to the rim of the vat.

He tested the liquid with one toe, playing the fool for Tom's benefit.

"Just right," he said, and he sank into the bubbling metal.

For one moment, Tom thought he had been released. He thought the god had killed himself, to free Tom because he loved him like a son and didn't want him to live like this anymore, and Tom could have cried for that love, because no one had loved him like that. He stepped closer to the vat and stared over, hoping for a glimpse to remember the god by.

The metal was drawing together and shaping.

It shaped a face, legs, a stomach. It shaped arms. And the god rose from his bath.

Tom whimpered now, because he knew he would die. He knew the god would not let him see this and live.

The god shook like a dog and drops of hot metal flew from him. One landed on Tom's cheek, and he smelt burnt flesh before he raised his sleeve to brush it away.

"Off to work," said the god, his voice molten, not strident or mean, but seductive, beautiful. "Why don't you come along?'

Tom hated to go out with the god. He watched things he could not stop without risking his own life.

They went walking through the city streets where Tom had done his best work. The god watched him collecting for a while. He amused himself while Tom worked. He passed his hand into the stomach of a woman who intended to sell her baby once it was born and he gave a squeeze. The mother barely felt a thing. She would not know until her baby was born dead.

Tom collected the coins and watched his god.

They found a blind man, standing on the curb of a road busy with cars but empty of people. He was puffing in an effort not to weep.

He could not see the purple eyes or the golden suit, he only heard the soft, seductive voice.

"Are you okay?" asked the god.

"I'm a bit lost," said the blind man, "I'm a bit stupid. I told my family I would be fine on my own, but I'm lost now. I can't cross the road."

"There's plenty of cars coming. Now, a break—no. Wait, after this car then—go."

Tom watched as the god led the blind man directly into the path of a bus. Both disappeared under the wheels. The god rolled out the other side, scratched and leaping with excitement.

Tom was not brave, but he was not happy to die, either. As he stirred the pot for the next suit, he thought and remembered and planned.

He heard every tale the god had to tell, and remembered much the god had forgotten telling him.

He had a little money of his own—paper money the god had no interest in.

He bought new coins, coins encased in plastic, never touched by human hands.

On the day he meant to leave the god, Tom tried to keep the excitement out of his step as he descended to the kitchen. The god never rose before afternoon. His business went late into the night and he slept in. Tom lit the large stove and set the cauldron ready. He began to drop the coins and watched each melt, watched the liquid spread, each coin becoming part of the golden fluid.

He waited till the pot was half full. He dropped more coins and more, then he heard the heavy footfall of the god pushing his body out of bed.

Tom's whole body shook as he took the plastic folders from his pocket and, still stirring, tore them open with his teeth. Being careful to keep the rhythm perfect, he plopped the brand new, untouched coins into the pot and stirred.

The plastic he shoved back into his pocket.

The god moved silently, and Tom smelt him first. A smell of metal and a smell of heat.

"When will the material be ready?" he asked, though he saw for himself. Tom thought the mixture smelt different, and hoped the god wouldn't notice.

"One more hour," said Tom. The god bent over the pot and sniffed deeply. He nodded and went to sun himself.

It was hot in the room.

The god made a new suit and went out. He didn't talk to Tom. Already, Tom barely existed.

The god did not return.

Tom's limbs began to ache, his hair grayed, fell out, his fingernails grew long and ragged. He couldn't see well. He couldn't hear. He breathed loudly through his nose.

He received back the fifty years stolen from him and he knew the god must be dead.

He took nothing from the house. He wanted nothing. He went to a hostel where, until he died, he swept floors and cleaned up vomit, in exchange for food and the freedom to come and go.

"You probably haven't had an unexplained cut or bruise for a while now, have you?" Tom asks everyone he sees. He cannot stop thinking how he never saw the god die—perhaps there is a new purple-eyed child. He asks everyone he sees, "How did you get that cut? Do you remember where you got that bruise? Have you seen a black-haired child with purple eyes, large teeth?" If Tom ever, receives the answer he fears, he has no plan but terror.

~

Two-time World Fantasy Award nominee and Shirley Jackson Award winner **Kaaron Warren** has lived in Melbourne, Sydney, Canberra, and Fiji. She's sold more than two hundred short stories, three novels (the award-winning *Slights, Walking the Tree,* and *Mistification*) and six short story collections including *Through Splintered Walls.* Her latest short story collection is *Cemetery Dance Select: Kaaron Warren.*

~

Even as Philo sashays down a street in Lagos, Nigeria, Rain is trying to right a wrong she's caused by mixing juju with technology. There is witchcraft in science and a science to witchcraft.

Hello, Moto
Nnedi Okorafor

"African women in general need to know that it's okay for them to be the way they are—to see the way they are as a strength, and to be liberated from fear and from silence."
—Wangari Maathai, Kenyan environmental activist and Nobel Laureate

This is a tale you will only hear once. Then it will be gone in a flash of green light. Maybe all will be well after that. Maybe the story has a happy ending. Maybe there is nothing but darkness when the story ends.

We were three women. Three friends. We had goals, hopes and dreams. We had careers. Two of us had boyfriends. We owned houses. We all had love. Then I made these . . . wigs. I gave them to my two friends. The three of us put them on. The wigs were supposed to make things better. But something went wrong. Like the nation we were trying to improve, we became backward. Instead of giving, we took.

Walk with me. This is the story of How the Smart Woman Tried to Right Her Great Wrong.

Dawn

With the wig finally off, Coco and Philo felt more distant to me. Thank God.

Even so, because it was sitting beside me, I could still see them. Clearly. In my head. Don't ever mix juju with technology. There is witchcraft in science and a science to witchcraft. Both will conspire against you eventually. I realized that now. I had to work fast.

It was just after dawn. The sky was heating up. I'd sneaked out of the compound while my boyfriend still slept. Even the house girl who always woke up early was not up yet. I hid behind the hedge of colorful pink and yellow lilies in the front. I needed to be around vibrant natural life, I needed to smell its scent. The flowers' shape reminded me of what my real hair would look like if the wig hadn't burned it off.

I opened my laptop and set it in the dirt. I put my wig beside it. It was jet-black, shiny, the "hairs" straight and long like a mermaid's. The hair on my head was less than a millimeter long: shorter than a man's and far more damaged. For a moment, as I looked at my wig, it flickered its electric blue. I could hear it whispering to me. It wanted me to put it back on. I ran my hand over my sore head. Then I quickly tore my eyes from the wig and plugged in the flash drive. As I waited, I brought out a small sack and reached in. I sprinkled cowry shells, alligator pepper and blue beads around the machine for protection. I wasn't taking chances.

I sat down, placed my fingers on the keyboard, shut my eyes and prayed to the God I didn't believe in. After all that had happened, who would believe in God? Philo had been in Jos when the riots happened. I knew it was her and her wig. A technology I had created. Neurotransmitters, mobile phones, incantation and hypnosis—even I knew my creation was genius. But all it sparked in the North was death and mayhem. During the riots there, some men had even burned a woman and her baby to death. A *woman* and her *baby*!

I didn't want to think of what Philo gained after causing it all. She never said a word to me about it. However, soon after, she went on a three-day shopping spree in Paris. We could leave Nigeria, but never for more than a few days.

"Oh God, I'm so sorry," I whispered. "I meant well." I opened my eyes and looked at my screen. The background was a plain blue. The screen was blank except for a single folder. I highlighted the folder and pressed *Delete*.

I paused, my hands shaking and my heart pounding in my chest.

"If this doesn't work, they will kill me," I whispered. Then I considered what they'd do if I didn't finish. So many others would die and Nigeria would be in further chaos, for sure. I continued typing. I was creating a computer virus. I would send it out in a few hours. When they'd both be busy. Then all hell would break loose . . . for me, just me. Sometimes things have to get worse before they get better.

My name is Rain and if I didn't get this right, the corruption already rife in this country would be nothing compared to what was to come. And it would all be my fault.

The Market

I am beast. I am lovely. I am in control. I was born beautiful.

All this Philo thought as she walked through the fruit and vegetable section of the open-air market. Around her, women slaved away. They sat behind tables and in booths selling tomatoes, peppers, plantain, egusi seeds, greens, yams. All those things that they'd have to cook at home for their families after a long day. Philo didn't live that life. She'd chosen better. She was above all of them.

Philo was tall and voluptuous, as she sashayed past women and men in her pricey high heels and a brown designer dress that clung to her every inch. Her foundation makeup made her skin look like chocolate porcelain. Her eyelids sparkled with purple eye shadow. Her lips glistened bright sensual pink. Perfect. Sexy. Hot. And her wig was awful. A washed-out black with auburn frosted tips, it looked as if it were made of colored straw and it sat on her head as if it knew it did not belong there.

"Here," a woman said, running up to Philo and handing her a roll of naira. "Take. You will make better use of it than me." The woman paused and frowned, obviously confused by her own actions and words.

"Thank you," Philo said, with a chuckle. She grabbed the money with her long-nailed painted fingers and stared into the woman's eyes. Philo felt her wig heat up and then a dull ache in the back of her head. Then she felt it behind her eyes, which turned from deep brown to glowing green. Philo sighed as the laser shot from her eyes into the woman's eyes. The woman slumped, looking sadly at her feet. It always felt so good to take from people, not just their money but their very essence. Philo quickly moved on, leaving the tired, sad-looking woman behind.

She passed a group of young men. They stared and she stared back, zapping and taking. Their ravenous looks grew blank. Philo smirked knowingly. She felt amazing. She strolled into a booth where a man sold hundreds of Nollywood movie DVDs. She glanced over the array of colorful dramatic covers where women and men scowled, wept, grinned, pointed, accused, laughed. "I'll take this one," she said, picking a DVD at random. She'd watch it. She'd enjoy it. She loved Nollywood. These days, she enjoyed everything. The world was hers. Soon it would be, at least.

She tucked the DVD into her purse and left the booth without paying. No one stopped her. As she stepped into the sunshine, she turned, absolutely loving herself. She knew everyone was looking at her, just as she knew she was sucking the life from them as they stared. Her wig's heat increased and her brown eyes glinted a bright green as she smiled at any man who caught her eye. By the time she left this market, she'd be weighed down with naira given and life juices taken. Market by market. It was like this every day.

Her cell phone went off. A male voice happily drawled, "Hellllo Moto," and then upbeat music began to play. Everything about Philo rattled as she stopped and lifted her purse—the jangling bangles on her arms, her jingling earrings and her three gold chain necklaces. She was clicks and clacks, shines and sparkles.

"Oh where is it," she said, digging in her purse, mindful of her long nails. "Where, where, where." She pushed aside her lipstick, her unnecessary wallet, tissues, compact case, a pack of gum, wads and rolls of naira. Her cell phone continued going off. She laughed. She already knew who it was. Rain, the weakest link in the chain. She could tell by the ringtone. However, she could also tell by more than that. In her mind's eye, Philo could see Rain standing outside her compound, next to some flowers, holding her cell phone to her ear, waiting. Philo found her phone, flipped it open and held it to her ear. It clicked against her long gold earring.

"What?" she said, grinning with all her teeth. She heard nothing. "Rain, I know it's you. Say someth . . ."

She felt it before she saw it. A coolness that contrasted horribly with the heat of her wig. She frowned as the phone made an odd beeping sound. She held it before her just as the phone glinted a deep green similar to the one her eyes flashed when she sucked psychic energy from those around her. Her phone buzzed, an electrical current zipping across it before disappearing. Green smoke began to dribble from it.

"*Chey!*" Philo exclaimed, staring at it. If she were smart, she'd have dropped it. But Philo was never really that intelligent. Just greedy. Rain didn't know that before, but she knew that now. A text message appeared on the screen but Philo could make no sense of it. It was a series of nonsensical symbols, rubbish. She dropped the phone, pressing a hand to her wig. "That bitch," she snarled, looking around with wide, enraged eyes. "How dare she even try." In the sunshine, her canines almost looked pointed.

Right then and there, Philo disappeared in a flash of green.

His House

Coco had just lit a cigarette. She leaned back on the plush white leather couch and crossed her legs. She held her glass of champagne up to the photo of her husband on the wall. He was out. He was always out. Working. For her. She laughed, scratching under her itchy wig with her long-nailed index finger. *Scritch scritch.* It was spiky, dark red and short and no one in his or her right mind would wear it. She got up and looked at her reflection in the glass that protected her husband's photo. Her skinny jeans and T-shirt fit wonderfully snug. Her face was flawless. And her hair was power.

"Mwah," she said, blowing herself a kiss.

She ambled into the living room, where two fans were blasting. She stood very still between them, her wig's "hairs" blowing about her face. It felt secure, despite the blowing air. She shut her eyes and inhaled deeply. Behind her eyelids, she could see. Then she began to draw it in from . . .

The busy street. People sitting in bustling bush taxis and perched atop hundreds of okada motorbikes. Market women walking alongside the road. The mishmash of old and modern buildings of Lagos. Disabled beggars in the road. Boys playing soccer on a field.

When she opened her eyes, they glowed a deep green and the wig glinted an electric blue. The blowing fans made the heat from her wig more bearable. Her cell phone went off and she nearly jumped. "Hellllo, Moto," it said as it played its dance music.

"*Ah ah*, what now?" she muttered. But she was smiling. The wig. It always left her feeling so *good*. Minus the heat, which left the actual wig feeling like a burning helmet. She ran to her cell phone on the couch. It was Rain. What did she want now? In her mind, the wig showed Rain standing outside her compound looking worried. The woman always looked so worried; she should have been at the top of the world.

Coco held the phone to her ear as she brought out some lipstick. "Hello?" she said, smearing on a fresh coat. She grinned, sure of what she'd hear. She frowned. "Hello? Rain, what is it? Speak up."

But she heard nothing. She held the phone to her face when it suddenly became like a chunk of ice in her hand. "Iiieeey!" she exclaimed, throwing it on the couch. As she stared at it, appalled, the cell phone began to dribble green smoke. A text box opened on its screen. Coco squinted, trying to read it. It looked like rubbish. But, like Philo, Coco understood what was happening.

"Oh," Coco said, out of breath. "You want to play now, eh? Okay." She threw her lipstick on the leather seat, the lid still off. It left a smear on the pillow. "Someone will die today, o. And it will *not* be me."

She disappeared.

I have made my choice. That's why I am still here, standing in these lilies. I run my hand over my shaved head. Waiting. The sun shines bright and happy in the sky, unaware of what's about to happen to me. Unaware of what I have done and will soon suffer the consequences for. Unconcerned.

Philo appears. She is standing on the lilies, mere feet away from me.

"What is wrong with you?" she shouts. She looks beautiful and ghastly in her tight brown dress, which probably cost more naira than a market woman makes in two years.

"I'm . . . " Fear pumps through my veins like adrenaline and blood.

"Why is your wig off, eh? You look horrible." Her wig flashes as the digital virus tries to cripple it. Notice I say "tries."

"I took it off," I snap. "This is wrong, o! This is wrong! Wake up!"

Philo chuckles. "And what is wrong about it? We have everything we want."

"Stealing from people is not what I made these for! I made them to help us give! To cure the deep-seated culture of corruption by giving people hope and a sense of patriotism. Remember?"

She looks at me as if I am crazy. The wig has made her forget. Na wao. Tricky tricky things, these wigs.

"Put it back on," she says, pointing a long nail at me.

"No," I say. "It has made us cruel witches. Look at you!"

Coco appears behind me. She hisses like a snake. She is in no mood for words. Her wig flashes. The virus is not working. When you mix juju with technology, you give up control. You are at the will of something far beyond yourself. I am done for.

See how it all ends? Or does it begin? I am watching them approach me now. I tell you while my life hangs on its last thread. I am putting my wig on. It is so hot. I should have paid more attention to the cooling system when I made these. I hear the heartbeat of everyone around me now, including the irregular rhythm of Coco's and Philo's. But oh, the power. It rushes into me like ogogoro down the throat of a drunk.

See Philo bare her teeth. They are indeed sharp like those of a bloodsucker. The virus is working through her wig now. But something has gone very wrong. They are both smiling. For a year, we have been psychic vampires, but now as they come at me, mouths open, teeth sharp, I see that they have become the bloodsucking kind.

I feel my own teeth sharpening too as I prepare to defend myself. This is new but I can't think about that right now. I tear the wig off and throw it aside.

"Come then!" I shout. Then, I . . .

~

Nnedi Okorafor's books include novels *Lagoon* (a British Science Fiction Association Award finalist), *Who Fears Death* (a World Fantasy Award winner), collection *Kabu Kabu* (a *Publishers Weekly* Best Book for Fall

2013), *Akata Witch* (an Amazon Best Book of the Year), *Zahrah the Windseeker* (winner of the Wole Soyinka Prize for African Literature), and *The Shadow Speaker* (a CBS Parallax Award winner). Her adult novel *The Book of Phoenix* was released in 2015 as was her novella *Binti*, which will be republished in *The Year's Best Science Fiction and Fantasy Novellas: 2016*. Her young adult novel *Akata Witch 2: Breaking Kola* will be out this year. Okorafor holds a PhD in literature/creative writing and is an associate professor at the University at Buffalo, New York (SUNY).

～

The Nightside lies deep within the city of London. It's always three A.M. there, the dark hour that tries men's souls. Its atmosphere is so saturated with magic, weird science, and general strangeness that even ghosts tend not to haunt it.

The Spirit of the Thing: A Nightside Story
Simon R. Green

In the Nightside, that secret hidden heart of London, where it's always the darkest part of the night and the dawn never comes, you can find some of the best and worst bars in the world.

There are places that will serve you liquid moonlight in a tall glass, or angel's tears, or a wine that was old when Rome was young.

And then there's the Jolly Cripple. You get to one of the worst bars in the world by walking down the kind of alley you'd normally have the sense to stay out of. The Cripple is tucked away behind more respectable establishments, and light from the street doesn't penetrate far. It's always half full of junk and garbage, and the only reason there aren't any bodies to step over is because the rats have eaten them all. You have to watch out for rats in the Nightside; some people say they're evolving. In fact, some people claim to have seen the damn things using knives and forks.

I wouldn't normally be seen dead in a dive like the Jolly Cripple, but I was working. At the time, I was in between clients and in need of some fast walking around money, so when the bar's owner got word to me that there was quick and easy money to be made, I swallowed my pride. I'm John Taylor, private investigator. I have a gift for finding things, and people. I always find the truth for my clients; even if it means having to walk into places where even angels would wince and turn their heads aside.

∼

The Jolly Cripple was a drinker's bar. Not a place for conversation, or companionship. More the kind of place you go when the world has kicked you out, your credit's no good, and your stomach couldn't handle the good stuff any more, even if you could afford it. In the Jolly Cripple the floor was sticky, the air was thick with half a dozen kinds of smoke, and the only thing you could be sure of was vomit in the corners and piss and blood in the toilets. The owner kept the lights down low, partly so you couldn't see how bad the place really was, but mostly because the patrons preferred it that way.

The owner and bartender was one Maxie Eliopoulos. A sleazy soul in an unwashed body, dark and hairy, always smiling.

Maxie wore a grimy T-shirt with the legend IT'S ALL GREEK TO ME, and showed off its various bloodstains like badges of honor. No one ever gave Maxie any trouble in his bar. Or at least, not twice. He was short and squat with broad shoulders, and a square brutal face under a shock of black hair. More dark hair covered his bare arms, hands, and knuckles. He never stopped smiling, but it never once reached his eyes. Maxie was always ready to sell you anything you could afford. Especially if it was bad for you.

Some people said he only served people drink so he could watch them die by inches.

Maxie had hired me to find out who'd been diluting his drinks and driving his customers away. (And that's about the only thing that could.) Didn't take me long to find out who. I sat down at the bar, raised my gift, and concentrated on the sample bottle of what should have been gin; but was now so watered down you could have kept goldfish in it. My mind leapt up and out, following the connection between the water and its source, right back to where it came from. My Sight shot down through the barroom floor, down and down, into the sewers below.

Long stone tunnels with curving walls, illuminated by phosphorescent moss and fungi, channeling thick dark water with things floating in it. All kinds of things. In the Nightside's sewers even trained workers tread carefully, and often carry flamethrowers, just in case. I looked around me, my Sight searching for the presence I'd felt; and something looked back. Something knew I was there, even if only in spirit. The murky waters churned and heaved, and then a great head rose up out of the dark water, followed by a body. It only took me a moment to realize both head and body were made up of water, and nothing else.

The face was broad and unlovely, the body obscenely female, like one of those ancient fertility goddess statues. Thick rivulets of water ran down her face like slow tears, and ripples bulged constantly around her body. A water elemental. I'd heard the Nightside had been using them to clean up the sewers; taking in all the bad stuff and purifying it inside themselves. The Nightside always finds cheap and practical ways to solve its problems, even if they aren't always very nice solutions.

"Who disturbs me?" said the sewer elemental, in a thick, glutinous voice.

"John Taylor," I said. Back in the bar my lips were moving, but my words could only be heard down in the sewer. "You've been interfering with one of the bars above. Using your power to infuse the bottles with your water. You know you're not supposed to get involved with the world above."

"I am old," said the elemental of the sewers. "So old, even I don't remember how old I am. I was worshipped, once. But the world changed and I could not, so even the once worshipped and adored must work for a living. I have fallen very far from what I was; but then, that's the Nightside for you. Now I deal in shit and piss and other things, and make them pure again. Because someone has to. It's a living. But, fallen as I am . . . no one insults me, defies me, cheats me! I serve all the bars in this area, and the owners and I have come to an understanding . . . all but Maxie Eliopoulos! He refuses my reasonable demands!"

"Oh hell," I said. "It's a labor dispute. What are you asking for, better working conditions?"

"I just want him to clean up his act," said the elemental of the sewers. "And if he won't, I'll do it for him. I can do a lot worse to him than just dilute his filthy drinks . . . "

"That is between you and him," I said firmly. "I don't do arbitration." And then I got the hell out of there.

Back in the bar and in my body, I confronted Maxie. "You didn't tell me this was a dispute between contractors, Maxie."

He laughed, and slapped one great palm hard against his grimy bartop. "I knew it! I knew it was that water bitch, down in her sewers! I just needed you to confirm it, Taylor."

"So why's she mad at you? Apart from the fact that you're a loathsome, disgusting individual."

He laughed again, and poured me a drink of what, in his bar, passed for the good stuff. "She wants me to serve better booze; says the impurities in the stuff I sell is polluting her system, and leaving a nasty taste in her mouth. I could leave a nasty taste in her mouth, heh heh heh . . . She pressured all the other bars and they gave in, but not me. Not me! No one tells Maxie Eliopoulos what to do in his own bar! Silly cow . . . Cheap and nasty is what my customers want, so cheap and nasty is what they get."

"So . . . for a while there, your patrons were drinking booze mixed with sewer water," I said. "I'm surprised so many stayed."

"I'm surprised so many of them noticed," said Maxie. "Good thing I never drink the tap water . . . All right, Taylor, you've confirmed what I needed to know. I'll take it from here. I can handle her. Thinks I can't get to her, down in the sewers, but I'll show that bitch. No one messes with me and gets away with it. Now—here's what we agreed on."

He pushed a thin stack of grubby bank notes across the bar, and I counted them quickly before making them disappear about my person. You don't want to attract attention in a bar like the Jolly Cripple, and nothing will do that faster than a display of cash, grubby or not. Maxie grinned at me in what he thought was an ingratiating way.

"No need to rush away, Taylor. Have another drink. Drinks are on the house for you; make yourself at home."

I should have left. I should have known better . . . but it was one of the few places my creditors wouldn't look for me, and besides . . . the drinks were on the house.

I sat at a table in the corner, working my way through a bottle of the kind of tequila that doesn't have a worm in it, because the tequila's strong enough to dissolve the worm. A woman in a long white dress walked up to my table. I didn't pay her much attention at first, except to wonder what someone so normal-looking was doing in a dive like this . . . and then she walked right through the table next to me, and the people sitting around it. She drifted through them as though they weren't even there, and each of them in turn shuddered briefly, and paid closer attention to their drinks. Their attitude said it all; they'd seen the woman in white before, and they didn't want to know. She stopped before me, looking at me with cool, quiet, desperate eyes.

"You have to help me. I've been murdered, I need you to find out who killed me."

That's what comes from hanging around in strange bars.

I gestured for her to sit down opposite me, and she did so perfectly easily. She still remembered what it felt like to have a body, which meant she hadn't been dead long. I looked her over carefully. I couldn't see any obvious death wounds, not even a ligature round her neck. Most murdered ghosts appear the way they did when they died. The trauma overrides everything else.

"What makes you think you were murdered?" I said bluntly.

"Because there's a hole in my memory," she said. "I don't remember coming here, don't remember dying here; but now I'm a ghost and I can't leave this bar. Something prevents me. Something must be put right; I can feel it. Help me, please. Don't leave me like this."

I always was a sucker for a sob story. Comes with the job, and the territory. She had no way of paying me, and I normally avoid charity work . . . But I'd just been paid, and I had nothing else to do, so I nodded briefly and considered the problem. It's a wonder there aren't more ghosts in the Nightside, when you think about it. We've got every other kind of supernatural phenomenon you can think of, and there's never any shortage of the suddenly deceased. Anyone with the Sight can see ghosts, from stone tape recordings, where moments from the Past imprint themselves on their surroundings, endlessly repeating, like insects trapped in amber . . . to lost souls, damned to wander the world through tragic misdeeds or unfinished business.

There are very few hauntings in the Nightside, as such. The atmosphere here is so saturated with magic and super-science and general weird business that it swamps and drowns out all the lesser signals. Though there are always a few stubborn souls who just won't be told. Like Long John Baldwin, who drank himself to death in my usual bar, Strangefellows.

Dropped stone dead while raising one last glass of Valhalla Venom to his lips, and hit the floor with the smile still on his face. The bar's owner, Alex Morrisey, had the body removed, but even before the funeral was over Long John was back in his familiar place at the bar, calling for a fresh bottle. Half a dozen unsuccessful exorcisms later, Alex gave up and hired Long John as his replacement bartender and security guard. Long John drinks the memories of old booze from empty bottles, and enjoys the company of his fellow drinkers, just as he always did (they're a hardened bunch, in Strangefellows). And as Alex says, a ghost is more intelligent than a watchdog or a security system, and a lot cheaper to maintain.

I could feel a subtle tension on the air, a wrongness; as though there was a reason why the ghost shouldn't be there. She was an unusually strong manifestation; no transparency, no fraying around the edges. That usually meant a strong character, when she was alive. She didn't flinch as I looked her over thoughtfully.

She was a tall, slender brunette, with neatly styled hair and understated makeup, in a long white dress of such ostentatious simplicity that it had to have cost a bundle.

"Do you know your name?" I said finally.

"Holly de Lint."

"And what's a nice girl like you doing in a dive like this?"

"I don't know. Normally, I wouldn't be seen dead in a place like this."

We both smiled slightly. "Could someone have brought you here, Holly? Could that person have . . . "

"Murdered me? Perhaps. But who would I know, in a place like this?"

She had a point. A woman like her didn't belong here. So I left her sitting at my table, and made my rounds of the bar, politely interrogating the regulars. Most of them didn't feel like talking, but I'm John Taylor. I have a reputation. Not a very nice one, but it means people will talk to me when they wouldn't talk to anyone else. They didn't know Holly. They didn't know anything. They hadn't seen anything, because they didn't come to a bar like this to take an interest in other people's problems. And they genuinely might not have noticed a ghost. One of the side effects of too much booze is that it shuts down the Sight; though you can still end up seeing things that aren't there.

I went back to Holly, still sitting patiently at the table. I sat down opposite her, and used my gift to find out what had happened in her recent past. Faint pastel images of Holly appeared all around the bar, blinking on and off, from where she'd tried to talk to people, or begged for help, or tried to leave and been thrown back. I concentrated, sorting through the various images until I found the memory of the last thing she'd done while still alive. I got up from the table and followed the last trace of the living Holly all the way to the back of the bar, to the toilets. She went into the Ladies, and I went in after her. Luckily, there was no one else there, then or now, so I could watch uninterrupted as Holly De Lint opened a cubicle, sat down, and then washed down a big handful of pills with most of a bottle of whisky. She went about it quite methodically, with no tears or hysterics, her face cold and even indifferent, though her eyes still seemed terribly sad. She killed herself, with pills and booze. The last image showed her slumping slowly sideways, the bottle slipping from her numbed fingers, as the last of the light went out of her eyes.

I went back into the bar, and sat down again opposite Holly.

She looked at me inquiringly, trustingly. So what could I do, except tell her the truth?

"There was no murderer, Holly. You took your own life. Can you tell me why . . . "

But she was gone. Disappeared in a moment, blinking out of existence like a punctured soap bubble. No sign to show that anyone had ever been sitting there.

So I went back to the bar and told Maxie what had happened, and he laughed in my face.

"You should have talked to me first, Taylor! I could have told you all about her. You aren't the first stranger she's approached. Look, you know the old urban legend, where the guy's just driving along, minding his own business, and then sees a woman in white signaling desperately from the side of the road? He's a good guy, so he stops and asks what's up. She says she needs a lift home, so he takes her where she wants to go. But the woman doesn't say a word, all through the drive, and when he finally gets there; she's disappeared. The guy at the address tells the driver the woman was killed out there on the road long ago; but she keeps stopping drivers, asking them to take her home. Old story, right? It's the same here, except our woman in white keeps telling people that she's been murdered, but doesn't remember how. And when our good Samaritans find out the truth, and tell her; she disappears. Until the next sucker comes along. You ready for another drink?"

"Can't you do something?" I said.

"I've tried all the usual shit," said Maxie. "But she's a hard one to shift. You think you could do something? That little bitch is seriously bad for business."

I went back to my table in the corner, to do some hard thinking. Most people would just walk away, on discovering the ghost was nothing more than a repeating cycle . . . But I'm not most people. I couldn't bear to think of Holly trapped in this place, maybe forever.

Why would a woman, with apparently everything to live for, kill herself in a dive like this? I raised my gift, and once again pastel-tinted semi-transparent images of the living Holly darted back and forth through the dimly-lit bar, lighting briefly at this table and that, like a flower fairy at midnight. It didn't take me long to realize there was one table she visited more than most. So I went over to the people sitting there, and made them tell me everything they knew.

Professor Hartnell was a gray-haired old gentlemen in a battered city suit. He used to be somebody, but he couldn't remember who. Igor was a shaven-headed kobold with more piercings than most, who'd run away from the German mines of his people to see the world. He didn't think much of the world, but he couldn't go back, so he settled in the Nightside. Where no one gave a damn he was gay. The third drinker was a battered old Russian, betrayed by the Revolution but appalled at what his country had become. No one mentioned the icepick sticking out the back of his head.

They didn't know Holly, as such, but they knew who she'd come here after. She came to the Jolly Cripple to save someone.

Someone who didn't want to be saved—her brother, Craig de Lint. He drank himself to death, right here in the bar, right at their table. Sometimes in their company, more often not, because the only company he was interested in came in a bottle. I used my gift again, and managed to pull up a few ghost images from the Past, of the living Craig. Stick thin, shabby clothes, the bones standing out in his gray face. Dead, dead eyes.

"You're wasting your time, sis," Craig de Lint said patiently. "You know I don't have any reason to drink. No great trauma, no terrible loss . . . I just like to drink, and I don't care about anything else. Started out in all the best places, and worked my way down to this. Where someone like me belongs. Go home, sis. You don't belong here. Go home, before something bad happens to you."

"I can't just leave you here! There must be something I can do!"

"And that's the difference between us, sis, right there. You always think there's something that can be done. But I know a lost cause when I am one."

The scene shifted abruptly, and there was Holly at the bar, arguing furiously with Maxie. He still smiled, even as he said things that cut her like knives.

"Of course I encouraged your brother to drink, sweetie. That's my job. That's what he was here for. And no, I don't give a damn that he's dead. He was dying when he walked in here, by his own choice; I just helped him on his way. Now either buy a drink or get out of my face. I've got work to do."

"I'll have you shut down!" said Holly, her voice fierce now, her small hands clenched into fists.

He laughed in her face. "Like to see you try, sweetie. This is the Nightside, where everyone's free to go to Hell in their own way."

"I know people! Important people! Money talks, Maxie, and I've got far more of it than you have."

He smiled easily. "You've got balls, sweetie. Okay, let's talk. Over a drink."

"I don't drink."

"My bar, my rules. You want to talk with me, you drink with me."

Holly shrugged, and looked away. Staring at the table where her brother died. Maxie poured two drinks from a bottle, and then slipped a little something into Holly's glass. He watched, smiling, as Holly turned back and gulped the stuff down, just to get rid of it; and then he smiled even more widely as all the expression went out of her face.

"There, that's better," said Maxie. "Little miss rich bitch. Come into my bar, throwing your weight about, telling me what to do? I don't think so. Feeling a little more . . . suggestible, are you? Good, good . . . Such a shame about your brother. You must be sad, very sad. So sad, you want to end it all. So here's a big handful of helpful pills, and a bottle of booze. So you can put an end to yourself, out back, in the toilets. Bye-bye, sweetie. Don't make a mess."

The ghost images snapped off as the memory ended. I was so choked with rage I could hardly breathe. I got up from the table and stormed over to the bar. Maxie leaned forward to say something, and I grabbed two handfuls of his grubby T-shirt and hauled him right over his bar, so I could stick my face right into his. He had enough sense not to struggle.

"You knew," I said. "You knew all along! You made her kill herself!"

"I had no choice!" said Maxie, still smiling. "It was self-defense! She was going to shut me down. And yeah, I knew all along. That's why I hired you! I knew you'd solve the elemental business right away, and then stick around for the free drinks. I knew the ghost would approach you, and you'd get involved. I needed someone to get rid of her; and you always were a soft touch, Taylor."

I let him go. I didn't want to touch him any more. He backed cautiously away, and sneered at me from a safe distance.

"You feel sorry for the bitch, help her on her way to the great Hereafter! You'll be doing her a favor, and me too. I told you she was bad for business."

I turned my back on him, and went back to the drinkers who'd known him best. And before any of them could even say anything, I focused my gift through them, through their memories of Craig, and reached out to him in a direction I knew but could not name. A door opened, that hadn't been there before, and a great light spilled out into the bar. A fierce and unrelenting light, too bright for the living to look at directly. The drinkers in the bar should have winced away from it, used as they were to the permanent gloom, but something in the light touched them despite themselves, waking old memories, of what might have been.

And out of that light came Craig de Lint, walking free and easy. He reached out a hand, smiling kindly, and out of the gloom came the ghost of Holly de Lint, also walking free and easy. She took his hand, and they smiled at each other, and then Craig led her through the doorway and into the light; and the door shut behind them and was gone.

In the renewed gloom of the bar, Maxie hooted and howled with glee, slapping his heavy hand on the bar top in triumph.

"Finally, free of the bitch! Free at last! Knew you had it in you, Taylor! Drinks on the house, people! On the house!" And they all came stumbling up to the bar, already forgetting what they might have seen in the light. Maxie busied himself serving them, and I considered him thoughtfully, from a distance. Maxie had murdered Holly, and got away with it, and used me to clean up after him, removing the only part of the business that still haunted him. So I raised my gift one last time, and made contact with the elemental of the sewers, deep under the bar.

"Maxie will never agree to the deal you want," I said. "He likes things just the way they are. But you might have better luck with a new owner. You put your sewer water into Maxie's bottles. There are other places you could put it."

"I take your meaning, John Taylor," said the elemental.

"You're everything they say you are."

Maxie lurched suddenly behind his bar, flailing desperately about him as his lungs filled up with water. I turned my back on the drowning man, and walked away. Though, being me, I couldn't resist having the last word.

"Have one on me, Maxie."

∾

Simon R. Green is a *New York Times* bestselling author of the Deathstalker, Nightside, Secret Histories, and (most recently) Ghost Finders series, among others. He lives in Bradford-on-Avon, Wiltshire, England.

∾

Babylon, Tennessee is located in a Lovecraftian (and otherwise strange)
alternate universe. Magic abounds and the streets lead to some very odd
locations—like Electric Squidland.

A Night in Electric Squidland
Sarah Monette

Some days, Mick Sharpton was almost normal.

Those were the good days, the days when he did his job and went
dancing after work, days when he enjoyed eating and slept well and sang
in the shower. Days when flirting with a good-looking man was fun, even
if it didn't lead to sex, and he didn't lose his temper with anyone unless
they deserved it. Those were the days when he liked himself and liked his
life, and some months there were more of them than others.

The bad days were when the world wouldn't stay out of his head, when
everyone he looked at wore a swirling crown of color, and everything
he touched carried the charge of someone else's life. Those days were
all about maintaining his increasingly precarious control, snarling and
snapping to keep anyone from getting too close. Trying not to drown.
Sometimes he succeeded; sometimes he didn't.

Today was a good day. He could almost pretend he wasn't clairvoyant.
His head was clear, and he felt light, balanced. He had not remembered
his dreams when he woke up, and that was always a positive sign.

Mick and his partner were wading through a backlog of paperwork
that afternoon. The sheer monumental bureaucracy was the downside
of working for a government agency like the Bureau of Paranormal
Investigations; left to his own devices, Mick would have let it slide, as he
had always done with schoolwork, but Jamie had a stern, Puritan attitude
toward unfinished reports, and it was useless to argue with him.

It was always useless to argue with Jamie Keller.

But the perpetually renewed struggle to find the right words—where "right" was a peculiar combination of "accurate" and "decorous" as applied to descriptions of interrupted Black Masses and the remains left on the subway lines by ghoul packs—was both tedious and frustrating, and Mick was positively grateful when the phone rang, summoning them to Jesperson's office. Jesperson would have something for them to do.

"It'll just be more paperwork later," Jamie warned.

"Oh, bite me, Keller."

"Not my thing," Jamie said placidly.

When they came into his office, Jesperson was leaning over a ley line map, spread out on the big table and weighted down with a fist-sized chunk of the Tunguska meteorite, two volumes of the *Directory of American Magic-Users*, and a lumpish pottery bowl with a deep green glaze, made for him by his daughter Ada and used for keeping paperclips and sticks of red chalk in. Ada lived with her mother in Seattle; Jesperson saw her for one week each year, at the Winter Solstice, and nothing was more sacred in the office than Jesperson's annual week of vacation, even if most of his employees politely pretended they had no idea why.

Jesperson looked up and said, "There you are," as if they should have known to be somewhere else, and waved at them impatiently to sit down.

They sat; Jesperson stalked over to stand between them and glowered at them both impartially. "What do you know about Electric Squidland?"

"It's a nightclub," Mick offered. "Goth scene. Lots of slumming yuppies."

"And?" Jesperson said, looking from one to the other of them.

Mick had told him all he knew—Electric Squidland had always been too trendy for his taste—and it was Jamie who finally said, reluctantly, "They get into some heavy shit on the lower levels."

"You've been to Electric Squidland?" Mick said.

"Used to work there," Jamie said and became unaccountably interested in the backs of his own hands.

"You *worked* at—"

"Sharpton."

"Yes, sir. Sorry, sir."

Jamie said, not looking up, "This is about Shawna Lafayette, ain't it?"

"It might be."

"Who's Shawna Lafayette?"

"A young woman from Murfreesboro. Three years ago—just after the Carolyn Witt scandal, if you remember it—she disappeared off the face of the Earth."

"Just like that?"

"She went into Electric Squidland," Jamie said in a low voice, "and she never came out."

"Vanished without a trace," Jesperson said, "and now it's happened again. Maybe."

"Maybe?" Jamie said. "You mean somebody sorta disappeared?"

"Actually, yes," Jesperson said and allowed himself a small, crooked smile at their expressions. "What we have are the remains of half a person."

"Um, which half, sir? Top? Bottom?"

"The right half, I believe, Mr. Sharpton."

Mick and Jamie looked at each other. "Well, that's a new one," Mick managed after a moment.

"Quite," Jesperson said dryly. "We got a tip this morning. Anonymous, of course. Here."

He pressed the *play* button on the recorder that sat, as always, on the corner of his desk, and a woman's voice, drawling with a hard nasal edge, spoke into the quiet room: "There's something y'all need to see. Right now it's out in the Sunny Creek Dump in a big black garbage bag, but I don't know how long it'll be there, so you better hurry. And if you wanna know more about it, go to Electric Squidland and ask 'em what happened to Brett Vincent." A solid clunk of metal and plastic as she hung up the phone, and Jesperson pushed the *stop* button.

And then both he and Mick were staring as Jamie lurched to his feet and said in a strangled voice, "I'll be right back." He almost fell against the door on his way out. Mick glanced at Jesperson for permission and followed him.

Jamie hadn't gone far; he was leaning against the wall next to the water fountain. Dark-skinned as he was, he couldn't go pale, but he was definitely gray around the edges. "Jamie?" Mick said, half-expecting his friend to slide to the floor in a dead faint.

"Sorry," Jamie said. His eyes were closed, and Mick thought he was doing one of the breathing exercises he'd learned from practicing yoga.

"About what, exactly? Are you okay?"

"I'll be fine. Just wasn't expecting . . . "

"Well, I wasn't expecting any of it, so I'm not sure how that gets you out here in the corridor looking like you're about to have a heart attack. You're not, are you?"

That got Jamie's eyes open. "Mick!"

"You look bad enough. And if you are, I want enough warning that I can call down for a gurney or something."

"Christ. No. I am not going to have a heart attack. I just wasn't ready for . . . "

"Oh," Mick said, feeling like an idiot. "You knew the guy, didn't you? Brett Whatsisface?"

"Vincent. Yeah, I knew him." Jamie smiled, but there was neither mirth nor pleasure in it. "All too well."

After a moment, Mick said, "I didn't know you were bisexual."

"What I am is monogamous," Jamie said—mildly enough, but it was a clear warning to back off.

"We're going to have Jesperson out here in a minute," Mick said obediently.

"Yeah," Jamie said. "You go on. Lemme get a drink of water. And, yes, you can tell him about me and Brett."

"Okay," Mick said, touched Jamie's shoulder lightly, awkwardly, wanting to give comfort but knowing he was no good at it, and went back into Jesperson's office.

"Jamie, um, had a relationship with the deceased," he said to Jesperson's raised eyebrows.

"Did he?" Jesperson said, and added just as Jamie came through the door, "Then perhaps he can identify the body."

An hour ago, this had been a good day. Now, it was beginning to feel more like a nightmare.

Mick and Jamie were in the BPI morgue. Cold, echoing, the lights harsh on gray tile and metal, the psychic residue of death like dirt on every spotless surface. Mick hated it.

He hated it more today, watching Jamie's grim impersonation of a hard-as-nails, ice-cold BPI agent. He wasn't fooling his partner, and Mick doubted he was fooling himself, which meant he was hanging onto the act because it was either that or go off in a corner and have a meltdown.

Mick spared some hate for Jesperson while he was at it.

He understood the logic, and Jesperson wouldn't have been competent to run the BPI's southeast hub if he didn't grab every advantage he could get and wring it bone-dry. But knowing that didn't make it any more bearable to watch the way Jamie's hands, carefully clasped behind his back, tightened and released against each other again and again, like the beating of some murderously overworked heart.

The morgue staffer seemed to catch the mood, for she was silent as she led them to the autopsy table, and remained silent as she pulled the sheet back.

Mick had to turn away. Even the mental images conjured up by the phrase "half a body" had not prepared him for the reality: the raw, ragged edges of bone and skin; the way what remained of the internal organs spilled untidily out of the body onto the table; the way that one staring dead eye was somehow even worse than two.

Jamie regarded the body for a long time, perfectly silent, then said in a level, almost uninterested voice, "Yes. That's Brett Vincent. I recognize him, and he's got the tattoo."

"Tattoo?" Mick said; his voice, unlike Jamie's, was a wavering croak.

"We went and got 'em together," Jamie said, touching Mick's shoulder to get him to turn around. He did, carefully not looking at the table, and saw that Jamie had rolled his right sleeve up, was indicating the bend of his elbow, where the Wild Hunt—who rode in somber, frenetic glory the length of his arm—broke like sea waves to either side of a design clearly the work of a different artist. For a moment, Mick couldn't make sense of the lines, and then it resolved into a circle made of two snakes, each biting the other's tail. Without knowing he was going to, Mick reached out and touched the tattoo gently, as if it might still be sore all these years later. His finger was shockingly white against Jamie's dark skin, and they both pretended they couldn't see how unsteady it was.

Jamie said, "Anyway, that body's got Brett's tattoo right where Brett had it. It's him."

"I'll write up the report," the morgue staffer said. "Thank you."

Jamie was unhurriedly rebuttoning his cuff. "And I guess we go see what Jesperson wants us to do now."

Jesperson wanted them to go to Electric Squidland.

"Never thought I'd see the day when the Old Man would send us clubbing," Jamie said when he picked Mick up that evening.

"Never thought I'd see the day when the Old Man would send us on a date," Mick countered, and was delighted when Jamie laughed.

They left the Skylark three blocks from the nightclub and walked the rest of the way, enjoying the mild night air. At 10:07 P.M. (Mick noted the exact time from force of habit) they walked into Kaleidoscope, the first level of Electric Squidland, mirrors and colored lights everywhere, and were greeted with a loud cry of, "Jamie! Lover!"

Mick stared disbelievingly at Jamie, who winced visibly before turning to greet an extremely pretty young man who was making the most of his Hispanic heritage with a pair of pale blue satin toreador pants. Mick, observing the pretty young man with the eye of an expert, saw that he was not as young as he was trying to appear, and he would be prettier if he admitted it.

"Ex-lover, Carlos," Jamie corrected, but he let Carlos kiss him.

"Oh, nonsense, darling. Once I let a man into my heart, he never leaves. But who is your Marilyn Manson here? This your new flame, sweetie?"

Mick opened his mouth to say something withering about blue satin toreador pants, but Jamie's abashed, apologetic expression stopped him. He swallowed his venom, said, "Mick Sharpton," and endured Carlos' cold fish handshake. He and Carlos understood each other very well.

"Mick's never been to Electric Squidland," Jamie said, adroitly avoiding the issue of whether Mick was or was not a "flame." "So I said I'd show him around. Suzanne working tonight?"

"Is it Wednesday and is the Pope Catholic?" Someone across the room was trying vigorously to attract Carlos' attention. He said, "We'll catch up later, sweetie. When you're not so busy."

When you've ditched your gothboy, Mick translated and was not sorry to see the last of Carlos. "I'll assume Carlos has hidden qualities," he said in Jamie's ear.

"Me-*ow*," Jamie said, and Mick felt himself blush. "C'mon. We won't find what we're looking for up here."

"What are we looking for, exactly?"

"Gal who has the Wednesday night show in Inferno."

"Oooo-kay."

Jamie grinned. "The two lower levels are Members Only. And I don't think Jesperson's going to let us put membership on our expense accounts. But Suzanne can get us badges, if she has a mind to."

"And will she?"

"Will she what?"

"Have a mind to?"

"Oh, I think so," Jamie said, and there was a private joke in there somewhere. Mick could feel it, and it made him a little uneasy. But only a little. He trusted Jamie, in a way he'd never been able to trust a partner before. He'd wondered sometimes, the first two years he was with the BPI, why he kept torturing himself, spending his days—and sometimes his nights—with a series of agents who disliked him, distrusted him. Some of them had openly hated him, and Mick had hated them back, fiercely and with no quarter given.

He had expected Jamie to be more of the same, Jamie with his bulk and his heavy hands and his deceptive eyes. And he still didn't understand what was different about Jamie, massive, gentle Jamie with his night-dark skin and his tattoos like clouds—didn't understand why Jamie had decided to like him and made that decision stick. Mick was painfully aware that he didn't deserve Jamie's liking—ever a proponent of "hit back first," he had been unconscionably nasty to Jamie in the early days of their partnership, until Jamie had proved, immutably, that he would not be nasty back. So whatever it was Jamie was waiting to spring on him, he knew it wouldn't be too bad.

He followed Jamie obediently from Kaleidoscope down the open corkscrew staircase that was the centerpiece of Electric Squidland's second level, Submarine. Submarine was classier, the level for those who fancied themselves Beautiful People. No disco balls here, and the music was dark, very techno, very European. Mick bet the bar on this level went through a lot of synthetic absinthe.

Jamie used their descent of the staircase to reconnoiter, and at the bottom, he grabbed Mick's elbow and said, "This way."

"Your gal's here?"

"Yup."

"Is she drinking synthetic absinthe?"

"What?"

"Never mind." By then, he could see the woman Jamie was aiming for, a petite woman with long plum-red hair, dressed in trailing, clinging black. The liquid in her glass was lurid green, and Mick moaned quietly to himself.

She looked up at their approach. Her eyes widened, and then she said, with apparently genuine delight, "Jamie! A very long time, and no see at all!" And then she gave Mick a once-over, seeming to take especial note of Jamie's hand on his elbow. "Are you attached to this delectable creature?"

"At the hip," Jamie muttered, only loud enough for Mick to hear, then said, "Sorta. I'm showing him around tonight."

"Well, you can just leave him to me." Suzanne extended a hand, the nails as long and black as Mick's own, and said, "Hi. I'm Suzanne."

"Mick." He did not let Suzanne's hand linger in his, although he knew he probably should have.

"Sit down, please," Suzanne said. "How have you been?"

"Oh, fine," Jamie said. "Listen, Suzanne, I really want Mick to see your act tonight."

It was hard to tell in Submarine's dim lighting, but Mick thought Suzanne blushed. "Jamie, how sweet of you."

Jamie kicked Mick's ankle; resigned, Mick picked up his cue: "Jamie's told me the most amazing things."

She was blushing. "He's probably exaggerating. But . . . " She looked at them, an expression in her eyes that Mick couldn't read. But whatever she saw pleased her; she smiled and said, "I'd hate to let you down. Let me see what I can do."

She left with a generous sway of her hips, and Mick leaned over to hiss in Jamie's ear, "She *can't* think I'm straight."

"I'm sure she doesn't." He shifted guiltily. "Suzanne, um. She has a thing for . . ."

"She's a fag hag," Mick said, several things falling into place; Jamie winced, but did not dispute the term. So that was Jamie's private joke. Mick grinned. "You son of a bitch. And you want me to—"

"Jesperson wants information. Of the two of us, I'm the one who knows where to look, which means you get to play distraction."

"But do I have to distract her?"

"You can distract her. And if you're distracting her, I can tell the bouncer at Inferno's side door I'm running an errand for her, and he's likely to believe me."

"Your plan sucks," Mick said.

"It's the only one we've got. And anyway, she's coming back, so it'll have to do."

"Your leadership technique also sucks," Mick said and forced himself to smile at Suzanne. Suzanne had brought them two pin-on black badges, each saying *Inferno* in fiery letters. "I've got to run and get ready," she said. "Sit where I can see you, and I'll talk to you after, okay?"

It was clear to both Mick and Jamie which one of them she was talking to, and Mick only barely managed not to sigh audibly.

"Be glad she brought two badges," Jamie said, then hesitated. "Suzanne's really not that bad. She's like a lot of the kids here—thinks it's exciting and sexy to work in a nightclub with a reputation. She doesn't know what goes on in Neon Cthulhu."

"And you do? What did you do, when you worked here?"

"Chief bouncer for Inferno. Adler called me Cerberus and thought he was being funny."

"You must've been good at it. Why'd you quit?"

Jamie smiled widely, mirthlessly, the same smile he'd had when he'd confessed to knowing Brett Vincent. "Because they were gonna give me a promotion."

"Most people," Mick said, cautious now because he didn't know this mood on Jamie, didn't know which way Jamie would jump, "don't find that offensive."

"They wanted to put me on the door of Neon Cthulhu, the lowest level. And I wasn't stupid enough to be interested. Inferno's bad enough, and it's really just play-acting." He held up one broad palm, anticipating Mick's objection. "Nothing illegal in the Neon Cthulhu. Leastways not out in the open. It's all consensual, and they got a license for public occultism. But it is nasty shit. I was only down there once." And he shuddered, as if even the memory made him ill.

"Jamie?" Mick said uncertainly. "You okay?"

Jamie shook his head, a weary gesture like a bull goaded by flies. "Don't like it here," he said. "Lot of real crappy memories."

"I'm sorry," Mick said helplessly, and was relieved when Jamie smiled at him, even if the smile was thin and forced.

"Not your fault, blue eyes. C'mon. Let's go to Hell."

Suzanne, it turned out, was a class eight magician; her act was very good, very smooth. She had a rather pretty young man as her assistant, and looking at him, looking at Suzanne, Mick saw his own twenty-year-old self and understood what Jamie had been trying to say about Suzanne. So eager to be wicked, but with no clear idea of how to go about it, so ready to admire anyone who seemed to have the secret information she lacked. He was able to relax a little, though, more confident she would not turn out to be the sort that would try to get him into bed.

After her curtain calls, Suzanne came and sat at Mick and Jamie's table, instantly making them the cynosure of all eyes; she preened herself, and Mick felt his patience with her slip another notch. Jamie, with his customary talent for evading the spotlight, went to get drinks, then muttered something about the restroom and disappeared—leaving Mick alone with Suzanne and several dozen interested spectators, including her seething pretty boy.

Mick knocked back a generous swallow of his screwdriver, and offered the first conversational gambit, asking a simple question about how she accomplished one of the effects in her act.

An hour later, he was wishing Suzanne's pretty boy would just go ahead and slip strychnine in his glass, because it would be less excruciating than this. The boy was hovering, green with jealousy; Suzanne, well aware, was flirting with Mick in a way he could have put *paid* to with a few pithy words, except that he was supposed to keep Suzanne distracted until Jamie got back, and where the hell was Jamie anyway?

Shouldn't have let him go running off to play James Bond on his own, Mick thought, while acknowledging ruefully that there was nothing else he could have done. He smiled at Suzanne—a little too hard, but she wouldn't notice in the dim light—and choked on his screwdriver when she asked, a trifle too nonchalantly, "Have you been Jamie's partner long?"

The coughing fit was merciful; by the time he recovered, and Suzanne was saying, "I'm so sorry, I didn't mean to embarrass you," he'd realized what she meant. She thought he and Jamie were lovers; her curiosity was prurient, not professional.

"You just surprised me," he said. "I didn't realize you . . . " and as he hesitated, trying to decide what he ought to say, whether he ought to play along, or whether he ought to tell her about Jamie's girlfriend, the image crashed into his mind, brutal as an SUV through plate glass—blood, black in lurid green light, and the harsh scent of cedar incense.

"Shit!" he said, setting his glass down hard enough to slop orange juice and vodka onto the table. "Jamie's in trouble."

Suzanne looked as if she couldn't decide whether to be offended or alarmed. "What, are you psychic or something?"

"Yeah, actually. Three-latent-eight."

She and her pretty boy stared at him with identical wide-eyed expressions.

"And I mean it," Mick said. "Jamie is in serious trouble. Will you help me find him?"

"But where would he . . . ?" She twisted around, and only then seemed to realize that Jamie was not lurking anywhere nearby.

"*Fuck,*" Mick said between his teeth. But Jamie needed him, and he knew he'd never find his partner without help. He gambled on the truth. "We work for the BPI. We're investigating the death of Brett Vincent, who was found out in Sunny Creek this morning."

"BPI? Jamie Keller went to work for the *BPI*?"

Mick wondered tangentially what Jamie had been like when he had worked here, and if that was why he'd been so unhappy to come back. "Yeah."

"And Brett?" Her eyes had gone even wider, and under her makeup, she'd gone pale. "Brett disappeared a week ago. Adler said he'd taken vacation, but Brett hadn't said anything about it, and that's not like him."

"Jamie identified the body. It really was him."

Suzanne thought a moment, her teeth worrying her lower lip, then turned to her pretty boy and snapped, "Give him your Cthulhu badge."

"But, Suzanne—"

"Do it!"

Pouting, frightened, the boy unpinned the badge—black like the Inferno badge, but with *Cthulhu* written on it in lurid green black-letter.

"Trade," Suzanne said. "Nobody wears both."

Mick did so quickly, lucky to avoid stabbing himself to the bone with the pin.

"Good. Come on."

"You don't have a badge," Mick said, getting up to follow her.

"I've worked here for years. They won't stop me."

Neither the bouncer at the top of the stairs, nor the bouncer at the bottom seemed at all inclined to argue with Suzanne. This was the job Jamie wouldn't take, Mick remembered and showed his Cthulhu badge. The bouncer waved him on with no further interest, and Mick felt a pang at how completely Jamie would have been wasted on this job.

He got out, he reminded himself fiercely. And you'll get him out again. Get him out and not come back.

Then he got his first good look at Neon Cthulhu. Mick was no stranger to S&M, and although he was not himself a magic user—and had no desire to be—he had been trained to recognize the more esoteric byways of the various disciplines. But Neon Cthulhu still rocked him back on his heels—almost literally—and it took him a moment to realize Suzanne looked as shocked as he felt. He remembered Jamie saying she didn't know about Neon Cthulhu, and it appeared that had been the truth.

"Stop looking like you're about to puke," he said, low and fierce. "C'mon, Suzanne. Pull yourself together."

"God," she said. "I mean, I knew it was a heavy scene down here, but—"

"It doesn't matter," he said, resisting the urge to shake her. "Help me find Jamie, and then you can get the hell out of Dodge."

"Okay." She took a deep breath and said it again, more firmly, "Okay. But where . . ."

Mick looked around, a quick, comprehensive glance. "That door," he said, with a jerk of his head toward the only other door that had a man on guard. "Can you distract the bouncer for me?"

"Can I . . ."

"For Jamie," Mick amended hastily, and that seemed to steady her. She nodded. "Good. Then pretend like this is all part of your stage act, and let's go."

That got her spine straight and her face, finally, settled, and they stepped away from the door together.

Having gone through all the stages from raw newbie to elite inner circle at more than one goth club, Mick knew perfectly well that the second most obvious sign of a tyro—after the wide-eyed gape—was the overdone look of blasé nonchalance. The trick was to look appreciative but not shocked, and he could manage that if he pretended strenuously to himself that the occult signs and mutterings and bits of ritual were just exceptionally impressive window-dressing for the S&M scenes being enacted in cages and on altars at various points around the room. He also reminded himself that Jamie had said Electric Squidland had a license for public occultism, and thus nothing going on here was illegal.

They stopped by a cage in which an ecstatic young man was being flogged by an Asian woman whose long braids snapped around her like another set of whips, and Mick pretended interest while Suzanne sashayed over, all hips and sex appeal, and engaged the bouncer's attention. Mick ghosted forward, aided by a sudden rapturous scream from the man in the cage that turned everybody's head for a split-second. Then Mick was at the door, wrenching the knob with clammy fingers, and then he was through, the door closed behind him, feeling his way down a much darker staircase, the bite of the cedar incense almost enough to make him cough. And he knew Jamie was close.

He could hear voices; as he reached the bottom of the stairs, his eyes adjusting to the darkness, he realized that the stairs were masked from the room beyond by a curtain. Green-tinged light seeped around its edges, and he drew close enough to make the voices come clear.

" . . . he must know something, or he wouldn't be here!"

"Could've been just listening to the rumors again. You always were a gossip, weren't you, Jamie boy?" A heavy thudding sound and a grunt: somebody had just kicked Jamie in the ribs. Mick's hands clenched.

"He's a threat, Adler," the first voice insisted.

"And I'm going to deal with him."

A beat of loaded silence, and the first voice said, appalled, "You're not going to give him to Brett's—!"

"I really don't think it will care." Adler sounded amused. "He certainly won't. At least not for long."

"We're not ready," the first voice said. "After last night . . . "

"Oh, Jamie will keep. No one's likely to come riding to his rescue."

Wrong, asshole, Mick thought with considerable satisfaction, listening as Adler and the other man, now discussing logistics and supplies for what sounded like a very complicated ritual, moved away from the stairs, growing distant and more muffled, until finally, with the click of a closing door, they became inaudible entirely.

Mick pushed the curtain aside only enough to slip through. The room beyond would have seemed ordinary enough—a waiting room with benches and chairs along the wall—if it had not been for the terrible greenness of the light, and Jamie Keller lying like a foundered ship in the middle of the floor, wrists bound, ankles bound, mouth stopped with a ball gag that could have been borrowed from any of the scenes going on in Neon Cthulhu's main room.

There was blood on Jamie's face—it looked like it was from his nose, and Mick was cursing Adler viciously under his breath as he dropped to his knees beside Jamie and fumbled at the buckle of the gag, trying not to pull Jamie's already disordered braids, trying not to hurt him more than he'd already been hurt.

He eased the ball out of Jamie's mouth, and Jamie took a deep, shuddering breath, and then another; Mick hadn't been the only one with visions of asphyxiation. Then Jamie let his head roll back on the carpet as Mick started working on his wrists, and croaked, "How'd you find me?"

"Had a flash," that being Jamie's term for the times when Mick's latent eight blindsided him.

"No shit?" Jamie sounded amazed and delighted, as if Mick had given him a birthday present he'd always wanted but never dared to ask for.

"Yeah," Mick said, and the leather thong around Jamie's wrists came loose. "But enough about me. What happened to you?"

"Being a Grade-A Prime fool, I walked slap into Mr. Henry Adler on my way back to the stairs."

"On your way back?" Mick said, untying Jamie's ankles. "Did you find out—"

"Yeah," Jamie said, his voice tight with the pain of returning circulation. "Only let's get out of here before we have Story Hour, if you don't mind."

"You could hardly have suggested anything I would mind less," Mick said and braced himself to help Jamie up. Jamie was perfectly steady on his feet, and Mick hoped that meant he had not been hurt too badly, despite the blood. He was glad to let Jamie take the lead as they proceeded cautiously into a positive rabbit-warren of storerooms and access tunnels.

"'You are in a maze of twisty little passages, all alike,'" Mick quoted uneasily. "Where the hell are we going?"

"Back door. Heck of a lot easier than trying to get out the way we came."

"And where's it gonna get us? Atlanta?"

Jamie laughed, and Mick was ridiculously glad to hear it. "Alley in back of the Kroeger's on Lichfield."

"That's three blocks away!"

"Halfway to Atlanta," Jamie said dryly.

"Adler can't own everything between here and there."

"Steam tunnels. Hell, Mick, you know how this city is. *Everything's* connected underground."

"Fucking ghouls." Much of the undercity of Babylon had been constructed in the late nineteenth century by a series of Reconstruction mayors who had preferred the local necromancers' money—and at a choice between the necromancers and the carpetbaggers, Mick wasn't entirely sure he blamed them—to the safety of their citizens. It was the ghouls, though, who kept those tunnels clear, as patient and industrious as moles.

"Works in our favor this time," Jamie said, and a voice said in answer, "It might."

Mick and Jamie both whipped around, and then Mick shied back, right into Jamie's unyielding bulk. He might have screamed; later, he could not remember and could not bring himself to ask.

The thing that had crept into the corridor behind them had once been human. It might still be able to pass, to anyone except a clairvoyant, although the way Jamie's arms tightened around Mick for a breath-stealing moment before letting him go suggested otherwise. Mick could see the broken wings it dragged behind itself, black as tar and shadows, and the way its eyes glowed fitfully sodium orange in the dim light. But the way its voice blurred and doubled, as if it were neither one person nor two, but perhaps one and a half—that, he thought, registered on the material plane, where Jamie could hear it just as well as he could.

And then there was the way it crawled, like a spider or a crab, and the fact that its legs ended in stumps where the ankle bones should have been; even if it could have passed for human, it could never have passed for normal.

Jamie said, his voice unnaturally steady, "You used to be Shawna Lafayette, didn't you?"

"'Used to be?'" Mick said, hearing the shrillness of his own voice. "Then what the fuck is she now?"

"I am ifrit," the thing said, its eyes flaring brilliantly, its voice warping and splintering, and it raised itself up like a cobra preparing to strike. Then it sank back again, the light in its eyes dulled. "And I think that, yes, this shell was once called Shawna. Much is lost."

There were several thousand questions demanding to be asked, and Mick couldn't find the words for any of them. Jamie cut straight to the heart of the matter: "What do you want?"

"I am hungry," the ifrit said in a plaintive, unconvincing whine. "I am hungry, and I am tired, and I am starting to lose my grip on this shell. You carry pain with you. You could release it to me." It licked its lips, not like a human being, but with the darting, flickering motion of a snake.

"No, thank you," Jamie said. "I did figure out what they're doing with Neon Cthulhu, you know. You got all the pain—and all the sex—you ever gonna need."

It hissed, again like a snake. "It would be better this way. Brighter."

Mick suddenly figured out what they were talking about and lurched back into Jamie again.

"He is eager," the ifrit said, its voice warbling with its own eagerness.

"*He* is scared out of his mind, thank you very much," Mick snapped. "Jamie, what—"

"Shut up, Mick," Jamie said, and very gently put him aside. "I have a better idea," he said to the ifrit, advancing slowly. "Why don't I help you let go of that body, before things get *really* ugly, and then you can go your way, and we can go ours?"

"Jamie—!"

"Shut *up*, Mick."

"You will not kill this shell," the ifrit said. "You know its name." It sounded certain, but it had backed itself against the wall, and it was watching Jamie with wide unblinking eyes, very orange now.

"And if you understood thing one about human beings, you'd know that's why I'm willing to kill you. That body's in misery, and it used to be someone I knew." He stopped, just out of arm's reach, and stared down at the ifrit. "It'll be quick, and then this whole clusterfuck will be over."

"I do not want . . . " But the ifrit's voice trailed off, as if it could no longer be certain what it did want, or didn't want; Mick remembered for no reason that mongooses were supposed to mesmerize their prey by dancing for them.

"Hold still, Shawna," Jamie said, his voice terribly kind, and then he moved.

Greased lightning had nothing on Jamie Keller, and Mick was still shocked at the idea that anyone so big could move so fast when he realized that small dry noise he had heard, like a twig breaking, had been Shawna Lafayette's neck. The body was just a body now, slumped and broken. The ifrit was gone.

"Is it dead, too?" Mick said hoarsely.

"Fucked if I know," Jamie said, and it was clear he didn't care, either. "Shawna's better off, though. I'm sure of that."

They reached the Skylark half an hour later, without another word being exchanged; Jamie folded down into the driver's seat with a sigh of relief and reached for the handset.

Mick caught his wrist. "Tell me first—are you okay?"

"Yeah. Adler got me down with a hex, not a cosh. Hadn't gone face-first, I wouldn't even have the bloody nose." He sounded disgusted at his own clumsiness.

Mick hadn't really meant physically. "Jamie . . . "

"I'm fine, Mick. Let's report in and get this over with, okay?"

Mick couldn't argue with that, although he had a vague feeling he should. He listened as Jamie called in; neither of them was surprised when Jesperson's voice interrupted to pepper Jamie with questions. Jesperson really *didn't* sleep, and he almost never went home. The first was the result of being a class nine necromancer—a *necromancer dux*, they called it in Britain—even if officially non-practicing; Mick often wondered if the second was as well.

"Did you find out what killed Brett Vincent?"

"Yes, sir. And Shawna Lafayette, too. Well, part of Shawna Lafayette, any way."

"I'm not going to like this, am I?"

"No, sir. Because Adler's hosting ifrits."

Jesperson's vocabulary became briefly unprintable. "Are you sure? Adler's only . . . "

"Class four, yessir. That's what happened to Shawna Lafayette. And Brett Vincent."

"That . . . oh. Oh, bloody hell."

"Yessir. Adler and his boys, they're talking 'bout it like a ritual, and I know for a fact Henry Adler ain't got the math. He can't figure a tip without a calculator."

"I like this even less than I thought I would. How long do you think this has been going on?"

"Dunno, sir. But I know what happened to Brett Vincent's body was on account of them getting the phase wrong, and the stupid bastards didn't even know the word."

Becoming aware of Mick's goggle-eyed stare, he covered the mike with his palm and hissed, *"What?"*

Mick just shook his head, and Jesperson said, "'Brett Vincent's body.' You don't think—"

"I think Brett Vincent's been dead for a long time. Same way I would've been if Echo hadn't come and got me out."

"Yes, what was November Echo's part in this evening's escapade?"

"Echo was invaluable, sir," Jamie said, and elbowed Mick hard in the ribs to make him stop laughing.

"Good," Jesperson said. A pause, probably while he wrote something on one of the legal pads that littered his office like shed snakeskins. "How many ifrits do you think there are in Electric Squidland?"

"There can't be that many," Mick said, and now it was Jamie's turn to look goggle-eyed at him.

"How do you figure that, November Echo?"

"Yeah," Jamie said. "How *do* you figure that?"

"Well, you said it yourself—and how did you get to learn so much about necromancy, anyway?"

"I don't spend my off-hours fornicating like a bunny rabbit. Go on— what did I say?"

"That they didn't know what they were doing. I mean, I don't either, but if they had to repeat the spell every so often—?"

"Yeah. 'Bout once every five years. Ifrit starts losing its grip, and that ain't pretty. Well, you saw."

"Yeah. And they've fucked up twice *that we know about* in the last three years—they can't be maintaining an army of ifrits, or we'd be up to our asses in Missing Persons."

"They must've lost the person who knew what they were doing."

"Carolyn Witt," Jesperson said, startling them both. "She was part owner of Electric Squidland. Sold her share to Adler just before her arrest. And she was class seven. I think a word with Ms. Witt might clear up a great many questions."

"Yessir," Jamie said and yawned.

"Go home, November Foxtrot and Echo," Jesperson said, and for a moment the rasp in his voice sounded less like irritation and more like concern. "You can finish the paperwork when you've got some sleep."

The BPI raided Electric Squidland that same night, discovering things in the rooms beneath Neon Cthulhu that would keep the state Office of

Necromantic Regulation and Assessment busy for years. Suzanne Parker was not among those arrested; she had taken Mick's advice and gotten the hell out of Dodge.

At 11:34 the next morning, Mick set two cups of coffee on the desk he and Jamie shared, and sat down opposite his partner. Although his head was clear this morning, and the world was coloring within the lines, Mick had a gloomy feeling today was not going to be a good day at all. They were facing a mountainous stack of paperwork, including closing the closing of the file on a seventeen-year-old boy named Daniel McKendrick who had disappeared from a Nashville suburb in 1983. His fingerprints matched those of Brett Vincent.

Jamie pushed back from the desk, stretching until his spine popped.

"Lila going to forgive you?" Mick asked.

"Maybe," Jamie said dolefully. "She hates my schedule."

"That's because you don't have one."

"Bite me." Jamie took a generous swallow of coffee and said, "Do you think we're right to say that body is Daniel McKendrick?"

"It *is* Daniel McKendrick."

"Not like that. I mean, his family's gonna be notified, and they been thinking he's dead all this time, and now they get half a fucking body to bury? Aside from which, Daniel McKendrick *has* been dead all this time—or at least most of it. That body was . . . somebody else, if it was a person at all."

"You mean, you think when you were sleeping with him . . . "

"Oh, I'm sure of it. Because he didn't give a shit when Shawna Lafayette disappeared, and now I know why."

"Do you want to talk about it?" Mick asked, red-faced at his own stupid clumsiness.

"No, but I'm gonna have to put it in the report anyway." Jamie sighed, took another slug of coffee. "It's the reason I quit Electric Squidland. Well, one of the reasons. Shawna was a waitress in Kaleidoscope. She caught Adler's eye, because she was pretty and not very bright, and I was worried about it— because she was pretty and not very bright. And then she disappeared, and nobody cared, and I asked Brett if he didn't think there was something strange about it, and he essentially told me to mind my own business. And, you know, I'd seen him talking to Shawna before she disappeared. Talking to her a *lot*."

"Persuading her."

"Seducing her," Jamie corrected. "And I don't know how many other people he seduced like that, or why he didn't try it on with me."

"Jamie, you're not helping yourself—"

"You know, that's the worst part. He let me go."

"Sorry?"

"*He let me go.* Oh, he tried to make me stay on, but when I wouldn't, he was okay with it. He never used magic on me, or tried to get me to play Adler's little games. Hell, he never even asked me to go down to Neon Cthulhu with him, and he must have known I would have. I think about the shit he could have pulled on me and the fact he didn't pull it, and the fact that he fucking let me go, and . . . Well, fuck it, Mick, I don't know. Was I just not worth it? Or do you think ifrits can love?"

"I don't know," Mick said, wanting desperately to give a better answer but simply not having one. "I really don't." And hesitantly, almost cringing, he reached out and put his hand over Jamie's, feeling the warmth and the strength and the roughness of Jamie's knuckles. And Jamie turned his hand over, folded his fingers around Mick's hand.

They sat that way for a moment, saying nothing. Jamie squeezed tighter, then let go and said briskly, "This ain't getting the paperwork done." But his eyes were clearer, as if some of the pain knotting him up had been released, and Mick returned to his share of their report feeling better himself.

Today might turn out to be a good day after all.

❧

Sarah Monette is the author of The Doctrine of Labyrinths series and co-author, with Elizabeth Bear, of *A Companion to Wolves* and *A Tempering of Men*. Some of her four dozen or so short stories have been collected in *The Bone Key* and *Somewhere Beneath the Waves*. Her 2014 novel *The Goblin Emperor*, published under the pseudonym Katherine Addison, received the Locus Award for Best Fantasy Novel and was nominated for the Nebula, Hugo, and World Fantasy Awards

❧

Although hidden from mundane eyes, The Library of the Hidden Arts is located somewhere on the rain-swept streets of Seattle. Its assets are a great help to a young man trying to become a full wizard.

Speechless in Seattle
Lisa Silverthorne

Thunder rumbled through the evening sky as storm clouds rolled off Elliot Bay where Brant Trenerry stood in Kerry Park, staff raised, ready to change the world.

The air prickled with energy, alive with the swirling of ancient forces as he summoned the power of all the wizards who'd carried this staff before him.

Already he smelled the acrid, almost electric tang of magic from the eye of the storm, a crisp, pungent odor that tingled his nose like cracked pepper.

He gripped the family staff tighter and whispered a spell he'd spent months crafting. It hissed from his lips, quickly joined by ancestral voices that echoed from the family grimoire he carried in the messenger bag underneath his cloak. He just needed to get the words right.

Brant was descended from House Trenerry, one of the five great houses of wizardry that settled in Seattle's sleepy streets nearly two hundred years ago. They lived quietly alongside mundanes who couldn't see or hear the trappings of their world.

He'd spent his whole life studying magic, schooled in the Arts before preschool and throughout his time in public schools. He'd lettered in all three schools of magic and passed all of his MHAATs. A senior at Seattle's College for the Performance of Magical Arts, he had a 3.8 average in Calefaction magic and a 4.0 in both Camber and Compulsion minors.

After committing the important spells of House Trenerry's grimoires to memory, he scoured Seattle's streets for a familiar, like all wizards-to-be. Just last month, he'd enticed a winged, tortoiseshell cat named Zipestra into the role. She'd been following him since his twentieth birthday, but it took him nearly a year to convince her to accept him as her wizard. Originally, he'd nicknamed her *Pest* for short, but the claw marks on his arm convinced him to choose Zip instead. *Cats.*

Now, on his twenty-first birthday, with his focus in place, he'd chosen a place of power to perform the spell. After the incantation, he'd inherit his house's power, becoming a full wizard in the eyes of the five great houses and Seattle's magical community.

If he completed the spell correctly.

All he had to do was say it.

He winced as he remembered his childhood struggle with stuttering. He'd grown out of it, but sometimes, when he was tired—or nervous—he stuttered.

Brant's staff glowed molten purple now, steaming in the mist-laden air, thrumming with pent-up forces ready for release. Carved out of myrtlewood on the steps of Glastonbury Abbey, honed with generations of Trenerry blood, sweat, and incantations, this staff had weathered continents and centuries. He was the seventh generation to carry it, an only child—which worried his parents.

Lightning fractured the sky, casting a neon yellow flash against Kerry Park's tall, steel sculpture. *Changing Form*, by Doris Totten Chase, consisted of two boxes with spherical cutouts that framed the skyline like a portal. For Brant, it was the most powerful place in Seattle.

Touched by the Puget Sound, Kerry Park carried elemental powers of earth, wind, and water. It pulsed with the constant energies of thousands of people who walked these worn red bricks every day. The walkways writhed with the hopes and dreams of tourists snapping countless photographs through the sculpture's circle. Each time, the world changed; storing bits and pieces of its magic into moments scattered throughout the Internet, framed on walls, and printed in the media—touching everything and everyone.

It just needed a spark. An element of fire to focus all the power he was about to summon.

Thunder roiled around him as he chanted the spell louder. The wind rose, strafing his face with rain. He stumbled over a word, then carefully spoke it again.

Brant's familiar fluttered around him, channeling his newfound energies into the staff, combining them into a single force. A task that familiars had performed for thousands of years.

The staff grew hot in his hand as lightning flashed overhead, crackling like pebbles against a tin roof. He shouted the spell's final line and slammed the end of the staff into the ground.

A massive fireball burst from the staff like a comet, shooting across the black, churning sky and exploding in a shower of sparks that rained down like fireworks. A jagged bolt of lightning tore across the horizon, thundering in a sharp, piercing clap.

Fire reigned from the clouds as a bright ring of fire rushed across the park, rolling over Seattle.

I'm free! It was Zip, his familiar's voice.

Brant turned, staring into the cat's deep copper eyes.

"Free?" he cried, shaking ashes out of his dark hair. "But . . . you're b-bound to me."

The winged cat rolled over in mid-air and stretched cream-speckled paws, arching her back as she clawed at the air.

Not anymore, Zip purred. *You spent so much time perfecting diction and crafting the spell, little wizard. You forgot about the words.*

"What are you talking about?" He glared at Zip as she licked her front paw. "I crafted my spell from the exact words in the Trenerry grimoire. And I didn't stutter!"

The pit of his stomach dropped into his feet. *What had he missed?*

Zip sighed. *That's the problem, little wizard. You forgot the first rule of magic: update all spells.*

He cringed, bristling at the smug, little furball. He wouldn't be lectured about magic by a flying cat.

A thousand years ago, each magical word was precise and had one meaning, Zip continued, rubbing against his elbow, her throaty purr soothing. *Today, those words have many meanings.*

He sighed and rubbed his forehead. "So what did I cast?"

You didn't call House Trenerry's magic into your staff, said Zip, *you set free every familiar in Seattle.*

Brant's eyes widened and he cursed under his breath. "I what? Oh, Gods, my father's gonna kill me! I've gotta fix this!"

He cast a Compulsion spell, transporting him to the one place that could help him, before anyone found out, The Seattle Library of the Hidden Arts.

Willa Rosewarren pulled her lavender cloak tight, head down, auburn hair tucked behind her ears as she shuffled through the angry crowd of wizards gathered at the steps of The Seattle Library of the Hidden Arts. Thunder rumbled in the distance. She smiled, hoping the storm would clear out these protestors.

Luna, the white dove on her shoulder, cooed in soothing warbles. The familiar scrubbed the impurities from Willa's magic until her Calefaction burned a pure, white flame. The five houses had mastered all three schools of magic, but only House Rosewarren exclusively practiced Calefaction, the manipulation of heat and light. Their wizards were the best at it, too—not that Willa liked to brag.

Willa loved practicing magic, but she preferred managing the library's collections, assisting researchers, and gathering rare, magical artifacts for her Seattle patrons. As the newest librarian, two weeks today, she'd volunteered for the evening shift, hoping to learn about the evening crowd's needs. She'd expected it to be busy, but she never dreamed there'd be protests.

Willa glanced at the two stone griffins perched on either side of the winding granite staircase that curved toward the library's oak doors, but the glowing slashes of blue, green, and orange runes obscured her view.

She groaned. Wizard graffiti.

The air smelled like melted plastic as she read the symbols flashing in the evening air.

Tomes Belong in Libraries. Grimoires Shouldn't be Digitized! Barcodes are Bad Magic!

Willa sighed, brushing away the runes. They turned to dust and floated away. Wizards. She rolled her eyes. Perfecting the magical arts for thousands of years, yet show them a barcode and they start a witch-hunt. Five great houses competing against each other since the Bronze Age, but mention digitizing family grimoires and they all band together.

Lightning flickered to the west as she swerved past two wizards, a man with black hair and a sable-haired, dark-skinned woman. They wore the royal blue robes of House Negus as they burned runes into the air, chanting, "Barcodes ruin grimoires!" as Willa reached the staircase. One had a shaggy brown dog that panted and wagged its tail. The other had a red squirrel perched on her shoulder, happily shelling an acorn. Willa loved seeing all the familiars.

House Rosewarren built this white two-story, gothic revival in the 1850s. At times, the black mansard roof with its wrought-iron widow's walk looked forbidding, but the spandreled portico softened its harsh appearance. It sat in stark contrast to the modern curves of the Seattle Art Museum, just a few blocks from Elliot Bay. Mundanes couldn't see House Rosewarren due to the extensive Camber magic that curved and refracted space around it.

A white-haired wizard dressed in a brown cloak and the yellow silk robes of House Kestell stepped in front of Willa. His familiar, a black stag, fidgeted beside him, rubbing its antlers against the granite stairs. The wizard smelled like stale smoke and decaying silk, his teeth clicking when he talked.

"This is an outrage!" he shouted. His features were sharp and hawk-like, small, dark eyes glaring. A goatee framed his angry pout as he shook a finger at her. "Just you wait until all the houses hear about what you've done here! It's desecration!"

A chestnut-haired sorceress wearing an orange pullover rushed out of the library, cupping blue orbs in each hand. "Have you seen my tiger?" she asked, looking upset, eyes glassy, a trail of blue sparkles trickling through her fingers and scattering down the steps.

Willa shook her head. "No, sorry."

She moved away from Willa. "Has anyone seen my white tiger, Freyja? Anyone? Please, my familiar's vanished! I can't focus spells without her!"

Distraught, she shuffled past Willa who tried to sidestep the angry House Kestell wizard, but other protesters blocked her path, tossing fireballs at the stone griffins.

The griffins let out a screech, broke free of their magical tethers, and fluttered into the night, halting the protestors' shouts.

Willa gasped, nearly falling down the stairs. The Library familiars!

She grabbed the railing as Luna took flight, following the griffins.

The deathly quiet on the stairs forced her to turn around. Every familiar was gone.

"What's happened?" someone whispered. The wizards looked lost, staring at each other as the protest runes faded into puffs of smoke.

"Where's my dog?"

Storm clouds broke, rain pattering against the granite steps, washing away dust and smoke. Panicked, the wizards scattered.

Willa didn't know what happened to the familiars, but she'd start researching possible causes—and solutions. She pulled open the heavy oak door and collided with a man in a black cloak.

Everything turned dark when the young man's cloak tangled around her head and she fell. She struggled to free herself, but the marble floor was too slick and she couldn't get to her feet. She groaned in frustration as the man struggled up from the floor.

He pulled back the edge of his cloak. She stared up at him, studying his kind face, warm brown eyes, and wavy brown hair. He looked mesmerized, his eyes wide and unblinking. He was quite attractive, tall and slim, tousled hair just above the collar of his gray henley, and wide-set brown eyes like a distraught puppy. His cloak almost hid his faded jeans. She brushed a tangle of auburn locks away from her face and smiled, but he seemed almost frightened of her. His lips moved, but no words came out.

Instead, the young man signed a spell, copper flashes dancing across her body, lifting her from the floor. Sweat misted his face as he seemed to struggle to hold the spell until she was on her feet. She grinned. A wizard!

"Thank you," said Willa, struggling to catch her breath.

She straightened her cloak, smoothing the Juliet sleeves of her pale mint blouse. Her black pencil skirt was hiked up, so she straightened the seam. Her rain-damp face was flushed, cheeks burning as she did her best not to stare—or make him feel more uncomfortable. After all, as a wizard of House Rosewarren, it was her duty to uphold the house's reputation of producing helpful, compassionate wizards and stewards of written magical knowledge.

At last, the young man returned her smile, looking calmer as he picked up his staff and bowed politely. But that distressed look returned to his face as he ducked into the east reading room.

Willa followed, hoping he needed help with his research.

"Can I help you find something?" she asked, hurrying down the long, narrow room, past wooden tables and brown leather couches. "I work here."

He turned away from a shelf of books against the far wall, smiling. "I . . . thought you were from House Rosewarren."

Bookshelves lined every wall, the room painted a pale aqua, and stood in neat rows of three between the tables and couches. The young wizard seemed fascinated by the rows of colorful books. Frosty white orbs floated across the ceilings in a slow, circular path, lighting the room with soft white light as he rushed from shelf to shelf, a look of desperation in his eyes.

Thick tomes and loosely bound manuscripts filled the shelves, some books glowing blue. Others had pictures that flashed along their spines, others were adorned with shiny jewels and fiery runes. Leather, colored cardstock, delicate silks, and vellums in frosty, crisp sheets.

He closed his eyes a moment, taking a deep breath, which seemed to calm him. Willa felt even more attracted to him now. He loved the smell of books. She was certain of it. When he opened his eyes, they had a dreamy quality, like someone who wanted to lose himself in every tome and text.

She breathed in the comforting scent of leather and old paper, knowing this man was someone she could have long conversations about magic and grimoires with over hot tea and scones. Someone who probably loved the rain and the ocean's nearness to the city. She desperately wanted to get to know him.

The wizard walked toward the large, glass-summoning spheres in the corner that bobbed in the air at eye level. They were the size of large melons and had more facets than a diamond.

"What are you searching for?" Willa asked, startling him. He reached toward the spheres and images danced across the clear glass. With a flick of his index finger, and a bit of Compulsion magic glowing lavender at his fingertips, he tried to use the spheres. He was probably new to the Library's new catalog system.

"Just say what you're looking for and the spheres will show you images from our collection."

"Familiars," he snapped.

Willa's eyes grew wide. No wonder he was distressed and struggling with his magic. He'd probably lost his familiar!

"Did you lose yours, too?" she asked.

The young man looked mortified now, his face pinching, mouth twisting into a grimace, eyes smashed closed.

Finally, he nodded and glanced at the shelves and the tomes, still looking for something. *Why didn't he just tell her what he needed? She couldn't help him if he wouldn't talk to her.*

"I lost my familiar, too, so I know how you feel," she said, touching his sleeve. He didn't pull away. "I'm here to help though. Just tell me what you're researching and I'll point you to the appropriate resources."

He stared at her in silence, a battle warring behind his eyes.

"I'm Willa," she said, extending her hand.

He pursed his lips. "Brant," he replied, his voice clipped. He smiled at her now.

"You're from House Trenerry, aren't you?" she said as she approached the glass spheres. "I recognize the staff."

He nodded.

"There are volumes written on familiars, Brant," she said, returning his smile. "Our new online system should help narrow down our choices."

She chanted a Calefaction spell, a force that controlled heat and light, and focused it on the books.

Across the room, two massive tomes floated off the shelves, scattering dust and sparks as they moved toward her. They hung in the air to her right. One had glowing orange runes on the cover and the other had blurry images rushing across its face.

"Here are two volumes on the subject," she said. "They haven't been digitized yet." She smiled, pointing to three small runes that sparkled red on the spine. "But I've barcoded them so the new system can find and retrieve them."

"That's n-n-nice," said Brant. Embarrassment flushed his face and he turned away, gripping his staff.

"What's wrong, Brant?"

He pitched the staff at the leather couch. It bounced off and hung in the air for a moment. Then it clattered against the marble floor.

"It's m-my f-fault!" His face burned with shame. "The f-f-familiars." He squeezed his eyes closed, balling his hands into fists. "I—I bungled the spell. I would have . . . been a full-fledged House Trenerry wizard. But that w-won't happen n-now."

Willa winced at his comments, feeling terrible for him. Tonight was the poor man's birthday! All wizards received their full power on their twenty-first birthday, but something had gone wrong for him. She laid a hand against his arm.

"Tonight was your twenty-first birthday, wasn't it?" she asked. "You were summoning your power, weren't you?"

He nodded, gritting his teeth. "I didn't u-update the spell. My fault." He let out a frustrated growl.

"Is that what happened?" Willa asked, turning him around to face her. "You crafted your spell using the original House spell?"

He cringed, nodding again.

"Do you have your family's grimoire with you?" she asked. "The one containing both spells?" She needed to see the whole text, including the spell he'd crafted.

"Y-yes," he answered in a quiet voice as he lifted the heavy tome out of his satchel.

The cover had a frosty sheen, inlaid with aquamarines and polished silver. It sparkled as he handed it to Willa who cradled the book in her arms.

She took his hand, flushing at the touch of his fingers against hers as she led him to the summoning spheres.

"I'll digitize the contents," said Willa. "Then we'll compare it to all known spells dealing with familiars."

She laid the book on a nearby table and summoned a crystal sphere.

She pressed her fingers against its smooth surface, reciting a Calefaction spell that lit Brant's grimoire. The spell illuminated every page, every pen stroke, every indentation as the sphere shifted colors and hummed with energy. Words and symbols burned images into the air as they traveled out of the book and into the sphere, turning and spinning.

Heat from the symbols and the Calefaction spell warmed Brant's face. He looked panicked now, as if he were reliving their casting and Willa couldn't help but feel badly for him.

"Once we get the spells captured, I'll compare them to the familiars spell." She smiled at him. "Don't worry, Brant. We can fix this."

"Hope . . . you're right."

It took several long, painful minutes before the sphere finished and went dark. Only then did Willa approach it.

"Locate all spells dealing with familiars," she said to the sphere.

Images and symbols flashed over the sphere's misty surface, whispers hissing as the runic signs glowed in the air. Willa walked among them, studying the information. Brant joined her, his shoulder touching hers now. He smelled of spring rain and a clean, woodsy scent that clouded her brain for a moment as she leaned closer to him.

Willa pointed at a cluster of pulsating runes.

"Do you remember this part of your spell, Brant?" She smiled. "It's beautifully crafted. Such a nice balance of Camber and Compulsion that builds with power into the Calefaction summons at the end."

"Yes," he replied, his face flushed. "It was-was tough . . . to cr-cr-craft."

Willa lifted a grouping of blue runes from the sphere. They floated in the air to her left, four double-spaced lines. She recited another spell as she reached into the sphere, teasing out a group of gold symbols. Four rows of double-spaced, gold runes hung at her right shoulder. She glanced left to right, reading each symbol, comparing one against the other.

"There it is," she said in a quiet voice.

Brant moved toward the symbols, studying them in silence.

"The blue symbols are part of the original Trenerry spell you spoke tonight," she said and motioned to her right. "The gold symbols are the spell you crafted."

Brant reached out and gathered the gold symbols in his palm. He dragged them over to the blue symbols and dropped them on top. Together, they compared the overlap of every symbol, the curve and brilliance of each one, blue against gold.

"Look for missteps," she said in a soft voice.

Brant nodded. "Right, anything that might have changed the spell's outcome or ruined the incantation somehow."

Brant's voice filled the room as Willa's spell called back the echo of his cast spell. The words floated through the world forever and she could call them back like a little capsule of time. She watched Brant wince at the sound of his own voice.

"My parents always w-worried about m-me," said Brant, bowing his head. "Guess they—they always knew I'd amount t-t-to n-nothing. That I'd n-n-never capture the energies of H-House Trenerry."

Willa's heart broke at his despair. She slid her arm around his shoulders. "Don't you talk like that, Brant! They believe in you and so do I. You *will* become a full wizard tonight. I just know it!"

At last, his face brightened. "Hope you're r-right, Willa." He paused a moment. "I s-stuttered as a kid, but now, only b-beautiful women make me s-s-stutter."

She couldn't hold back her smile as she watched him concentrate on the symbols again, studying the agreements in the magic. Looking for the green tint wherever the blue and gold symbols matched.

They stood in silence for a long time, studying the symbols, but finally, Brant cried out and pointed at three, tiny symbols that didn't match.

"Here . . . they are! Three symbols that broke the familiars' bonds," he said, pointing. He winced. "I used an old h-homonym from my grimoire."

"It strictly meant a wizard's talisman once."

Willa nodded. "Yes, you're right! That symbol's become slang for familiars. Any wizard might have used that symbol to mean staff, Brant."

"That damned cat's gonna gloat for weeks over my mistake."

Willa captured the three symbols, scattering the rest into a shower of sparks that dissolved in a puff of smoke.

"Show counter signs to this magical break," she said into the sphere. "Then show us the spell to re-forge our familiars' bonds."

"And focus only on the staff," Brant added.

Vivid purple letters appeared beside three gold symbols. Brant read through the line of purple symbols and then studied the three gold signs.

"That's the fix then," he said, his hands shaking. "I'll uh—recast with those symbols. But without my familiar, it won't work." He sighed in exasperation and kicked the leather couch.

Willa grabbed his arm as she turned toward the sphere. He didn't understand that he controlled the power he was summoning, not his familiar. Familiars were there for focus and tempering, nothing more.

She laid a crisp piece of blank parchment onto the table. With both hands, she lifted the symbols out of the air and pressed them against the parchment, a spell of Calefaction on her lips.

Her words were precise, the diction flawless as thin blades of fire carved Brant's eleven symbols into the parchment. She blew on the paper until it cooled and all the blackened edges had hardened. Then she rolled up the scroll and handed it to Brant. She loved the feel of his warm, strong fingers against her palm, wanting to entwine her fingers in his.

"There," she said. "You won't have to rely on memory."

With a loud thud, the library doors slammed open as dozens of wizards poured inside, demanding assistance. They brushed past Willa and Brant, making their way down the long hallway toward the library's main service desk. A big, round walnut desk stood in the center of the vaulted foyer. Four librarians cowered behind it as the herd descended on them.

A huge chandelier hung over the service desk, dripping with hundreds of multifaceted, teardrop crystals. Swirls of light danced across the cold marble floor as the growing crowd clacked across it, heaping themselves around the desk in tangles three and four people deep. The roar of their voices echoed through the chamber. On either side of the round, ornate desk were two sets of wrought-iron staircases winding gracefully upstairs to special collections and more reading rooms. The two staircases met at the top in an elegant balcony overlooking the marble foyer. Brant eyed the balcony and Willa worried that he might jump from it.

"My familiar's just disappeared," someone shouted. "Now, I can't cast any spells! You've got to help me!"

"Please, my familiar's missing!" shouted another wizard. "I need that hawk to strengthen my Compulsion spells!"

Librarians huddled behind the desk, calling up tomes that flew off reading room shelves to the hands of Willa's colleagues who were desperate to help.

Brant tugged on her sleeve. "There's only one way to f-fix this. Will you. Help—me?"

Willa nodded. She was afraid he wouldn't ask. "Of course!"

Brant retrieved his staff and then folded her arm in his. He fought his way through the growing crowd of wizards, pulling her along until they reached Seattle's rain-swept streets.

Brant signed his way through a series of Camber spells that shifted and refracted space, allowing him to twist magical forces into a portal that brought them back to Kerry Park. He tugged her up the red brick stairs to the strange, steel geometric sculpture.

Through the steel's round cutouts, he gazed at Elliot Bay through a haze of blackness and rain-smeared city lights framing the Space Needle and Seattle's unforgettable skyline. The storm had passed to the east, clouds faded to wispy trails allowing stars to burn through the swath of midnight sky.

Brant lifted the staff toward the sky. He unfurled Willa's parchment that burned with the new incantation. Eleven symbols that would re-bond the familiars and make him Seattle's newest full wizard.

"Ready?" Willa called above the rush of wind.

She stood beside him, so encouraging, so inspiring. Maybe she'd see him as more than a stuttering fool?

Nodding, he gripped the parchment and the myrtlewood staff, staring at the fiery symbols. He whispered them, practicing each one.

Fear gripped him as he clenched the staff and cast the corrected spell. Only eleven symbols stood between him and his birthright. This time, he would get it right.

Brant cleared his throat and held the parchment out to Willa.

"Will you hold this while I cast?"

She nodded, taking the stiff parchment and holding it in front of him.

One last time, he ran through the spell in his head, pausing to insert the eleven corrected signs.

Then, concentrating on each symbol, Brant spoke the crafted spell with precision, working through each section with confidence. He felt the uneven flow of energy through him, untempered and unfocused without his familiar. He continued the spell, pausing for the final eleven symbols to correct the incantation. Fix what he'd broken. Summon his birthright at last.

The myrtlewood staff gleamed brilliant red, the surface warm against his fingers. A fiery glow pulsed, rushing down the length of the staff and then rolling back again, turning deep orange, then gold, then white. And finally blue.

His hands shook as he took a deep breath, focusing all his concentration, and chanted the last symbols. Without a stutter or bobble.

Energy crackled, the sound like a gunshot. With tremendous force, the entire flow of magical energy contained in House Trenerry slammed into the myrtlewood staff and then Brant's body. The impact threw him across the brick stairs and onto the cold, wet ground.

Dazed, Brant laid there listening to the staff sizzle as rain misted the air and grass.

The sudden flutter of wings startled him, a deep, thrumming purr resonating across his cheek. Something brushed against his leg, beating past his stomach to hover at his shoulder.

Zip! The winged tortoiseshell cat arched her back, wings thumping the cool air as she lifted a fat, cream-colored paw to her mouth and licked it with her tiny, pink tongue.

You fixed the spell, little wizard, she said with a throaty purr between licks. *Well done.*

Brant reached out to pet the winged furball, but she slid just out of his reach.

"You did it," said Willa, kneeling beside him. "Great job, Brant! It took courage to recast that spell."

He smiled as she helped him up from the cold grass.

"I couldn't have done it without your help," he said. "And the library. How can I thank you?"

A gleam touched her deep green eyes. "Actually, you might be of some help at the library."

He raised an eyebrow. "How so?"

Willa sighed. "A testimonial on having your family grimoire digitized might go a long way with your fellow wizards."

Brant laughed. "You mean showing them it was painless and I still have the intact book?"

She nodded. "Exactly."

"Anything to help," he said. "It's the least I can do."

He reached out and stroked Zip who licked his hand then nipped it. He sighed. *Cats.*

He stepped closer to Willa, staring into her eyes as he held her hand.

"As Seattle's newest full wizard, I could give a talk reminding wizards to always um . . . update their spells."

Willa smiled when a white dove landed on her shoulder. Laughing, she squeezed his hand and moved closer to him.

"I'd love to discuss it over tea."

"Love to," he said, squeezing her hand.

≈

Lisa Silverthorne has published nearly seventy short stories and novelettes of many genres. *Isabel's Tears*, her first novel, was released last year.

≈

Palimpsest, as author Valente has stated, is a "sexually transmitted city." The only way to reach it is through the magic of streetmaps that appear on a lover's skin.

Palimpsest
Catherynne M. Valente

16th and Hieratica

A fortuneteller's shop: palm-fronds cross before the door. Inside are four red chairs with four lustral basins before them, filled with ink, swirling and black. A woman lumbers in, wrapped in ragged fox-fur. Her head amid heaps of scarves is that of a frog, mottled green and bulbous-eyed, and a licking pink tongue keeps its place in her wide mouth. She does not see individual clients. Thus it is that four strangers sit in the red chairs, strip off their socks, plunge their feet into the ink-baths, and hold hands under an amphibian stare. This is the first act of anyone entering Palimpsest: Orlande will take your coats, sit you down, and make you family. She will fold you four together like quartos. She will draw you each a card— look, for you it is the Broken Ship reversed, which signifies perversion, a long journey without enlightenment, gout—and tie your hands together with red yarn. Wherever you go in Palimpsest, you are bound to these strangers who happened onto Orlande's salon just when you did, and you will go nowhere, eat no capon or dormouse, drink no oversweet port that they do not also taste, and they will visit no whore that you do not also feel beneath you, and until that ink washes from your feet—which, given that Orlande is a creature of the marsh and no stranger to mud, will be some time—you cannot breathe but that they breathe also.

The other side of the street: a factory. Its thin spires are green, and spit long loops of white flame into the night. Casimira owns this place, as did her father and her grandmother and probably her most distant progenitor, curling and uncurling their proboscis-fingers against machines of stick and bone. There has always been a Casimira, except when, occasionally, there is a Casimir. Workers carry their lunches in clamshells. They wear extraordinary uniforms: white and green scales laid one over the other, clinging obscenely to the skin, glittering in the spirelight. They wear nothing else; every wrinkle and curve is visible. They dance into the factory, their serpentine bodies writhing a shift-change, undulating under the punch-clock with its cheerful metronomic chime. Their eyes are piscine, third eyelid half-drawn in drowsy pleasure as they side-step and gambol and spin to the rhythm of the machines.

And what do they make in this factory? Why, the vermin of Palimpest. There is a machine for stamping cockroaches with glistening green carapaces, their maker's mark hidden cleverly under the left wing. There is a machine for shaping and pounding rats, soft gray fur stiff and shining when they are first released. There is another mold for squirrels, one for chipmunks and one for plain mice. There is a centrifuge for spiders, a lizard-pour, a delicate and ancient machine which turns out flies and mosquitoes by turn, so exquisite, so perfect that they seem to be made of nothing but copper wire, spun sugar, and light. There is a printing press for graffiti which spits out effervescent letters in scarlet, black, angry yellows, and the trademark green of Casimira. They fly from the high windows and flatten themselves against walls, trestles, train cars.

When the shift-horn sounds at the factory, the long antler-trumpet passed down to Casimira by the one uncle in her line who defied tradition and became a humble hunter, setting the whole clan to a vociferous but well-fed consternation, a wave of life wafts from the service exit: moles and beetles and starlings and bats, ants and worms and moths and mantises. Each gleaming with its last coat of sealant, each quivering with near-invisible devices which whisper into their atavistic minds that their mistress loves them, that she thinks of them always, and longs to hold them to her breast.

In her office, Casimira closes her eyes and listens to the teeming masses as they whisper back to their mother. At the end of each day they tell her all they have learned of living.

It is necessary work. No family has been so often formally thanked by the city as hers.

The first time I saw it was in the pit of a woman's elbow. The orange and violet lights of the raucous dancefloor played over her skin, made her look like a decadent leopardess at my table. I asked her about it; she pulled her sleeve over her arm self-consciously, like a clam pulling its stomach in.

"It's not cancer," she said loudly, over the droning, repetitive music, "I had it checked out. It was just there one day, popping up out of me like fucking track marks. I have to wear long sleeves to work all the time now, even in summer. But it's nothing—well, not nothing, but if it's something it's benign, just some kind of late-arriving birthmark."

I took her home. Not because of it, but because her hair was very red, in that obviously dyed way—and I like that way. Some shades of red genetics will never produce, but she sat in the blinking green and blue lights haloed in defiant scarlet.

She tasted like new bread and lemon-water.

As she drifted to sleep, one arm thrown over her eyes, the other lying open and soft on my sheets, I stroked her elbow gently, the mark there like a tattoo: a spidery network of blue-black lines, intersecting each other, intersecting her pores, turning at sharp angles, rounding out into clear and unbroken skin just outside the hollow of her joint. It looked like her veins had darkened and hardened, organized themselves into something more than veins, and determined to escape the borders of their mistress's flesh. She murmured my name in her sleep: *Lucia.*

"It looks like a streetmap," I whispered sleepily, brushing her hair from a flushed ear.

I dreamed against her breast of the four black pools in Orlande's house. I stared straight ahead into her pink and gray-speckled mouth, and the red thread swept tight against my wrist. On my leather-skirted lap the Flayed Horse was lain, signifying sacrifice in vain, loveless pursuit, an empty larder. A man sat beside me with an old-fashioned felt hat askance on his bald head, his lips deeply rosy and full, as though he had been kissing someone a moment before. We laced our hands together as she lashed us—he had an extra finger, and I tried not to recoil. Before me were two women: one with a green scarf wrapping thin golden hair, a silver mantis-pendant dangling between her breasts, and another, Turkish, or Armenian, perhaps, her eyes heavily made-up, streaked in black like an Egyptian icon.

The frog-woman showed me a small card, red words printed neatly on yellowed paper:

You have been quartered.

The knots slackened. I walked out, across the frond-threshold, into the night which smelled of sassafras and rum, and onto Hieratica Street. The others scattered, like ashes. The road stretched before and beyond, lit by streetlamps like swollen pumpkins, and the gutters ran with rain.

212th, Vituperation, Seraphim, and Alphabet

In the center of the roundabout: the Cast-Iron Memorial. It is tall and thin, a baroque spire sheltering a single black figure—a gagged child with the corded, elastic legs of an ostrich, fashioned from linked hoops of iron—through the gaps in her knees you can see the weeds with their flame-tipped flowers. She is seated in the grass, her arms thrown out in supplication. Bronze and titanium chariots click by in endless circles, drawn on runners in the street, ticking as they pass like shining clocks. Between her knock-knees is a plaque of white stone:

IN MEMORIAM:

THE SONS AND DAUGHTERS OF PALIMPSEST

WHO FOUGHT AND FELL IN THE SILENT WAR.

752-759

SILENT STILL

ARE THE FIELDS

IN WHICH THEY ARE PLANTED.

Once, though the tourists could not know of it, on this spot a thousand died without a gasp. Legions were volunteered to have their limbs replaced with better articles, fleeter and wiser and stronger and newer.

These soldiers also had their larynxes cut out, so they could not give away their positions with an unfortunate cry, or tell tales of what they had done in the desert, by the sea, in the city which then was new and toddling. Whole armies altered thus wrangled without screams, without sound. In the center of the roundabout, the ostrich-girl died unweeping while her giraffe-father had his long, spotted neck slashed with an ivory bayonet.

Down the mahogany alleys of Seraphim Street, clothes shops line the spotless, polished road. In the window of one is a dress in the latest style: startlingly blue, sweeping up to the shoulders of a golden mannequin. It cuts away to reveal a glittering belly; the belt is fastened with tiny cerulean eyes which blink lazily, in succession. The whites are diamonds, the pupils ebony. The skirt winds down in deep, hard creases which tumble out of the window in a carefully arranged train, hemmed in crow feathers. The shopkeeper, Aloysius, keeps a pale green Casimira grasshopper on a beaded leash. It rubs its legs together while he works in a heap of black quills, sewing an identical trio of gowns like the one in the window for triplet girls who demanded them in violet, not blue.

At night, he ties the leash to his bedpost and the little thing lies next to his broad, lined face, clicking a binary lullaby into the old man's beard. He dreams of endless bodies, unclothed and beautiful.

I can be forgiven, I think, for not noticing it for days afterward. I caught a glimpse in my mirror as I turned to catch a loose thread in my skirt—behind my knee, a dark network of lines and angles, and, I thought I could see, tiny words scrawled above them, names and numbers, snaking over the grid.

After that, I began to look for them.

I found the second in a sushi restaurant with black tablecloths—he was sitting two tables over, but when he gripped his chopsticks, I could see the map pulsing on his palm. I joined him—he did not object. We ate eels and cucumbers thinner than vellum and drank enough clear, steaming sake that I did not have to lean over to kiss him in the taxi. He smashed his lips against mine and I dug my nails into his neck—when we parted I seized his hand and licked the web of avenues that criss-crossed so: heart and fate lines.

In his lonely apartment I kissed his stomach. In his lonely apartment, on a bed without a frame which lay wretched between milk crates and cinder blocks, the moon shone through broken blinds and slashed my back into a tiger's long stripes.

In his lonely apartment, on a pillow pounded thin by dozens of night-fists, I dreamed. Perhaps he dreamed, too. I thought I saw him wandering down a street filled with balloons and leering gazelles—but I did not follow. I stood on a boulevard paved with prim orange poppies, and suddenly I tasted brandy rolling down my throat, and pale smoke filling up my lungs. My green-scarved quarter was savoring her snifter and her opium somewhere far from me. I saw the ostrich-child that night. I smelled the Seraphim sidewalks, rich and red, and traded, with only some hesitation, my long brown hair for the dress. Aloysius cut it with crystal scissors, and I walked over wood, under sulfurous stars, trailing dark feathers behind me. The wind was warm on my bare neck. My fingers were warm, too— my bald quarter was stroking a woman with skin like a snake's.

There were others. A man with a silver tooth—a depth-chart crawled over his toes. With him I dreamed I walked the tenements, raised on stilts over a blue river, and ate goulash with a veteran whose head was a snarling lion, tearing his meat with fangs savage and yellow. He had a kind of sign language, but I could only guess correctly the gestures for mother, southeast, and sleep.

There was a woman with two children and a mole on her left thigh— between her shoulder blades severe turns and old closes poked on an arrondissement-wheel. With her I dreamed I worked a night's shift in a restaurant that served but one dish: broiled elephant liver, soaked in lavender honey and jeweled with pomegranate seeds. The staff wore tunics sewn from peacock feathers, and were not allowed to look the patrons in the eye. When I set a shimmering plate before a man with long, gray fingers, I felt my black-eyed quarter pick up her golden fork and bite into a snail dipped in rum.

There was a sweet boy with a thin little beard—his thumb was nearly black with gridlock and unplanned alleys, as though he had been fingerprinted in an unnameable jail. He fell asleep in my arms, and we dreamed together, like mating dragonflies flying in unison. With him,

I saw the foundries throwing fire into the sky. With him I danced in pearlescent scales, and pressed into being exactly fifty-seven wild hares, each one marked on its left ear with Casimira's green seal.

Lucia! They all cry out when they lie over me. Lucia! Where will I find you?

Yet in those shadow-stitched streets I am always alone.

I sought out the dream-city on all those skins. What were plain, yellow-lined streets next to Seraphim? What was my time-clock stamping out its inane days next to the jeweled factory of Casimira? How could any touch equal the seizures of feeling in my dreams, in which each gesture was a quartet? I would touch no one who didn't carry the map. Only once that year, after the snow, did I make an exception, for a young woman with cedar-colored breasts and a nose ring like a bull's, or a minotaur's. She wore bindi on her face like a splatter of blood. Her body was without blemish or mark, so alien and strange to me by then, so blank and empty. But she was beautiful, and her voice was a glass-cutting soprano, and I am weak. I begged her to sing to me after we made love, and when we dreamed, I found her dancing with a jackal-tailed man in the lantern-light of a bar that served butterfly-liquor in a hundred colors. I separated them; he wilted and slunk away, and I took her to the sea, its foam shattering into glass on the beach, and we walked along a strand of shards, glittering and wet.

When I woke, the grid brachiated out from her navel, its angles dark and bright. I smiled. Before she stirred, I kissed the striated lines, and left her house without coffee or farewells.

Quiescent and Rapine

There are two churches in Palimpsest, and they are identical in every way. They stand together, wrapping the street-corner like a hinge. Seven white columns each, wound around with black characters which are not Cyrillic, but to the idle glance might seem so. Two peaked roofs of red lacquer and two stone horses with the heads of fork-tongued lizards stand guard on either side of each door. They were made with stones from the same quarry, on the far southern border of the city, pale green and dusty, each round and perfect as a ball. There is more mortar in the edifices than stones, mortar crushed from Casimira dragonflies donated by the vat, tufa dust, and mackerel tails. The pews are scrubbed and polished with lime-oil, and each Thursday, parishioners share a communion of slivers of whale meat and cinnamon wine. The only difference between the two is in the basement—two great mausoleums with alabaster coffins lining the walls, calligraphied with infinite care and delicacy in the blood of the departed beloved contained within. In the far north corner is a raised platform covered in offerings of cornskin, chocolate, tobacco. In one church, the coffin contains a blind man. In the other, it contains a deaf woman. Both have narwhal's horns extending from their foreheads; both died young. The faithful visit these basement-saints and leave what they can at the feet of the one they love best. Giustizia has been a devotee of the Unhearing since she was a girl—her yellow veil and turquoise-ringed thumbs are familiar to all in the Left-Hand Church, and it is she who brings the cornskins, regular as sunrise. When she dies, they will bury her here, in a coffin of her own.

She will plug your ears with wax when you enter, and demand silence. You may notice the long rattlesnake tail peeking from under her skirt and clattering on the mosaic floor, but it is not polite to mention it–when she says silence, you listen. It is the worst word she knows.

The suburbs of Palimpsest spread out from the edges of the city proper like ladies' fans. First the houses, uniformly red, in even lines like veins, branching off into lanes and courts and cul-de-sacs. There are parks full of grass that smells like oranges and little creeks filled with floating roses, blue and black. Children scratch pictures of antelope-footed girls and sparrow-winged boys on the pavement, hop from one to the other. Their laughter spills from their mouths and turns to orange leaves, drifting lazily onto wide lawns. Eventually the houses fade into fields: amaranth, spinach, strawberries. Shaggy cows graze; black-faced sheep bleat. Palimpsest is ever-hungry.

But these too fade as they extend out, fade into the empty land not yet colonized by the city, not yet peopled, not yet known. The empty meadows stretch to the horizon, pale and dark, rich and soft.

A wind picks up, blowing hot and dusty and salt-scented, and gooseflesh rises over miles and miles of barren skin.

I saw her in November. It was raining—her scarf was soaked and plastered against her head. She passed by me and I knew her smell, I knew the shape of her wrist. In the holiday crowds, she disappeared quickly, and I ran after her, without a name to call out.

"Wait!" I cried.

She stopped and turned towards me, her square jaw and huge brown eyes familiar as a pillow. We stood together in the rainy street, beside a makeshift watch-stand.

"It's you," I whispered.

And I showed my knee. She pursed her lips for a moment, her green scarf blown against her neck like a wet leaf. Then she extended her tongue, and I saw it there, splashed with raindrops, the map of Palimpsest, blazing blue-bright. She closed her mouth, and I put my arm around her waist.

"I felt you, the pipe of bone, the white smoke," I said.

"I felt the dress on your shoulders," she answered, and her voice was thick and low, grating, like a gate opening.

"Come to my house. There is brandy there, if you want it."

She cocked her head, thin golden hair snaking sodden over her coat. "What would happen, do you think?"

I smiled. "Maybe our feet would come clean."

She stroked my cheek, put her long fingers into my hair. We kissed, and the watches gleamed beside us, gold and silver.

125th and Peregrine

On the south corner: the lit globes, covered with thick wrought- iron serpents which break the light, of a subway entrance. The trains barrel along at the bottom of the stairs every fifteen minutes. On the glass platform stands Adalgiso, playing his viola with six fingers on each hand. He is bald, with a felt hat that does not sit quite right on his head. Beside him is Assia, singing tenor, her smoke-throated voice pressing against his strings like kisses. Her eyes are heavily made-up, like a pharaoh's portrait, her hair long and coarse and black. His playing is so quick and lovely that the trains stop to listen, inclining on the rails and opening their doors to catch the glissandos spilling from him. His instrument case lies open at his feet, and each passenger who takes the Marginalia Line brings his fee—single pearls, dropped one by one into the leather case until it overflows like a pitcher of milk. In the corners of the station, cockroaches with fiber optic wings scrape the tiles with their feet, and their scraping keeps the beat for the player and his singer.

On the north corner: a cartographer's studio. There are pots of ink in every crevice, parchment spread out over dozens of tables. A Casimira pigeon perches in a baleen cage and trills out the hours faithfully. Its droppings are pure squid-ink, and they are collected in a little tin trough. Lucia and Paola have run this place for as long as anyone can remember—Lucia with her silver compass draws the maps, her exactitude radiant and unerring, while Paola illuminates them with exquisite miniatures, dancing in the spaces between streets. They each wear dozens of watches on their forearms. This is the second stop, after the amphibian-salon, of Palimpsest's visitors, and especially of her immigrants, for whom the two women are especial patrons. Everyone needs a map, and Lucia supplies them: subway maps and street-maps and historical maps and topographical maps, false maps and correct-to-the-minute maps and maps of cities far and far from this one. Look—for you she has made a folding pamphlet that shows the famous sights: the factory, the churches, the salon, the memorial. Follow it, and you will be safe.

Each morning, Lucia places her latest map on the windowsill like a fresh pie. Slowly, as it cools, it opens along its own creases, its corners like wings, and takes halting flight, flapping over the city with susurring strokes. It folds itself, origami-exact, in mid-air: it has papery eyes, inky feathers, vellum claws.

It stares down the long avenues, searching for mice.

≈

Catherynne M. Valente is the *New York Times* bestselling author of over two dozen works of fiction and poetry, including (the novel version of) *Palimpsest*, the Orphan's Tales series, *Deathless*, *Radiance*, and the crowdfunded phenomenon *The Girl Who Circumnavigated Fairyland in a Ship of Her Own Making*. She is the winner of the Andre Norton, Tiptree, Mythopoeic, Rhysling, Lambda, Locus, and Hugo awards. Valente has been a finalist for the Nebula and World Fantasy Awards. She lives on an island off the coast of Maine with a small but growing menagerie of beasts, some of which are human.

⁓

In San Francisco's Mission District, West African magical powers reveal the consequences of Mr. Ash's unfortunate actions as well as the innermost reality of the city.

Ash

John Shirley

A police car pulled up to the entrance of the Casa Valencia. The door to the apartment building, on the edge of San Francisco's Mission District, was almost camouflaged by the businesses around it, wedged between the standout orange and blue colors of the Any Kind Check Cashing Center and the San Salvador restaurant. Ash made a note on his pad, and sipped his cappuccino as a bus hulked around the corner, blocking his view through the window of the espresso shop. The cops had shown up a good thirteen minutes after he'd called in the anonymous tip on a robbery at the Casa Valencia. Which worked out good. But when it was time to pop the armored car at the Any Kind Check Cashing Center next door, they might show up more briskly. Especially if a cashier hit a silent alarm.

The bus pulled away. Only a few cars passed, impatiently clogging the corner of 16th and Valencia, then dispersing; pedestrians, with clothes flapping, hurried along in tight groups, as if they were being tumbled by the moist February wind.

Just around the corner from the first car, double-parking with its lights flashing, the second police car arrived. By now, though, the bruise-eyed hotel manager from New Delhi or Calcutta or wherever was telling the first cop that he hadn't called anyone; it was a false alarm, probably called in by some junkie he'd evicted, just to harass him. The cop nodded in watery sympathy. The second cop called through the window of his

SFPD cruiser. Then they both split, off to Dunkin' Donuts. Ash relaxed, checking his watch. Any minute now the armored car would be showing up for the evening money drop-off. There was a run of check cashing after five o'clock.

Ash sipped the dregs of his cappuccino. He thought about the .45 in the shoebox under his bed. He needed target practice. On the slim chance he had to use the gun. The thought made his heart thud, his mouth go dry, his groin tighten. He wasn't sure if the reaction was fear or anticipation.

This, now, this was being alive. Planning a robbery, executing a robbery. Pushing back at the world. Making a dent in it, this time. For thirty-nine years his responses to the world's bullying and indifference had been measured and careful and more or less passive. He'd played the game, pretending that he didn't know the dealer was stacking the cards. He'd worked faithfully, first for Grenoble Insurance, then for Serenity Insurance, a total of seventeen years. And it had made no difference at all. When the recession came, Ash's middle management job was jettisoned like so much trash.

It shouldn't have surprised him. First at Grenoble, then at Serenity, Ash had watched helplessly as policyholders had been summarily cut off by the insurance companies at the time of their greatest need. Every year, thousands of people with cancer, with AIDS, with accident paraplegia, cut off from the benefits they'd spent years paying for; shoved through the numerous loopholes that insurance industry lobbyists worked into the laws. That should have told him: if they'd do it to some ten-year-old kid with leukemia—and, God, they did it every day—they'd do it to Ash. Come the recession, bang, Ash was out on his ear with the minimum in retirement benefits.

And the minimum wasn't enough.

Fumbling through the "casing process," Ash made a few more perfunctory notes as he waited for the armored car. His hobbyhorse reading was books about crime and the books had told him that professional criminals cased the place by taking copious notes about the surroundings. Next to Any Kind Check Cashing was Lee Zong, Hairstyling for Men and Women. Next to that, Starshine Video, owned by a Pakistani. On the Valencia side was the Casa Valencia entrance—the hotel rooms were layered above the Salvadoran restaurant, a dry cleaners, a leftist bookstore. Across the street, opposite the espresso place, was Casa Lucas Productos, a Hispanic supermarket, selling fruit and cactus pears and red bananas and plantains and beans by the fifty-pound bag. It was a hardy leftover from the days when this was an entirely Hispanic neighborhood. Now it was as much Korean and Vietnamese and Pakistani and Indian and Middle Eastern.

Two doors down from the check-cashing scam, in front of a liquor store, a black guy in a dirty, hooded sweatshirt stationed himself in front of passing pedestrians, blocking them like a linebacker to make it harder to avoid his outstretched hand.

That could be me, soon, Ash thought. I'm doing the right thing. One good hit to pay for a business franchise of some kind, something that'd do well in a recession. Maybe a movie theater. People needed to escape. Or maybe his own check cashing business—with better security.

Ash glanced to the left, down the street, toward the entrance to the BART station—San Francisco's subway—this entrance only one short block from the check-cashing center. At five-eighteen, give or take a minute, a northbound subway would hit the platform, pause for a moment, then zip off down the tunnel. Ash would be on it with the money, escaping more efficiently than he could ever hope to, driving a car in city traffic. And more anonymously.

The only problem would be getting to the subway station handily. He was five-six, and pudgy, his legs a bit short, his wind even shorter. He was going to have to sprint that block and hope no one played hero. If he knew San Francisco, though, no one would.

He looked back at the check-cashing center just in time to see the Armored Transport of California truck pull up. He checked his watch: as with last week, just about five-twelve. There was a picture insignia of a knight's helmet on the side of the truck. The rest of the truck painted half black and half white, which was supposed to suggest police colors, scare thieves. Ash wouldn't be intimidated by a paint job.

He'd heard that on Monday afternoons they brought about fifteen grand into that check-cashing center. Enough for a down payment on a franchise, somewhere, once he'd laundered the money in Reno.

Now, he watched as the old, white-haired black guard, in his blue and white uniform, wheezed out the back of the armored car, carrying the canvas sacks of cash. Not looking to the right or left, no one covering him. His gun strapped into its holster.

The old nitwit was as ridiculously overconfident as he was overweight, Ash thought. He'd never had any trouble. First time for everything, Uncle Remus.

Ash watched intently as the guard waddled into the check-cashing center. He checked his watch, timing him, though he wasn't sure why he should, since he was planning to rob him on the way in, not on the way out. But he had the impression from the books you were supposed to time everything. The reasons would come clear later.

A bony, stooped Chicano street eccentric—aging, toothless, with a squiggle of black mustache and sloppily dyed black hair—paraded up the sidewalk to stand directly in front of Ash's window. Crazy old fruit, Ash thought. A familiar figure on the street here. He was wearing a Santa Claus hat tricked out with junk jewelry, a tattered gold lamé jacket, thick mascara and eyeliner, and a rose erupting a penis crudely painted on his weathered cheek. The inevitable trash-brimmed shopping bag in one hand, in the other a cane made into a mystical staff of office with the gold-painted plastic roses duct-taped to the top end.

As usual the crazy old fuck was babbling free-form imprecations, his spittle making whiteheads on the window glass. "Damnfuckya!" came muffled through the glass. "Damnfuckya for ya abandoned city, ya abandoned city and now their gods are taking away, taking like a bend-over boy yes, damnfuckya! Yoruba Orisha! The Orisha, *cabrón*! Holy shit on a wheel! *Hijo de puta!* Ya doot, ya pay, they watch, they pray, they take like a bend-over boy ya! *Eshu-Elegba* at your crossroads shithead *pendejo*! LSD not the godblood now praise the days! Damnfuckya be sorry! Orisha them Yoruba *cabrones!*"

Yoruba Orisha. Sounded familiar.

"Godfuckya Orisha sniff 'round, *vamanos! Chinga tu madre!*"

Maybe the old fruit was a Santeria loony. Santeria was the Hispanic equivalent of Yoruba, and now he was foaming at the mouth about the growth in Yoruba's power. Or maybe he'd done too much acid in the sixties.

The Lebanese guys who ran the espresso place, trying to fake it as a chic croissant espresso parlor, went out onto the sidewalk to chase the old shrieker away. But Ash was through here, anyway. It was time to go to the indoor range, to practice with the gun.

On the BART train over to the East Bay, on his way to the target range, Ash let his mind wander. He had only fired the automatic once before—and before that hadn't fired a gun since his boyhood, when he'd gone hunting with his father. He'd never hit anything, in those days. He wasn't sure he could hit anything now. But he had been researching gun handling, and even if he didn't turn into Wild Bill Hickok, he would be able to stop a man. How hard could that be? He didn't want to have to shoot the old waddler. Chances were, he wouldn't have to shoot. The old guard would be terrified, paralyzed. Putty. Still . . .

He scanned the interior of the humming train car, as if somebody or something might be able to read his mind. But none of the passengers were paying attention. His eyes focused on a page of a morning paper abandoned on the seat beside him. It was a back-section page of the *Examiner,* and it was the word *Yoruba* in a headline that focused his eyes. Lurching with the motion of the train, Ash crossed the aisle and sat down next to the paper, read the article without picking it up.

Yoruba, it said, was the growing religion of inner city blacks—an amalgam of African and Western mysticism. Ancestor worship with African roots. Supposed to be millions of people into it now. Orisha were spirits. Eshu Elegba was some god or other.

So the Chicano street freak had been squeaking about Yoruba because it was getting stronger. His latest attack of paranoia. Next week he'd be warning people about some plot by the Vatican.

Ash shrugged, and the train pulled into his station.

Ash was glad the week was over; relieved the waiting was nearly done. He'd begun to have second thoughts. The attrition on his nerves had been almost unbearable.

But now it was Monday again. Seven minutes after five. He sat in the espresso shop, sipping, achingly and sensuously aware of the weight of the pistol in the pocket of his trench coat.

The street crazy with the gold roses on his cane was stumping along a little ways up, across the street, as if coming to meet Ash. And then the armored car pulled around the corner.

Legs rubbery, Ash made himself get up. He picked up the empty, frameless backpack, carried it in his left hand. Went out the door, into the bash of cold wind. The traffic light was with him. He took that as a sign, and crossed with growing alacrity, one hand closing around the grip of the gun in his coat pocket. The ski mask was folded up onto his forehead like a watch cap. As he reached the corner where the fat black security guard was just getting out of the back of the armored car, he pulled the ski mask down over his face. And he jerked the gun out.

"Give me the bag or you're dead right now!" Ash barked, just as he'd rehearsed it, leveling the gun at the old man's unmissable belly.

For a split second, as the old man hesitated, Ash's eyes focused on something anomalous in the guard's uniform; an African charm dangling down the front of his shirt, where a tie should be. A spirit-mask face that seemed to grimace at Ash. Then the rasping plop of the bag dropping to the sidewalk snagged his attention, and Ash waved the gun, yelling, "Back away and drop your gun! Take it out with thumb and forefinger only!" All according to rehearsal.

The gun clanked on the sidewalk. The old man backed stumblingly away. Ash scooped up the bag, shoved it into the backpack. *Take the old guy's gun too.* But people were yelling, across the street, for someone to call the cops, and he just wanted away. He sprinted into the street, into a tunnel of panic, hearing shouts and car horns blaring at him, the squeal of tires, but never looking around. His eyes fixed on the downhill block that was his path to the BART station.

Somehow he was across the street without being run over, was five paces past the wooden, poster-swathed newspaper kiosk on the opposite corner, when the Chicano street crazy with the gold roses on his cane popped into his path from a doorway, shrieking, the whites showing all the way around his eyes, foam spiraling from his mouth, his whole body pirouetting, spinning like a cop car's red light. Ash bellowed something at him and waved the gun, but momentum carried him directly into the crazy fuck and they went down, one skidding atop the other, the stinking, clownishly made-up face howling two inches from his, the loon's cocked knee knocking the wind out of Ash.

He forced himself to take air and rolled aside, wrenched free, gun in one hand and backpack in the other, his heart screaming. People yelling around him. He got to his feet, the effort making him feel like Atlas lifting the world. Then he heard a deep voice. "Drop 'em both or down you go motherfucker!" And, wheezing, the fat old guard was there, gun retrieved and shining in his hand, breath steaming from his nostrils, dripping sweat, eyes wild. The crazy was up, flailing indiscriminately, this time in the fat guard's face. The old guy's gun once more went spinning away from him.

Now's your chance, Ash. Go.

But his shaking hands had leveled his own gun.

Thinking: *The guy's going to pick up his piece and shoot me in the back unless I gun him down.*

No he won't, he won't chance hitting passersby, just run—

But the crazy threw himself aside and the black guard was a clear-cut target and something in Ash erupted out through his hands. The gun banged four times and the old man went down. Screams in the background. The guard clutched his torn-up belly. One hand went to the grimacing African charm hanging around his neck. His lips moved.

Ash ran. He ran into another tunnel of perception, and down the hill.

Ash was on the BART platform, and the train was pulling in. He didn't remember coming here. Where was the gun? Where was the money? The mask? Why was his mouth full of paper?

He took stock. The gun was back in his coat pocket, like a scorpion retreated into its hole. His ski mask was where it was supposed to be, too, with the canvas bag in the backpack. There was no paper in his mouth. It just felt that way, it was so dry.

The train pulled in and, for a moment, it seemed to Ash that it was *feeding* on the people in the platform. Trains and buses all over the city puffing up, feeding, moving on, stopping to feed again

Strange thought. Just get on the train. He had maybe one minute before the city police would coordinate with the BART Police and they'd all come clattering down here looking to shoot him.

He stepped onto the train just as the doors closed.

It took an unusually long time to get to the next station. That was his imagination; the adrenaline affecting him, he supposed. He didn't look at anyone else on the train. No one looked at him. They were all damned quiet.

He got off at the next stop. That was his plan—get out before the transit cops staked out the station—but he half expected them to be there when he got out of the train.

He felt a weight spiral away from him: no cops on the platform, or at the top of the escalator.

Next thing, go to ground and *stay.* They'd expect him to go much farther, maybe the airport.

God it was dark out. The night had come so quickly, in just the few minutes he'd spent on the train. Well, it came fast in the winter.

He didn't recognize the neighborhood. Maybe he was around Hunter's Point somewhere. It looked mostly black and Hispanic here. He'd be conspicuous. No matter, he was committed.

You killed a man.

Don't think about it now. Think about shelter.

He moved off down the street, scanning the signs for a cheap hotel. Had to get off the streets fast. With luck, no one would get around to telling the cops he'd ducked into the Mission Street BART station. Street people at 16th and Mission didn't confide in the cops.

It was all open-air discount stores and flyblown barbecue stands and bars. The corners were clumped up, as they always were, with drinkers and loafers and hustlers and people on errands stopping to trade gossip with their cousins. Black guys and Hispanic guys, turning to look at Ash as he passed, never pausing in their murmur. All wearing dark glasses—it must be some kind of fad in this neighborhood to wear shades at night. It didn't make much sense. The blacks and Hispanics stood about in mixed groups, which was kind of strange. They communicated at times, especially in the drug trade, but they were usually more segregated. The streetlights seemed a cat-eye yellow here, but somehow gave out no illumination—everything above the street level was pitch black. Below, a leprous mist smudged the neon of the bars, the adult bookstores, the beer signs in the liquor stores. He stared at a beer sign as he passed. "Drink the Piss of Hope," it said. He must have read that wrong. But farther down he read it again in another window: "Piss of Hope: The Beer That Sweetly Lies."

Piss of Hope?

Another sign advertised Heartblood Wine Cooler. *Heartblood*, now. It was so easy to get out of touch with things. But . . .

There was something wrong with the sunglasses people were wearing. Looking close at a black guy and a Hispanic guy standing together, he saw that their glasses weren't sunglasses, exactly. They were the miniatures of house windows, thickly painted over. Dull gray paint, dull red paint.

Stress. It's stress, and the weird light here and what you've been through.

He could feel them watching him. All of them. He passed a group of children playing a game. The children had no eyes—they had plucked them, were casting the eyes, tumbling them along the sidewalk like jacks—

You're really freaked out, Ash thought. It's the shooting. It's natural. It'll pass.

The cars in the street were lit from underneath with oily yellow light. There were no headlights. Their windows were painted out. (That is *not* a pickup truck filled with dirty, stark-naked children vomiting blood.) The crowds to either side of the sidewalk thickened. It was like a parade day; like people waiting for a procession. (The old wino sleeping in the doorway is *not* made out of dog shit.) In the window of a bar, he saw a hissing, flickering neon sign shaped like a face. A grimacing face of lurid strokes of neon, amalgamated from goat and hyena and man, a mask he'd seen before. He felt the sign's impossible warmth as he pushed through the muttering crowds.

The place smelled like rotten meat and sour beer. Now and then, on the walls above the shop doors, rusty public address speakers, between bursts of static and feedback, gave out filtered announcements that seemed threaded together into one long harangue as he proceeded from block to block.

"Today we have large pieces available . . . the fever calls from below to offer new bargains, discount prices . . . prices slashed . . . slashed . . . We're slashing . . . prices are . . . from below, we offer . . . "

A police car careened by. Ash froze till he saw it was apparently driving at random, weaving drunkenly through the street and then plowing into the crowd on the opposite side of the street, sending bodies flying. No one on Ash's side of the street more than glanced over with their painted-out eyes. The cop car only stopped crushing pedestrians when it plowed into a telephone pole and its front windows shattered, revealing cracked mannequins inside twitching and sparking.

Shooting the old guard has fucked up your head, Ash thought. Just stare at the street, look down, look away, Ash.

He pushed on. A hotel a hotel a hotel. Go in somewhere, ask, get directions, get away from this street. (That is not a whore straddling a smashed man, squatting over the broken bone-end of a man's arm to flick it in the back of that van.) Go into this bar advertising Lifeblood Beer and Finehurt Vodka.

Inside the bar. It was a smoky room; the smoke smelled like burnt meat and tasted of iron filings on his tongue. One of those sports bars, photos on the walls of football players smashing open the other players' helmets with sledgehammers; on the TV screen at the end of the bar a blurry hockey game. (The hockey players are not beating a naked woman bloody with their sticks, blood spattering their inhuman masks, no they're not.) Men and women of all colors at the bar were dead things (no they're not, it's just . . .), and they were smoking something, not drinking. They had crack pipes in their hands and they were using tiny ornate silver spoons to scoop something from the furred buckets on the bar to put in their pipes and burn; when they inhaled, their emaciated faces puffed out: aged, sunken, wrinkled, blue-veined, disease-pocked faces that filled out, briefly healed, became healthy for a few moments, wrinkles blurring away with each hit, eyes clearing, hair darkening as each man and woman applied lighter to the pipe and sucked gray smoke. (Don't look under the bar.) Then the smokers instantly atrophied again, becoming dead, or near-dead, mummies who smoked pipes, shriveled—until the next hit. The bartender was a dark-skinned man with gold teeth and white-painted eyelids, wearing a sort of gold and black gown. He stood polishing a whimpering skull behind the bar, and said, "Brotherman you looking for de hotel, it's on de corner, de Crossroads Hotel—You take a hit too? One money, give me one money and I give you de fine—"

"No, no thanks," Ash said, with rubbery lips.

His eyes adjusting so he could see under the bar, in front of the stools— there were people under the bar locked into metal braces, writhing in restraints: their heads were clamped up through holes in the bars and the furry buckets in front of each smoker were the tops of their heads, the crowns of their skulls cut away, brains exposed, gray and pink; the clamped heads were facing the bartender who fed them something that wriggled, from time to time. The smokers used their petite, glimmering spoons to scoop bits of quivering brain tissue from the living skulls and dollop the gelatinous stuff into the bowls of their pipes—*basing the brains* of the women and men clamped under the bars, taking a hit and filling out with strength and health for a moment. Was the man under the bar a copy of the one smoking him? Ash ran before he knew for sure.

Just get to the hotel and it'll pass, it'll pass.

Out the door and past the shops, a butcher's (those are *not* skinned children hanging on the hooks) and over the sidewalk which he saw now was imprinted with fossils, fossils of faces that looked like people pushing their faces against glass till they pressed out of shape and distorted like putty; impressions in concrete of crushed faces underfoot. The PA speakers rattling echoing.

" . . . *prices slashed and bent over sawhorses, every price and every avenue, discounts and bargains, latest in designer footwear . . . "*

Past a doorway of a boarding house—was this the place? But the door bulged outward, wood going to rubber, then the lock buckling and the door flying open to erupt people, vomiting them onto the sidewalk in a Keystone Kops heap, but moving only as their limbs flopped with inertia: they were dead, their eyes stamped with hunger and madness, each one clutching a shopping bag of trash, one of them the Chicano street crazy who'd tried to warn him: gold roses clamped in his teeth dead now; some of them crushed into shopping carts; two of them, yes, all curled up and crushed, trash compacted into a shopping cart so their flesh burst out through the metal gaps. Flies that spoke with the voices of radio DJs cycled over them, yammering in little buzzing parodic voices: "This Wild Bob at KMEL and hey did we tell ya about our super countdown contest, we're buzzing with it, buzzzzzzing wizzzz-zzzz—"

A bus at the corner. Maybe get in it and ride the hell out of the neighborhood. But the bus's sides were striated like a centipede and when it stopped at the bus stop its doorway was wet, it fed on the willing people waiting at the bus stop, and from its underside crushed and sticky-ochre bodies were expelled to spatter the street.

"*. . . one money sale, the window smoke waits. One money and inside an hour we'll find the paste that lives and chews, prices slashed, three money and we'll throw in a—*"

He paused on the corner. There: the Crossroads Hotel. A piss-in-the-sink hotel, the sort filled with junkies and pensioned winos. Crammed crammed between other buildings like the Casa Valencia had been. He was afraid to go in.

Across the street: whores, with crotch-high skirts and bulging, wattled cleavages and missing limbs that waved to him with the squeezed out, curly ends of the stumps. (It's not true that they have no feet, that their ankles are melded into the sidewalk.)

"*One money will buy you two women whose tongues can reach deeply into a garbage disposal, we also have, for two money—*"

The whores beckoned; the crowd thickened. He went into the hotel.

A steep, narrow climb up groaning stairs to the half door where the manager waited. The hotel manager was Indian, and behind him were three small children with their faces covered in black cloth (the children do not have three disfigured arms apiece), gabbling in Hindi. The manager smiling broadly. Gold teeth. Identical face to the bartender but long straight hair, heavy accent as he said: "Hello hello, you want a room, we have one vacancy, I am sorry we have no linen now, no, there are no visitors unless you pay five money extra, no visitors, no—"

"I understand, I don't care about that stuff," Ash babbled. Still carrying the backpack, he noted, taking stock of himself again. *You're okay. Hallucinating but okay. Just get into the room and work out the stress, maybe send for a bottle.*

Then he passed over all the money in his wallet and signed a paper whose print ran like ink in rainwater, and the manager led him down the hall to the room. No number on the door. Something crudely, pen-knifed into the old wooden door panel: a face like an African mask, hyena and goat and man. But momentum carried him into the room—the manager didn't even use a key, just opened it—and closed the door behind him. Ash turned and saw that it was a bare room with a single bed and a window and a dangling naked bulb and a sink in one corner, no bathroom. Smelling of urine and mold. The light was on.

There were six people in the room.

"Shit!" Ash turned to the door, wondering where his panic had been till now. "Hey!" He opened the door and the manager came back to it, grinning at him in the hallway. "Hey there's already people in here—"

"Yes hello yes they live with you, you know, they are the wife and daughter and grandchildren of the man you killed you know—"

"What?"

"The man you killed, you know, yes—"

"*What?*"

"Yes they are in you now at the crossroads and here are more, oh yes—" He gestured, happy as a church usher at a revival, ushering in seven more people, who crowded past Ash to throng the room, shifting aimlessly from foot to foot, gaping sightlessly, *whining* to themselves, bumping into one another at random. Blocking Ash, without seeming to try, every time he made for the door. Pushing him gently but relentlessly back toward the window.

The manager was no longer speaking in English, nor was he speaking Hindi; his face was no longer a man's, but something resembling that of a hyena and a goat and a man, and he was speaking in an African tongue—Yoruba?—with a sound that was as strange to Ash as the cry of an animal on the veldt, but Ash knew, anyway, with a kind of *a priori* knowledge, what the man was saying. Saying . . .

That these people were those disenfranchised by the old man's death: the old armored-car guard's death meant that his wife will not be able to provide the money to help her son-in-law start that business and he goes instead into crime and then to life in prison, and his children, fatherless, slide into drugs, and lose their hope and then their lives and as a direct result they beat and abuse their own children and those children have children which *they* beat and abuse (because they themselves were beaten and abused) and they all grow up into psychopaths and aimless, sleepwalking automatons . . . Who shoved, now, into this room with him, made it more and more crushingly crowded, murmuring and whining as they elbowed Ash back to the window. There were thirty of them in the little room, and then forty, and then forty-five and fifty, the crowd humid with body heat and sullen and dully urgent as it crowded Ash against the window frame. He looked over his shoulder, peered through the window glass. Maybe there was escape, out there.

But outside the window it was a straight drop four floors to a trash heap. It was an air shaft, an enclosed space between buildings intended to provide air and light for the hotel windows. Air shafts filled up with trash, in places like this; bottles and paper sacks and wrappers and wet boxes and shapeless sneakers and bent syringes and mold-carpeted garbage and brittle condoms and crimped cans. The trash was thicker, deeper, than in any air shaft he'd ever seen. It was a cauldron of trash, subtly seething, moving in places, wet sections of cardboard shifting, cans scuttling; bottles rattling and strips of tar paper humping up, worming; the wet, stinking motley of the air shaft weaving itself into a glutinous tapestry.

No, he couldn't go out there. But there was no space to breathe now, inside, and no way to the door; they were piling in still, all the victims of his shooting. The ones killed or maimed by the ones abandoned by the ones lost by the one he had killed. How many people now in this room made for one, people crawling atop people, piling up so that the light was in danger of being crushed out against the ceiling?

One killing can't lead to so much misery, he thought.

Oh but the gunshot's echoes go on and on, the happy, mocking Eshu said. *On and on, white devil cocksucker man.*

What is this place? Ash asked, in his head. Is it Hell?

Oh no, this is the city. Just the city. Where you have always lived. Now you can see it, merely, white demon cocksucker man. Now stay here with us, with your new family, where he called you with his dying breath . . .

Ash couldn't bear it. The claustrophobia was of infinite weight. He turned again to the window, and looked once more into the air shaft; the trash decomposing and almost cubistically recomposed into a great garbage disposal churn, that chewed and digested itself and everything that fell into it.

The press of people pushed him against the window so that the glass creaked.

And then thirty more, from generations hence, came through the door, and pushed their way in. The window glass protested. The newcomers pushed, vaguely and sullenly, toward the window. The glass cracked—and shrieked once.

Only the glass shrieked. Ash, though, was silent, as he was heaved through the shattering glass and out the window, down into the airshaft, and into the innermost reality of the city.

~

John Shirley is an Emmy-nominated author of novels, short stories, TV scripts, and screenplays. More than forty of his novels have been published. Many of his numerous short stories have been gathered in eight collections including the Stoker Award-winning *Black Butterflies*, which was also listed as a Best Book of the Year by *Publishers Weekly*. As a musician, Shirley has fronted his own bands and written lyrics for Blue Öyster Cult and others.

~

Welcome to a very odd street in a small American town where some rather unusual folks with weird—or perhaps alien or who-knows-what-kind-of—magic settle.

In Our Block

R. A. Lafferty

There were a lot of funny people in that block.

"You ever walk down that street?" Art Slick asked Jim Boomer, who had just come onto him there.

"Not since I was a boy. After the overall factory burned down, there was a faith healer had his tent pitched there one summer. The street's just one block long and it dead-ends on the railroad embankment. Nothing but a bunch of shanties and weed-filled lots. The shanties looked different today, though, and there seem to be more of them. I thought they pulled them all down a few months ago."

"Jim, I've been watching that first little building for two hours. There was a tractor-truck there this morning with a forty-foot trailer, and it loaded out of that little shanty. Cartons about eight inches by eight inches by three feet came down that chute. They weighed about thirty-five pounds each from the way the men handled them. Jim, they filled that trailer up with them, and then pulled it off."

"What's wrong with that, Art?"

"Jim, I said they filled that trailer up. From the drag on it, it had about a sixty-thousand-pound load when it pulled out. They loaded a carton every three and a half seconds for two hours; that's two thousand cartons."

"Sure, lots of trailers run over the load limit nowadays. They don't enforce it very well."

"Jim, that shack's no more than a cracker box seven feet on a side.

Half of it is taken up by a door, and inside a man in a chair behind a small table. You couldn't get anything else in that half. The other half is taken up by whatever that chute comes out of. You could pack six of those little shacks on that trailer."

"Let's measure it," Jim Boomer said. "Maybe it's bigger than it looks." The shack had a sign on it: *Make Sell Ship Anything Cut Price*. Jim Boomer measured the building with an old steel tape. The shack was a seven-foot cube, and there were no hidden places. It was set up on a few piers of broken bricks, and you could see under it.

"Sell you a new fifty-foot steel tape for a dollar," said the man in the chair in the little shack. "Throw that old one away." The man pulled a steel tape out of a drawer of his table-desk, though Art Slick was sure it had been a plain flat-top table with no place for a drawer.

"Fully retractable, rhodium-plated, Dort glide, Ramsey swivel, and it forms its own carrying case. One dollar," the man said.

Jim Boomer paid him a dollar for it. "How many of them you got?"

"I can have a hundred thousand ready to load out in ten minutes," the man said. "Eighty-eight cents each in hundred-thousand lots."

"Was that a trailer-load of steel tapes you shipped out this morning?" Art asked the man.

"No, that must have been something else. This is the first steel tape I ever made. Just got the idea when I saw you measuring my shack with that old beat-up one."

Art Slick and Jim Boomer went to the rundown building next door. It was smaller, about a six-foot cube, and the sign said *Public Stenographer*. The clatter of a typewriter was coming from it, but the noise stopped when they opened the door.

A dark, pretty girl was sitting in a chair before a small table. There was nothing else in the room, and no typewriter.

"I thought I heard a typewriter in here," Art said.

"Oh, that is me." The girl smiled. "Sometimes I amuse myself, make typewriter noises like a public stenographer is supposed to."

"What would you do if someone came in to have some typing done?"

"What are you think? I do it of course."

"Could you type a letter for me?"

"Sure I can, man friend, two bits a page, good work, carbon copy, envelope, and stamp."

"Ah, let's see how you do it. I will dictate to you while you type."

"You dictate first. Then I write. No sense mix up two things at one time."

Art dictated a long and involved letter that he had been meaning to write for several days. He felt like a fool droning it to the girl as she filed her nails. "Why is public stenographer always sit filing her nails?" she asked as Art droned. "But I try to do it right, file them down, grow them out again, then file them down some more. Been doing it all morning. It seems silly."

"Ah—that is all," Art said when he had finished dictating.

"Not P.S. Love and Kisses?" the girl asked.

"Hardly. It's a business letter to a person I barely know."

"I always say P.S. Love and Kisses to persons I barely know," the girl said. "Your letter will make three pages, six bits. Please you both step outside about ten seconds and I write it. Can't do it when you watch." She pushed them out and closed the door.

Then there was silence.

"What are you doing in there, girl?" Art called.

"Want I sell you a memory course too? You forget already? I type a letter," the girl called.

"But I don't hear a typewriter going."

"What is? You want verisimilitude too? I should charge extra." There was a giggle, and then the sound of very rapid typing for about five seconds.

The girl opened the door and handed Art the three-page letter. It was typed perfectly, of course.

"There is something a little odd about this," Art said.

"Oh? The ungrammar of the letter is your own, sir. Should I have correct?"

"No. It is something else. Tell me the truth, girl: how does the man next door ship out trailer-loads of material from a building ten times too small to hold the stuff?"

"He cuts prices."

"Well, what are you people? The man next door resembles you."

"My brother-uncle. We tell everybody we are Innominee Indians."

"There is no such tribe," Jim Boomer said flatly.

"Is there not? Then we will have to tell people we are something else. You got to admit it sounds like Indian. What's the best Indian to be?"

"Shawnee," said Jim Boomer.

"Okay then we be Shawnee Indians. See how easy it is."

"We're already taken," Boomer said. "I'm a Shawnee and I know every Shawnee in town."

"Hi cousin!" the girl cried, and winked. "That's from a joke I learn, only the begin was different. See how foxy I turn all your questions."

"I have two-bits coming out of my dollar," Art said.

"I know," the girl said. "I forgot for a minute what design is on the back of the two-bitser piece, so I stall while I remember it. Yes, the funny bird standing on the bundle of firewood. One moment till I finish it. Here." She handed the quarter to Art Slick. "And you tell everybody there's a smoothie public stenographer here who types letters good."

"Without a typewriter," said Art Slick. "Let's go, Jim."

"P.S. Love and Kisses," the girl called after them.

The Cool Man Club was next door, a small and shabby beer bar. The bar girl could have been a sister of the public stenographer.

"We'd like a couple of Buds, but you don't seem to have a stock of anything," Art said.

"Who needs stock?" the girl asked. "Here is beers." Art would have believed that she brought them out of her sleeves, but she had no sleeves. The beers were cold and good.

"Girl, do you know how the fellow on the corner can ship a whole trailer-load of material out of a space that wouldn't hold a tenth of it?" Art asked the girl.

"Sure. He makes it and loads it out at the same time. That way it doesn't take up space, like if he made it before time."

"But he has to make it out of something," Jim Boomer cut in.

"No, no," the girl said. "I study your language. I know words. Out of something is to assemble, not to make. He makes."

"This is funny." Slick gaped. "*Budweiser* is misspelled on this bottle, the *i* before the *e*."

"Oh, I goof," the bar girl said. "I couldn't remember which way it goes so I make it one way on one bottle and the other way on the other. Yesterday a man ordered a bottle of Progress beer, and I spelled it Progers on the bottle. Sometimes I get things wrong. Here, I fix yours." She ran her hand over the label, and then it was spelled correctly.

"But that thing is engraved and then reproduced," Slick protested.

"Oh, sure, all fancy stuff like that," the girl said. "I got to be more careful. One time I forget and make Jax-taste beer in Schlitz bottle and the man didn't like it. I had to swish swish change the taste while I pretended to give him a different bottle. One time I forgot and produced a green-bottle beer in a brown bottle. 'It is the light in here, it just makes it look brown,' I told the man. Hell, we don't even have a light in here. I go swish fast and make the bottle green. It's hard to keep from making mistake when you're stupid."

"No, you don't have a light or a window in here, and it's light," Slick said. "You don't have refrigeration. There are no power lines to any of the shanties in this block. How do you keep the beer cold?"

"Yes, is the beer not nice and cold? Notice how tricky I evade your question. Will you good men have two more beers?"

"Yes, we will. And I'm interested in seeing where you get them," Slick said.

"Oh look, is snakes behind you!" the girl cried.

"Oh how you startle and jump!" she laughed. "It's all joke. Do you think I will have snakes in my nice bar?" But she had produced two more beers, and the place was as bare as before.

"How long have you tumble-bugs been in this block?" Boomer asked.

"Who keep track?" the girl said. "People come and go."

"You're not from around here," Slick said. "You're not from anywhere I know. Where do you come from? Jupiter?"

"Who wants Jupiter?" the girl seemed indignant. "Do business with a bunch of insects there, is all! Freeze your tail too."

"You wouldn't be a kidder, would you, girl?" Slick asked.

"I sure do try hard. I learn a lot of jokes but I tell them all wrong yet. I get better, though. I try to be the witty bar girl so people will come back."

"What's in the shanty next door toward the tracks?"

"My cousin-sister," said the girl. "She set up shop just today. She grow any color hair on bald-headed men. I tell her she's crazy. No business. If they wanted hair they wouldn't be bald-headed in the first place."

"Well, can she grow hair on bald-headed men?" Slick asked.

"Oh sure. Can't you?"

There were three or four more shanty shops in the block.

It didn't seem that there had been that many when the men went into the Cool Man Club.

"I don't remember seeing this shack a few minutes ago," Boomer said to the man standing in front of the last shanty on the line.

"Oh, I just made it," the man said.

Weathered boards, rusty nails . . . and he had just made it.

"Why didn't you—ah—make a decent building while you were at it?" Slick asked.

"'This is more inconspicuous," the man said. "Who notices when an old building appears suddenly? We're new here and want to feel our way in before we attract attention. Now I'm trying to figure out what to make. Do you think there's a market for a luxury automobile to sell for a hundred dollars? I suspect I would have to respect the local religious feeling when I make them though."

"What is that?" Slick asked.

"Ancestor worship. The old gas tank and fuel system still carried as vestiges after natural power is available. Oh, well, I'll put them in. I'll have one done in about three minutes if you want to wait."

"No, I've already got a car," Slick said. "Let's go, Jim." That was the last shanty in the block, so they turned back.

"I was just wondering what was down in this block where nobody ever goes," Slick said. "There's a lot of odd corners in our town if you look them out."

"There are some queer guys in the shanties that were here before this bunch," Boomer said. "Some of them used to come up to the Red Rooster to drink. One of them could gobble like a turkey. One of them could roll one eye in one direction and the other eye the other way. They shoveled hulls at the cottonseed oil float before it burned down."

They went by the public stenographer shack again.

"No kidding, honey, how do you type without a typewriter?" Slick asked.

"Typewriter is too slow," the girl said.

"I asked how, not why," Slick said.

"I know. Is it not nifty the way I turn away a phrase? I think I will have a big oak tree growing in front of my shop tomorrow for shade. Either of you nice men have an acorn in your pocket?"

"Ah—no. How do you really do the typing, girl?"

"You promise you won't tell anybody."

"I promise."

"I make the marks with my tongue," the girl said.

They started slowly on up the block.

"Hey, how do you make the carbon copies?" Jim Boomer called back.

"With my other tongue," the girl said.

There was another forty-foot trailer loading out of the first shanty in the block. It was bundles of half-inch plumbers' pipe coming out of the chute—in twenty-foot lengths. Twenty-foot rigid pipe out of a seven-foot shed.

"I wonder how he can sell trailer-loads of such stuff out of a little shack like that," Slick puzzled, still not satisfied.

"Like the girl says, he cuts prices," Boomer said. "Let's go over to the Red Rooster and see if there's anything going on. There always were a lot of funny people in that block."

≈

R. A. Lafferty (1914-2002) wrote more than two hundred short stories and twenty-one novels—historical as well as science fictional. He received a Hugo Award in 1973 for his short story "Eurema's Dam" and was honored with a World Fantasy Lifetime Achievement Award in 1993. As his *New York Times* obituary stated, Lafferty was " . . . a prolific science fiction writer best known for his short stories and his fresh, eccentric . . . satirical style [who] pushed the limits of his genre."

≈

Acknowledgements

"One-Eyed Jack and the Suicide King" © 2005 Elizabeth Bear. First publication: *Lenox Avenue*, March-April 2005.

"Last Call" © 2009 Jim Butcher. First publication: *Strange Brew*, ed. P. N. Elrod (St. Martin's Griffin).

"The Last Triangle" © 2011 Jeffrey Ford. First publication: *Supernatural Noir*, ed. Ellen Datlow (Dark Horse).

"The Goldfish Pond and Other Stories" © 1996 Neil Gaiman. First publication: *David Copperfield's Beyond Imagination*, eds. David Copperfield & Janet Berliner (HarperPrism).

"The Spirit of the Thing" © 2011 Simon R. Green. First publication: *Those Who Fight Monsters: Tales of Occult Detectives*, ed. Justin Gustainis (EDGE Science Fiction and Fantasy Publishing).

"Painted Birds and Shivered Bones" © 2013 Kat Howard. First publication: *Subterranean Press Magazine*, Spring 2013.

"Bridle" © 2006 Caitlín R. Kiernan. First publication: *The Ammonite Violin & Others* (Subterranean Press).

"Caligo Lane" © 2014 Ellen Klages. First publication: *Subterranean Press Magazine*, Winter 2014.

"In Our Block" © 1965 R. A. Lafferty. Published with the permission of the author's estate and the JABberwocky Literary Agency. First publication: *Worlds of If*, July 1965.

"A Water Matter" © 2008 Joseph F. Lake, Jr. Published with the permission of the Lake Family Trust and the Donald Maass Literary Agency. First publication: *Tor.com*, 29 October 2008.